To Jimmy

Thank you [for sharing?] your poetry with [me]. You publish [...] Holly.

No Such Thing As Secrets

a fictional story based on the diaries of Holly Robinson

P.S. you are the real Zohan!

Holly Robinson

Copyright © 2012 by Holly Robinson
First Edition – November 2012

ISBN
978-1-4602-0476-4 (Hardcover)
978-1-4602-0474-0 (Paperback)
978-1-4602-0475-7 (eBook)

All rights reserved.

No part of this publication may be reproduced in any form, or by any means, electronic or mechanical, including photocopying, recording, or any information browsing, storage, or retrieval system, without permission in writing from the publisher.

Produced by:

FriesenPress
Suite 300 – 852 Fort Street
Victoria, BC, Canada V8W 1H8

www.friesenpress.com

Distributed to the trade by The Ingram Book Company

"Part of the beauty of literature is that you discover that your longings are universal longings, that you're not lonely and isolated from anyone. You belong."
F Scott Fitzgerald

"Throughout our lives, we seek to understand ourselves, our emotions, our experiences, and our relationships with others. We also attempt to define our connections to larger social and cultural institutions. One way that we do so is through literature, for works of literature are the records of individual response to the world in which we live"
The Harbrace Anthology of Poetry

FORWARD BY THE EDITOR
BRETT LEIGH EASTERBROOK

This fictional book is written from the perspective of Betty Benson's diary entries. We watch Betty grow into a woman who deals with familial and personal problems and relationships. Her love of baseball and snowboarding provide relief from the never ending piles of laundry, her work as a bartender, and the typical insecurities in life we all experience. Betty struggles with the uncertainties of work, life, and love, as she constantly pursues her dreams of acting. But Betty has a secret life that she shares with us through her diary. Betty is an internet porn star.

INTRODUCTION

The Handbook of Chinese Horoscopes by Theodora Lau breaks down everyone as to the year they were born in and the astrological sign they were born in. I found it to be quite accurate for me:

CAPRICORN HORSE: EARTH + POSITIVE FIRE

"The Mountain Goat's most welcome gift to this combination is consistency. The Horse should have more permanent and reliable qualities because of it. Both signs in this match spur the subject toward continuous activity and industry. Responsive but careful to check the sources of his information, the Capricorn Horse likes to mind his own business while tuning in on the nuances others give out. A less solid carefree spirit, the Horse here will lend speed and grace to Capricorn's solid resolve. This person will know how to set his priorities and be able to accomplish much."

I've written this intro to my book numerous times and I'm still trying to get it right. I've been keeping a diary since I was eleven years old and to this day it's been a constant in my life. For some reason, somewhere along the way, I thought that when I wrote in my diary about my feelings, it validated them for me. It was like someone was listening and someone heard my exact thoughts on the matter. Over the years I thought this chat I might hand down my diaries to my daughter or grand-daughter, both of whom I haven't met yet.

~2004

I now have a four year old daughter that has brightened my life and given me a new found joy and gusto for living. I have wanted to publish my diaries for many years and although I am concerned that none of my friends or family will ever again speak to me again after reading this book; it is my life mission to publish. My diaries have always inspired me to elaborate and create a story that people would want to read. This book is completely fictional and not intended to implicate any real person to any fictional character. I think I could live through almost anything as long as I have a pen and paper to write my thoughts down on. The world isn't always fare and just, but living in North America we have the privilege of speaking our minds and talking about the good, the bad, and the obscene.

~2012

CHAPTER ONE

Dec. 27, 1989

Dear Diary,
Right now my little sister Belle is being a real pain. After I'm done this I have to go and brush my teeth or they will soon fall out of my mouth. Then tomorrow when I wake up I have to meditate than go wake up my mom than I'm going to see the little mermaid. Well my sister wants to sleep and is getting to be a pain so bye till whenever! I'm done brushing my teeth! Betty Benson

Dec. 28, 1989

Dear Diary,
I have to have a shower but it is so cold I can barely write! I haven't even got out of any blanket for a second. What am I going to do? Well if I haven't died from coldness I'll probably talk to you later. I saw the Little Mermaid and was it ever good! But I almost didn't because Brooklyn my big sister sort of ran away because of my oldest sister Beatrice, I would tell you but I'm too tired. Well tomorrow we're going skating so I need my sleep. Betty Benson

Feb. 13, 1990

Dear Diary,
I know I haven't written to you for a long time! The reason I have the time now is because I'm staying home for the first time this year except when school was cancelled for half a day because of snow. So you can see that I must be really sick. You know I think spring is here early. Well I have to go because the pain is back. P.S. it's 9:07 am right now!

Feb. 14, 1990

Dear Diary,
Can we cut this dear diary crap? Thank you! So Happy Valentine's Day. You know spring didn't come early it's a blizzard out there! Oh guess what I got a Valentine's Day card from Wyatt today! It said: hum hum "Guess what I'd like most to be today? Valentines with you! Happy Valentine's Day". Man, I think he is so cute and his personality, I love it. I also got about 15 other cards. I got them from my teacher Mrs. Beaches, Kristy, Deacon, Randy, Abby, Belle, Leleigh, Kandice, John, Minka also some big candy hearts from her, Eddie, Kaitlyn, Allison, Burt, Kat, and Garret oh I'm forgetting Tim Crize. Got You. What a sucker! Until next time write you later. You're Friend Betty

July 14, 1990

It is finally summer time and my family has not done a thing we haven't gone anywhere we could of went to the waterslides in Capsville but Mom was working or Beatrice was. We probably won't go for another week or so! My dad might take Belle and me to the park today I hope I can take a friend like Mindy! I'm supposed to clean my room but I'm just not into it yet so I decided to write to you. Oh next year I'm going into gr.6!!

Aug. 12, 1990

Today nothing really happened; I went to the river this morning and might go again in about half an hour! But yesterday I went over my head and jumped off the rocks and then jumped off the diving board. Well I'm going to see if I'm going swimming so until whenever. Betty

Dec. 15, 1990

Yipes it's almost Christmas! Sometimes I just don't know what to do. Beatrice treats me like such dirt. In this house people swear. So any way tonight it's (Beatrice's) having some friends over and so she wanted the house a bit cleaner. So we started to work and she had already torn a strip off Belle. I would have just left. So anyway I was pretty mad already when we were putting the dishes away when I was going to put the measuring cup away when I saw the big mess. A cup with icing in it. So I went to put it in the fridge when she said "NO, NO, NO!" I just felt like saying fuck you bitch. So I went to put it in the pantry when she said NO again so I said, "Then where the fuck does it go?" And she slapped me across the face and said don't swear at me! Well that did it. It has NO right to punish me in any way so I left. I mean why should I have to spend any more time with the most inconsiderate person on the face of this planet any longer than I had to. I went upstairs and told my parents on her and came in my room. Ever since I can remember she put us down and then asks us sisters to do something for it. Betty

Dec. 23, 1990

Tomorrow is X-mas eve, so I guess you could say I'm a bit excited! But I just try not to be so before I know it, it will be x-mas. Tonight I hope Kaitlyn can stay the night. Kaitlyn is a really good friend of mine but so is Mindy.

Jan. 21, 1991

Beatrice went to a Poison concert and do I ever wish I was in her shoes. Poison is the best and they always will be. She snuck a camera in and she got pictures of all of them. I can't wait until they are developed. I might get some copies for Kaitlyn's birthday present. Kaitlyn's birthdays Feb.18. Poison Rules over all forever!

No Such Thing As Secrets

Mar. 21, 1991

I am going out with Jerrod he is in gr.7 but still cute. We started to go out on the 19th of March 91. I am mad at Beatrice, Brooklyn, and Gordy. Beatrice and Gordy were listening to one of my phone calls with Kristy. Kristy asked me if I would ever French Jerrod and I said yeah probably. When Beatrice and Gordy were listening they thought Kristy said fuck. So they went and told my mom and Brooklyn. First Brooklyn came in and said a speech. Then my Mom started to when I set her straight. But I'm not going to tell Beatrice or Brooklyn about what they heard. I'm just going to let them sweat it out for a while. I don't know, maybe I'll pretend to confess to mom at the dinner table when they are all there. In a way I feel like I should listen into one of her phone calls. But I guess I won't because I've already read her diary. Both of theirs actually!

Date unknown

Mozart is dead. He died on Thursday, April 11th 1991. He turned on Brooklyn so my dad had to shoot him. It took a lot of bullets but he's dead. Gordy had to hold him. He was hysterical after. Beatrice was a wreck. We watched as my Dad shot him. I just kept to myself. I do that. That night I cried more than I did when G.T. (great grandma Tiff) died. I guess I really miss him. That night I had a dream that Mozart was there and here in spirit. I remember me and him snuggling together. Mom said he would purr like a cat. I love Mozart. I sure do miss Mozart. The next day at school I almost cried at school. But I held it in. Nobody knows how I've been doing except you, me, Mozart. I'll leave you with this last thought. I love Mozart and I always will for forever more.

Date Unknown

I miss Motzy.

Apr. 28, 1991

I broke up with Jerrod yesterday. First I called him to dump him but he had to go. So I called Kristy and told her to do it for me. She did and while she was talking to him he said he didn't want to go out with me. So we dumped each other. So now I like Ralph. I hope Ralph's a better kisser.

June 3, 1991

I'm not going out with Jerrod anymore. I'm going out with Ralph and thinking of dumping him. Should I or not. Kaitlyn is still my best friend. Oh Ralph got such a bad haircut. He is turning into a total dog. Oh, Mozart is dead; he turned on Brooklyn so dad shot him. I've cried more tears than you could think. Our class went to Strethcun and it was very fun.

June 4, 1991

Guess what it's almost summer. I can't wait until this hell of a year is done. I know I'm not a good speller, that's why there are so many spelling mistakes. Gordy got a job yesterday; he'll be making a lot so hopefully Beatrice and Gordy will move out. Then mom promised me Beatrice's room. Belle wants it but that's just too bad. I'll be going into gr.7 next year and I'll have Mr.Leeaoh or however you spell it!

June 17, 1991

I was going out with Jep for a while then we broke up. (He dumped me for a dog with a motor bike)! Too bad for him. I was reading Kaitlyn's diary (she let me). It said "I love Jep, I wish he would ask me out" and it went on and on! Neat colored pen I'm writing with! Its 9:39 or later so I have to go to sleep. Tomorrow I'm going to go to school looking so good. Hopefully Jep will ask me out so I can say Fuck You and NO right in his face!

June 27, 1991

Last night Kaitlyn stayed the night. We got out of school on the 25th. I'm just about to go to the beach with Kaitlyn. No one is home except me. I've pigged out and snuck things so there are no more things to do. Kaitlyn will pick me up in around ten minutes. We got a new truck and camper. We'll probably go to Pentickle to see Piggy and Eve and the waterslides. On my report card I got 31

G's, 3 S+'s, 1 S, 3 A's, 2 B's and no money. Beatrice and Gordy might move out soon but I hope even sooner than that. I've been helping Dad with the truck a lot. I helped put on and take off the drive shaft. Being a mechanic isn't that bad. It's a lot better than house work. Jep is such a dog and he is so conceited it's not funny.

Thursday, July 4, 1991

We are going to go camping on Sunday; it will just be my parents, Belle and I. Everyone else has to work. I'm glad I don't have a job! I can hardly wait until we go. We'll finally get to test out our new camper and truck. We're going up to Little Beach. The McKinnon's (Mike + Geena + Chrissy + Betty) are meeting us up there. I hope the sand is nice and it's not boring on the way up or down. I have to sleep because it's 10:20 pm.

July 6, 1991

Tomorrow morning we're going camping up at Little Beach. We'll leave at around 6:00 or 7:00 am. Kaitlyn is going at the same time so I'll see her there. But I'm not supposed to know. I'm going to put a piece of paper on our camp site number sign so she can tell I'm there. She's doing the same. I'm taking my dairy up there. So I'll write again. Time 7:05 pm.

July 7, 1991

It's early but it's been a very tiring day. We didn't get up till 7:15am because we slept in. We didn't' leave our house till around 10:30am. We arrived around 2:30pm. Our number was 17. After that we went to Little Beach and ate some food (hot dogs). We left the beach around 7:00pm. The planes were flying really low because the airport was across the street from the beach. We had to find a place to sleep. We finally decided on Kan Lake. We just parked the camper and ate dinner around 20 min's ago the time right now is 9:36pm. We had wieners and beans. Kaitlyn is coming with her family up to Blue Point (that's the place we're going tomorrow). So I'll have a friend. I'm almost asleep as I write this so I'll write tomorrow night at Blue Point. Where we're camping now, there's bear shit all over the place so I guess bears.

Aug. 12, 1991

I got back from the fair yesterday. I was showing my chickens. Today Brooklyn tried to wear my jeans but she couldn't get the zipper done up. They're too big for me. I have to get back to cleaning my room.

Aug. 31, 1991

If you didn't already know we got a puppy. We named her Topaz. We had to get her put to sleep because my Dad threw her outside after she peed and she dislocated her arm and the vet couldn't fix her. In only 1 year, the year of 1991, 3 dogs and 1 hamster have died. 1st Candy, 2nd Mozart, 3rd Topaz and Brooklyn's hamster Taz. If this is what happens whenever I get a dog I don't want any more. All they bring me is heartache. Betty

Sept. 28, 1991

I no longer wish to be as pretty and popular as Brooklyn or even anything like her because she let me down. She smokes, now I look up to myself. If Beatrice can't make it and Brooklyn can't make it well than I'm going to. That I vow as you as my witness. I'm NOT going to smoke. I never thought I could be this disappointed in my family!! I never thought Brooklyn was so stupid. I guess I was wrong. Now Belle can fallow in my footsteps and so can I. What's this world coming to anyways? Oh yeah I'm going out with Jep. I was going to go with him to the movies tonight but he had to stay home because it is his brother's birthday. Oh well I'm going anyways with some friends of mine. We're going to see Naked Gun 1 + 2 ½.

Date Unknown

I'm going out with Corey P. And I think I really like him. We baby-sit for the same people. I started going out with him on Friday Oct. 25th 1991. This makes me happy because I'm going out with him but I'm sad because one of my chickens died. Her name was Friendly!

No Such Thing As Secrets

Oct. 27, 1991 | **5:47pm**

Guess what Kristy's Mom is in labor. I hope it's a girl for Kristy. I still love Corey.

Nov. 10, 1991

Well I'm going to get my ears pierced soon. I'll get them done Dec. 26th (my birthday). I bought a magazine and I found on all of Poison's birthdays. I'm going out with Corey now. He's cute. I really badly want to go to the next Poison concert. If Mom says no I'll be so mad she'll regret it! Poison Rules forever.

Nov. 22, 1991

For Belle's Christmas present I got her a pair of boots. Brooklyn and I went in on it together! Betty

Jan. 1, 1992

I'm not going out with Jep anymore! I dumped him before the Christmas Holidays. Guess who I like now. Chris Slayer!! He's a very cute movie star. Oh well I might not even meet him. But I'm planning to become an actress, I will too! Betty R.

Mar. 19, 1992

Well I haven't written to you in a long time. My best friend Kaitlyn just got back from Disneyland yesterday. So I'm going to her house at 1:00pm. I need a boyfriend but there isn't one worth it. I'll find one soon I hope. I am going to be an actress some day. I'm sure I'll find one then. Anyway it was nice writing you. Oh on my report card I got four A's and a B in language arts because I'm a bad speller. But I'm improving. I still have to share a room with Belle. But when Beatrice moves out I can get my own room. She's 20 in June. I got lots of great things for X-mas but I don't feel like saying them all. Oh well write you later! Party on.

Thursday, May 14, 1992

This isn't about guys this is about me. I'm in 4H, softball, and I take horse riding lessons. But my parents don't care. I have a softball game tonight and my parents can't come because they don't want to. They never come to any of my games. All the other kids' parents go to every game except for one girl. I used to feel sorry for her until I realized my parents are the same. I really don't care if my parents come. It's just that if they did it would show me something. I don't know what just something. At band concerts my parents hear me play then leave. We had a concert last night they heard me play and five seconds later we were gone. Today in school my teacher was talking to us about how he couldn't understand why parents would listen to their kids then leave. When I heard it I was laughing on the outside but crying on the inside. I have a friend who I've had for eleven years. Her parents are going way out of their way to drive me to the softball game because Mindy (my friend) is getting a ride with someone on the team. So Mindy's Mom is driving me to Mindy's Dad's work then she's driving Emily (Mindy's sister) back to her game. Then Tim (Mindy's Dad) will drive me to the game. At the last game we had to sign something and our parents had to too. My parents weren't there. Then Mindy said to the coach, how is Betty going to get her parents to sign they never come. It's true. I felt like... It's hard to explain all I know is I felt so bad. My dad wants to see my game but he has to work but my mom could come. Oh well, she doesn't want to. One of my friends called while I was at softball and she told them I was at T-ball. She doesn't even care to know what I play. Sometimes I wonder if she really loves me. I mean I know she loves me and I know if she knew how much it hurts when there's no parents of mine around she would.

June 26, 1992

Well I got my last report card. 3 A's + 2 B's, pretty bad eh. Well we're going on a holiday for two weeks and my mom wants me to bring a journal or diary so I'll bring this. Any way Beatrice is being a bitch (as usual). I can't stand her. Oh well I guess I won't have to soon. I hope we're leaving tomorrow or tonight. Betty

No Such Thing As Secrets

Nov. 29, 1992

We left that night. While we were gone we went to Elmaton Mall. We went horse riding (Brooklyn, Belle, and I) with our 3rd cousin Buck. When we got back from a four hour ride, five miles up a mountain then five back, Justine (the horse I was riding) took off running and slipped in the mud and we both went down. I got whip lash. Mom still doesn't know. I'm in gr.8 and we got our first reports card. I got straight A's. My classes were math, science, band, gym, and an elective.

Dec. 13, 1992

My marks are dropping in everything. I went skiing with Kaitlyn, her family, and some people at Mt. Laundryton. It was perfect weather. They got a new chair up there called "The Sunrise Quad". It's kind of like the blue. I got back today. I went on the 11th, 12th, 13th. I noticed this on my bed and my drawer open, so someone read it. I put all the cool stuff in another place. Belle don't put "read it ****" or I'll be pissed off. Anyway I have more to say so I'll put it in the other place. Oh I got an in-school suspension for throwing a hat, which kind of (not really) started a fight. My principal is such a dick. I really hate how he takes his fucking job so seriously. Well I hope one day I can look at this and remember each word written, already it's been three years. Any way that's that. I still want to be a famous actress. I don't think anyone takes me seriously though, except Kaitlyn. So be it.

Dec. 15, 1992 | **9:20pm**

Tomorrow is our band concert at Roperfurd. I get to miss school. Kandice is going out with Dion Hexter. Kandice is really short and Dion is kind of tall. She comes up to just past his elbow. Dion's in gr.10 she's in gr.8. No problem there. I want a boyfriend but there isn't anyone. I guess that might sound a bit conceited but no one should read this but me anyway. I went to the chiropractor today, I was really out. Tina Miths is a bitch and Tom Awahl likes her. Make me want to gag. Tina is my age and Tom went out with Brooklyn for a while, a while ago. Fuck is life fucked up sometimes. But it's all in the eyes of the beholder. I don't know what to do my guy life is asleep, in a coma. Oh I'm dropping in science and math, 2 B's.

Dec. 16, 1992 | **8:42pm**

This is getting pretty regular. Belle and I wrestled with my diary for a half hour. I'm watching 90210. It's a X-mas one. We (our band) played at Roperfurd today. It was snowing out there and it was sticking. I have to remember to bring food for our "sally ann" food drive at school. 10 days till my birthday and 9 days till X-mas. Tomorrow we make pizza. I want to be a famous actress really soon. No one really understands though. I don't know maybe they think it's a childish dream, maybe it is. All I know is that I want to be an actress and to be famous would be a big plus. Open up a lot of guy possibilities! I'd want to do movies on the side while doing a sitcom. I could buy a car when I'm 16, help my parents' money wise and give better Christmas presents. Anyway, so be it.

Feb. 2, 1993 | **8:53pm**

I went to Kandice's after school. When I got home everyone was in a bad mood. Brooklyn and Beatrice got in a fistfight and mom's stuck in the middle. Dad doesn't do enough around the house and everyone is grounded until things start to shape up. You know its funny seeing how funny people are when they're in a bad mood. So I being my happy good self say O.K. and that's that. It's as if they don't realize I could have my own problems. Looking at my friends and seeing their lives. Mine looks so different. The funny thing is none of my friends are like me. I look at the world around me and just see how strange it really is. I have a boyfriend named Barney; he's sweet, nice, and shy. I hate it when he smokes pot though. I think I want to be an actress because I get to be so many different people and happy at the same time. I think I'm going to grow up; do my laundry, clean my room, save my money, do house chores, keep to myself and just weird everyone out for a while. Or I could be the slob I'm "acting" like now!!!

Aug. 19, 1993

Maybe I did grow up, I doubt it. On Valentine's Day Barney got me a necklace with a charm in it. When we broke up (I dumped him) I had it in my bag to give it to him when he got his friend Shawn to ask for it, what a wimp. After I broke up with Barney I decided not to go out with burnouts anymore. Most of them care more about drugs then you. There is someone I like and have liked for a long time. I won't say who because I don't want you to know Belle. Brooklyn is pregnant, due on Nov.30th-93. Rant (who else) is the daddy. I think it's going to be a boy. Just so I don't forget, when Barney and I met I invited him along with other people to a bon fire party at my house. I got really wasted (so did Mindy) and I puked on Barney's shoes. He kept telling me I didn't to make me feel better. Not long after the party he got a new pair of shoes and a girlfriend (me). Belle is growing up too fast, she already going out with boys and she even wore one boy's jacket. I'm just glad she hasn't started to kiss yet. All of us girls (sisters) are different.

Sept. 6, 1993

Tomorrow I go back to school. The summer is over!! Beatrice has been trying to set me up with this guy at Grocery Country. I finally met him a couple of days ago. He is nice. He is a skater. His name is Zarren Zanderbee. He is fourteen and has worked at Grocery Country for a year. I'll phone him today. Tomorrow I'll be going into grade 9. I'll write more later.

Sept. 7, 1993

Yesterday I called Zarren at 11:30 over at Mindy's house. We talked for about five minutes then he had to go to work. He called me after he got home at about 10:30. We talked for about an hour. He was really nice and easy to talk to. He mentioned that he knew Mary-Ann L. and I found out she is in my homeroom today. I asked her about him and their parents are good friends. Zarren and I are not going out but he's phoning me again after work tonight. Hopefully not so late this time because I have to get up at 7a.m. tomorrow. And no one is supposed to call after 9:30 because it would wake my dad up. Zarren just called but I had to go outside with Belle to feed her bunny so he's going to call me back soon. I was at Kandice's house today and her sister went to Bibsbey last year, so did Zarren. So I found him in the yearbook and showed him to Kandice and her boyfriend Dion. I don't know why but when I'm not talking to Zarren he sounds like Barney to me. But, he's not. I'm glad he is really different than Barney. I just talked to him and I don't think I'd mind going out with him. Anyway it's late and I have a long school day tomorrow.

Sept. 13, 1993

Yesterday the worst thing in the world happened to me. My best friend died. But before I get into this I'll tell you something funny my best friend Ozzy did. At about two in the morning Ozzy came in and started sniffing around me. I thought she had to go to the bathroom so I threw her out. The next morning I woke up to a dead mouse lying beside me. The mouse got away from her and was running around in my bed while I was sleeping. Now the bad news. The most upsetting thing I thought could happen to me, happened. Ozzy died. Belle found her in Rufus' (next door dog) mouth, dead. She was screaming so loud Mindy's (best friend) whole family ran over. Then my mom didn't even tell me, she just hugged me while I started to cry, because I knew. Then Beatrice and my father got into a fight about killing Nicky (my dog). My dad had Beatrice in a headlock and Gordy separated them and I stayed the night at Mindy's house. We went for a walk down to the beach and it was dark out. A car had two girls and two guys in it parked on the boat ramp and they started making out. We could see them because the interior light was on. Then a boat came in but the people didn't see it for about five minutes. Then they left and so did we. When we got to Mindy's house I cried again till I fell asleep. Then in the morning I woke up and started to cry. Then I went to school and barely made it through the first class. Geenie asked me if my cat left any mouse on my pillow this morning so Mindy & I went home. On the weekend I had fun though. This skater guy named John that I've kinda liked for a while liked me. We didn't do anything but we still had fun doing nothing. That's all folks. P.S. I miss Ozzy.

Sunday, Feb. 27, 1994

Ozzy did come back. I was half asleep when my dad brought her in. I was half asleep so I thought they buried my cat alive. But, it was the neighbour's cat. That happened long ago! Lots have happened. I'm sick of almost everything about school. The teachers, students, and there's no guys worthwhile. Anyway I've been staying home or skipping out too much so I decided Friday (the 25th) would be my last fun day. I somehow missed the bus, didn't leave the house or something. So I went back to bed, then got up and watched TV for a while. The last time I had been drunk was in November so I decided, oh wait, first I took the car for a ride. I'm only fifteen but I can still drive. It had snowed the day before, not too much. My parents left the car at home because they thought it had shitty tires for the snow. But I was feeling adventurous, stupid is more like it, and took the car out. I went out of the driveway then down the road a bit. I backed into Tweeney's driveway to turn around when the tires had no grip and the car was stuck. I got out and kicked some snow out of the way and got back in and said "if I get out, I promise to put the car right back". Then I was out. Too close, considering that the Tweeney's were home and would have jumped at the chance to bust me. After my little "joy" (not right word) ride I watched more TV. Then at about 11:30 I found some vodka. Actually I knew where it was, I just noticed it. We didn't have orange juice, but pineapple did just fine. So fine that I got tanked. I had the stereo cranked and was dancing around having a great time. Our dog Nick thought I was crazy, but I didn't care. Mindy and Kenzie called me from school. When Mindy got home I was tipped over in the chair. But I was happy. Mindy and Kenzie came over after school; I was sober by the time Kenzie arrived. I wanted to show them where I got stuck before my mom got home. So instead of walking I decided to drive. Both of them can't drive worth shit. As we went down the deserted snow covered road the car starting doing fish tails but it was nothing I hadn't seen before. We made it home safe and before my mom got home. Then that night I went with Tori-leigh to a place called "Waves". It was all right. Before I went inside I finished my beers. Tori and I split a case of Molson or something. I was drunk again for the second time. I saw lots of people and had some fun flirting. Then a guy named Mark gave us a ride home. Mark was pretty cute. He isn't even that old only 17, 18, maybe 19. The next day Rant picked me up before noon and then I got home. I'm still waiting for mom to notice the vodka gone or the car looking different. Saturday night I went to Duncan with Mindy. We got back at about 1:30am and then crashed in her room. Today I went for an 8km jog and visited Jordan and co. and Debbie and co. anyway.

Oct.11, 1994

A lot has happened to me in the last seven months. I have drank too much, necked with two different guys in the same night, had two other one night make outs, quit drinking, got a job at Grocery Country, had Kenzie move away and come back, almost fucked a twenty-two year old, was drinking and driving (but doing good for standard), fell in and out of crushes with some of the guys at work, smoked pot, made new friends, lost old friends, and a lot more that I don't remember. After waking up beside three different guys I decided it was time to quit drinking. Kevin was twenty-two and it was Sept 5th 94. I was really drunk. Things almost got carried away but it never got too far. I often think of him and wonder if I should have stuck it out. But I guess I shouldn't have. The first time I met Terry at work I thought wow! But now that we have become friends I know that that's all it ever will be. Teddy is one of Kris' friends who I have always thought of. Then one night we got together. I didn't sleep with him in that way, but literally. I stopped that one too. Why do I always end up with the dead-beats? I have never been in love or even happy with a boyfriend. My life will change I'm sure. I know Mindy has often thought about suicide and it scares me because she means a lot to me. I like working with the people at Grocery Country. All the guys in grocery are nice, they all are different though. Tate is a sweetheart always picking me up over his shoulders, Terry is a friend always there for me, Zarren is a very nice person, Chase is the most like a brother in the way that he is always teaching me how to play cards or making sure I'm alright, Jay is a nice person but I can see pain in him, Brent is a jerk but he sometimes tries to be nice, Ray is in love with Beatrice but is still nice, Will is also in love with Beatrice desperately and can be a snob at times, and Ricky, as annoying as he can be at times, is always in a good mood, oh and Tim the really cute guy who is married at twenty-one. There should be a law against that. I'm going to remember them for the rest of my life even when I'm rich and famous. I think I have to learn to enjoy what I have.

Oct.19, 1994

I started seeing a guy named Lee on Sunday (Sat night). But today (Wednesday) I broke up with him. Maybe I am afraid of love. I keep breaking up and waiting for someone better to come along. They may come along but nothing ever happens. I feel like such a bitch hurting Lee. He was nice but he was a boy, a young boy. It was cute; Terry, Tate, and Ray all told me that Lee had better be nice to me or they'd have to kick his ass (in more or less words). I guess in a way I do have brothers, and Rant and Tyson would do the same.

No Such Thing As Secrets

Nov. 2, 1994

Terry and I have become good friends over the time we've spent talking on the phone, working together, and just hanging out. Last weekend he took me shopping. Tonight he came over for a last visit because tomorrow morning he is leaving to Mt. Lora to be a ski instructor and live with Lela. He gave me a big hug good-bye and then he left. I won't see him again for six months. I think I'll miss him. I've also decided just now that I am tired of being a fragile weak helpless girl. I want to start lifting weights. I'll start off at home on mom's weight set then I'll start going to a gym. I will be able to take Brooklyn on even and no guy will think he is so much stronger than me that I can't hurt him. I wish I could get strong over night. But I've made the first step. I'm also going to try to eat better. My body will be astonishing by the. time I'm done (will power)

Sunday, Mar. 22, 1995 | **1:00am**

Tonight I let loose and got drunk then I smoked lots of pot. I'm sitting here chi-eyed and fucked up. I then realized that fuck sounds the same no matter what vowel you use. I feel really dizzy and burnt. Kenzie is down, I miss her lots, but I don't really like her boyfriend that much. But I won't say nothing till it's over because she is happy. I can't even see to write because the book is weird looking. I drank coolers that Rant bought me. Then I tried some fish food at Casper's house. You know men suck. You think you like them, and then you realize you don't. Then you remember dreams, then you fall in love with love, then you go through singles, then you get anxious and upset. I tell ya, men suck!

Oct. 17, 1995

I know I have a problem. But I'm the only one who knows. I'm bulimic. I am 5'5" and weigh 115lbs. I look at myself and see fat. I know that I'm not most of the time, but sometimes I feel so gross. If I eat and feel full I have to throw it up until my eyes water, my nose runs, and my throat hurts. I couldn't count the number of times I've done this. I guess it's been going on for about ten months. It stopped for a while when I started going out with Clint, but lately it's been getting bad again. I notice my stomach rolls and feel ugly and undesirable. I have to stop, but I don't know how. If I start jogging and eating right it will go away. If you let out all of your air then stick your finger down your throat it is very easy to puke. I haven't just done it at home but at work, the chiropractor's office, friend's houses, and at parties. People think I puke because of other things but I make myself do it. At least I know it is wrong and I've made the first step by admitting that I am bulimic.

CHAPTER TWO

Feb. 15, 1996

Clint and I have been going out for over seven months now and I love him very much. For Valentine's Day he got me an anklet and a bracelet to match my necklace that I got for my birthday. I think about him all of the time and can't imagine him not in my life. I will remember him forever. He is smart, cute, sexy, a strong person, generous, and caring. I could go on and on! Only a couple of nights ago I opened up to him. It was very hard for me but it was nice to have someone to listen. He has told me many things about his life before this, quite a while before. My parents are getting a divorce most likely from what I can see. I think that this has opened up a lot of feelings for me. I am angry at them for not watching my ball games, or my plays, my award ceremonies, not making us dinner, not buying nice furniture. All of the sudden it just hit me that I was very upset and very angry. I'm glad that Clint is here for me, and I can be there for him. He needs a vacation and wants to leave for a month. He wanted to know if I would still be around in a month. I can't think of one person I would rather be with in my life than him and a month isn't that long. Although I would love to go with him I do have school. Although I'd miss him so much and probably spend the last week of it in tears if he needs to go, I want him to go. I can't just up and leave with my family the way it is lately anyway and school. Clint wonders if I would sleep with anyone else. I think even the thought of having sex with anyone else even disgusts me though. Mindy hates Clint because I spend so much time with him. My life isn't simple right now. I just can't wait for summer. Maybe I'll have more fun then.

Apr. 25, 1996

Most girls wish they were beautiful. Me, I wish I was average. I work with men who hit on me constantly and when they're not, they're talking about me. No matter how hard I try they'll never see me for more than a sex symbol. No matter how nice of a person or how interesting or how smart or how athletic I am; they see me as sex. Nine out of ten males between the ages of thirteen and forty-three hit on me because they look at my outside appearance. I have been dealing with men (the good but mostly the bad) since I was very young. And I have been dealing with females who are jealous for a long time. I try to ignore, hoping it will get better and it might go away. But will it ever? Clint hates all the men who hit on me and he takes out all of his negative energy on me. He doesn't, or I should say hasn't, stopped to think about how I feel, how I deal with it every day of my life. I don't think I should change my image for Clint or any man, just so they don't hit on me or get jealous. When Clint and I started going out I never told him anything, and now that I've started to he's always mad at me. So I cry, and tonight he told me to go cry my eyes out to someone else because he didn't want to hear about it. He hangs up on me all the time. Why do I always have to be the one who calls back? The one man I want to love never shows me that he loves me back. Well I shouldn't say never, sometimes he does. I used to want to fall in love, now that I have I wish I was more specific when I was wishing. I wish I had someone to talk to. Clint is someone, the first someone that I can cry in front of, and now he tells me that he doesn't want to hear it. I guess he only want to hear some of my problems but not all. Maybe he's scared to love or maybe he just doesn't know how to show his feelings. He is embarrassed of my age. He doesn't tell people how old I am, but I do. I tell people because my age is a part of me, and I want to remember the day, month, and year that I was born. Jordan (Brooklyn's son) is the one boy I truly love because his love for me is real. I'm not saying I don't love Clint and my dad, but they sometimes say things that hurt me so much. Then still expect me to love them. I have to learn how to stand up for myself, when I'm not drunk. If the roles were reversed right now and I was Clint I would come to my house and just hold me. I try so hard to be a good girlfriend but why? Sure he buys me gold and lends me his truck, but I guess that old saying is true "money can't buy love". I already love him, why can't he just love me back. There's more to loving than words, it's the action you do to show it. I wonder what he is thinking of me. Does he really think I'm playing head games with him, maybe he's the one playing head games with me. Why do I always have to be the one trying?

May 16, 1996

It's hard to believe that I've had this diary for six years. I hope I always write in one so I remember my life. I'm still with Clint. I talked about that night and he didn't mean to sound mad at me because he wasn't. I dropped my physics class. I don't need it to graduate and I'm getting a horrible mark and I find it boring. Maybe it's the teacher, maybe it's me, or maybe the subject. Clint is mad at me for not trying harder and dropping it. Well it's a good thing that it's my life! Sure it would be nice to have, but it's too late. Judy dropped it too. Why do I have to be perfect? The only people that are even near perfect are just acting. Clint says I should have physics because my acting thing might not work out. Well first of all I want to be a director, second I wouldn't want a job that had to do with physics, and third, I will make it. I'll die before I accept failure on my dream. I am an enabler as my mom says. I help people use me. She's taking a course on something or other and she wants us kids to as well. Lately I'm beginning to think it's not such a bad idea. Anyway I guess Clint wont phone tonight after all. I need… well, where should I start?

May 25, 1996

Tonight I "went out" with my friends because it was Mindy's B-day. But all I could think about was going home or to Clint's house to snuggle with him. Clint and I are a lot the same, we both used to party hard and take control and liven up any party, but now we would both rather be with each other just relaxing. It doesn't make our "friends" too happy. I love my friends but I'm tired of partying with them, which is a horrible thought. Oh well at least I have my family and Clint and some friends.

No Such Thing As Secrets

May 29, 1996

Tonight I'll try something different, I'll write in this when I'm not upset. I hope I never forget how much Clint loves me or how much I love him. I know it's only my first love but I really could spend the rest of my life with him. Relationships are just so hard when you're young. Not spending every night together, having to move away for work or school, no home to call your own, even the smallest age difference can be a challenge. The fact that Clint and I don't fight often is amazing, not that I would waste my time fighting. He loves me very much and although he doesn't show it like the way that I express my feelings, he does. The only thing that is bugging me now is my dad. He feels so sorry for himself. Why I don't know. He has a good job, money, a new truck, and a great family. If he can take control of something he will. His truck, I can't drive Beatrice home in it because he doesn't trust me. A car loan, he won't co-sign because I "can't pay it". His sleep and rest, has to have lots of it, and don't try to spend time with him if there is a program to do. The chores he does once in a while but only if he can make you feel bad about him working so hard.

June 10, 1996 | **10:29pm**

Only five more days of gr.11!! The last day Judy and I are going to get drunk then go to school. Well also bring a camera. I'm still with Clint, but lately he's been distant. I think I'll try to spend less time with him, so he can think. I want a job so bad after leaving Grocery County. I'm sick of sitting at home in this house with my piggy parents. The Tap is hiring and there are interviews on Wednesday from two to four. I'm not keeping my hopes up but I hope I have the best summer ever. I also hope that Clint gets a job that he likes because he's getting grumpy. I would too if I worked at the gas bar that long. I keep wishing for time to go by quickly and I'm older with a loving family, a good job (director of motion pictures) and making a difference with my life. I guess what I should be doing is enjoying my high school days, cause they'll never come again and I hear they're the best. I'm starting to feel fat; my weight is up to 120 lbs, which is just gross. I'm starting to do push-ups and sit-ups every night. I should start jogging too! I need to trim up and fast. Summer bathing suit season is here and I don't want to look like a fat pig. I'll work out and eat and keep it down. I hope.

June 17, 1996

Clint and I are quite fond of each other. In fact we've talked about how someday we'll be married and live on our own in a nice house with good jobs. There is something that bothers him though. It bothers him that he doesn't know my friends and they don't know him. He can be very jealous, not that I do anything to make him jealous. Whenever I go out, he gets very drunk. So I'm stuck, I want to make him at ease and not go out (he still tells me to go out a lot) but I don't have fun, or I could drink and be young more. He doesn't want to go to parties with me anyhow. He knows nothing about the other part of my life except what I tell him. I know he should have trust in me and not even wonder but I can see where he's coming from. I really hope that we stay together but I know it could be difficult. Two years, four months, and twenty-four days may not seem that big of a difference but at this point it has been the biggest obstacle to overcome. I just hope our love lasts.

July 6, 1996

Clint and I have been going out for 1 year today. He stayed most of the night last night until 6am. I got almost no affection but we had been active earlier so I didn't care. It is now 8:30pm and I haven't talked to him. I called him and one of his friends answered. I said for Clint to call me. I left a message on his machine for when he gets home. I talked to his friend three hours ago. I tried calling his cell again and it's out of service or turned off. I was looking forward to going out on the same date we went out on a year ago today. Maybe I should just go by myself! I am tempted to, but somehow I don't think dinner, and mini golf and a walk along the beach would be as fun alone. I keep wondering why he hasn't called me, did he forget, is he mad at me for some reason, didn't Arnie give him the message.

Guess who I just got a call from three hours and twenty minutes later. He lost his birthday $250.00 Oakley sunglasses that I got him at the lake and he lost track of time, and he didn't get the message that I called. Am I mad? I thought I was going to get a night out. Instead I had to settle for pizza my dad bought. I bet he'll be another hour at least till he gets here. I don't even feel like curling my hair so it will wreck before he gets to see it. If I was Angela Panderson or if he thought of me like that, he wouldn't have lost track of time. I could go out with other guys; problem is I don't want to. But I am sick and tired of being upset all the time.

July 19, 1996

I went to a B.C. softball tournament and had back pains but my coach really wanted me to play. Turned out I stole home to win the game. My team came in seventh out of sixteen top teams in B.C. After the tourney I got sick. So sick I had to go to emergency the next day. Turned out I had a kidney infection and that was what the back pain was. I had to stay in the hospital for four nights. Clint was really good to me; he would fall asleep rubbing my feet. I think he was very worried. He got me a teddy bear and roses. I got emotional at night so he would stay late even though he had to work in the morning until I felt better and could sleep. I'll never want anyone else but him. The only thing that could break us up is if he cheats on me, which he never would. I also got a job at the Tap. I'm really happy about it and hope it works into something good. I'm still working for Will at the lottery booth as well. I wish summer would last forever or at least let school get better or school time fly by. I should just enjoy my life while I'm young.

Aug.10, 1996

Today was horrible. Clint and I had our first fight, at least he yelled and I stood there stunned. I have never felt so insulted and hurt in my life. He ended the conversation by saying "just get the fuck out of here" and slamming the door. I just phoned and left a message on his machine even though I didn't want to. I don't know what the outcome of this will be. We've been going out for thirteen months. I love him but I don't want to ever, ever, go through what I did earlier today. I left & started hyperventilating so I had to slow down, roll down the window and pull onto a quieter road. Somewhere inside I know he loves me, but he doesn't have an ounce of trust for me. Now I wish I didn't call. We're fighting because I didn't call him back and stayed the night with some friends at a lake. He accused me of sleeping with a bunch of guys and didn't believe I slept with Lillian and Mindy. Part of me wants to forget about him, but he means so much to me I don't think I can. I tell him more than anyone, I love him very much, I spend more time with him than anyone, and I think about him every minute

it seems like. I want him to have everything, and I would trust him with
So really he just means too much to me. And he can't even call me. I can't
I'm not hungry, and I'm crying a tear a minute. He thinks I'm playing a ga
with him. Obviously I'm not. I really feel so nothing. I have too many thought
running through my head to think. You can't even imagine how sad I am. I never
want to smile again. I thought I didn't have any lessons to learn this life but I'm
right in the middle of this one. I'm not saying either of us is right because it takes
two and I don't think either of us will come out of this a winner alone.

Aug. 31, 1996

What can I say, I'm finding out a lot about myself and why I am the way I am. I've been just thinking. The reason I feel unloved so much is because my parents told me they loved me lots but weren't interested in my life. No matter how exciting I made it, they weren't interested in band concerts, ball games, report cards, plays, etc. So I never tell Clint anything about my life just because I expect him not to want to know. Then when he doesn't say I love you every day I think he doesn't love me. It's very hard to tell yourself that your way of thinking is wrong and it's even harder to figure out what the right way of thinking is. I also am more worried about what the people I care about think of me than what I think of me. Before I die I'll have it figured out.

Sept. 4, 1996

Today was the first real day of gr.12. It was alright except for the fact that I have to catch the fucking bus. I get up at 6:30 for a 7:30 bus when school starts at 8:30. I get out of school at 3:00 but not home until 4:05. But last night Clint told me that he was going shopping today so I asked him to buy me something, and he did. He bought me a very nice ring; he should have been spending his money on his truck that he lets me drive all over and drives me around in. I wish I had a car so I wasn't such a burden, but that time will come. The ring is 14k with eighteen diamonds in it. I started crying because it meant so much. He has never given a ring to anyone and swore he never would. But he gave me one. I think I'll be with him forever, as long as he never yells at me again. I love him. Whenever I see him I want to hold onto him and just be with him. I love him so much that when I think of how much tears come to my eyes. I think that's a lot. I hope I never lose him to anything.

Today or night, I phoned a kung-fu place and I'm going to go and sit in on a class and get an introductory. It is a really good feeling I'm getting. I want to feel confident that I can protect myself against any man or woman that may challenge me in any way. I was at one point, but somewhere I've lost that courage, but don't worry it will come back.

Oct. 10, 1996

All I can say is that life is like a box of chocolates. You never know what you're going to get. My life is going pretty good right now. I would like a better job though and a more affectionate Clint. I have to be more honest with people when I'm mad or I'll never get rid of my soft heart when it comes to people judging me. I don't know if Clint and I are going to manage to stay together our whole lives or not, but at least it won't end too quickly as far as I know, because he's a pretty special guy who needs lots of TLC.

Oct. 25, 1996

I have been very stressed today because of work. I've been trying to get today off and trade for a week and they didn't tell me I could until I got there. Up until then it was "I'll get back to you" tomorrow, next day, in an hour, five minutes, on hold for ten minutes. I was so upset plus it was a full moon. So Clint and I went to Capsville five hours after we had planned to but we made it. We shopped and had Chinese food, even though the msg makes Clint sick. I was upset all day and I even got mad about the way he was ordering his food. After we got out I cried in the truck. He gave me a big hug and made me feel a lot better. In the past week it has been really good or maybe I just don't get so upset so easily. One of those. The point is I love him even if he sometimes can be a jerk, because a lot of the time he's not. And although he can't show it that well, I know he loves me a lot. A whole lot. I just forget that sometimes. Everything else in my life is fine.

Nov. 23, 1996

What is there to say? I used to want to be in love and now I hate it because no matter how mad I am at Clint I can't hate him. My parents are really getting on my nerves. Well my dad anyway. I need (can't live without) a car. But do they see that, no. Last night I thought Clint and I would do something after I got off work. Instead of me driving in the snow my dad drove me. When I got off I had no way of getting home. No Clint, Beatrice, parents, Brooklyn. No one gave a flying fuck. I finally got a hold of Clint and an hour after I got off, I left work. Clint was mad that he had to pick me up. He was mad at my parents for not getting me a car. I was very upset so when I got home (he didn't want to take me out with him, I'm just his dumb old lady that is only good for yelling at and having sex with) I started yelling, well, bitching at my parents. They calmed me down and assured me that I would get a car soon, very soon. Clint was supposed to call me an hour after he dropped me off. I didn't think he would, I was right. I fell asleep anyway and woke up at 7:15am. I couldn't sleep. I called him and he said that he just fell asleep when he got home. In other worlds he didn't feel like dealing with me. Then he was tired and told me that if I couldn't sleep in half an hour phone him back and he'd come over. I was very upset and forty minutes passed so I called him. He was asleep. Why couldn't he just come over after the first time I called? He said I was a pain in the ass so I said he could call me whenever he got up. I think I need a hobby. On my report card I got straight A's. I was really happy about it. It is 9:00am; I've been up for two hours wasting my energy on nonsense. I guess I have to not care. I have to accept that Clint is mean-hearted and doesn't mean anything by it. My parents are immature and too involved in themselves to notice that I am their kid. I work my butt off to be perfect for everyone and it's getting me nowhere. I should tell how I'm feeling inside, not shut up and hope that someone will care enough to ask. I'm the only person that gives a flying fuck.

Feb. 7/8, 1997

I don't know what to do, I really don't. I love Clint but it hurts more than it doesn't. Tonight I went to comedy night with Tiffany and the whole time I wished to be with Clint. Then he was there but didn't even come say hi to me. Before I knew it he, Mac, Jake left to another bar. When I got to that one (following him like a puppy) he didn't say a word to me. So I didn't say anything to him and got madder and madder. So he thought I was giving him "attitude". Clint left by saying go back to your boyfriend Betty (Zarren that I pecked once three or four years ago). I was very hurt. I'm sick of feeling useless, unloved, and unwanted by Clint. I called him because I couldn't sleep. He doesn't care enough to open up to me, just gets madder and accuses me of "attitude" and thinking that he'd cheat on me, when I honestly trust him. I may have been cold to him but I was sick of being the only one hurting. I learned my lesson though, "you play with the bull, and you get the horns". I don't want to play.

Feb. 18, 1997

Belle is getting older right before my eyes. She even has a crush on a twenty-one year old! My Auntie Callie, Uncle Richard, and Debbie are moving out to Calgary. Clint doesn't get horny over seeing me in a sexy cute little outfit. And he makes fun of my candy, and he won't let me cut his hair, but I would love a man that let me do whatever I want to him.

Mar. 30, 1997

I think that C.M. and I have come to a point in our relationship where it will either stop or keep going. Lately he has been blowing me off. Not intentionally to be mean, he just doesn't want to spend as much time with me anymore (so I conclude). He cares more about drinking with the boys, getting his sleep, and saving money, than he does enjoying time with me. I really don't know what to think. I sometimes wonder if he is still as attracted to me as he used to be, not a great thing to think about. Lillian has started to come out with me and Clint the last two weekends and I almost think he's flirting with her. It's not that I'm mad at Lillian, because she doesn't flirt back. I don't flirt with his friends. Clint just doesn't treat me the same way as he used to. When I think back to how he used to talk to me, give me flowers for no reason, ask me out on a date, flirt with me, tell me he liked my bum, call me gorgeous, invite me to go out with him, want me around, etc… I realize that he has changed. He didn't use to tease me as much, say rude things, ditch me, and not miss me when I'm not around. I don't think I even got an Easter card. Last night he did give me a rose but I feel like he's only doing things with me because he thinks he has to and he doesn't have the guts to break up with me. I guess what I'll do is just lay low for a while. Let him have some time to think and give myself a chance to get back in touch with my friends and my dreams and my future life. I shouldn't need him to make me happy and I shouldn't let him make me sad.

Apr. 14, 1997

I have been trying not to write in my diary in order to remember the good things in my life. But if Clint is going to hang up on me then I can do whatever the hell I want. I really don't know why he's so mad. I guess it's because I worked late last night and he didn't know where I was. He called me at work and my boss was around so I told him I'd call him when I got home. I guess he was mad about that so when I called at 10:30, he hung up on me. I thought he didn't mean to, so I called him back again and he hung up on me again. I'm not going to bother calling again, I can take a hint. I had a long shower and it calmed me down a bit. But I just can't sleep so I decided to write. It allows me to get some of my feelings and anger out. I just wonder what's going on in his head! Clint claims that he doesn't remember me phoning and was mad today because I didn't call. How could I not believe him?

Apr. 22, 1997

C.M. and I are doing really good. I love him just as much now as I ever have! I went away on a softball tournament and when I got back Clint missed me because he got into way too much trouble while I was gone. If only I knew what that was that it took for him to appreciate me. That "point we came to", well we decided (s UNPonsciously), was to keep on going, just as strong as ever. Sure we don't have as much sex as we once did but it is still very good.

May 28, 1997

I've almost graduated. Only twelve more days of school and two exams. I'm going to go to Capsville and get a tattoo along with Clint, Mac and Mindy. I'm sure by the time I read this I'll know what I got. I know that Clint doesn't love me as much as I love him, but I'm okay with it. He just doesn't know how or is afraid of loving me completely. I wonder how he can get sick of me, when I don't get sick of him. We've spent five evenings together and tonight (I saw him then called to say good night) he was tired and didn't want to talk very long. I know I'm over reacting and I'm sure that he loves me very much but I have an active imagination. I should just think of all of the good things and how much I love him. I love his curly hair, his soft feet, his cute smile, his dimpled bum, his good taste, and the fact that he would never ever cheat on me. I wonder if I will always love him, if he will always love me, and if I will spend the rest of my life with Clint. I hope I never experience a broken heart.

June 1, 1997

Today I got my tattoo. It took about twenty-five minutes for mine, ten minutes for Mindy's, and fifteen for Clint and Mac's. They got matching hockey Canada tattoos. I took pictures and mine cost $85.60. I really like it. I showed my parents and at first my dad seemed a little mad, but soon he gave me a hug and said he liked it and hopes I'll always like it. I can't believe that "sweet" Betty got a tattoo. It hurt but not too much. I'm glad I went through with it. It feels cool or something. I don't know.

Aug. 1, 1997

Clint's mom went to Europe for a whole month so I lived with C.M. for that long. It was kind of cool not sleeping alone for a month. Now things are back to normal and I miss Clint. Because of work schedules we hardly see each other. Now he's going camping with the boys for August long weekend. I guess I'll have fun without him; I've got tons of stuff to do. I have a new kitten named Elliot Thomas (E.T.) and he is very comforting while C.W. isn't around. Except when he wants to play in the middle of the night. Oh well he is still the best male I've come across.

Aug. 3, 1997

For Clint's birthday I ended up getting him a ring. This was a very big step for me but I'm glad I did. Clint has invited me to go camping with him and the boys at Stem Lake. I'll go later today providing I won't be the only girl there. Clay and I would be better off if we lived together (I know scary thought). I think we both liked spending time together when his mom was away. But it's not like either of us could afford to move out. I hope I go camping and have a really good time with my Clint bear.

Aug. 13, 1997

Tonight Clint came over and worked on our roof with my dad. Then they talked and we all watched a movie together. Clint went home and I came into my room to my bed on the floor. I'm sick of living in a messy house. I'm sick of not sleeping with Clint beside me for more than three nights a month. I'm just sick of living at home. I haven't told Clint but I want to move out with him. I've been thinking about it for a while. I'll take Elliot and we'll manage. I just can't wait any longer; it's getting to that point. I don't want to live with mom, dad, and Belle. I love them all but I need to get out on my own. I need to do my own laundry for my own bathroom. I want to decorate my home the way that I want. It is a lot of money to throw away on rent every month but maybe it would be worth it. Clint and I would be happy spending every night together. I wish I won the lottery and had a ton of money, doesn't everyone. I just wish Clint and I lived together and slept beside one another every night. It's hard being young.

Nov. 7, 1997

I should really stop reading this. The more I do I get angry with C.M. We do have a lot of good times when he tickles me, playing psycho killer, going out for dinner, going shopping, sleeping in together, and all our sports. Last night was the opening night for the college play 'Billy the Kid'. I didn't get a part in the play and its' been hard for me. Last night was the night you get the flowers, you get the audience, you get every ones congrats, and all of your hard work finally pays off. I wasn't even allowed back stage. I felt like shit, like worthless scum. I felt bad, really bad. I hope I get a part in the spring production. If I don't I'll feel even worse. All I did was hold the door and collect tickets. I helped build the set but that wasn't enough. I should have gone on the running crew, because there is more to theatre than just acting. It has been a long time since I've been in a good play. It takes up a lot of your time but it is worth it at the end, very worth it. It is a nice day outside and I have a lot of homework to do and I'm lying in bed, watching the people's court and writing in this… so I'll get up.

No Such Thing As Secrets

Dec. 9, 1997 | 2:00am

I had my X-mas staff party last… well tonight. C.M. didn't go with me because he thinks everyone at the Tap is a loser, so I took Lillian. I don't know what's wrong with C.M. and me. It seems like I'm always mad at him and he's always complaining about spending time with me. I think I need some time alone, just to think and be myself.

Dec. 22, 1997 | 10:00am

It's almost Christmas and almost my birthday. Life is full of decisions, and hard ones at that. Clint and I have been having trouble. I work every Friday and Saturday so he goes out to the bar till who knows what hour. I just go to work, go home, and go to bed. I have often wanted to go out after work but haven't because of what Clint would say. So I went out on Friday and I had a lot of fun. Clint drove by my house, expecting me to be patiently waiting for him and I wasn't there. So he got really mad. He was yelling and swearing, and saying I was cheating on him and I'm sneaky and he's really fucking had it. So this upset me and I was crying. Then we were just about to go out to his staff party later that day and he started talking about it again. I didn't want to start crying just before we left so I told him that I didn't want to talk about it. Then we didn't end up talking about it until today (Monday). I find myself getting less attracted to Clint and more attracted to being single. I love Clint lots, but I have cried so many tears over him. And I don't think he's cried any over me. I don't want to let him get the opportunity to hurt me again and again. He won't dance with me, he won't meet any of my friends or co-workers, he won't stay home on Friday or Saturday or any night if I'm working, he's always too tired to see me, he doesn't trust me at all, he doesn't open up to me anymore. He thinks my job is dumb, he thinks my school is dumb, he thinks my family is dumb, he even thinks my dog is dumb. I can't argue with him because he goes out of control. He never tells me he loves me or I look pretty anymore. He doesn't seem as interested in me. Sex isn't the same; there are no feelings, just him getting it off. He doesn't appreciate anything I do for him. He takes me for granted. He doesn't want me to have a life one minute, but if I'm bugging him then I need to get a life. Sure he has a cabin, nice truck, jet-ski, boat, etc., but I've never been much for material possessions. I'm tired of feeling unloved and like I'm not worth anything.

Jan. 17, 1998

C.M. and I got in a big fight, so I broke up with him. But he was so upset and told me he would change and he's been trying very hard. I find myself not wanting to be with him though. I love him because he's my Clint bear. But I don't lust over him anymore. He is still the same old Clint, that I can't talk to and feel way too controlled by. I went to the bar on Friday and Jack was there, we danced and I find myself so attracted to him. It would be wrong of me to pretend to Clint that I love him and then flirt with Jack. I am constantly thinking about Pluto. He is cute and I wish I could see him in his birthday suit. I love Clint but I lust Pluto. I want to end it completely with Clint, I just don't know how to without hurting him. The last thing that I would ever want to do is hurt C.M. But I know what I have to do. I am nineteen and I want to go out with my friends and have fun and be young (without worrying what C.M. would say). I want and need the strength to walk away from Clint because I'm not being fare to either of us right now.

Feb. 2, 1998

Clint went to Mexico with all of his guy friends for a week. I thought it would be a good time to see how life was without him. He comes back today and I'm going to end it with him. I really had a great time without him and can't stay with him just so he's not upset. To make matters more complicated I ended up rear ending someone in his truck on Thursday. So I thought okay, I can't really say here's your truck and I don't want to see you anymore, but I'll pay the deductible. Then on Friday I went out with everyone from work. We went to Colonels, then to Kings and then Pluto and I walked back to our cars together flirting the whole way. When it came time for him to go his way and me to go mine we started kissing. It felt really natural to just kiss goodbye and his body felt so good up against mine. I wish I could re-live that moment over and over again. I felt his hard nipples and his wash board tummy. So anyway, I can't be with Clint now, it wouldn't be right.

No Such Thing As Secrets

Feb. 13, 1998

I broke up with Clint on the fifth. It was hard and it didn't happen the way I thought it would, but it happened. Clint is crushed by it; it is so hard to see him so upset. But I can't come this far and go back to him. He hasn't been sleeping, won't eat, is throwing up blood, and cries a lot. I'm very confused. A big part of me wants to give him a big hug and not ever let go and just hope that things will be different. But what if I still feel the same way and I'm just pretending for him. I still think Jack is cute but the last thing I want is a relationship. I'm worried that I will turn around one day and I'll want Clint back but he won't go back to me. But I know that there is plenty of fish in the sea and there will be someone perfect for me. Now I get to go out and have fun and not worry about anything!

Feb. 14, 1998

I had a great day. I woke up this morning and my mom left me some Purdy's Valentines treats. Then I talked to C.M. at work this afternoon and that wasn't so great. He's in a hate Betty stage. Then I worked my ass off because I was so busy. But Lillian dropped off a Valentines surprise for me. It almost made me cry it was so thoughtful. Then I drove Jack home and we kissed. That was exhilarating. Then I got home to a secret present, a rose and a little wolf teddy bear. But no one signed it except "not your x". So I'm puzzled and flattered and very happy. I would have to be some one that knows my address because it looks like it was delivered. Who could it be? Maybe a family member? Maybe Mindy, Kaitlyn, Jenny, or Lillian again? I'm puzzled. You know I feel the most loved I ever have right now, maybe I'm exaggerating. Maybe it was someone from my theatre program. I'm really happy right now. Really very, very happy!

Mar. 27, 1998

Clint and I are back together. After one month without him, I really missed him. Everything is so great now. I know he loves me and I know I love him.

July 14, 1998

I finally got another diary, four months after I finished my old one. My last diary lasted me eight and a half years! I wonder what stories this book will hold. Clint is done plumbing school but not working steady, so we can't afford to move out. I think that I should look for a second job but the summer is almost over now! I'm only working two to three nights a week and my two days of office work. That's only twenty hours a week. I wonder if I should go apply somewhere. I guess it wouldn't hurt to try. But who is going to hire me Mon-Fri during the day for the little bit of summer left? I'm getting really sick of living at home. Every time I mention moving out to Clint he doesn't answer, or he says "if the circumstances are right". I want to have him beside me every night, but I don't think that he feels the same way. But I guess that there aren't too many guys willing to snuggle. Clint and I have been together for three years now and it's almost like we're still dating. Most people get engaged by this point. Most couples move in together after one year. I'm so sick of living in this house. It is always messy. Belle and I are the only ones who ever clean. Everything in the house is so junky; you can't make it look good no matter how hard you try! I'd love to have my own place to keep clean (spotless), to decorate, to come home happily to. Once school starts I'll never see Clint unless we live together. It would cost us each a minimum of $150/paycheck for rent, so is $600/month worth it? Not to mention all the furniture, etc. we'll need. I think I'll start keeping my eyes open for kitchen stuff, etc. I guess I could come home for the computer or use the one at school. I guess the wisest thing to do is to paint my room and live with it, for what will (already does) seem like forever.

Aug. 2, 1998

Clint gave me a very nice TV for last Christmas and it is a beautiful TV. Well for some reason my dad wants it to be the family TV. I want it in my room, to keep nice and watch at my convenience. My fucking Dad keeps moving it out of my room and down stairs to the living room for the family to use. He has a smaller TV or an older TV the same size that he could use. Instead he disregards my wishes and takes my TV. It really annoys me that he doesn't respect my decision. I work hard for my money, really hard. I work hard so I can have a bed and bedroom furniture, nice clothes, and new shoes, put myself through school, and go out for dinner or lunch. Because I have things everyone seems to think that they are up for grabs. I like to share my clothes. I like to drive Belle everywhere as long as my mom and dad realize that I'm also doing them a favor. I develop all of everyone's film because they all use my camera. I don't mind buying Chinese food and pizza so everyone can eat it. I don't mind that my parents give everyone else money every month while I work my ass off to get ahead. Everyone thinks I'm rich so they take advantage of me. I only make about $800/month. No one ever thanks me; instead they treat me like I have too much. If I say anything they'll think I'm being selfish. Maybe I am being selfish. I don't know. One day when I'm rich I'll buy everything for everyone and love doing it, but I hope they would realize that it would be a gift from the heart, not the wallet. And a respectful thank you is all I would want.

Aug. 12, 1998

I'm bored waiting up for Clint to come over, and I've read everything, watched all the movies, and done my laundry and no cable so I'll write. I've also talked to or left messages with all my friends. Only three and a half weeks of summer left! Wow, back to school before I know it. I'm looking forward to seeing all of my theatre friends again, I miss all of them. It's Mick's birthday tomorrow so I might see him and Mel then. I'm helping Mindy and Cindy move during the day. I can't believe they're moving out together. I mean I would love to move out but I can't afford to spend that kind of money when I can live at home for free. All my friends are starting to do their own thing. Kaitlyn is moving to Cityville and going to U.B.C. in September. Janelle has a twenty thousand dollar car loan so she's working full time at 49th Parallel meat department and not going to school this year. Mindy is moving but can't afford to (more guts than me). Suzanne doesn't know what she wants to do with her life, so she works at the Horse and Barn Pub, sees Wayne and smokes cigarettes every day. Lillian has low self-esteem so she lets guys treat her badly and she worries too much about how she looks. Judy has to stop spending so much time with Stan. She never phones or does enough with Lillian, Mindy and me because of her family (long story) and Stan. Helga is living in Cityville after having a love affair with her married boss Tharon. He got her to leave town and then dumped her! Melissa is going to the gym every single day because she wants to become a body builder champion. Erica and Minka do coke. I don't know how often but I don't think too often. In high school we used to all sit in the cafeteria and all be kids, talk, and just hang out. What happened? Oh, Clint's here.

Sept. 7, 1998

Tomorrow is my first day of school, second year at Millispi College in the theatre program. I'm looking forward to seeing all my old theatre friends; I haven't seen any of them all summer. I went to a Shanty Swain concert with Mick, Suzanne, and Helga. I went shopping with Mel once. That's it! Kaitlyn is over at UNP in dorms. I'm very excited for her; it's a whole new life for her now! I am hopefully going to be going to SWU next year and living in Cityville (well Burnaby). I hope that Clint decides to go with me. I don't know what I'll do if he decides to stay here. I would just miss him too much. Clint and I just got back from Horne Lake (our annual ten day summer vacation). We didn't get any time alone! All of our friends and family were always there, which was fine because I enjoyed their company but next year we'll go to Mexico for less of a headache and more romance.

Sept. 25, 1998

School is going by so quickly. I love my second year at Mill-U! I love Mel and Mick and my other friends. I see Mindy, Suzanne, Lillian, and Cindy rarely because all my classes are at different times than theirs. I am in a script writing class and I think I'm a bit over my head! I have to write a hundred and twenty page movie script by the end of the semester! I've started on it, and I know that I can finish it, but it'll be hard. Rick is doing the Tempest for our fall production and auditions are in three days. I really hope that I get a good part! But what if I don't? I know that I can do a great job, if I get the chance.

Oct. 9, 1998

Rick gave me the part of Miranda, the lead! I'm so excited; I'm giving it my all. My prince is Tyler Scotts, a first year. My father is Richard, my friend who is also second year. Mick got a shitty part. Mel got a good part. After rehearsal last night my car was acting funny. I didn't know what was wrong. I thought that I needed oil and I did. My car engine seized on the way home. I had to walk from my car to Malway in the dark to use a phone. I'm sure that I'm never going to hear the end of it from my dad. My dad will be surprised if my car ever works again. So I'm fucked! I'll just have to get a little loan and get a new car I guess. My grandma is in the hospital again. The stupid doctors put a pace maker in her and something's wrong her heart. It's enflamed she's having severe chest pains and trouble breathing. The doctors have no clue what's going on so they just pump her full of Demerol and "run tests". In my opinion those doctors just keep on fucking her up more and more! I'm really scared that my grandma won't make it out of the hospital. My grandma is the closest thing to perfect that I know. She is wonderful; she is so pure and full of love. My grandma loves me no matter what… that's something that not everyone can do. I want her to see me star in this play; I want her to be there when I get accepted into SWU! I want to tell her all about my life and hear all about hers. Did you know my grandpa was the "milk man"? When they met she was a cashier at the dairy. I guess there will never be the right time for her to go, but now isn't right! I'll just miss her so much. We love each other exactly the way we are, the most honest love.

Oct. 9, 1998

I had rehearsal tonight and loved every minute of it. I feel so loved all night (due to the script). My father, Prospero, and my prince, Ferdinand, tell me how much they love me. So I walk away feeling so loved. I haven't seen Clint for a couple of days and I don't miss him. I'm just having so much fun with rehearsal that I haven't had a chance to. My prince is really good looking! He keeps looking into my eyes and me into his. He tells me his love in beautiful Shakespearean iambic pentameter. He is tall, strong, funny and young. I feel butterflies when he puts his arms around me. I know that I'm falling in love with the prince, not Tyler Scotts, but what if I'm wrong. I don't think he has any feelings for me outside of the play. I want so, so much to just share one little kiss. I love Clint and the thought of us breaking up is upsetting but how can I feel this strong interest in some guy I don't even know?

Oct. 23, 1998

I love Clint with all of my heart but he's jealous and it bugs me. Here I am again feeling unloved and ugly. I feel like guys aren't attracted to me once they get to know me (once the initial "I'd fuck her" wears off). I've been with Clint and Clint only for three years, three months, and seventeen days. Is that a long time? Is there a magical unbelievable prince out there for me? Have I already met him?

Nov. 5, 1998

Tonight is opening night for the Tempest, my big dramatic role as Miranda! I think that I play comedy much better, but beggars can't be choosers! My Mom, Dad, Belle, Clint and his friend Randy, Lillian and her Dad, Jessie and her two friends, maybe some people from work and maybe even Beatrice and Tyson are coming! So yes, lots of eyes on me. We've reserved about two hundred tickets for tonight. I'm going to school at 4pm to work on scenes again and the play starts at 8pm. I'm a little nervous but it's not bad at all. Clint and Randy went out shopping last night for new clothes and Clint got his hair cut. They're going to look so cute. We'll see how Clint does mixing with the theatre people tonight. If he's totally cool than that will make me love him more. But if he's a jealous loser saying stupid shit then I'll be mad and take a good look at our relationship. So rather than worry about tonight, I'll just take it as a chance to see what kind of guy he can be.

Nov. 9, 1998

Well Clint fucked up royally on opening night. He and Randy got really drunk and he said he was cramping my style. He said I couldn't be myself and I was two different people. He left saying that he didn't know where he was going, and he made fun of every guy there. Tyler and I got a picture together and he was "joking" about how he was going to beat Tyler up. I asked if I would see him later and he said "well you won't be home" so I asked him where I would be and he said "I don't know, wherever you usually are". I let him go and I had fun without him there. Then he went to the Bearzly and got in a fight with Ray from Grocery Country. I got two different stories about why. One from Clint and one from the Grocery Country staff. Why do I have to be in love with him? Anyways, he came over the next morning and said he was sorry and he would never drink again. So he didn't go out Friday or Saturday night. Wow, is all I have to say. Anyway Clint has been suck holing ever since and I've been so busy that I haven't had time to really think about it. Clint's talking about moving to Cityville with me and basically putting me through school. But I don't want that. So what do I do, what should I do, what will I do??? Beatrice went into labor Saturday morning and had Tabitha at 6:25am on Sunday morning.

Nov. 15, 1998 | **5:55am**

I'm going to bed now! I've been high on mushrooms all night and it was so cool. I had so much fun, they're awesome. I told Clint that I was doing an all night strike at school which was half lying. I felt bad, but hmmm, I don't know, I wouldn't give up the fun that I had tonight with everyone for anything! I felt like such a little kid all night. I'm so coming down now. I didn't hang out with just one group, instead I ran around seeing everyone. I felt like everyone wanted to be around me, and I was blessing them with my high presence. Then I got soaked (it was raining) so Tyler gave me his sweatshirt and pants to wear. I'm still in the top, it smells so good. Hmmm, I think if he goes to SWU and I go there we'll totally get together. Smells so good, interesting eh.

Dec. 12, 1998

Life is full of decisions. Some of them are easy, but most are hard. How do you ever know if you're going down the right path?

Feb. 18, 1999

I haven't written in my diary for a while. Clint read my diary on my birthday. He read about Tyler. So I thought he was cute, big deal. Clint thought I was in love or something. So I haven't written since then. But tonight I will. Clint is away in Capsville going to school.

Mar. 21, 1999

Clint and I broke up on March 14th, 1999. It is forever this time. I just finally realized that I don't want to spend the rest of my life with him. He didn't take it well. He and I were both crying and looking at each other's sad faces. He said "if you're sure that this is it then I'll go, are you sure?" so I nodded my head to say yes. He said "fine I want you to remember what I tell you, fuck you! I hope someone

fucks you over the way you've fucked me over because this fuckin hurts". Then he said a few other things too, and left slamming the door as hard as he could. Then he came back in and said "I want my stuff. Anything of yours I'm throwing out. Give me my stuff." I told him I'd drop it off. He said "no I don't ever want to see you or speak to you again, go and get it now." So I said "fine I'll get someone else to drop it off". Then he left again saying more kind words. I got his stuff together and Mindy dropped it off. I haven't spoken or heard from him since. It's been one week today. I just wonder how he's doing and if he's okay, but he and I are not right for each other. I need to get back to the girl that I used to be. I'm not going to make sacrifices like I did with Clint. This is my life and I have to live it for me. Life is full of learning experiences.
(The Tap burnt down that same week and I lost my job too. It was a really bad week for me.)

Mar. 28, 1999

Well shortly after Clint and I have broken up I heard a ton of rumors. It seems that half of Newsville knows that he's a little slut who can't keep his hands, lips, or dick to himself. He denies everything, but I'm tired of believing his lies. Too many people have said too much. It's all of them who are lying or him. He was at Martha's house on my prom night, he told me he spent the night at Johan's, but Martha told Jane that he spent the night with her. That doesn't make me feel too good. All of Newsville knows he's a cheater and a mean drunk. A big part of me wants to break his nose and then run over him. Lillian's Dad has heard that Clint cheated on me in Mexico. I mean full out cheating, fucked another girl! I've confronted him but he just gets mad and says that everyone just wants to get into my pants and that's why they're telling me bad things. Zeus' girlfriend Rona has heard the boys joke about some of the girls; they've gone as far as to joke about Clint fucking some girl in Cityville. I don't find it all too funny. I'm really scared to ever go out with a guy ever again. But I also want so badly to have a man's strong arms around me. I would just lie on a man's chest and feel protected from the world. But then what if he just gets up all of the sudden and leaves me for another girl? I don't know what to do with myself. I know that my prince charming is out there somewhere and we'll be happy together some day and we'll love each other, be very attracted to each other, and have a lot of fun together… some day, right?

No Such Thing As Secrets

Apr. 6, 1999

Tonight Annie is sleeping with Auntie Betty. Annie is helping me write in my diary, in my house. Annie is three years old and very cute. "My dad smokes just outside" says Annie. "On my lights… I in your bed" says Annie. "Say you have a picture… of guys". Annie is snuggled up right beside me. This will be the first time she slept over with me. She has me pushed up against the side of the bed not letting an inch go between us. I wonder if some day she'll be older and we'll look back at this together. I should "say I got my necklace on"…she wants me to stop writing. Annie brought all sorts of animals into bed to keep us company. She wants to go now, but Annie I want you to know that you are very special and I love you forever. I'll give you anything that you ever need.

Apr. 18, 1999

Well it's been five weeks today since I've seen Clint. I don't know how to explain how this all feels. A part of me misses his body next to me at night. I miss the hugs, I miss the holding hands. I miss the comfort of having someone. At the same time I hate what he has done to me. He is a mean person who doesn't know how to love anything. He is immature, racist, a bully, judgmental, insecure, and he can't keep his dick in his pants! I know that he wasn't right for me for many reasons, but it is so hard to go from having a best friend to not even talking on the phone in weeks. When I think about our relationship sometimes I just want to cry and other times I just want to yell and hit him and then I think that I should hide or just run away. My life makes no sense right now. There are tons of guys that I could date and they're hot too, but I just can't. I hate men. I just find them only interested in fucking. All of them only care about their dicks and so I'll just be single for a while.

May 5, 1999

My life is full of order once again. Lillian and I are moving out June first. I'm very excited. I'm working more than full time, so that's great. I would love to love someone but I don't know if I'm ready to have someone cheat on me and leave me so I just can't let myself get committed to anyone. I'm the girl that loves to get dirty playing sports, the girl who spits and farts, the girl that loves her family and stands by her friends, the girl who is quiet and shy at times and goofy and wacked out at others, the girl with no make-up, lying in bed in her pajamas, the girl who needs to be loved and protected but scared of looking like a pansy-ass. The girl who wants to trust a man and have a man that trusts her in return. The girl, who needs to be hugged, not screwed! Maybe I'll have to see what Dirk Manly thinks about average girls with mild fears hidden by bullshit and a smile. What I really want is someone to talk to.

May 27, 1999

On Monday May 17th, 99, Pete and I went on our first date. We went to the casino, played pool, and we went to subway. It wasn't really a date. We just hung out. We kissed when I dropped him off. I enjoyed kissing him. We stayed the night at Roper ford for StarWars opening on the 18th and saw StarWars the 19th. I met his mom and dad the 21st. He met Belle the 23rd. A lot of my girlfriends (Mindy, Lillian, Judy, and Suzanne) met him the 19th. We slept together on May 25th –99. It was very passionate. Yes, I think this is moving way too quickly but I can't help it. I love spending time with him. So far I like everything about him. I worry that he'll stop liking me or he'll like some other girl. I worry that I want to spend too much time together. I know you're always supposed to choose love over fear, so I'll try not to worry.

June 1, 1999

Well I'm still happy with Pete. The poor boy is confused about what he should do in life. I guess his parents weren't always saying "life is what you make of it" and "you can do anything" like mine. I'm very thankful that I know exactly what I want to do with my life. I'm going to school so I can make movies and show people how wonderful our world is. I think the world is good and full of good people who have a few problems. I think that life can be perfect if you follow your heart, not your head. Your head worries way too much about money and getting hurt in some way. Maybe I'm supposed to help Pete relax and that is why our higher selves brought us together. Well I'm hoping that he'll show me that men can be nice and they don't always think with their dicks. I can only hope that he won't take advantage of my trust and I can't fear.

No Such Thing As Secrets

June 27, 1999

I'm not with Pete anymore, too wimpy. He just wasn't for me. I quit Chicago Pizza too. The owner was mean to me so I told him off and walked out. I got hired the next day at the Springset Pub. It's really cool there, lots of regulars. It's also cool because it's all girls that work there. So far they all seem very nice. The tips are good, 15% average at the end of the night. I'm going to apply at the Real Room as well; it's a night club in town. Lillian and I have two kittens. Our little apartment is very nice and our kittens are like little babies. I do miss Elliot a lot; I wish that I could have brought him with me. I do miss seeing my family every day, but I love this place too.

July 10, 1999

I just got off work at the Springset Pub. I'm working at the Real Room too. It's the hottest club in town. Look at me! I'm such a waitress… I had a bad night tonight. I guess my bad day started yesterday. I've had a little crush on Caiden since I met him, but I've always been with Clint. Anyway we got together the other night. As much as I didn't want to go anywhere with it cause he has a girlfriend I couldn't help it. I've always liked him. We ended up sleeping together a few days later. It was awkward, but good. Anyways, he's going to stay together with his girlfriend so that's the end of that. I did a one-night stand. He doesn't like me and I feel horrible over the fact that he had a girlfriend and I was "the other woman". Every time my dad cheated on my mom there was the "whore", the "bitch", the "other woman". I hate all the "cunts" Clint cheated on me with. Now I'm no better than the rest of them. I was coming home from work tonight and someone was following me and I was scared. I was thinking oh great, which psycho that I served tonight is following me? I deeked them out, but they kept on following me. It turned out to be the cops, but for five minutes they followed me before putting their lights on. They let me go after I told them that I was scared. It just made me wish that I had a boyfriend to protect me. I came home to no one to comfort me and tell me to stop being a baby. It would have been Clint and my four year mark a few days ago. Oh well, some day my prince will come and he'll be single I hope… or I'll just die an unhappy, old, grumpy lady.

Aug. 12, 1999

Caiden left his girlfriend for me. How nice… Everything was going fine. We went on a few dates and spent time together. I felt comfortable talking to him. Then I didn't hear from him for like a week. I phoned a couple times and left messages but he never called back. I don't know what to say except I've been played. He played me for the fool that I am.

Aug. 16, 1999

What am I doing with my life? I guess being young and having fun, almost too much fun! I haven't even applied to film school yet. I'm very disappointed in myself for letting days go by without working on my application. I'm working at the Real Room and the Grub co. now. They are both nice places to work with nice co-workers. I work with a lot of hot guys at RR, but don't worry I'll stay away from guys I work with. But some of them are so cute though…

Sept. 1, 1999

I should focus on school and career right now. I have to get accepted into Cityville Film School, which is my new priority.

CHAPTER THREE

Sept. 17, 1999

How do you decide what your morals are and if they're right or not? I can go on the internet and on a webcam and show my body while typing dirty things to a bunch of old pigs watching. It pays a lot of money. I could make around $100 U.S. for an hour and a half of work. Only it's not even really work. I make my own hours, I do what I choose to do, and I can turn it off at anytime that I want. So is this a bad thing or a good thing? Is the human body so bad that I can't show mine? I need over $30,000 for school and I can't make more money serving beer to a bunch of drunks. I have drunk guys hit on me all night at the Press Room, putting their arms around me, touching my waist, rubbing my arm. I don't like to be touched! Just because they order a beer and maybe tip me a dollar doesn't mean they can touch me! Then at the restaurant I smile and put up with people, biting my tongue the whole time. Just because I serve someone a meal and cater to there every need doesn't mean I'm not as good as them. They wave their hands to shoe me away and snap their fingers to bring me to them. I put up with it for a five dollar tip. Now is that worth it? Some tables are very nice and they treat me like a person, but no one ever respects me. A waitress is not a respectful job like a lawyer or even a bank teller. My body aches by the end of a day at both jobs. I make about one hundred dollars in tips for the whole eight hours! So why shouldn't I paint my nails in my underwear while old men whack it? I'd rather work for myself because I know that I'll never treat myself like shit for $7.15/hr. I'll respect me more than any boss of mine ever has. I'll have time to go to the gym every day, spend time with my family, and clean up this house. So once again I'm asking is this a bad thing or a good thing?

Sept. 26, 1999

It's amazing how much I write in this when I don't have a boyfriend taking up all of my time. Boys are nothing but trouble. I don't even know how to react with boys anymore. I have trouble being nice to them. I don't trust them. I think they're all full of crap. They tell you what you want to hear and think something else.

Oct. 13, 1999

Well I don't know if anything is really new with me. Judy is going to teach me how to flirt. I just don't do a good job of it. If I see a guy that I think is cute then I just don't look at him. It doesn't make any sense, eh. I went to Cowgary to get my Auntie Dana and that was fun. I needed a friend there to have more fun though. I haven't talked to Clint in a long time. I just don't know if I should or not, so I don't. I do know that I don't love him anymore. I don't want to be passionate with him. He still has his mean side of him and I don't need that in my life. I still think Kenny Smalls is kind of cute. Judy thinks that he is just a player though. I don't need that either. Mind you to look at me people would probably say the same about me. Kent at work told me that guys are scared to talk to me and I'm unapproachable. I'm nice. Why are they scared to talk to me? It makes no sense to me. Well maybe if Judy teaches me how to flirt that will change. I don't understand why there has to be all of these games involved with dating. Why can't we all just be honest? Why can't a guy just come up and ask a girl out if he likes her? I look forward to the day that my husband and I can look back at my notes and laugh about how naive I was. Whoever he is I wonder if he's having this much trouble dating. I wonder if he thinks about getting married to someone like me. I hope he's having fun and getting it out of his system so he's ready to settle down with me and our five kids!! He's going to be perfect, or I'm not marrying him!

Oct. 19, 1999

I have to make myself more motivated. I have all these things to do and I don't do them. I'm just tired or I go out with friends or watch a movie instead. I'm going to have to start writing a list of things to do in a day and start doing them! I have to find a school and apply to it, go online more often, buy a new computer, keep up with laundry, fix up my truck, work at the Real Room, get into tanning, edit videos, edit my movie, etc etc. There is always something to do, always.

Oct. 21, 1999

Tonight the coolest thing in the world happened to me. Thank you spirit guides! We went to the Real Room. We did E and so I didn't feel like going to bed after the bar closed. Lillian went to Kyle's house and Judy went home to bed. So I would be all alone, high and energized. So on the way home I was thinking "how am I going to amuse myself, I'll be so bored" etc. Then I pull into my driveway and there in front of me there are 2 horses in my yard. Do you believe it; I have to be the luckiest girl alive! I'm in need of something to do and there is my favorite thing in the world in my yard. I love horses so much and someone gave me a beautiful present tonight. I woke up Bonnie, Mom and Dad and said "there are horses in the yard and I'm feeding them apples!" Of course no one believed me until I made them look out the window. I was outside with those beautiful animals in my yard feeding them apples. I phoned Judy and Lillian and told them too. They're happy for me. This was the best present anyone could have given me ever and I thank whoever did this! Very much! My life is wonderful; I don't have any man bringing me down. If I'm lonely the universe gives me wonderful horses in my yard! I love my life; I'm so happy right now (because there are horses in my yard). I thought about Kenny tonight. He wasn't out but all night I wished to see him. I hope I'm not being stupid with this. I like him no matter how hard I try not to. I like Kenny Smalls, but I like horses way more!

No Such Thing As Secrets

Oct. 25, 1999

Well I went to the gym today to see Kenny and work out. I'm getting pretty buff indeed! That's a good thing, I don't ever think about not eating something or throwing up because I'm in great shape.

Nov. 5, 1999

Well a few things have happened. Halloween at the Real Room went well. I'm proud of myself for all my hard work, it paid off. Saturday night was great, 95% of the packed full bar were dressed up in some really cool costumes. Everyone had a lot of fun. But at one point earlier I went to Clint's to drop off tickets (nice of me). He once again got into the why can't we be together and blamed me for ruining his life. So the question of cheating came up and the answer was an absolute no, I never would, hostile to me for asking. At the bar that night I saw Nick and I asked him again "did Clint cheat on me" and he nodded his head yes. I said "thank you, that's why you're my favorite monkey" (they were all dressed like apes). I was on E so it didn't totally click right away but I was upset and I needed my friends. So there you have it, Clint is the biggest liar in the world who thinks only of himself. I'm so angry with him, it's not even funny. I believed him when he told me that he didn't do it. Now I believe everyone who ever told me that he cheated, so that means Mexico, Cityville trip, my prom, and more. I haven't called him on it yet. I'm told that it will only make me feel worse. I think it would be great myself. But he's gone out of my guilt now at least.

Nov. 3, 1999

I got my tongue pierced. This is the most painful body art that I've experienced. My tongue is so swollen, it really sucks. It will be all good soon though (by the 6th or 7th). I went over to Mace's house on the third too. We've been out a few times now. He's so sweet the way he's so gentle. So now what???

Nov. 9, 1999

Well I've decided to quit my job at the Real Room and work online full time. The money is good and I'm helping lonely people out. I'm my own boss. I set my own hours and I do what I want to do. I'm going to get a $4000.00 Imac computer. It's $136/month for three years. I can do everything all in the comfort of my own bedroom. With this computer I'll be able to edit videos at home on it. It has everything! That night Mace and I were together I told him office gossip and he blabbed it and in turn got me in hot water with a couple people at work. So there you go, I thought he was cool but he just ran and told people the second he could. That shows that you can't trust him.

Nov. 12, 1999

So what am I doing with my life now? I've decided that I want to quit the Real Room and work online full time. I need to save a lot of money for school and that's the only way how. I'm excited because I've found a couple of guys that I can go snowboarding with this year. So yeah, I won't have to go by myself. One of the guys I think is very cute but Lillian used to like him and maybe still does. That means that I can't like him. I'm sure he wouldn't like me anyway. Oh well, I'll still have fun boarding with them. I'm so nervous about quitting the RR. I hate quitting jobs, but it's what I have to do. I really think that I'll be happy if I stay at home more and make tons of money on-line. For social fun, I'll go boarding. That will cost me just as much as it would to go out drinking one night, only much better for me.

Nov. 14, 1999

I'd like to know what is wrong with me that I can't ever find a boy. I'm a nice girl, I'm kind of cute, and I'm funny. It seems like unless you're really forward you don't get a guy. Lillian talked me into putting a note on Kenny's truck after the gym saying "call me" more or less. Well he never called. So now I feel like a really big looser and I never want him to see me again. Then I thought I would kind of talk to Mace but he doesn't seem interested. Lillian was working at the real Room and they were joking around and he tackled her to the ground and was lying on top of her. I guess he was only interested in one thing from me. They want my body or nothing at all.

No Such Thing As Secrets

Nov. 24, 1999

I went down to Capsville last weekend with Jessie and I saw Pluto (Jack Halt). He looked just as cute as he always has. He kissed my hand at the end of the night (he was working in a lounge). I left and nothing was said. I'm really hoping my bad luck streak will end and I'll have good fortune with Jack. I think he could be charming to a girl. Well I'm hoping for that anyway. Maybe I shouldn't even bother and save myself the trouble. All I'll say is it sure would be nice to be treated well by a boy who wanted more than one thing from me…

Nov. 26, 1999

1 month till my birthday! Well today is my last day of work at the Real Room. Brenda (owner) came up to me on Wednesday and asked if I would reconsider and how much she appreciated the work I've done and I've done a great job, etc. I've decided that Mace is nothing more than a self centered PIG! It was like he was only out for one thing and once he got it he wasn't interested in anything else. Is that all I am to men, a conquest? Oh well at least today is my last day of work at the RR, and then I don't have to leave my room.

Nov. 30, 1999

Today I get my computer and video camera! I'm very excited about it. I haven't slept that well last night because I've been excited. I'm getting an iMac with fire wire and DVD and a DV Sony camera. Both will have a three year warranty on them. Elliot just jumped up to snuggle. He's such a good cat, he keeps me company every night. He's a great companion. I went to a Christmas party of Tyson's with Tyson, Beatrice and a friend Tyson works with, Eddie. Eddie met me at Beatrice and Tyson's house one night and has been talking to Tyson about me ever since. He was very nice; he brought me flowers and was complimenting me all night. He was dressed very nice, but alas, no sparks. I wonder what the future holds…

Dec. 2, 1999

I had a dream last night. I dreamt that Belle and Lillian wrote and told Opal how much I love Dirk Manly. Then I went on Opal to see him but I didn't know why I was on the show. Then I met him and he was wearing Mickey Mouse socks like I do and we got along really well. I think he was even flirting with me. I wonder what he's like in real life. Who knows, he could be a loser or a big pig or a jerk, etc. I'm just listening to that Christmas Figgie pudding song. I always thought those kids were so rude demanding Figgie pudding like they do. Anyway I have my computer and video camera now. It's very cool, but I don't know how to work it all yet. I will soon I'm sure. I wonder if I'll ever meet Dirk Manly...

Dec. 5, 1999

I saw the movie Madog, starring Abe Benson and Dirk Manly. I can only hope that he is as wonderful as I perceive him to be. Think of how cute our kids would be. Still though, even if Dirk Manly was in some weird way put on my doorstep, I think I would hold back right now. I'm so scared of getting hurt and not getting loved back I don't know if I can trust. I'm going to try not to fear and to love and to trust my higher self. There is the perfect guy for me out there and we will be happy together and knowing that will keep me warm at night, that and Elliot. Life is what you make it and my life is full of love and happiness (hopefully someday soon)...

Dec. 16, 1999

Well, Kenny Smalls likes Lillian. He asked for her phone number and said he'd like to call her. She told me to be a friend. I felt like a big loser! What is wrong with me? Not to sound mean, but Lillian has head problems, she cheats on all her boyfriends, she has a very bad temper, she's anorexic, and she flirts with every guy she sees. Don't get me wrong, she's one of my best friends, but I wouldn't set her up with anyone I didn't want to hurt. I sometimes wonder if I'll ever love again or be loved, I mean truly and deeply loved by that same person that I truly and deeply love. Is there that perfect love? Where you can't imagine a better person, who you're proud of, devoted to, attracted to and all round in love with. I want that love where I know deep down I'm loved. I know that I can open up and talk to him. Tell him all my deepest feelings and not fear what he'll tell me after. I want to spend days relaxing together and not get sick of each other. I want to go to parties together and actually have a good time. I want ten times better than the best sex that I've ever had, every night. I want to have a family with him and not worry about the way he treats my kids or me. I want to have a trust stronger than an infant's trust of their mother. I want to play sports with him, laugh with him, and grow with him. I want to love everything about him, good and bad, just because it's him. I want to share the passion of life together. I want to spend my life being in love with that one person who was put on earth for me. I want to share happiness with him (wherever he may be). All I can say is he better come…

Dec. 19, 1999

Well I went to Cityville with Judy to meet Mitch and his Aussie friend Skylar and we were maybe going to stay at their friend Phil's house. We arrived at Phil's at 1:30 and Mitch was sick so he went to bed. Phil and Skylar were out snowboard shopping so it was just Judy, Phil's family, and I. We went to the fish market. His family was very nice and made us feel very welcome. Phil's sister was showing us her favorite toys, a bouncing tiger and monster that Phil gave her for Christmas last year. So I instantly thought, what a sweetheart. I was thinking that he sounded likeable before I even met him. So Judy and I were watching a movie when Phil and Skylar got home. As soon as I saw him I thought, wow he's pretty hot. But I didn't think anymore about it. I didn't think that he would be single or like me, you know etc. So Skylar, Phil, Judy and I went in the hot tub and we were talking and I thought that he might have been flirting with me but I didn't know. I of course was more and more attracted to him as the night went on. So then Phil and I go to pick up pizza together and we got a chance to break the ice. He asked if I had a boyfriend, etc. We got back, had pizza, got ready and went to the Roxby where we met some of Phil's friends. We went in very deep mud in his jeep on the way there (4X4ing) which I didn't think city boys even knew how to do. We had fun at the bar, dancing and me attempting to flirt back with him. I had so much fun dancing with him. Then we were sitting at our table and he came up from behind me and started massaging my neck. All I could think to myself besides this is so nice to have a cool guy massage my neck was, it's about time I was the lucky one. So we went back to his house after the bar.

When we got home he suggested that him and I go in the hot tub and I wasn't about to say no. We were in the hot tub talking and talking. I felt that there was so much to talk about. It's like I wanted to tell him all about my life and I wanted to learn all about him. Anyway we started kissing and I actually wasn't thinking about it too much. I was just kissing him. So we were kissing in his hot tub and I was having a really good time doing just that. But his mom came out and so we went to bed and I spent half an hour lying in bed remembering the kissing with a little smile on my face. The next morning I didn't know what he would think but he did give me his number and told me to call him when I got home. I didn't because I was so late getting home and I didn't want to call too late. I've been thinking about him all day. Wondering what this means, if anything. I hope I wasn't just "some chick" to him but I wouldn't presume to know what he feels. I'm scared to call him but I will.

Dec. 29, 1999

Well the biggest New Years Eve is coming up. I'm going to Mt.Laundryton for it with some friends. It should be fun; I bought a really nice dress for it. Janelle and I are going dress shopping for her dress today. Part of me thinks that I should be at home with my family but they're all couples and so I'd rather be with lots of people.

Jan. 5, 2000

I can't believe I'm writing that date, "2000". Anyways I had an awesome New Years, except I hurt my arm pretty bad trying to clear a jump snowboarding. I had to dance with one arm all night because I couldn't move the other one, but oh well. I had lots of compliments on my dress from boys and mostly girls. I threw up at the stroke of twelve, that champagne didn't go down too well. No one caught me, I just grabbed Janelle's cup, spit it out, put it down, and kept on going! All and all it was a good New Years. I've talked to Phil since then and so the phone flirting continues. He is so hard to read. I don't know if he likes me or doesn't or what. Anyway he was saying that he and his friends were thinking about coming to Newsville one weekend. So I told him that they could stay here. Now that means that I'll have to make this house presentable ASAP. Its times that I want to invite people here that I really hate living in such a messy house. It would be so nice to want to show people where I live. Well I guess complaining about it won't help any. If you want something done than do it yourself, right. I'll just spend time fixing up the place and hopefully it will be ready to go in a couple of weeks. Besides, I'm almost certain that we whom live here care more than our guests ever do.

Jan. 14, 2000

I think I have a problem where I have to be the best at everything I do, or it's not good enough. I was watching snowboarding on TV and I was getting mad at myself for not jumping bigger and being the best. Already when I go up the mountain I don't see any girls better than me, but this is a small island. There is lots of girl's way better than me in the world. You look at my relationship with Clint. I constantly tried to be the "perfect girlfriend". I would not let things bother me just to be the perfect understanding cool girlfriend. When I look at my body I see imperfection, it's not perfect. I shouldn't care, it's good enough. In school I always wanted good grades to be the perfect daughter. Why am I obsessed with being perfect? Whenever there is a competition, I have to win. It drives me nuts not to win. I'm especially like this with sports, and even more so against other women. Everything I do, I try to do perfectly. Maybe it's because a lot of people expect me to be perfect. If I ended up not going back to school, that would appall people. My grandma expects me to be the one who goes all the way with school and gets out of poverty. And I honestly think I will. Sometimes I wonder why I try so hard to impress everyone. Live up to everyone's expectations of me. I don't know why I can't stop trying to be perfect. There is this thing inside me that keeps saying "that's not good enough Betty", "you could have done better", "why can't you do that", "be a good person", "don't judge people", "say thank you", "smile", "don't argue", "he won't like you anyway", "pretend you don't care", "don't be a pansy ass", "your being stupid", "don't really tell them how you feel". Does everyone hear these pressures?

Jan. 15, 2000

Brooklyn and Rant had a few people over at their house tonight. They had a bonfire. I had a few drinks and a couple of hoots. That's only three ciders and two hoots. And I'm pretty tipsy. Hey maybe I'll call Mindy. I'm talking to Mindy right now. Mindy says I'm a fickle person. She says that cause it's an inside joke, hmmm, men are bad. I've learned this. I'm telling Mindy about Phil now; I don't think she cares though. She just wants to know if he has a friend. Now look who is fickle. I like Rob. I hate Clint. Mindy says I'm a cheap drunk. She also says that Lillian is always doing stupid things. I can't wait; I'm going to Cityville on Tuesday to see Phil. I'm so excited! I can't wait to see Phil much better than only talk, talk, talking all of the time. Anyway I'm just going to bed now; I'm too intoxicated to talk now.

Jan. 19, 2000

I told Phil about my internet porn. He kind of guessed something was up. He asked a couple of questions and I told him little details. And he still wants to see me. He didn't care. But who knows what he really thinks. I'm glad that he still wants to see me. As Mindy says Phil has passed the first test. He wants to go skiing at Mt.Cook this Tuesday with me. I think that that will be fun. I'm looking forward to seeing him. If he cancels on me again I'm going to be very upset. I don't want to get my hopes up yet I'm excited about Tuesday already. Mindy can't wait for him to come over here so she can test him. I don't want to show him my messy house. Mindy says that my house is test #2. My friends are #3. My cat Elliot is #4 and I forget what we said #5 was. I don't believe in testing myself. Mind you Clint did fail every one of Mindy's "tests" so…

Jan. 23, 2000

I'm going to Cityville tomorrow night to see Phil. Then the two of us are going snowboarding at Mt. Cook. It should be quite fun. I'm worried because we haven't seen each other in so long. I know I worry too much. I don't know what to do when I get off the ferry. I hope we can recognize each other. I went out for a "truths" dinner (sat. 22nd night) that Clint invited me on. He brought flowers, took me to Capsville to dinner and a play. He had tickets reserved. He opened my door, etc., but I didn't fall for it. He's still the same jerk underneath his lies and acting.

No Such Thing As Secrets

Feb. 6, 2000

The world is a mystery to me. Everyone wants to feel self-worth and we do all sorts of strange things to be "liked", to be "adored" and "cool" and "popular" and "the best". Really we should feel good about ourselves, stop judging ourselves and others and feel confident that we are decent people. I look around and I see a lot of troubled people. Everyone needs to feel that love and self worth. I wish I had a magic wand to give it to everyone, including me. My parents are right in the middle of divorce and this time it's real and horrible. My dad is self-centered and cares for no one, not even himself. He keeps on cheating and using my mom. My poor mom feels guilty for wanting to end the marriage, and feels a lot of pain and anger towards dad. I feel bad for their pain and wish my magic wand could take it away for them. I want to separate them quickly, like a Band-Aid. It hurts more if you pull slowly. I must admit that I've found this divorce very hard so far and I know it's just beginning. I don't like Phil too much anymore. I went to Cityville, had a great time. Too great, we slept together. Now I hear from him once in a while. He might come over this week but I don't know if I want him to. I know I'm a fickle girl. I can't say I'm glad that I slept with him, but shit happens.

Feb. 15, 2000

I went snowboarding yesterday for Valentine's Day. It was fun and sunny all day. I was working on my jumps. They are slowly they're getting bigger and bigger and still smooth. I don't know how to throw in any tweaks or grabs yet. But that will come. I was going to see Phil last week but he was late calling me, he called from a bar on a cell (so couldn't talk long) and wanted me to call and wake him up the next morning to make sure he wouldn't miss the ferry. I figured if he really wanted to come, he wouldn't need a wake-up call. So I phoned him and told him to stay in bed. He didn't understand why I didn't want to see him. Anyway, I've decided to give up on dating men for now. It's not the right time and all I'm finding are losers. I know my destiny; I know what I want to do with my life. Now I have to save enough money to go to school and make movies. I want to make movies and show the world that everyone can make life good. Life is what you make it. Sometimes in life we get confused and we all get confused; even the richest movie stars, even the smartest people alive. I think it's important to send out love to the world instead of hate or judgment. Don't worry about money.

Money is stupid, I hate money, but I understand why we need it at this point. I try to see the good in everyone and my life is easier for it. Rather than judging and feeling inadequate I see people and think of how they're confused. It's hard at times, but it gets easier. I don't believe in violence. I think that violence is very wrong and unnecessary. So how do you stop violence, and is it best to let people learn that lesson on their own? I can't wait to go to school. I need like thirty grand so I'm going to submit pictures to playboy and try to be a model for them. Its' all just a thought…

Feb. 19, 2000

I know what I want to do with my life; make movies. Sometimes I wonder if I'll make it. I'm sure that is a question every person asks at one or more points in their life. I also want to find more people that I click with. I have lots of friends that I love dearly but I sometimes, ok most of the time, I don't open up to them. They don't believe in the things that I do and they judge people and lecture me on life when theirs is a mess. So now I pretend nothing is ever wrong cause they say things like "you need to tell your parents to go fuck themselves" because my parents are going through a divorce??? Does that make any sense? Or they're mean to people, people that they feel they're better than. It's just not right to be mean. No one likes being judged or treated like shit. Just honestly love any stranger you see on the street, the way you love every baby you see for no reason. I want to be around people who aren't confused, who are honestly nice people. The world is as good as you make it. The universe will provide. Positive thinking. I have doubts all the time that all I believe is shit. I will say though, since I've made a conscious effort not to judge and to send love; my life has been better. Guilt makes us think that we can't have what we want easily. It's so easy that in four days (twenty hours max) I made $1000.00 American, $1500.00 Canadian. I made this money sharing love to ones who feel that they don't deserve the real thing. Yes I type dirty language about how my character would love to sixty-nine and get fucked. But I also make these men feel important, feel loved, and feel "cool". Sex is a weird thing, a thing that I could do without for a while. I want to wait for "him", my soul mate.

No Such Thing As Secrets

Mar. 2, 2000

I realized something today about myself. You see I was at a job assessment and I was with about forty people and I knew about five people there. We were put into small groups and had to make games and market them, then one person had to sell them to the big group. So for I don't know what reason I was picked to market my group's game? Whenever I'm in that sort of situation my group always wants me to be the "speaker" or "marketer" or "director" etc. Now here is a group of people who don't even know me and want me to be the leader. The whole game was basically my idea. Then there were five groups and as we went and looked at the games and each person talked about the game. Everyone laughed and thought it was fun…. until me. Everyone was silent and paying close attention to my every word. Why? What is it about me that makes people listen like I'm so serious? I was trying to have fun with the assessment too, but everyone took me so seriously then even the big bosses told me what a good job I did afterwards. I hope I don't come across as a harsh bitch. I'm really just an easy going girl who for some reason commands respect?!? I don't get it but know that I think about it, it's always been this way. Weird eh. I want to go to Apex again this year, but we most likely can't. There are no rooms left up there. I want to go with my old Keg boys. They're great guys who love to party. Oh well at least I already had two great years up there, even if we can't go this year. I'm still doing internet porn, trying to get my huge tuition money. I'm going to send pictures to playboy too. If I get picked to pose for them I get paid twenty-five grand, which means film school baby! That is all I want, to go to school. I will soon. Hopefully real soon!!!

Mar. 25, 2000

I don't know but I think I'm turning cold hearted. I went to the movies tonight with Nick. It was a sad movie, "Cider House Rules". I didn't cry. I thought it was sad, but no tears. I didn't cry in "The Green Mile" either. I haven't cried in a long time, even in real life. I felt no urge to flirt with Nick. I feel no urge to look any guy over. Nick was rubbing and holding my arm during the movie. I didn't offer my hand. Instead I got up and went to the bathroom. I see someone cute and I instantly think it won't work. My life is full of things to do right now. I don't want any more friends especially if they're male. My dad cheating on my mom as much as he had has really turned me off men and relationships. I feel like it's impossible for a guy to want to spend time with a woman other than sex. I feel like men think all women are dumb, naive, bitchy, and can't carry on a conversation. Personally I have no urge to talk to men about anything; I don't want to hear their bullshit. I don't want to be a part of their lies. I don't want to be used for sex. I get paid by men to get them off. I lie to them and I'm sure they must know I'm lying. I don't think they care, as long as they see some pussy and blow their load. I sing to music which, with the three second delay looks like I'm moaning and having an orgasm. Most of these guys are way too old for me. They are there because their wives don't do it for them anymore or they're too busy to spend time with a girl. Or they don't have the courage or charm. At least the men online are honest with me. They are there to get off and get out. Most men cum really easily. I just type "don't stop", "keep fucking me", "I'm almost there", "I'm cumming", then arch my back and their done. I think some of them do it because its dirty sex and some of them do it to reach out to someone. Some of these guys fall in love with us. They like thinking that a young beautiful woman wants them. I never ask how old they are because I want to picture Abe Benson on the other side and they'd rather be that good looking anyway. You know I don't want much from a guy. I'm low maintenance. I just want to be loved and not cheated on. I'm getting so used to being alone I don't know if I can go back…

Apr. 1, 2000

I've spent the day with Brooklyn pretty much. We've been driving around in her '67 Camero and she had a BBQ deck party tonight. I was having some Canadian beer and talking to this person and that person, and BBQing steaks. Steaks are one thing that I can cook. Sometimes I get lonely. It's been over a year now since C.M. and I have been together. A year of not bonding, not talking seriously, not loving any man. I come home, put on my pj's and go to sleep… no hot sex here!

Apr. 19, 2000

I don't understand people. Why can't we all think the same? So many people I know are so fucked up, I mean really fucked up. I don't understand how they think it's alright to pull the shit they pull. Maybe I'm just growing up and my friends are just staying the same. Lillian has gone off the deep end over nothing? Judy never really did make sense to me and still doesn't. Mindy and I get along great; she's like a sister to me. Some people need so much maintenance. I'm sick of it. I can only say poor baby so many times. I can only smile and nod and bite my tongue so many times. I try to be a good person. I try to be honest and fare. I just can't agree with everyone all the time. I try not to judge but sometimes I tell people when they're being an idiot, I can't help it. Right now Lillian is being a manipulating bitch and I don't agree with it and so I told her. I said mostly nothing but I didn't agree with her behavior. She's mad at me now. So do I want to be friends with someone who is so messed up? She thinks it's alright to cheat as long as she's doing the cheating. She has double standards for everyone. She expects the world to praise her every ten seconds or she starts being "depressed". I just don't feel sorry for people who expect it and thrive off it. Maybe I'm being wrong here. Maybe I'm finally being right. Everyone has their own issues to deal with, everyone. I think I like the rules by Maharishi, don't analyze, don't complain, problems are all in your head, and hold yourself together!

May 5, 2000

Well the Lillian and Marty thing continues with me in the middle. I've just tried to not talk about it to not get into any arguments. It was my Dad's b-day yesterday; we're having a party for him Saturday night. My dad moved out on April 15th. He's renting Beatrice's mobile home from her. He's starting to see how good he had it here. He's lonely now but still sleeping around. I really don't understand that. Poor Brooklyn. Her and Rant are going to separate and it's so hard on them. Rant has hurt her too many times so she doesn't love him anymore. She loves him but doesn't trust or lust him. It's tearing him apart to go through this but what can she do? Is she supposed to stay with him so he won't be unhappy? She's done that for the last 3 years. Now she is finding herself wanting more in a relationship. I just feel so bad for them; I would go through the pain for them if I could. I guess they are both learning from their experiences and pain. I think I'm going to go and see her for a bit. I'm keeping an eye on Jordan and Annie to make sure they're not upset about all of this. I know one problem that I have. I'm living in the future. Some people dwell on the past, some fantasize about the future, we're supposed to enjoy the moment and live for the present. I'm trying to get myself to start enjoying today. I'm going to make a note to self *no one likes a whiner* I'm so sick of hearing my friends complain. I just want to shake them and say "stop feeling sorry for yourself; you have nothing to cry about". I see real pain and I feel compassion for those but I don't feel compassion for those people who just want attention and sympathy over nothing. I'll stop complaining now. I know I shouldn't whine about whiners!!

May 9, 2000

The Lillian and Marty thing exploded with me and Mindy in Lillian's bad books. Long story. Anyway Lillian was being harsh and saying mean things so I wrote her a letter. If she wanted me to say oh poor Lillian, I'm sorry I was going to say more. So I gave her the letter and she slit her wrists. I felt like a harsh person when she told me. I'm going to keep a copy of the letter in case I want someone dead in the future. I was just being honest, I guess the truth hurts! I'm going to continue to be friends with Marty and Lillian. How this will work, I don't know. On a lighter side, I'm really ripping it up in slo-pitch. I'm hitting great, farther than any other girl and some of the boys. I'm getting every ball hit into left field. I'm looking and feeling good on the ball field. I wish that I could become a professional baseball player. Maybe next lifetime!!

May 22, 2000

I have a confession. Marty Trees and I had sex May 8th. After our ball game we were out drinking beer with Jake and Kyle. We were drunk and watching Forces of Nature then we started kissing and didn't stop. I wasn't sure if it was just a one-time thing or not. Now I know it's something special. It's different than anything else I've ever been a part of. Our bodies melt together. I feel so comfortable around him. It's the best sex either of us has ever had. I don't know how to explain how I feel. I've never been happier to spend time with anyone. I want to be around him all the time. It's like he's perfect. I know that something will probably happen and actually I can't see anything happening. We're so much the same. I enjoy his company so much. I don't know what is going on…
Things are going very well with Marty and I except the Lillian part of it. She was pretty mad for a while but I think she's coming out of it… maybe. I tried everything to get her to be ok with it but she just kept shutting me down. I think she likes being "hurt" even if she's not. She likes the attention it gets her

from everybody she tells her fabricated story to. Oh well, I don't even want to talk about her and her many personalities. You know if all those guys that drool over her only knew that it's all an act. She's one of the most fake people I know and also one of the prettiest. But she knows it. I think I'm beginning to see the difference between outside fake beauty and a beautiful person who could look like anyone. So many people try so hard to be perfect, they forget who they are. They forget how they feel because it's only cool to be a certain way. I don't know where I fall into that. I don't know how fake or real I am. I'm sure one day I'll have it all figured out. Back to Marty though, he is wonderful. So sweet, loving, and handsome. It's so good; I'm scared I'm holding back from him. I'm worried that it will end and I'll get hurt. I guess I should stop worrying and try to enjoy him. I don't think he would ever hurt me. He has a good heart. He is a nice person. I'm just scared that I'm being gullible or he'll realize I'm not so great. Maybe he only likes me because I'm running and not really ready for commitment. I'm myself around him. I don't try, we just work. What if he wants a girl who tries? A girl who is lovey-dovey and cute and breakable. I'm not breakable, I'm not sexy, and I don't wear skirts and pretend to be dumb. What if he decides that he wants a girl who flirts with him and doesn't play catch and jokes with him? I'm just me with him and I love that he is okay with that. He says he loves everything about me and I'm amazing. What if he is just saying that? Well I guess only time will tell…

Aug. 5, 2000

A lot has happened in the last month. I broke up with Marty. Lillian won't let it all go and I'm tired of her talking about me. I will never trust Lillian again. I now see a side of her that manipulates and lies to get people to see her as perfect and to get attention. Part of me wants to knock her out but I know that isn't the answer. Although she has said sorry, deep down I don't forgive her for everything she's done. It will always stick in my mind as to what to believe when she talks to me about other people. I guess there's a reason she doesn't have a lot of friends and none of her ex boyfriends will talk to her. Speaking of ex's, I phoned Clint to wish him a happy birthday Aug 2nd. I don't hate him anymore. I know he cheated and didn't always treat me well but we were young and it wasn't all bad times. Brooklyn moved home. She's having a hard time with it all. Rant is the guilt trip king. He's always over here and calling her and telling the kids that they have to help him get Brooklyn to move back home. It's really hard to see the kids so different. They don't listen at all, they cry over anything and they don't understand any of it. I'm leaving tomorrow to visit family and ride horses. I'll be gone for a week and ½ and it's just what I need. It will give me a chance to think about school and life and what I'm doing with mine and it will let me think.

Aug. 24, 2000

Taking the first big step into the adult world is a hard one. Something I didn't expect to have trouble with. It's that step of leaving everything you know for everything you don't know. For me going to school in Cityville is the first step. I don't really know anyone in Cityville. I don't know if getting a big huge student loan is a big waste of money. I don't know if I'm choosing the right school. I don't know if I'm going to like it. I'm scared I won't make it but I have to go. I can't stay in Newsville, I just can't. It would kill me and turn me into something I'm not. I know that I can always come back to Newsville and see all my friends and I will always be close with my family no matter where I am. I find myself bored to death of this town and the narrow minded attitude. My family is closer to me than family, they are my friends. I enjoy spending time with them more than anyone. I'll always talk to them, they'll always be here. I have to go and take the step into the next phase of life.

Aug. 28, 2000

Mindy and I are going to Cebattle today for the Mariners/Yankee's games. It should be great. Something I was thinking is that if you go out with a guy and it doesn't work once, it won't work the second time for the same reason. I quit the Tap. I'm going to put all of my spare energy into going to school. I want to go to the Jan 2nd –2001 start date at VFS. I'm going to get a huge student loan and work online when I can while I go. There are so many things that I need to do and buy. I'm going to work online as much as possible to get $$$. I wonder if I'll meet "him" in Cityville. I wonder when I'll meet lots of people. I'm just really looking forward to meeting new people. I'll always come back here to my old friends, but I want to meet tons of new people and see tons of new things.

Sept. 8, 2000

Mindy and I have decided that the sexiest uniform on a man is a pro baseball player. I find Allen Richards to be the hottest one. Mindy doesn't agree. We did have lots of fun. I wish that I could be a pro baseball player. I would work really hard to be the best. I'm getting tired of life here. I want to move on, go to school, and move out into the world. I'm quite happy to do it alone. I look forward to one day meeting "the one". Sometimes I wonder who he'll be.

Sept. 10, 2000

Tiffany, Lance and I were rear-ended a couple of day ago. It's pretty painful now. I have to smoke joints all the time for the pain. I was thinking that whoever I'm going to meet someday and fall in love with should hurry up and find me. Sometimes it's hard to believe, I'm going to be a Mom one day, a wife, a grandma. I wonder when I will meet the person who will share my life with me…

Oct. 7, 2000

I got back from Disneyland yesterday. We had a great time. It was really nice to get away for a couple of weeks. It was weird being in California. It felt like I could live there and will live there soon. We were picked to be in the parade one night, which was so cool. We met some guys down there and I learned from them that we are all just people all over the world. We're all the same once you get to know us. We are different but we're similar everywhere. I sent off my school application on Sept 20th. It felt SO good to put it in the mail. I haven't heard back from them yet but I also haven't been home. I applied for the Feb 26th start date of classes. This will mean moving to Cityville (all alone), meeting new people, doing something that actually stimulates me, and moving into the next phase of my life. This is a very big step to take, but one I can't wait to leap over…

Oct. 11, 2000

I've had a long day. I need to come up with a lot of money for school ($9000.00 in 3 months) and fast. I'm going to have to work online every day in order to try to make enough money. I can do it and I've made up my mind, I will do it. I'm just stressing about it. It makes me happy to do it on my own; it makes it more of an accomplishment. I can't wait to go to school though. Working online can be very upsetting if you break out of character at all. What keeps me going is that one day I'll be in love and it will be wonderful. One day I'll have a job that I love and that I'm very, very good at. I would like to be the first big female director. There are lots of famous excellent female directors but I want to be up there with Stan Steinberg. Every one of his films are so touching, so amazing. I want to learn how to do that.

Friday, Oct. 20, 2000

Today has been one of the saddest days in my life. My dog Nick was put to sleep. In grade six three of our dogs died in one year. I said that I would never love another dog because they died too easy. Then Beatrice and Brooklyn brought home Nick in the summer of 1992. He was a very cute puppy. My plan didn't work; I fell in love. I must say that he was the best dog I've ever met. Nick grew to be as tall as my belly button and over the years he put on a healthy weight. He was a very friendly giant. He's been with me through so much. He used to go rollerblading with Mindy and I. He walked us to the bus stop every morning. He saw me grow up. He protected us all so well. Just knowing he was here made me feel safe because I knew no one could get past him. He was with us every moment that we were outside or inside for the past eight and a half years. I don't think I've ever felt this sad before. I've never lost anyone close to me. In the past every time I'm sad, I go jogging and Nick goes too. I can't even explain how sad I am. Nick was there when I broke up with Clint. Nick was there all the time if ever needed. He did such a good job with us kids. He loves kids; he'll make some kids very happy in his next life time. He loved to play in the snow all day, build forts all summer, go swimming, and play tag. He never would fetch, he'd just steel whatever you had and run away with it. He'd drop it for a bit to make you think you'd get it but before you could, he'd get it and run. He ran circles around all of us and it was sometimes all of us against him. He loved truck rides. He would always want in the back of my truck. He was scared of storms and loud noises, and he howled at the fire alarm in Hemlock. He never fought with other dogs; he knew he could beat them. He always listened. Making the choice to put him down was so painful, but he was in pain with a big cancerous tumor sticking out of his skin on his butt. He'll always hold the most special spot in my heart. He was always there for me.

Oct. 25, 2000

If there is one thing that really bugs me, it's rumors about me. Even if it was true I hate people talking about me. I don't know how many people know I do the internet thing, but a lot of people know that shouldn't. And the rumors are very stupid too. Mindy heard from Lillian that my sisters and I all work online and we all celebrate about it. There are lots of other examples I just don't feel like writing down. Why is it any of anyone's business? All I know is that working online is going to help me go to school and get me my dream. We all do things in life we're not proud of for different reasons. You know the whole world is perverted and yet they judge people who are more open. They are hypocrites. I honestly don't like narrow minded fuck heads who only know how to judge. Fuck anyone who talks about me, their karma will get them! (If I don't first).

Oct. 30, 2000

I've calmed down about the town gossip, that's just the way this town is. I'm not ashamed for working online. Sometimes in life we have to work hard to get where we want. Sometimes we have to do things we don't want to do, to get our dreams. I will not give up on my dream and if that means that I have to please men for the next three months, I'll do it. I will never let my daughter do it. I wonder if I'll ever get attracted to a man after I'm done working. I feel like men will use me for sex. I feel like they don't see me as a person. I just try not to think about it most of the time. I try to stay in character while working, so they don't use "Betty", they use my character. I understand the world more after this work. I understand that people need to "fuck" a stranger to feel good. I don't think I'll ever "fuck" again in real life. I only want to make love, I want romance, and I want the best. I can get down on myself sometimes for not having my goal. Then I think, I'm only twenty-one, relax. I still can't help it. I need to be involved in making movies. Not Hollywood movies, but touching, real life, lesson learning movies. I also want to start a family one day and have a career to take a break from then go back to. Right now I don't have that. I don't have a career. Lately I think about Dirk Manly. I feel like a freak, why do I think about someone I've never met so much. For all I know he's a jerk. I want to meet him, and I don't know why. Am I some silly crazed fan? That doesn't sound like me and I don't feel this way about other stars. What's the deal? Right now he's my motivation while working, not in a sexual way, but in a work hard for school so I can work with him kind of way. Is it some past life thing? I don't know what's up with that but I think I'd better meet him before I get married…

Nov. 7, 2000

Tonight I went and tied one on. It was a blast, very fun. I saw tons of people I knew at Kings. I had a few too many I'm sure, because the room is feeling sick. I saw Cam Canes from the real Room. He's a good snowboarder. I saw Zarren there so I introduced them because they're both so good and Zarren told Cam that I rip shit up. So I was stoked. Lillian was there. I was nice to her, but she was a bitch as always. (To my future husband, don't let me ever trust her again). She has been the worst friend I could ever have. I do have tons of real good friends. I sure love my life being single, but I'm sure I'll love being married when I'm much, much older. Elliot sure is good to me, he's always snuggling me. My sisters are so close to me, they're each my best friends. I love them more than I could ever love anyone. I look forward to meeting my husband, I think of him even now. I guess only time will tell…

Nov. 20, 2000

I'm really tripped out right now because I smoked a doob with Brooklyn tonight and watched "Fear and Loathing in Las Vegas", then I came home and started thinking about Cam Canes. He's a guy I've known for a year and a half, but hadn't really met totally honestly with till yesterday. We went on a thirty-three hour date to Cityville. We talked and talked and talked the whole time. I was honest with him and I think he was honest with me. I guess one problem is that he was in a relationship for a year that ended only two months ago. I think he's still upset about that. I can tell you that I really like him. I bet we would get along so well, like two peas in a pod. So good for each other in every way. I'd love to feel his body next to mine. His chest against my chest, skin to warm skin. Looking into each other's eyes so happy to have found each other. Exploring each other's bodies with our soft hands. The anticipation of what is to come is so strong and exciting sexually. Wrapping my legs around him as he holds my weight. Kissing, wonderful, tender, passionate, gentle, on fire, deep and perfect. Like the most perfect feeling of a kiss that you may have experienced once or three times out of every kiss in your life. But that wonderful kiss would be like that for hours. We could spend whole days making love and snuggling and talking. The sex would be better than I can imagine. Someone who can keep up with me in the bedroom. Someone who turns even me into more of a tigress, and I drive him wild too. Oh my god! I would orgasm so many times and he would be hard 24/7…

Nov. 25, 2000

Well I've calmed down since my last entry (note to self, no more writing high). I went to the Barley tonight then we went into town to the Real Room. I guess I had fun. I saw lots of people I hadn't seen in a while but the aura is very negative there. Everyone is very judging and self conscious. I'm glad to be home and I won't do that again soon. I like my "pub" atmosphere; I guess I'm getting old. I'm almost twenty-two. I just have to say that I have a great life. Everything is positive and I have lots of wonderful people in my life. Maybe the reason I have so many very cool male friends is because I don't have a boyfriend. So I guess a few lonely nights that I get are worth it to be free to be friends with lots of different guys. I feel sorry for everyone trapped into club life; there's just so much more to life than that. Life is what you make it, and I'm going to make mine great.

Nov. 30, 2000

There's something cool to be said about recreational mary-jane. When I'm ripped I feel so calm and I know the future, everything seems so clear. I have a pretty good life. I'm not complaining. Right now I'm lying in my big warm bed with Elliot beside me, eating Duncan Hines Vanilla with licorice. I don't have to get up in the morning and I'm listening to country love songs on my disc man. I'm dreaming of my future and I make my first tuition payment tomorrow. I worked my butt of online to get the money. I have lots of great friends and my family is so great, each one!

Dec. 1, 2000

I'm not sure why but I feel very lonely tonight. I'm waiting for my computer to download some stuff before I start work. I feel like I need a companion. Someone who I can talk to, I mean really talk to. Someone who is attracted to me would be nice too. I have lots of guys who think I'm hot but once they get to know me I'm there buddy. D.J. said today that he "doesn't even see me as a chick". Cam never calls me or if I ask him to do something he doesn't jump at it. I have tons of guys who love my online character but they just like "Betty". I guess its cause I don't flirt with boys, I just don't know how in real life. I wonder if I'll ever be in a good relationship. Whoever I'm supposed to meet next better hurry up cause I'm getting tired of not talking, not sharing, not kissing, not hugging, not snuggling. I think hugging is a big one. I miss not having someone I trust. Maybe I'm ready to trust and love again, just maybe. I might go out to RR for Lillian's B-day tomorrow. Maybe I'll even have fun, or maybe I'll just stay home and save my money for school…

Dec. 14, 2000

Once again I'm alone with my thoughts. Big snowfall today. There are lots of cars in the ditch up the S-bend. I just put chains on if I got stuck, and I drove all over rescuing people. I love doing manly things like that. Went to the Barley tonight, I love those guys, they're so real and cool. They are all so wonderful. Each one in a different way. I don't know what's wrong with me but all I want to do at the end of a day is smoke a joint. That's the only thing I look forward to. I don't think anyone even guesses how depressed I get when night after night I'm alone. The sad part is that I think everyone feels the same way, so alone. I just look forward to the day that I have my husband to be with, to love, to hold, to understand. I saw Cam last night and we kissed and made out a bit. It was very passionate and it was nice to be kissed. I don't know what will happen with it, but he's cute and has a good heart. I can see that he's real. We stayed up till 6:30am, just kissing. It was so nice. Now tonight he goes his way and I go to the Barley. I like it that way. You know what's really funny. I meet guys, date them, whatever else, and all I think about is Dirk Manly. It's starting to bug me really, I just want to get to know him, really know him. Oh, so yes, back to Cam. I had such an enjoyable night, I was savoring every kiss, every touch, everything. It was nice to feel wanted. Cam is very cute. I keep half falling asleep while writing this and listening to music. I like half pass out and think of something else to write. I sure love hanging around with the Barley guys, they're all really cool.

Dec. 17, 2000

Lately I've been smoking pot. It's all I want to do when the day is over to just escape the loneliness. I'm so alone. The only thing I have close to being with me, like a part of me, is Brooklyn and Elliot. I'm always holding back from people.

Jan. 1, 2001

Wow, the years go by so quick. I can't say that 2000 was all that wonderful, it's been an eventful year full of learning. I hope I don't have to learn so much this year; in life's lessons that is. I'm so happy to have learned what I've learned, but I'd like some more joy and less drugs, etc. New Years Eve was great. I was at Beatrice's, then the Barley, then the fire hall, then our friend's house party. Next New Years I wouldn't mind someone to kiss, but only if he's a really cool person. I do have a great group of guy friends though. On my birthday Brooklyn had a little party for me and at one point all my friends stood around the fire and sang happy birthday to me. It was very nice; most of them were guys. Only Suzanne, Judy, Belle, and Brooklyn were girls, and then twenty guy friends. That's sort of strange but nice that I have so many nice, caring friends.

CHAPTER FOUR

Jan. 15, 2001

I have to work for like six-eight hours a day till February just so I can make my tuition payment. So to make working alone in my room more fun I smoke pot, listen to music, and don't be disturbed for hours at a time. So I have a lot of thoughts go through my mind as I work. I want to name my first daughter Miranda Brooklyn _____. I wonder how many years it will be till I meet my children. I'm having fun with my life now, being a kid (except for internet porn). I'm very secluded right now. I don't open up too much to anyone. I haven't had sex in like 6 months but I'm fine with that. I'm glad I don't have to be clung onto 24/7. Men are needy or at least they can be. I don't know, I guess I might like a boyfriend but no one really turns my crank right now. Besides I'm too busy getting ripped and whacking off for money so I can go to film school, who has time for a boyfriend.

Jan. 24, 2001

I don't know how much more of online work I can take. All I do is sit in my room and work and get ripped. I start school soon at least. I wish I could magically just get enough money for school and I didn't have to do internet. I'm tired of being all twisted characters in roll play for men. Who are all crazy! I want to get back in tip top shape again too. Feb is a whole new beginning for me, and I can't wait. I hate my life right now, its lame. All I do is work as a porn star in my room for hours every day. I don't have any spare money. I don't know if I even want any stupid man, it's not like they're good for anything! Seriously all I want is a man that can give as much as he takes, I doubt it's possible. I don't know why I'm so negative right now, I'm just depressed I guess, living this alone life. All by myself for hours with only the stupid internet for company. Oh well it will be all worth it for school.

Feb. 13, 2001

I'm in my room, working, ripped, and watching TV. I'm getting used to being alone in my room ripped. It's a good way to really get to know that relaxed calm, positive side of you. When I'm ripped, I'm content. I'm happy that no one can disturb me if "I'm working". I like watching much music, much more music too. I go to school on the 15th for orientation. That's when I'll meet everyone. I'm nervous and excited. I'm going to miss my old life, but I have to give something new a try. I wonder what life will be in a year from now. Life will be so different. I can't believe how close I am, a few more years. My mom is helping me with lending me $2500.00 of $20,000.00 and my bus pass. I'll come home some weekends and work online. I'm sick of Brooklyn and Rant being together. Rant treats her so horribly. He doesn't even work, or get U.I. He's a bum and he's so nasty and moody. I just hope she will be ok, and Rant still blames me for all his and Brooklyn's troubles because we hang out all the time.

Feb. 26, 2001

Well I'm here at McKinnon's, home from my first day of school. I went through a very hard time to get here. I found out on February 14th that Wonder and Dean Bossley died on Brooklyn's b-day. They were driving too fast and totaled Dean's jeep up near Pintnay. I had never gone through anything so horrible in my life. I can't even explain the pain I felt. I'm still dealing with it. I can't believe they're dead. They were at my birthday singing Happy Birthday. We were all bowling just three days before. Wonder and I were partners and we were doing horribly but we were having fun. There is no pain like the one you get when someone dies. Going through all this pain and now I've been thrown into school. I'm all on my own now. D.J. and I were together and now we're not and I really miss him. Everyone at school is really nice but I don't feel any connections yet. You wouldn't even believe the hell I went through in the last twelve days. I won't get into it, but I'm still upset, very upset. Oh well I guess it's made me stronger. My friends died and my parents were fighting over who would take me, and only after I complained when they said I could just throw some stuff in a bag on the ferry. My Mom and Brooklyn moved me and they were great. Beatrice yelled at me over some stupid internet stuff and I'm the only one that took responsibility for it. Then I was all upset about Lillian and D.J. and all of that. But mostly I just can't believe that Wonder and Dean died. I couldn't sleep or eat for days. I lost ten lbs in one week. I got a tattoo and it's not healing that well. I don't have a bed yet so I sleep on a foamy on the floor in a sleeping bag. But I'm not complaining because I know it's the best place for me to live while in school. D.J. and Lillian have too much of a history for me to go mess with it, but I sure miss him. I hope bad things stop happening. I'm going to work hard at school.

Mar. 2, 2001

It's all good baby. My life is coming together now. The key to life is to live in the now. My new goal is to not live in the future or the past, but the now. My friend Tim from school and I had a great talk last night. I know that the things he told me last night all made sense. His wife predicted me. He has four daughters. Last night I felt as high as or higher than on E, but I wasn't on any drugs. Tim and his wife are very old souls and he is one of the people I was supposed to meet at VFS. Trippy shit man, but so cool. I love my new school although I'm still adjusting to some of it. I miss my friends and family terribly but that's why there is phone and email. Brooklyn is coming over next weekend and I hope Belle comes soon. I miss Beatrice, the kids, Tiffany, Jacquie, Grandma's kitchen table, smoking pot, all my friends, Auntie Dana, my Mom and Dad. But I'm not sad, I just miss them. I really want Dad to meet Tim, he's in tune. The sky is the limit.

Mar. 5, 2001

Well it's Sunday already and time to go back to school. I still think about Wonder and Dean all the time. I would give anything to see them again. I think it's hard for me because I'm all alone here. I can't use the phone all the time cause of long distance and someone here usually needs to use it. It takes so long to try to go anywhere cause of the bus and I don't know my way yet. I wish I could have afforded a place down town. This place doesn't feel like home yet. I wonder when it will. It makes me feel alone. Most of the kids in my class are rich and they don't understand life so I won't bother talking about anything personal with them. I guess I'm learning about myself being alone all the time, on the bus, walking, in my room. No one really cares about me except for everyone at home but they're not here. You know they say that only few people make it because it is so hard. Well I deserve a break, I deserve a nice life, and I promise I'll appreciate it.

Mar. 14, 2001

Well life is all about learning and there are always lessons to be learned. I keep thinking about D.J. and I don't know what to do. I don't know how I feel about him. I love him like a friend but maybe more. He still wants to get together but he understands that I need to concentrate on school right now. I would hate to go out with him and then have it not work and then we couldn't be friends. Of course, I'd be crushed if he got a girlfriend. I'll just have to wait and see because there's no point in worrying about it now because he's in Newsville and I'm in Cityville. I do really miss him, but what about the whole Lillian thing. I just don't want to get hurt or hurt anyone else if I don't have to. VFS is going good, I'm still getting used to it. I like all the people in my class, I wouldn't want to work with all of them but I like going to school with them. Some of them are there for the wrong reasons, some of them still need more growing, but all of them are fun to watch and secretly analyze.

Mar. 16, 2001

Last night was our first big party for VFS. I got a chance to see people's real sides. I of course got ripped before hand and then to my surprise everyone (almost) got ripped too. Hans, (I found out) loves to snowboard so I'm going to get Brooklyn to bring my board over and go riding with him. I figured out that Jean and Darren like each other, so I told Darren that Jean likes him just to make the show more interesting. I figured out the whole D.J. thing. I asked a star for guidance and it came to me in my dream. The reason he wants to go out is because he thinks that will make the pain of losing Wonder and Dean go. So now I know, thanks to a little help. It's fun watching everyone in my class, their behavior. I'm known as the friendly talkative one.

Mar. 22, 2001

Today I've been faced with a very big life decision. Should I leave VFS while I can still get eighty percent of my money back? This school I am learning is not worth the money they are charging. It is a very poor investment. One third of the class (all the smart foreign kids) is dropping out and getting their money back. Hans is going back to Switzerland but coming back this summer to go to a better school in Sept. and Dibbs is very unhappy about the school. I haven't been challenged at all in school yet. I'm not sure what all of the kids are going to do, but I might go for my degree using my Mil -U or maybe more at SWU or UNP. I have to look into the schools and find out what is the best for my dollar. So far I think I could learn more than VFS can offer in my spare time. I don't know why or how I could have been so foolish. At least I have had the chance to meet other students who have some ideas and knowledge on movies, and so now we can keep in touch through email.

Apr. 29, 2001

Last night Sat April 28th 2001 was Belle and Jacquie's prom. We all had fun and I could go into detail but I won't. Belle drank a bottle of tequila and ate the worm from an old bottle I had gotten from Janet and Ryan for house-sitting while in Mexico. I'm not really sure where my head has been lately. I've been wake and baking too much, and last night Tiffany, Jacquie, Judy and I did E. I'm awake in bed feeling like shit wishing I never took it. I am done with E. That man made drug isn't as nice to your body as pot or mushrooms. I've been trying to find people to go to Van with me to live and no one wants to move. Oh I even almost feel too sick to write. I think I'm such an idiot for doing this to myself. Well I've been lying in my bed with Elliot, he's sleeping, and I'm not. The house is sleeping; I'm feeling way too gross to sleep.

No Such Thing As Secrets

May 1, 2001

I made it through the day with a little help from mary-jane. I even got a lot done around the house. I've actually been thinking a lot more positively since I had a good party night to let out some stress. I just hope I didn't embarrass myself too badly. I'm going to work online today, I'm just lying in my bed procrastinating. I should go eat breakfast too or make it and eat while working. I guess first I'll put on my whore make-up. Beatrice phoned to go for a walk and Suzanne phoned to go rollerblading. I'd love to but I must make myself work. Internet work isn't that bad. It's definitely always interesting, weird, funny, gross, and educating. It's hard to believe that I have been doing this work as long as I have. I started out doing it because I had friends that were doing it and telling me how much money I could make. The first time I tried it I went to my girlfriend's house and just sat in my clothes and made $80 US in twenty minutes. Back then there was next to no competition and the money would fly into the account. Now the viewers are a bit fewer and farther between, but they are still there. My one friend had so much luck with the dominatrix side of internet porn that I thought I would try it. She had one subbie slave guy buy her a fridge and stand up freezer, because she was his Mistress and she needed one. These men just want someone to worship. It's a fetish. They want to feel unworthy and used. I'll admit it's a weird fetish, but every person out there has a bit different taste in sex. It's not big deal, I understand all the fetishes. Some people shock me though, like the guy that said his dream was to walk in on his girlfriend being fucked by another dude. That was his sexual fantasy because he used to watch his mom get fucked by different guys growing up. Some guys are into the whole pregnant milk in titties thing. One guy even asked my friend who had milk at the time (she had a newborn) to change his diaper. He was wearing a fake diaper and had this total mommy fetish thing going on. I will never understand the guys who want to eat shit though. Come on, that's just gross. I'm not attracted to men in lingerie. I prefer to be the one wearing the sexy outfits, but I deal with a lot of those guys so I'm pretty used to seeing the pictures. Sometimes I can't hold in the laughter, so I stand up and show my body and not my face so I can laugh a bit. I want a manly man, not a man dressed up like a girl and putting toys in his ass. The man's G-spot is apparently between the ball sack and the butt hole so maybe that's why they like toys up there so much? I can't imagine doing a guy with a strap-on in real life, but I talk about it a lot online and even wear one. I have two actually. It's just an act. In my life I'm not into the dominatrix. I want a man to take charge in the bedroom and show me what's up for once. Every show is different and very entertaining to say the least. I make money, never deal with anyone face to face, and I'm my own boss. Ok, hair and make-up now. The other day I went to meet Suzanne at the Horse and Barn and I guess I had forgotten to wipe the make-up off before leaving the house because she had to warn me that I looked a bit odd. I have to wear heavy blush and I usually over elongate my eyeliner and have bright red lipstick on. It looks normal online but not in person. So happy I get to smoke doobs at work and watch TV.

May 9, 2001 | **1:48am**

Here I am awake, thinking, ripped, and tonight my thoughts are scattered. I'm listening to music and thinking (if only I didn't think so much). I miss Dean and Wonder; death is such an interesting thing. I feel like I should be able to see them, but I can't, they are dead. I guess one day I will talk with them again, when I die. I would give anything to see them again. Death is so unlike any other pain. Death is the end of communication. I only wish I could talk to the dead. I don't know who else I will have to live through dying but I'm not looking forward to it. Wonder's parents put a picture from the Christmas party at my house in his coffin with him because of how much he loved his friends. I never saw his tattoo. I looked in all my year books and he only signed one. All I think about is the last time I saw him. We went bowling. D.J., Suzanne, Lillian, Wonder and Dean were there for my going away thing. My birthday they all sang Happy Birthday around the fire. That was the best birthday ever! I felt like a princess that night, with all my prince charmings. What are the chances that I would go through my first "death" two days before my dream school orientation day? Then my school sucks!!! I lose all my savings and my dream and I'm back at home right where I started. My mom and dad bitch about my smoking pot and not having money (when I make more than most of my friends doing internet fucking porn). I fucking hate it but I don't have a choice! I have to degrade myself everyday and people make fun of me and I'm not proud of what I do. But at least I've learned more than money can buy, over this whole nightmare. I cleaned my closet and my drawers and I found old letters to Clint (hate mail). I went to dinner tonight and gave the letters to him. I'm not going to hold on to the pain anymore. I don't hate him and I can now remember all of the good times that we had together! We really did have fun together and still do, just in another way. He is one of the few people who makes fun of my quirks. He got me to sign an old picture of myself and he had it in a frame. It felt good to let go of him in this way. I guess now he'll know how much he hurt me and I can let the pain go. I'm ready to move on in my life. I'm ready to see all the wonderful things this world has to offer me. I'm even ready to love again; I just hope he's hot. I want to be randy every time I see him… Oh well I can dream. I don't think I'm asking for so much. A job I enjoy and I work hard at, and a paycheck that helps the whole family out financially. One day, one day… I hate lying in bed, awake and bored and wishing you could fall asleep but almost too afraid to try. I know I do too much marijuana, but I'm not doing everything else so it's not too bad. It's now 2:23, what's the point in sleeping anyway? LOL, I guess I should get my sleep. I just don't have a clue as to how I'm supposed to get from burn out in Hemlock to director all over the world??? I probably stress out about it too much, I just wonder about the future all the time. I wonder about my life and how it will turn out. I think I'll see how this one ends though. It's been very entertaining so far. Well maybe I should try to fall asleep now; it is past my bed time. It is easier to sleep with a man, I know but oh well you can have it all!

May 22, 2001

I've gone on two dates with Talon now and no kiss, we're both shy. That's a good thing though. When the time is right I guess. I've figured out what to do to become a production assistant. It's not too hard and I'm hoping to be working by fall. I'm playing mixed ortho with the Barley team this year and I'm having such a great time. Here's to summer fun!

May 29, 2001

On May 24th (late to 25th) Talon and I went on a date. We went to Pizza Palace to see Mindy, then to Mindy's and Jack's then back to Talon's. He invited me in and he kissed me. We then started getting hot n heavy and we had sex. I'm the second girl he's ever French kissed/sex/etc. I don't know why but I feel really comfortable around him. He is so sweet and sexy! Looks like I'v6:25ame got some sweet summer loving coming my way this year. I'm very happy with him and it's so nice to have someone care about me. The way he looks at me and touches me makes me feel like he actually cares. Belle and I are fighting; I'm staying in bed till she leaves. She's always mad at me for some stupid, petty reason. Her whole life she's been mad and jealous at me and I'm sick of it. But I won't fight because she's seventeen and you can't be right when talking to a seventeen year old who knows everything. It's 11:15, when will she go to school? I want to get up! Between her and Mom, they just bitch, bitch, bitch. I never bitch to them; they think I have a stress free life. I think with my first big paycheck I'm just going to give it to mom and say "here, have it, now stop bugging me for having no money or smoking pot". Now Belle's mad at me for not going to the Barley with her on Sat night. For one day I'd like for those two to not be mad at me. Oh well maybe one day. Belle is taking my truck now. Good, now I can get up. Mom just phoned again to say, "I wish you and Belle wouldn't fight". Do I look like I'm fighting? I stay quietly in my room and give her my truck all fucking day and night. If I don't give her my truck I have to drive her cause princess won't ride the bus.

June 10, 2001

I'm not mad at Belle anymore. She and Jace broke up so she's upset. She is only seventeen, so I understand. I was nice to her and I didn't even bring up anything. My mom and I went to Combes and Baiters yesterday and we had a lot of fun. I can hear Annie singing and playing guitar, she sounds so cute! An iridologist told me that I have a brown spot in my eye because an ancestor had a drug overdose. Maybe it was even Grandma and her drinking. Not the answer I was looking for. I understand how easy it is for people to worry about money. I can't wait till money isn't an issue in my life. I guess I'd better get a job and start working my way up the ladder. I'm always thinking about my career. It would be nice to have it all planned out a whole lot more. Annie just crawled into bed with me and she says she can read my diarrhea book but not Jordan. I'm getting tired of Talon already, I don't know why. I just don't want to have a boyfriend. I just want to flirt with all the boys and leave it at that.

June 16, 2001

Today is father's day and my Dad is with Jan going to Whiteswan. Jan is my Dad's girlfriend, but I've never met her. He says it's not serious but he's taking her to see relatives. I didn't really want to get him anything anyway. He didn't even show up for Belle's prom. I've tried to figure my Dad out and I can't. It's weird but I don't see him as my Dad. He's more of someone I have to take care of then someone who takes care of me. I'm not complaining but my parents are like friends, not parents. I guess there's most of the world the same. I can remember making my own breakfast (eggs at age five) while my parents were meditating. I made my own school lunch by gr.2 and we made what we wanted for dinner. I ate a lot of cereal growing up. Maybe one day I'll write about my childhood, it was full of adventure!!

July 4, 2001

Well, I've met someone. Actually, I've known him for years and then last Sat (June 23rd) he gave me a ride home from the Real Room. Then we went on a few dates and on June 29th we slept together. So far, so good. His name is Rambo and he's twenty-four. He makes me laugh with his quick wit and I like the way he teases me. It's weird to be in a relationship but I think I really like him. I start working at RR again this Friday. I'll be a bartender in the new back lounge. I think I'll like being the bartender. I'll still work online too. I can't wait to get back to Cityville working again. I guess everything happens for a reason and I have to just forget about Cityville for the summer. It's starting to get really hot this summer. I sure do love summers in Hemlock.

July 24, 2001

Everything is going good with Rambo. I like him more and more all the time. It's nice to actually like someone! I wonder how long we'll stay together. I wonder if he'll end up moving to Cityville with me. You never know what the future brings I guess. Rambo might become a fireman and that would be a sexy boy toy. I feel really comfortable around him, totally at ease. Right now we (mom, Belle and I) took Rambo's roommate's dog Cline because he's a pit-bull and got kicked out of his old house. He has to take classes before he can go back. He's on my bed right now. Everything is so different all of the sudden. I think I'm maybe falling in love with Rambo. I know it's too soon to tell, but I like everything so far. Everything is good at Real Room and bartending. I kind of like being a bartender!!

Aug. 17, 2001

Rambo and I are still together. I wasn't expecting this but we're having a good summer. I'm sick of working at the Real Room already. I just don't like the late hours and the ass kissing that I don't have to do online. I think about Wonder a lot, but I feel a lot better about it. When it's your time, it's your time to go. Cline is gone now, back at Rambo's. It was nice having a dog while it lasted. I'm smoking too much pot still, I'm sure. Oh well, no more chemical drugs at least. I don't really drink lately, so pot is my fun. Rambo doesn't smoke that much so we don't smoke that much together. It gives me a reason to be mellow. We're going camping this weekend though. I'm sure we'll both be drinking and smoking. I can't wait to move to Cityville and get working in the movie industry. I just keep telling myself I'll get there, now I've got to just go and do it. Question is what will happen with Rambo?

Sept. 24, 2001

Rambo and I will be together three months on the 27th. I can't believe how quickly three months has gone by. We spend time together almost every day. My friends and family are jealous, but I'm happiest with him. He treats me very well and he is a new relationship for me all together. Rambo will move to Cityville with me. We're hoping to be ready in November. I can't wait to live with him. Snuggle up to his warm body every night. I don't know what it is, but I really love Rambo. The only problem is getting him ok with the whole internet thing. I wish he would work with me or something. I just want him to look at it the same way I do. Money and that's all, just money. He feels like I'm cheating on him, I would never cheat on him or want him to feel that way. I love Rambo and working online is just a job. It's not a big deal at all. I sit there in sexy lingerie and have on my make-up and maybe some lace up boots or high heels. The viewer enters the video chat and I ask them what they are wearing. I then make them get on their knees and hold their cock in either the left or right hand. It's better to be specific and pick a hand but really it doesn't matter what hand. Anyways, I ask what toys or props they have and get them to start using them. I don't show them anything unless they are good and pay me a lot. At the end when they cum me tell them they can cum on my count of three. On the one I show them my tits usually, on two maybe I will show them my ass, and on three I show them my pussy and they can cum. They don't dare cum until I command them to, and I don't tell them to until I think I have gotten all the money I can out of them. I have told Rambo that he can watch me or be a part of it with me, and how it's just money. He says he'll work with me. I hope he will soon.

Oct. 3, 2001

It looks like Rambo is going to build a house on his parents property and I'm going to move in with him. We're hoping it will be done by Christmas. I'm excited to live with Rambo even if it wasn't a new home. I plan to go to Cityville for my weekend classes and commute over as I need to. If it gets to the point I'm doing it too much and we have the money to move then we'll rent out his cabin and go from there. I'm looking forward to moving out so much. I'm going to have to work lots to afford everything but that would be good to get some extra cash flow. It would be so nice to have a place with Rambo to call home. I'm more than ready to move out. I think maybe even I'll get along better with Mom and Belle if I move out. They won't be able to get mad at me anymore!! Tiffany is getting an abortion and it's made me think a lot about what I would do. I think at my age, I would keep it. Well, I just couldn't kill my baby when I know I could be a good mom and take care of it. I'm not saying Tiffany is bad for getting an abortion, but I don't think it's justified. I think she and Zarren would be good parents and she and the baby could live for free at Grandma's. Poor Tiffany has Grandma, Auntie Vicky, and Jacquie all telling her to get an abortion. Brooklyn, Beatrice, Mom and I think she should keep it. She's twenty-seven and thinking of trying for a child in a year or two. It's made me realize that I would keep it. But, I'm on the pill so I'm not put in that position. Tiffany, Belle, and Jacquie are all not on the pill. Brooklyn's coming over to hang out. It's a good harvest this year for Rant and Brooklyn. We've all been snip, snip, snipping all the time. But, free weed for me now!! I don't see Lillian, Mindy, Suzanne and Judy too much anymore. Between Rambo and my family I don't have any time off. Lillian is moving to England soon. Suzanne is there touring now. Judy's in Capsville. Mindy and Jack got a nice new house in town.

Oct. 13, 2001

I'm very upset right now. Life just seems the worst right now. I have no job except online and Rambo hates it so I never get to work and I can barely make truck payments and I don't even have a spare loony in my purse. I have no money and I don't know how to get any. Rambo treats me like I'm cheating on him if I even want to work. So I can't work without a big fight or it being a big deal. He just won't understand that it's just a job for money. I'm not cheating! I don't know what to do. It's sat night and should I work to make money or should I go to Rambo's. But I don't even have five dollars for a drink if I want. I can't stand it. I've never been so broke. I'm so upset, why can't I just get a good job? That's all I want. I'll work hard. A job I can be proud of. A job that pays well. I've been borrowing too much money as is. I need to be making money. I'm too sad to work tonight anyways. I guess I'll go put on some make-up and try to feel/look better. I hate men, I really do!

Nov. 8, 2001

A lot has happened since the last entry. Rambo spied on my chat room while I was working. It makes him feel like I'm cheating on him when I work. So I quit online for good. I'm selling my computer and back at the Tap. I'll miss the money but not the rest of it. Rambo just can't see it the way I do, he thinks it's cheating. I see it as money. So of course I compromised and quit. So now I'm a stupid hostess at the Tap, making eight dollars an hour and no tips. But Rambo and I are living together, with Max (Rambo's friend). Rambo keeps teasing me about the internet; he doesn't realize how much that hurts I guess. Oh and he says he can't trust me. I'm so trust worthy, but how do you tell someone that? It really bothers me that he doesn't trust me, because without trust how can you love? I feel like he doesn't love me, he hasn't said it in so long I don't remember. Part of me wonders what he thinks of me, the other part doesn't care. I just wish he could see me for who I am. I don't think he does, he thinks I'm conniving or something. I feel like there's nothing I can say to make him understand, so I say nothing. I guess next time he says something about me being worth 2.99/minute I should call him on it, but instead I just get hurt feelings and say nothing and thinking shut up asshole, etc, etc. I hope he doesn't realize what he's saying too late. I won't be made fun of forever. I'll walk and be alone first!

No Such Thing As Secrets

There's nothing wrong with being alone. Sure I like having someone to sleep next to, I have more love for Rambo then he has for me. I look at him and I love him so why does he look at me and see pothead who is a retired porn star. One day I will have made a better name for myself, one day…

Nov. 13, 2001

I was talking to Judy the other day and she has quit drugs all together. She said she didn't know what she was running from till she quit and faced her pain. Whenever I feel hurt in a relationship I feel like the other person doesn't love me. All these years I thought it was the other person being an asshole, but you can't blame another person for the way you feel. So I kept thinking and I remember how unloved I felt as a child growing up. Maybe my parents did love me and just didn't know how to show it. Maybe they never loved me the way other kids parents loved them. My parents didn't know anything about me and still don't. My friends' parents have been better "parents" to me. I guess that's why I'm like a daughter to so many of my friends parents. I remember little bits from my past, my childhood, but only little bits. I know for sure I didn't think my mom loved me, but my dad I thought was the greatest guy alive. He was always pretty happy (ripped) and he never lost his temper on me. I was dad's girl and Beatrice, Brooklyn, and Belle were all Moms. They would crawl into mom's side of the bed and I'd go to Dad's. My dad even went to the odd ball game of mine when no one else cared. My mom thought I played t-ball still. She always got mad at me for bugging Belle. Beatrice and Brooklyn always teased and bugged me but they never got in trouble. Even today my mom says, "When are you going to quit smoking pot"? So why do I smoke pot? I guess I feel like I've seen enough of this cruel world and I love the escape of pot. It puts me in a good mood and I see all the good in life. My parents made me feel unloved because they never took interest in my life or tried to help me reach any of my goals. They would rather see their daughter be a porn star than to try to help her with school funding. I put myself through school, me. I'm the one who encourages myself to follow my dreams. My parents didn't do a whole lot for me other than to say I can do anything. When my Dad wouldn't quit cheating on our family even after I asked him, it really crushed me. Even to this day if I need help, I go to my sisters before I go to my parents. Beatrice has cooked me dinner way more than my parents. I was cooking for myself for as long as I can remember. I guess I keep all these thoughts inside because I don't want to complain. It's time to face my fears and talk about it. I love my parents very much and I don't want them to ever know how much they hurt me. I never tell anyone when they hurt my feelings. I guess writing about it helps get it out anyways.

Dec. 6, 2001

Rambo is in California visiting his Dad in intensive care. He's been there since Saturday. I've missed him so much and who knows when he'll be back. I know he's going through so much pain right now and I feel like I'm not there for him. I guess there's nothing I can do for him anyways. All he wants is his Dad to be ok and I don't know if that will happen. I really wish he didn't have to go through this horrible time. He's worried that this will change him. I'm worried he'll want to leave town and me if something happens. Why am I always thinking and worrying he'll leave me? I guess all I can do is wait for him to come home. I had my tea leaves read with Belle and Harry and that was neat. It said that I should start taking pictures. Black and white ones. So I'll get Dad's camera and take some pictures. I'm getting my hair permed today. I hope it looks good for when Rambo gets home.

Dec. 20, 2001

Unfortunately Rambo's Dad passed away late Dec 6th. Rambo drove home and got home on the 7th. As time goes by, he seems to be getting better. I hate working at the Keg. I'm just sick of serving people and all the BS of it. I'm sick of kissing ass for no money. It's not worth it. I have my work computer set up here so I can at least make money. I'm just doing dominatrix so Rambo doesn't get mad. I'm going to have to borrow money off my mom this Christmas. I just have no money. I need a new job that pays very well and I enjoy working. My life is still upside down. I want my health back too. I'm down to 110 lbs and I feel so ill and ugly and weak. Only time will help me, I guess…

Dec. 26, 2001

I can't believe I'm twenty-three! Yesterday was Christmas but it doesn't feel like it. Oh well, I guess some years are like that. This is the first year I don't have a penny, not a loony to go shopping with. It's just not fare, I don't make enough money. I really want to go shopping today and buy new clothes, but I guess it's not in the cards this year. I can't even think of anything I want to do tonight. I can't drink, or I would! I can smoke, so I will smoke big fat doobies all day. Everything is going good with Rambo. We want a house but who knows where we'll be in a year. My career had better start this year. Where are my millions? I hope 2002 is a lot better of a year. I've done a lot of learning in the past year, now I'm ready for some fun. All I want is fun. I just want to feel truly happy.

Jan. 7, 2002

It's hard to believe it's 2002. Rambo and I have been fighting a lot lately. He's just always a bitch!!! Relationships are so hard. I feel like I'm never good enough for him or that he thinks that I'm not good enough for him. I feel like he doesn't love me or most of the time even like me. Then his "attitude" puts me in a bad mood and we don't talk to each other. My eye is twitching. Why is he like this? Does he even care about me at all? He keeps getting so mad at me over nothing. Over telling him what to do when he's driving – he should hear what I don't say! Or now he's mad at me because he screwed up on his Dad's video that he won't let me help with. He said "you've been enough help" and said I told him how to do it wrong. All I've said was "are you sure you don't want my help". Fucking men! What good are men? No good! All they do is make you cry and are extremely self-centered! Yes all men are very self-centered! I guess I should try telling Rambo how I feel, but I'm too mad still. Why is my life like this? Also Rambo calls me a "porn star" and says things that hurt about me "showing my tits all over the internet". I get that hurt feeling in my chest, my eyes water up and I hold it in, as always. I feel like he hates so much about me and I think I'm feeling way less self esteem because of it. All I want is to be happy. I just want a job that pays well and a boyfriend that loves me and respects me. I feel lost. I feel like my life is hell and I can't do a thing about it. I feel unloved and tired of trying. How can he be so cold to me? I'm just the fool who moved in with him so he could have a live-in fuck partner. That's all he cares about and he doesn't care about my happiness. All I want is to be happy, is that too much to ask? I have nowhere to go, I just feel like writing. I have nothing to write I've already said enough. I don't want to leave my room and I don't want to go anywhere. So I guess I have a lot to learn because I can't be happy. I try and try and things just keep going wrong.

I've put so much into this relationship and does he even care or am I the one making more out of this than it is. Did I just push myself into living with him and he just secretly doesn't care about me and is just going along with it? Or does he love me and it's my childhood insecurities that make me feel unloved? Or is it him not showing his feelings and me taking it too sensitively? Well, I guess we have to talk and express our feelings so we know how each other feels. All I know is I feel sad and unloved and unappreciated and not respected. Maybe this year I'll find more happiness… maybe.

Jan. 23, 2002

I need to change my life! I need to change everything. One big thing is that I'm tired of smoking pot all the time. I'm tired of wasting my life not happy. I want to start doing more and being busier. I guess I need my health back first. I should get the test back from helicobacter in two weeks. Then I can hopefully go on medication for one week. I just want my good life back. I want to focus on my health and what makes me happy. I want to get my dad's camera and learn how to develop my own pictures. I'll start with black and white. Rambo and I have been doing better and I think he's starting to feel better. A part of me wonders if we should move in together and jump into a mortgage. I'm sick of this apartment and I need out of here. I feel like all I do here is clean up after, buy food, and cook for two boys and it's so small in here. So, part of me wants to move home and part of me wants to move out with Rambo. I just wonder what would make me happy. I don't want to feel trapped. I don't want to live somewhere that I can't invite my friends to (Rambo won't let me invite Lillian over). God, why can't life be easier? I love Rambo but is he "the one" I want to build or buy a house with. Maybe Rambo would be happier living at his house in Greenpoint with his mom and brother. I want him to go to Mexico with his friends too. Because I think I want to go to Thailand with Belle. What is the right thing to do? I think it will be hard for me to live without Rambo and I'm not ready to let him go. But I don't want to live like we are now. I don't want to be some ones housemaid. I want to be happy, very happy. I just don't know what steps to take to be happy. I have tanning this morning so I'll go there and just go on with my day thinking as usual. I keep waiting for a miracle but I guess I have to figure it out on my own and make my life good.

No Such Thing As Secrets

Jan. 24, 2002

Rambo and I had a big fight last night. Yesterday he was so mad and he left in a puff being an asshole to me. Then he went to a girl's house and I asked why and he said "because I needed to talk to someone and you were too busy with internet porn". So I asked about my letter I wrote him while he was at that girl's house and he said nothing. I said, "Do you love me?", and he said "I don't know we've only been together 6 ½ months". Well why am I living with him then! And I guess everything in my head tells me to move home because of all the signs he's showing me. He's not here now. I got up this morning and left to Brooklyn's for tea. I went to moms and started cleaning out my old room. I talked to Tiffany, Beatrice, Belle, Brooklyn, Mom, Lillian, and even Rant, and they all say by what I've told them that I should move home and he's not being fair to me. He's being immature and they all make good points. I just think what should I do? And Rambo won't talk to me about if I should move home or not because he says "that's your decision" but I need his input. He says "don't try to make me make the decision". He also says that he can't be worried about not being in a bad mood so maybe I should move home. My heart hurts so much and my eyes are swollen and I look a wreck. Also, I'm 110 lbs cause of helicobacter and Rambo says "I bet your not even sick and it's all in your head". I'm lying in "our" apartment and I don't feel like packing but my head says "wake up girl; you deserve to be treated better". Rambo should just go to Mexico like he wants and go to all the fucking girls and ex fucking girl friends houses he wants! And I'll stop kissing his spoiled ass! If he "doesn't know" if he loves me then why am I living like this? Am I that stupid – why does this hurt so much?

Jan. 27, 2002

It's Sunday morning, it's snowing and I'll make Rambo drive me to work. I think with Rambo, I have to do what makes me happy and stop sacrificing my life for him, because he doesn't even know what I do and don't do for him. So the key is for me to not be like my mom, but to do whatever I want every day. Rambo needs to be my boyfriend but not my life. I need to go out with all my girls more and not care how long I'm out. I need to not take his moods to heart – but I will never marry anyone like Uncle Richard or dad with all those stupid self-centered moods. Rambo needs to be told how to treat a girl. It's hard but I have to learn how to talk about my feelings anyways. Mom and Belle want me to move home, but I really don't want to. I've lived at home forever and I don't want to be under mom's control either. I guess I really need to just do whatever will make me happy. Get guitar lessons, acting groups, normal great job, better house to live in and a new car. Now I'm on my balcony having a doob. Part of me thinks I should quit or cut back. But the other part of me thinks I'm young and it does so much for me. It makes me have a better outlook on life, makes me hungry so I eat, and makes me think clearer and a lot more positive. When I'm not ripped I'm grumpy and I feel like there's no hope in my life and I have a tummy ache. Snow makes everything so pretty and quiet and simple. Too bad I can't drive anywhere in it. I love the snow. Rambo and I are going to look at a house that sounds wonderful. I really want a new place to live and a new full time Mon-Fri day job. I could get up and shower and get dressed nice every day and have money that I can count on. I can do Keg/internet for extra money nights and weekends. I just need to do more with my life. I'm so bored. It would be nice to have a time chart/ hand book on life so I would stop worrying and just know what's going to happen. I guess no one would learn from their mistakes then. The wind is starting to pick up. I was thinking that I should write more – about what I'm not sure. I guess just write about what I think all day as I watch the world. Just write about what I see. I was also thinking about interviewing people and asking them the same questions that I think they'd answer the same, then tell my own opinions on the questions and edit it all together. Just to show people how we're all the same. So it would have a ton of editing involved and lots of interviewing. What questions should I ask? What is your most valuable possession? For me it's my diary, I would be very upset if I lost it. It can't be a person. Do you believe in life after death and who you think will be there to greet you when you die. I think people who have lost someone are more likely to think there is life after death. I need a ton of 8mm tapes and money to buy them. This movie is going to be about people and how I see them. I think I could even enter this into a film festival. I need that insurance money.

Feb. 4, 2002

I'm down to 105 lbs because I'm so sick and have been for months. You would think that doctors could help me, but they don't even care or listen to me. Maybe if they were paid less then less doctors would be doing it for the money and more would be good and want to help. I just don't know how much more of this I can take. I feel like I'm dying and I look disgustingly thin. I was up puking and dry heaving all night and I don't have any energy left- none. If I puke tonight and don't eat all day I'm going to the hospital and not leaving till I feel better. I know that I want to move home – I need my mom to take care of me! I went to a healer last Wed to Sat (today's Mon morning) and I'm feeling better except my tummy. I don't have the urge to smoke. I finally can have happiness and think clearer without pot. But I haven't eaten that much in days and I'm getting dehydrated from vomiting and I'm supposed to be on medication for a bladder infection. I've never been so sick. If today doesn't go better I have to go to the hospital, I'm just at that point. I want to move home 100% now. It's just the best thing for me and I need my mom. We have better communication since the healer so I feel good about moving home. I really feel hopeless and like I can't go on. I see my very small arms and wrists and hands and I see how weak I am. I should take pictures. I don't know how I'm going to make it through the day. I have the worst painful pain in my stomach - it's unbearable and been going on way too long. Day after day, month after month and no fucking asshole doctor cares! I hate doctors!

Feb. 10, 2002

I went to the hospital from the 5th to the 8th and was put on IV for all those days and nights so I could get my medication into my system. So I'm feeling better than I was, but still no energy and sore etc. Oh and I weigh 102 lbs now at 5'5"! Those stupid doctors are such assholes they don't care about helping me at all. I had a scope done on the 6th and the idiot did it wrong and put a hole in my tummy and tortured me. It was the worst pain I'd ever been through and I don't think I'll ever forget the experience. Blood was pulse spurting into my stomach and I was gagging and throwing up the whole time and then he put 6 shots of adrenalin around the wound to stop it from bleeding and then they loaded me full of more drugs to try to ease the pain, so I was moaning and groaning and tears were streaming down my face and I was in the worst pain imaginable. Then I was throwing up brown old blood every half hour for five hours and I wondered if the pain and throwing up would ever stop. I couldn't even think about what they did for a while because it hurt to think about. At the time I was thinking, break my wrist or any bone, just no more of this pain. The nurse was holding my head down and even with the drugs I could feel the pain so much. I was knocked out for hours after and didn't come to till later that night. Then I had to have a morphine shot in my arm for the pain to help me sleep. I tell you, morphine is one cool drug! They wanted to give it to me again but I don't like putting harsh drugs into me. So I came home late Friday day and have been on the couch since. I can't believe they did that to me. The doctor said, "Oh I've never seen that before, your one in a million". Is that supposed to make me feel better for the hell you just put me through asshole!??! Then I get home only an hour and Rambo came over and he starts being a dink. Saying, "well I can't see us making it if you move home and if you go to Thailand with Belle". Well fuck him man, I'll do whatever makes me happy and if he don't like it, there's the door honey! I couldn't believe the way he was treating me and I still had my hospital bracelet on! What an asshole! He starts going off about online and pot and shit and I was crying and he didn't even care. So he left and came over Sat and I told him it was over. I can't stand to be treated that way and it's like he didn't hear me. I was crying again and I've been really good about saying everything on my mind since the healer. I don't hang onto it, I just let it go. So I told him to go out last night and have fun and decide if he wants to be single or in a relationship. Then we hugged good-bye for a while and it felt so good to have him hold me. As much as I love him I won't be treated badly, I'd rather be alone so we'll see what happens from here.

Feb. 11, 2002

Rambo and I watched a movie and had dinner together last night and also had make-up sex. It felt so good to be in his arms. We snuggled all night together and I stayed at the apartment. Today I went shopping for Brooklyn's b-day present and that was fun. My tummy still gives me trouble but I just keep the hope of getting better soon in me. I have to or sometimes it overwhelms me and I wonder if I'll ever get better. I don't know what I'm doing with my life or what steps to take to go in the movie career direction. I just keep thinking up ideas. I guess that's all I can do. Moving home is the best thing for me, but I don't want to pack all my stuff and move it all again. Oh well, I'll worry about that when I'm feeling better. I always have this problem where I feel that Rambo doesn't love me and I don't know if it's me or him or maybe both. I just worry if I miss a call from him way too much and stuff like that. No one said life was going to be easy, but I'm ready for a whole lot less stress in my life. I'm ready for happiness. I'm still off the pot. It's weird but since the healing I feel no urge to smoke it. It's not on my mind 24/7 anymore. But my stomach has been way worse since I quit. Well they prescribe pot to cancer patients for their stomachs, so it makes sense. I also have so much more time now that I'm not spending ½ my days rolling and smoking and finding more pot. And I'm happier on the real joys of life like my nieces and nephew and just stuff. I can't believe how good that healer was for me, now all I need is for my tummy to be better and get my appetite back. I'll just keep drinking lots of water and try to keep my stress and activities low. Easier said than done for a worrier like me. I've even started to meditate again, not twice a day but around once a day so far. Well Rambo better phone again soon or I'll never relax enough to eat my lunch…

Feb. 13, 2002

Well what a year it's been! Yesterday I wanted to drive up to Pintnay where my friends died and I put some flowers and pictures up and something I wrote. It felt really good to spend the day doing that. Annie went with me and she was the perfect company. She asked me lots of questions about Wonder and Dean and death and she made it all seem funny. I got home late in the afternoon and then my mom wanted me to try on shoes for Brooklyn so I went shopping with her and then we stopped at Beatrice's on the way home and went for a quick dip in the hot tub, then we went to Hemlock. I took my truck to Rambo's and I had about two and a half hours with him before he had to go to work. He was so rude to me and mad at me for not spending the day with him, and that was a special day for me that I wanted to share with him. He handled it wrong and he spent the time I was there being mad at me and he left without saying or kissing me good-bye. All he said was "lock the door when you leave". I just took it as the last straw, the final fight, and I was planning to pack my stuff while he was gone to work. I wrote him a letter – again saying why I was doing what I had to do. I need to have my days free to do what I want with who I want. I don't need someone bringing me down anymore. It's just everything that was wrong with our relationship was adding up to us having to split up. So Tiffany, Jacquie, and Belle came over to help me pack. Belle, Tiffany, and Jacquie were my saviors and they helped me pack up everything and do tons of trips up and down stairs, and we loaded up Jacquie's car and my truck and I left the apartment looking nice and not ransacked. I left the heat on and a movie in the room ready to play and I just tried to make it as easy on him to come home to as I could. I'm glad I got everything out when he wasn't there, it made it easier. But now I have the biggest mountain of stuff downstairs waiting for me to sort through it. So I need to paint my room and pack my stuff back up there again. So I got home and finally crawled into bed with mom and had maybe two hours of sleep before Rambo woke me up when mom went for a shower. We went to the living room and talked and he said he would try and made me feel so horribly guilty for my decision to leave. But if we're going to break up one day, why not now and get it over with. I didn't want to hurt him; I really didn't want to hurt him. All I wanted was to try to make him happy and no matter what I tried I couldn't make him happy. I just got tired of trying and I was tired of putting my life on hold to kiss his ass. I love him and this will be a hard one to get over but it's for the best this way. I need to go and find myself and travel and follow my dreams and work guilt free and do whatever I want every day. I'm just not ready for him and me to have a live in relationship. I won't move in with another man or woman because I'm not ready to give up any person in my life. I should be allowed to go put some flowers up for my friends ~ its one year ago today. I should be able to move home when I want and have someone mature enough to handle the truth. I need to work on my career and Rambo didn't/doesn't even believe I'll make it. He says I have high school dreams. Oh well, at least I'm happy. I'm happiest alone at this point in my life. I can't believe how hard this was/is. I hope I start to feel better soon. It was Chinese New Year yesterday when all this happened. It was the 1st day of the year of the horse. This is my year!

Feb. 17, 2002

Rambo and I are still broken up and I'm happy about that. He's come over saying he'll change and he loves me so much and all that BS and I'm very nice but I won't go back out with him. D.J. is back in town and he, Lillian, and I went to Mindy's last night and it was fun. It feels great to see my old friends again. I feel so good; my room is painted; now I just have to move everything in. I'm going to start my own company called "Picture Perfect Productions" and I think it will do very well. I'm taking my iMac in to get fixed on Monday so it's all ready to go for my company. Lillian's dad says I can use his digital camera and computer to edit colour pictures anytime, and I'm going to get my own dark room for black and whites. I need some business cards and a price list and my equipment all ready to go then it's just going to snowball. So I'm excited about this year and I get to redecorate the house on Mom's budget so I'm happy about that too. Life is good and here to be enjoyed!

Feb. 21, 2002

He's chewing on my pen while I try to write. Jose's the cutest little puppy in the world. It's so nice to meet my baby boy and I'm going to take him everywhere with me. I'm happy to be single again. I just love being free and single. Rambo is still trying but I just don't want to go back to that relationship. I don't want any relationship right now except for Jose's. I'm so worried about him. He's so little and breakable. I have a new understanding why mom worries so much about us. I hope Jose lives forever with me. I feel like I had a son. He pees and poops everywhere but they're small and easy to clean up. I just have to do lots of laundry. Belle's puppy Molly is a handful too. She chews and bites everything and everyone. I'm going to spend my time training my puppies and enjoying life to the fullest. Jose loves Brooklyn's Chihuahua's (Rocko and Eddie) and I'm working on our cats Elliot and Tykera. I don't know how I'm going to make this place picture perfect but I will very soon…

Feb. 22, 2002

My pokey little puppy takes up all of my time, not that I'm complaining. I love my little puppy so much, he's my baby. I'm so worried that he'll die on me but I try not to think about that. I'm thinking about the future and how close it is for me. I don't know when or how but I know it's my destiny to "make it". I know I'll act and direct and one day produce and open up women shelters around the world. I've been thinking about D.J. too. He thinks he loves me still but I just don't know. Maybe I'll end up marrying him or maybe not. All I know is I don't want to hurt him ever or our friendship. Rambo is still lost without me and whenever we talk I just end up crying because I fall for his whole "feel sorry for me" act. But at times he sounds fake like Clint so I don't totally fall for it. I know that I don't want to marry Rambo so there's no point in pro-longing the agony. I have the cutest puppy to keep me company and I think that I don't even want anymore meaningless sex. I'm going off the pill and I really don't want to have sex with men that I don't love anymore. I'd rather grow a friendship with any suitors and learn more about them that way, and if they can't handle it than they can go find some other girl to fuck because this girl has been fucked over enough and is worth more than sex. I have a mind and a free spirit. That should be enough to attract the right man. I'm thinking I might want to wait till I'm married but I know that probably won't happen. I just don't want to regret any more of my sexual partners and some of them I regret. I have my little puppy now. Who needs a boy? Now if only I could get Jose to poop and pee outside. I can't wait to grow closer and closer to Jose and have him understand how much I love him and I'm his mom now. I can't wait till I understand how much he loves me too. I think he's still worried that I will leave him like everyone else has ~ but I never will!!!

Feb. 28, 2002

Wow, a new diary. I wonder what experiences will be written in here. My mom found and bought me this journal because she knew my old one was running out. My puppy Jose needs a friend, too bad I'll have to wait till I get my insurance money. I'm up to owing my mom two grand. I hate owing money to everyone and being so broke. I'm so happy to be single again; dating always seems to cost me money! I'll take Jose over any man any day. He's so cute when he wakes up in the morning. He just lies beside me and bites my fingers then he wakes up a bit more and starts for my nose. I feel like he's my little angel from the universe sent to me to make me happy. Now I just need a little friend for him. I don't know if I'll get a girl or another boy friend for him but as soon as I get some extra cash I need a puppy, black and white picture stuff, another editing system, a studio, and money in the bank so I can relax and landscape the yard. Well I'm going to go to Brooklyn's to enjoy the day.

Mar. 3, 2002

I wrote a letter to Dirk Manly the other day and now I can't stop thinking about it. I know he probably won't even get it or read it, but he might. Maybe he'll say here's an audition and I'll take it from there. I guess I should just forget about it. I'm such a big dreamer, a wishful thinker, but is that so bad? I guess only time will tell. Rambo keeps phoning and wanting to get back together but I don't want to. I just can't go back in life and I know that people don't change, especially after three weeks of being broken up. I'm tired of having no money and no career. I want a job that I really enjoy and I want it today! I'll just keep working on my business and see what the future brings. Well this is a new diary and I'm ready for a new section of my life. Jose and I are ready to see the world and experience the most happiness. With Jose I'll never be alone because I can take him everywhere…

Mar. 4, 2002 | **6:25am**

Well I tried everything to make money today and it just isn't there. I made like twenty bucks and I need more than that. I'll work at the Tap and the World doing bookwork and make some money that way. I went to bed last night at 10pm so I woke up at 6am. I have to work at the Tap at eleven so I have a few hours to spare. I think I'm going to go to work online before work. Any extra moola helps. I'm just going to work online / Tap / World. Last night while I was working I started writing my movie. I have my two old diaries to work with but I'm not sure of the plot and all that yet, but I think so far it's about my life. I'm using quotes from my diaries and the only problem is that there is too much to write about.

Mar. 18, 2002

I've had Jose one month today!! I'm going snowboarding today with Belle and we're taking Dad's truck. I was house sitting for Brooklyn all weekend and Dad kept stopping by to smoke one with me so we had lots of good talks. He even knew I was real low on weed so he brought over some he had from the trailer. So I'm going to roll it up and take it with me. He tells me all the time all the reasons I should quit and why I smoke it. If nothing else it's a secret bond we have that we both hide from Mom. Dad stops and smokes with Brooklyn and Rant all the time. Dad's always trying to quit but "falls off the wagon". My mom has been lending me tons of money lately. I can't wait to pay her back. I think I will start serving again for extra cash and get my insurance money ASAP. So much boring stuff to do, no wonder I put it off…

Mar. 19, 2002

Good Morning! It's 8:30am and I'm lighting my second doobie so I'm nice and ripped. Then I'm going to do some laundry, tidy my room, and then hopefully be online by 11:00 and work till 5pm. I need a cable splitter so I can watch TV. Then I could go to cheap night movies with someone. I hope I get money soon. I just have no money because I wasn't working for a month while I was sick. So I hope to get my first check back this week and only like $100 US, so not much but I've had zero. I've been borrowing off mom which I hate doing! I'm going to light some incense and candles when I get up. Mom's at work. Jose likes to chew on my dirty panties; I don't let the little pervert, although sometimes he finds a pair. Oh, and I'm going to clean my room. I wonder what this life will bring for me. I wonder when I'll get a great job. I wonder when I'll get my insurance money. I wonder…

Mar. 24, 2002

I'm lying in bed listening to Van Morrison and snuggling with Jose. He's the cutest little puppy. It sucks having no money. It sucks working a job you hate too, but I guess these are the problems the whole world has. At least I have a nice bed to lie in and good family and friends to keep me company. I go to do my weekend office work at the World then the Tap then home and I'll maybe work online tonight. I love my little puppy so much. Well I'm ready to move on in life. I'm ready to have a career in the movie industry. I'm ready to act and work hard at my job. I'm ready to go where I have to go to have my dreams come true. I'm ready to leave all this behind in a second (I know I can always return again). I'm ready to see the world and all the people in it. I'm ready to take my place and live my life. I'm ready when life is ready for me…

Mar. 26, 2002

I went to cheap night tonight with Tiffany, Jacquie, and Lillian. We all smoked Tiffany's weed she's kind of selling. I wish I was growing or had money so I could have tons of weed to smoke with all my friends. It's actually 1:05am so I guess it's the 27th. On my way home I saw a car head light down at Rope Bay trail. It's late so I started to drive down there because Rant's uncle is stealing off them and some murders are involved ~ it's a long story that Brooklyn will have to write about. So I got half way down the Rope Bay part when they turned off the lights. Then I got scared and put it in reverse and backed up and went to Brooklyn's to get Rant. I was scared they'd kill me maybe if I'd cornered them down there. So Brooklyn and Rant sent me home with Jose and I bet they're lurking around the neighborhood now. I guess it's best to stay away from those crazy coke/heroin/etc junkies... Those guys are too scary for even Rant.

Mar. 28, 2002

I was at Brooklyn's and had a doob with her and Rantly. So I'm ripped because I have no moola to buy weed, so I haven't smoked much green, and today my stomach has been upset. I even bought some cigarettes because I had the craving to smoke so badly and the cigarette got me just ripped. It was ok but I don't like the taste and it's nowhere near as good as pot. And today I had two cigs close to each other and I felt so ill. So ill in fact that I don't even want to smoke cigarettes again. But now I just had a few hoots with Brooklyn and Rant-o and I'm feeling much better. So point being I'm sticking to weed, sweet weed. The true friend of Mary-Jane. I guess I should stop waiting for some miracle and I should do something about my life. I guess I just don't know what to do. I need a full time desk job but all I want to do with all my heart is run off and be an actress. I'll take my start however I have to and roll with it, whether it's TV, movies, or Broadway even, but I'd rather be in front of the camera for now. I just want it so bad and I've been waiting my whole life for it. I can't put off getting a desk job much longer. I just want a show for Brooklyn and I, one we can travel with and have fun. I can't wait any longer; I'm at my wits ends. Please spirit guides give me that dream. I've tried to be good and I really think I deserve my dreams coming true and much more.

Saturday, Mar. 30, 2002 | **3:25am**

I just got home from the bar. Jose is at Brooklyn's and Tykera is here with me. Elliot is around somewhere. I had a good night out tonight. I saw lots of people at the Station. Belle was puking by the end of the night. I have to work in five and a half hours so I'm going to sleep. D.J. was all over me tonight, and so was Caiden. Gary Greens gave me his email and a few boys bought me drinks. Elliot just came into my room now. I'm working on my first grow room down in the tin shed. I insolated it all by myself. Marty's girlfriend phoned me the other day to play ball with them so I don't know I guess I will, no better offers yet. I gave her a hard time and asked what position.

Thursday, Apr. 4, 2002

Today is Thursday and nothing exciting is happening in Hemlock. Brooklyn rented a carpet cleaner so I have to clean mom's carpets. I think I'll work on that chicken house/grow room more too.

Tuesday, Apr. 9, 2002

I worked at the Tap Saturday night and last night. Each night I made fifty dollars, so not bad I guess. Short three and a half hour shifts both times. I'm using a bit of my computer skills with my men customers at the Tap. Last night I had a table of five old men and they all tipped me well and said what a great job I did. It's really hard to explain how I talked to them because it was in a very subtle way with my eyes and my smile. I was saying Tap info but with internet facial (well on a much smaller scale). It's weird but I really think I could figure out any mans sexual fetish, quickly too. I can just tell the character the man is looking for. It's almost like a super power really.

Apr. 15, 2002 | 7:46am

Jose thinks there's a strange little dog in my room (him in the mirror). He's barking at himself and no matter what I do he goes back and finds that little dog to bark at. He doesn't think it's himself. "Yap yap yap". I had a long weekend working at the Tap. I worked eleven hours and played ball at my first practice in between my split shifts. Monday is my big "day off". I think Brooklyn and I will work on our demo tape today. I'm going to take my iMac down (and camera) because Rant's uncle stole all of their goods. Poor Rant has some pretty harsh family members. Some are good but a lot are crack heads. I love getting up in the morning and enjoying that first "puff puff", especially when I have a big bag for the rest of the day... 8:00am

No Such Thing As Secrets

Tuesday, Apr. 16, 2002 | 12:10am (17th)

I went to cheap night at the movies tonight with Lillian. We saw Abe Benson's new movie. Lillian went to her boyfriend's house after the show and I came home to get Jose and a doobie. I think the weed is a bit wet because it's hard to get this sucker to burn. Mmm, puff, puff, puff. I guess I was feeling alone so I thought I would write in here. I like to write and smoke weed!! Lillian is funny; she changes her boyfriends all the time. Now she doesn't smoke as much and did coke with her bf and E a couple of times. So for me I guess I'm a hypocrite because I think E is pushing it and coke I won't ever even try. Why bother when weed gets me high, or mushrooms if I really want, or I could go out drinking if I want to. I guess when I write in my diary it's like writing to the future me who is reading. Hi future Betty (older Betty reading back). I hope we're happy and if not, let's ask ourselves why? Jose is sleeping under the covers. My window is slightly cracked and I hear the hum of the woodstove, and the faint sound of crickets mixed with the mill docks far off, and the rain dripping off the roof onto the 2nd roof – just lightly. My room is messy as it has been my whole life. I wear pink flannel pj's with donuts on them and my room is cluttered with toys. It is a room that has been lived in for a very long time, and a house that I helped build at age two.

Thursday, Apr. 18, 2002 | 8:10am

My mom wants me to go see Larry Harry (talks to dead people). She went and thinks everyone should go now. I'm thinking I'll go but I'm not sure when yet. There is a lot to do, but nothing new and fun. I think I smoke weed because I'm bored. If I was always busy I wouldn't have time to smoke it as much. Reilly helped me tune and put on new strings on my guitar and I've started to play again. He just did it last night and it's lying on the bed beside me now because I've already played this morning. Belle doesn't like it when I play when she's sleeping though. Today I need to have a shower, finish my laundry, work online, get "welcome home" flowers for grandma and visit her. I really should visit Sammy too. I was going to buy Mariners tickets for Mindy for her birthday so we can go do that this summer. See, I'll need a new car by then. I need to make an appt with Monroe's Law and I'm set to settle I guess. Well who knows how long this will take. Brooklyn will hopefully get a good computer job today. She has another interview.

Saturday, Apr. 20, 2002 | **3:30am (21st)**

Tiffany, Belle, and I just got home from the bar. I worked eleven hours then went out and I have to work tomorrow morning. All the Tap guys were out and I was in my street clothes looking good and it was fun to get their attention. Its good having my cousin Harry there too cause I have an in with the kitchen boys. Not that I couldn't get in on my own, but I don't look like some desperate girl, I look like I'm chilling with my cousin.

Apr. 23, 2002 | **7:55am**

Tuesday morning and there's lots I should do today but who knows how much I'll get done. I have ball tonight. Every Tuesday is a double header of slo-pitch at McGrowl. Last week's first game was cancelled due to too much water on the field. The sun is shining so far today so I should play. It will be fun. I'm picking up Mindy like the good old days and we'll go play ball together.

Apr. 24, 2002 | **11:30pm**

I had the worst night last night and day today. I have this cold that has taken everything out of me. I've been sleeping on and off all day and haven't even thought about getting dressed. Belle just dropped into my room I offered her a hoot but she said no she was burnt (Tiffany, Jacquie, and her went to a movie) and I tried again and again then gave up. If she doesn't want to smoke pot, more for me. Lillian has done coke a couple times. Brooklyn and Rant are worried; Rant says that's it she's hooked. So I guess I'd better have a chat with her. Her boyfriend deals it and does it and now has her doing it. I'm not going to even try it. I'm sure it's great, but I won't ever know. Lillian said she didn't like it, so why'd she do it again, and by herself before meeting up with me at the Tap on Sat. We were all smoking doobs there but she chose to do a couple lines then smoke weed. Oh well each to their own I guess. I really hope tonight goes well. I hate colds. I have to tape Brooklyn's friend's stagette tomorrow.

Apr. 25, 2002 | **9:00am**

Not much has changed since last night. Belle is still sleeping. I've been up since 7am. I looked through some pictures and now I'm having a puff and writing. I had a better night last night but I'm still feeling sick. My stupid truck is broken again. I still owe from the last fix and now it's broken again. I've been using Brooklyn's car but I need a new car for myself. I need something that I don't have to fix ever. I like the new VW bugs; I wish it came in convertible. I wish a lot of things. Jose is up growling at that darn dog in the mirror again. He's a funny boy. There's the phone, too bad I don't have one in my room. I bet its Brooklyn, I'll just call her in 2 sec's when I'm done my smoke. I'm going to go see "Larry Harry" a guy who talks to dead people. Mom, Brooklyn, Uncle Abe, and Alison from work have all been and say he's for real. And so I think I should go. Everyone thinks I should go. I guess my spirit guides could come through or anyone you've lost and are now on the other side. It's like confirmation on spirits and if they are really watching and with you all the time. And I hope they give me advice on my life. Tell me what I'm supposed to be doing?? I wish I could talk to spirits. I'd ask a lot about life, time travel, and all those weird things I wonder. I'd love for Wonder or Dean to come to me. Maybe he'll go to Larry Harry. I could pass on messages for him. I don't know maybe I'm crazy. I guess I'll just have to check it out and see what he says. It's $95 and the reading lasts about forty-five minutes. Brooklyn and Mom both loved theirs. So ok, well who knows when I'll go? I need money to go. So, we'll see… 9:20am

Apr. 26, 2002

Thank God the stagette went well for Brooklyn and her friend. We had a BBQ at Brooklyn's then went to the Station for strippers. Then it was off to the casino where I spent my usual ten dollars on quarters for slot machines. It was fun, but Newsville doesn't get very good strippers man. The ones I saw in Cowgary were one hundred times better. But Brooklyn's friend got pulled up on stage a few times and everyone knew it was her stag. I don't know, but I guess I should go back to the "commercial" today at 6pm and drop off a resume. I'm not sure if I even want to work there, but no movie deal and online has been really dead. I need a more secure income. As far as tip money, I'd probably make the most there in town. And in the summer, it's even busier. So why not? I need a change.

I can work Tap on weekends and Democ during the week. And hopefully get some sort of set schedule. I just took Jose out for a pee and I saw my Moms car. So she's home. I hope she doesn't come in here and find me with a cloud of smoke around me. I'd better get out of here. I'll take Jose (I can't go in my truck because it's broken) and I'll go down to Brooklyn's and go from there I guess. You see, my room will never get done. I feel like I can't be myself living with M and B. I feel like I just don't fit with them. They're different than me. Oh well, I'm going to go now.

Sunday, Apr. 28, 2002 | 11:11pm

Well I'm in bed with a hot neocitrin and Jose. I fell asleep watching TV earlier and now I woke up and might be up for a bit, but maybe the neo will work. I slept from like 5:30 – 10:30 moving from the couch to my bed and kept on sleeping. Brooklyn starts training for her new job tomorrow so I have to go down and make sure the kids are off to school in the morning. Everyone is too busy to help me and I have no bf so no one has to make time for me, or my truck. On Saturday night at the Tap I was working and I saw my old college professors. It was good to see them but they were both surprised to see me at the Tap and not making movies yet. Maybe next time I see them I'll be making movies?! I find myself really enjoying music more than I ever have before. I like to dance too. Maybe the idea of a band isn't so bad? Or a TV show with Brooklyn would be fun. Caiden wants me to come and see him tomorrow till Wed, but I have no moola. And its Brooklyn's first week of work so she asked me to help with her kids. But I might not have ball this week so that would be good to go then. The money thing is a big one. It would be fun to go but I'm not one hundred percent sure if I want to go. I guess I'll just see how tomorrow goes. I wish I had my iMac in my room so I could watch that movie (still haven't returned it) damn late charges. They always get me…

May 6, 2002 | 11:30am

On May 2nd I went to Capsville with Suzanne, Barron, and Tim. We met up with a couple girls from high school down there, and Ben and Stinky ended up coming down and getting a room in the same hotel. We went out to dinner, then dancing, and it was so much fun. I got really drunk and was having a blast.

Then Judy showed up for a bit. Then we went back to the hotel and we smoked weed. We went up and down from room to room and almost got kicked out. Then I fell asleep while I was watching TV in Ben's bed and we were lying there and he put his hand on my tummy and I was thinking "I should put my hand on his", so then I did. It was very slow moving, just touching. Then we kissed and snuggled all night. It was the best night. I even got a guy. I went over to his place Friday night and Kent and Stinky were there. We all blazed and Kent left early but Stinky stayed up till 2:30am. We didn't have a chance to talk till then so it was a bit awkward. We kissed a little bit, but then I left. I got kind of mixed signals that night. But then he called Sunday (I was so busy all day Sat with Brooklyn's friend's wedding). He came over and we watched a DVD in my room. We kissed a lot more and then fell asleep together, and he was softly rubbing my back as I laid on his chest and it felt so comfortable as we were kissing, I would forget it was my old high school buddy and just be into the kiss and feel really attracted to him. The more we talk, the more I like him. I'm intrigued by him. I said to him Sunday "I think I like you Ben" and he smiled and said "yeah we kind of click", and I do feel some connection. So I'm definitely expecting to end up with Ben as a boyfriend, but I'm enjoying it so far. He's cute, he's nice, he's my friend, he's funny, he's witty, he's trustworthy, he smokes weed, he seems like the perfect guy ~ where's the catch… is there one?

May 10, 2002 | **5:30pm**

I'm going to go to Ben's parents place for a summer staff party of the company he and his Dad work at. It should be fine, but I'm a bit worried about meeting his parents. No, I don't want to get married at this young age. I haven't done internet work since before the second so it's been a new life for me. I really like my new life.

May 15, 2002

I had fun at ball last night with Mindy. I played better, still not one hundred percent though. I went to Ben's after and we were talking and he said something like he "can't forget" about the past but he's trying to live in the moment. "The past" being my "internet". It hurt me that he thinks less of me because of it. I'm not a bad person or some "horny internet porn diva". Can't he see that? I think

I'm a very misunderstood person. I don't want to deal with internet ever again. No matter what happens with Ben, I'm tired of it in my life. I know it was brought to me so I can help the women who have no choice every day and who need a break in life. A life changing break. The way I really need a life changing break right now.

May 17, 2002 | 3:15pm

I went to StarWars Episode II yesterday. I went to the matinee with Brooklyn, Jordan, Annie, Rita, Suzanne, Mindy, and Jake. Then I went again at night with Suzanne, Mindy, Jake, Tim, Barron, Ben, and Stinky. I stayed the night at Ben's after. There's a contest through JRFM. The best act to wins ten grand and a record deal. So Brooklyn and I have been writing a song and practicing all day for a few days now. It has to be in by next Friday, one week from now. Then the top ten go on to compete in Cityville, then in Cowgary for the finals. I really think we can do this. I think this is it; we're joining up with Stinky and his band mates that I've known since kindergarten. And we're all from Hemlock so we need some Hemlock in the name of the band, maybe Hemlock Melody. I just hope we get the song done in time. I should write the song out but that would take a while. The title is "we were meant to be". Brooklyn and I wrote it together. I really want to win this contest because I really want that new life. I'm just going to go for the music deal because what else can I do this week.

May 20, 2002 | 3:14pm

I'm sitting on the roof puffing and writing. I've been cleaning house all day and now I'm going to edit the wedding video. I have so many things I should/could be doing with my life, but I don't want them. I want the impossible dream instead. That's all I can think about. We met with the band last night. It was interesting, to say the least. They were punk/metal and we were country/pop. But if we somehow could mix the two we'd be starting something of our own and I think it would have a big following. It's hard when you have "impossible" dreams. People always saying how "you can't make it" and "what steps are you taking to get there?" and "I don't see how you're going to get there living here" and "do you know how hard it is to make it". The world can be broken into two groups, positive and negative. Belle and Tiffany just drove in. They caught me smoking on the roof. They said "save me a hoot" so I'll save them a hoot. It's a good thing I always roll two…

May 26, 2002 | **4:00pm**

Yesterday was Mindy's 23rd birthday. She had some people over. I had fun but not as much fun as I would have if I was single. Ben was by me all night and I felt like I couldn't chat with my work friends because he didn't know them. I just felt like I wished I was single and could stay longer. Being single has so many advantages. I don't see Jose enough or my video company when I'm "attached". And how long do I think we would last? All these thoughts are going through my head. I guess when I think of marriage I think of Hollywood hunks not the guy's I've met. I guess I don't think I'll marry Ben. But that doesn't mean I have to break up with him. I guess I'll just stick it out and stay happy. But then there's that internet thing.

June 5, 2002 | **11:44am**

Last night after ball Ben and I stopped at Mindy's and she told him I'm a liar. And they were ripped and going on about it and it bothered me. Cause I try not to lie. Then at Ben's after he was saying, "your best friend says you're a liar, not the kind of thing I want to hear". I just think what? The shit I've heard about him and put aside. I don't know if I'm mad at Mindy or if she seriously thinks I'm a big liar?? I can't stop thinking about it. I hate liars, I would never be one! I'm probably the most honest person I know! I pretend to be happy when I'm mad at someone, does that make me a liar? I'm not worried about Ben and Mindy, they were just ripped and thinking they were funny. I'm editing the wedding ceremony and it's looking really good. Brooklyn and I are both working on it. We make an unbeatable team. She doesn't think I'm a liar and she knows me better than anyone…

June 6, 2002 | **12:14pm**

I'm downstairs waiting for a movie to export (the wedding video actually). Belle and Lillian both assure me that I'm not a liar. I will avoid the truth to be nice but I won't ever lie to your face. And I think they're right. Lillian, Ben, and I went into

Ben's hot tub last night. We smoked weed and I had some of my favorite black cherry Okanogan coolers and Ben had Corona. Lillian just smoked. I like having a boyfriend I can hang out with my friends with. The last thing I need is complications in my life, so as long as this is fun and not stres SWUI, I'll enjoy it.

Friday, June 14, 2002 | 1:30pm

I'm sitting down at the iMac puffin a puffer with Brooklyn. She is editing the video. I'm making copies of the "Wonder and Dean in Chilliwack" tape and cleaning up. Ever since Larry Harry I feel closer to Dean and Wonder but I miss them still. I wish we had more time together. I'm sick of the Tap job. I have fun at work but I make so little of money and I would rather be making movies ~ for tons of money with huge budgets. All I need is a new career.

June 20, 2002

Today has been a bad day, for 'Island Films' anyways. We lost thirty-eight edited minutes from the wedding. I phoned a 1-800 number for an iMac tech help and everything but we still lost it. And we have tons of work to do on other projects. I have no money till I get tips on Friday.

June 21, 2002

Today is a good day. The pre-school video is looking good. Jose is feeling better and Brooklyn and Rant bought me a beautiful pair of gold earrings. I have to get ready for work. I already worked this morning, picked the kids up from school, visited Ben, worked on the preschool video, and now I'm listening to the radio and getting ready for work. This song is "you can leave your hat on".

June 23, 2002 | 8:05pm

What a bad night last night was. We were all out for Tim's B-day on Saturday night. It should have been fun for me but D.J. was being a bitch to me and saying I picked my relationship with Ben over him and our friendship. And Rambo was at the Real Room too and he was being really bitchy too. I was drunk and trying to have a good time but D.J. ruined that. Then Ben and I left in a cab to his house in Rabbitwood. He told me he's heard bad things about me and Marty. "We had taped sex" (oooh, big deal. It's not like there are copies). He's very jealous of me playing ball with Marty so I've had it. He made me feel like an internet whore and that I'm not. Fuck him if he can't see that and fuck D.J. for treating me with no respect. He was just being a complete asshole. Why the fuck should I cry all day cause of them – my so called friends. It's over between me and Ben for one more reason and this is the clincher. When we went camping we all had a shower in Brooklyn's trailer one day (Brooklyn, Ben, and I). The next day Brooklyn and Rant showered. Brooklyn just rinsed her hair over the tub but Rant got in and stepped in cum. Ben and I were out for a walk and Brooklyn said Rant was gagging. She remembered she didn't bring conditioner and she had it in her hair! I shit you not. So that's it. I can't stay with him anymore, I like being single anyways way more. And so I should break up with him but I'm not in the mood to tonight. I just want to lie in bed and forget my problems.

Monday, July 1, 2002 | **3:30pm**

Yesterday was Jacquie's 19th birthday. We all went up to Little Beach and Tiffany, Jacquie, Belle, Lillian, Jacquie's boyfriend, a couple of his friends, and I all did mushrooms. I didn't take too many because I didn't want to get too high. Lillian got very high and so did Belle. My mom and Auntie Dana were up there in a cabin and Brooklyn, Rant, and co. were in a campsite. Some other hemlock folk were also camping there! So it was a big party weekend. Last night we were drinking, smoking, and singing songs around the camp fire. I just had a bath and I made Jose join me at the end because we both smelled after three days of camping. I could go to Fun Island with Suzanne tonight. I'm not sure. I just got a phone call about filming another wedding! So that's Leena's on July 27th and the new one is on August 3rd I think. I am so busy. Who needs to work at the Tap? Really, I don't have the time. I have no time between all my 'island film' work and the Tap. Really my days off are few and far between and full of guilt because I should be working. I should phone Suzanne too and talk to her. Really I should edit tomorrow but sun tanning on Fun Island would be fun… it's hard to balance pleasure with work. But I try. I think I'm doing alright. I like Brooklyn and my co. "Island Film Productions".

July 3, 2002

I ended up leaving my room and going to Fun Island with Suzanne and Jose. I had to come back Tuesday for ball. I'm going to go to Kelly's now and work on videos. Our business bought a web page name called 'islandfilm.ca'. We (well Rant's credit card) bought it last night. We have lots of deadlines and projects to work on and people to call. All we need now is our studio. We just need to send out a bill for the pre-school job and finish the editing wedding one. Send out demo tapes to Leena and the new wedding. Every time we mention our business someone wants us to look at something or knows someone who would like our work. The plumbing video has to get done in the next couple of weeks. I want it out of the way before Leena's wedding. So much work and softball I don't have time for a boyfriend or even the Tap. I've been thinking about quitting but I really like the staff so I'll probably stay. I'm just so busy.

July 4, 2002 | **9:10am**

The kids (J.A.R.) are down stairs. I let them stay last night. They all stayed in the living room. I've got so much to do today. Way too much to do actually. I have to clean up mom's house. I need to go to the Tap and see if I can get Saturday off for ball. Right now I'm supposed to work 9 –3 and 5-9, and play ball with my team for league games (4 games). The fun Molson tourney is Friday and Saturday and I'm supposed to be organizing it, so I have to go work shit out big time. I hope I can play all those games. I don't know how I'll play four games at McGrowl out by Stonetrees, and 2 – 4 games in Hemlock at the Barley?? I need the wedding promo ready for Saturday's game to give to my coach. Oh boy and today is Thursday! My cousin Warren and his wife Beemer stopped by Brooklyn's the other night with two of their friends. They (Warren and Beemer) are doing great. They went from being broke with no work, to super busy with tons of work in a month like me. I just had a thought that I could teach a course on how to beat the depression of life. I was thinking Brooklyn needs to convince Rant that he can do it on his own and he doesn't need her, for business that is. Once his mind is around it, his bobcat business will fly.

No Such Thing As Secrets

Wednesday, July 10, 2002 | **11:00pm**

It was a very hot day today. Lillian, Belle, and I took Molly and Tiger to the river and we all went swimming. Now I'm eating cheese and crackers in bed with Jose and there are mosquito's buzzing around. Last weekend was crazy. I played lots of ball. Jose got sick on Tap meat (meant for Brooklyn's pit-bull Lisa) and went to the vet. I worked and on Sunday night I went out with Kyle. I'm broke right now, so he took me out for dinner. I had a great time but two bottles of wine and whatever we were shooting made me sick the next day. I promised to never drink again. It was a horrible puke session. I puked driving home. I had to pull over! Then on Brooklyn's deck twice, her bathroom three times, and the other bathroom. Drinking isn't worth how sick I got. The next day I saw Kyle for a bit but then left for my staff party. Then everyone was doing mushrooms and since I can't drink anymore Tiffany and I did a bit. Just a bit and it was fun. Belle and Jacquie were there too but they didn't – oh wait Jacquie did later in the night then left with her boyfriend. Harry got tweaked on mushies too. Everyone did. It was a big camping staff party. Kyle offered me a job at the Democ but it got me thinking of leaving the Tap, but I'm already thinking of leaving the Tap and just doing internet and island films. I'm too busy for the Tap and I'd rather not serve anymore. Time to move on. I have way too much on the go right now and I need to delete something. Kyle made me really think of quitting, but not for commie. You just have to try to make yourself happy. I've been working at the Tap for everyone, but me. My opinion counts and I don't want to be a waitress anymore!!! So, I'm going to quit. 11:20pm.

July 13, 2002 | **3:35am**

It's Beatrice's 30th birthday party. She's pregnant with baby number three who is going to be born a little horse like me.

July 14, 2002 | **10:20pm**

Well, where to start. Beatrice had her 30th birthday party on Saturday night. I got there late after work and Brooklyn and Rant were already gone so I didn't think much of it. It turns out that Dad was being an asshole so they left. They were smoking and out of nowhere he started yelling at Rant and his brother Al.

It made them leave and they were both in tears. Next time I see him I'm going to say a few words to him! He's lucky I didn't find out while I was at the party. And if I was there, it would have been him leaving not Brooklyn and Rant-o. Brooklyn said that Rant was very upset. They don't even want to talk to him. What a dink my dad can be! He's a spoiled brat at times. And the coward goes after the one person there who wouldn't fight back. Oh, I wish I was there. If I don't say something to him – who will? No one else cares about him enough to discipline him. They just want the easy way out – ignore him. Fuck him man, he will not be allowed to treat any of us like that again and I'll see to it.

July 16, 2002 | **8:40am**

Well as always I have tons to do and not enough money to do it all. Today I should go to the gym with Harry, work, clean my still messy room, and I have ball at 6pm. I'm smoking my last doobie, I really need some cash so I can buy more weed. I'm just going to smoke n write till my room looks better. Right now it's looking like a lot of work. I have too many clothes. Oh well, I guess that's a good thing. We don't even use the iMac now. Why should we use it when the other program does a way better finished product? We went from eight transitions to like a hundred and fifty! So it's a big difference. I talked to Leena last night and set up the July 27th wedding. It should be a very easy and fun one to film. I get to see it all more clearly next Thursday for the rehearsal. I wasn't really thinking about all the people who will be there. Leena is my age and her husband is probably Rambo's and the wedding is in Girlsville. Oh well, at least I'll have my faithful partner Brooklyn with me. I told her I want head sets, which would be fun. Boy, I need money! So much I want to buy and things to do. At least I have my internet job; it pays better than Tap on a bad day in way less time. And the Tap isn't a bad job. I guess my point is that there are a lot of shitty jobs out there for real shitty pay. It's just not fare. It shouldn't be so hard to get ahead. There has to be a better world. I'm lucky, very lucky compared to a lot of women in this world. I have a beautiful (but still messy) room and my mom is so sweet to me. I have everything any woman would love to have. I am rich in so many ways and there are way more poor people than me. So I better clean my clothes and appreciate my life more.

July 18, 2002 | 12:45am

I'm lying in bed, sleepy and burnt. Today I talked to my Dad. I'm reminded of what a weird relationship I have with my Dad. I don't even know how I feel about him anymore. It's hard when you don't know how you feel about your Dad. I don't know if I'm very mad at him and feel abandoned or if he's always been distant. I never talk about how I feel with him, just idle chit chat. I don't know if I've ever been real with him. When I was younger I got straight A's and even meditated but that was grade 8. Then in gr.9 and 10, Mindy and I skipped all the time and my parents didn't know and mostly didn't care to know. I even drank at school. Then I worked at the RR and did E all the time but they never knew. They thought it was ok to drink because it's legal. Now I'm more real with them than I've been. I don't hide my weed and they think I'm the worst I've ever been. Parents, can't teach them.

July 26, 2002

A lot has happened. I went to Fun Island with Suzanne and Tim on Mon and Tuesday night. D.J. and Barron came over for the Tuesday night. That was the first time D.J. and I saw each other since the Big Tim's B-day blow up! I wasn't even going to stay but he asked over the phone Monday night to stay for his B-day Tuesday night. We didn't get a chance to talk about it all though because there were always other people around. So it was awkward for all. We had fun but felt the uncomfortable-ness. So I'm not sure what to do today. My room is a mess as always. I should work. I phoned D.J. last night to see if he wanted to hang out but he was busy and wanted me to call him today. So I guess I'll call him when I think of what to say. I'm going to work for a bit I think, why not man? My room can wait. I need someone to keep me company while I clean it. Suzanne would I'm sure. I need to think up a movie – a six minute movie on 11:58. It's another contest. On Fun Island everyone was thinking of it. All we came up with was a dog race #1158 and 11+58=69. My dad thinks I should enter and blow them out of the water. So I better write it. My cousin Harry told me about it and so did my Dad (eight months ago he said). I slightly remember. Oh well I'll start now. I'm just going to go to work on the Fun Island video and see what happens. Maybe I'll find something in it. Maybe because we were talking about it so much, I could get six great minutes out of it. It would be a real story about people thinking up 1158. I'll check the tape today, right now even…

July 28, 2002

The wedding was yesterday and it went well. It was a long day but it went by quick. I got up just after 6am and didn't get home till just after 11pm. Today my new puppy Kandy came home and with Belle's puppy Chip. Kandy is so cute and friendly. She compliments Jose nicely. Kandy, Chip, Jose are all on my bed and I'm out the window having a puff, waiting for D.J. to call. I asked him if he wanted to watch a movie. I'm hoping we'll get a chance to chat. Who knows when the jerk will phone! Ah, life, what can you do with it; it will do whatever it wants to you. All you can do is try to keep your chin up and stay in the game. Then again, maybe society's game is what we should steer clear from? Who knows? I'm not sure what to say to D.J. I just want our friendship back. I'm sure I've hurt him and we know he's hurt me but I'm willing to put all that behind me. I'm just going to try to be honest. I'll try to tell him how I feel or have felt. But it's hard to talk when you don't know what to say. I'm bad at feeling emotions. Maybe I found myself upset on the wedding, seeing the perfect wedding with the perfect parents. The bride's father gave such a nice speech. The way the sister hugged her Dad after the ceremony, it was real. I know I don't hug my Dad like that. She (well they both were) was Daddy's little princess and I know my Dad doesn't believe in that. My Dad keeps bugging me to get firewood. To make it worse it's all burnt black char around the outside so I'm going to get all dirty helping him. My Dad loves me I know. He just has a weird way of showing it. My Momsy is great – I know how much she loves me. Well she just told me she missed a beep, so I'll go call D.J.!!

July 31, 2002

Well D.J. came over but we didn't talk because you know me, and I guess he doesn't like to talk either. I kept falling asleep and he did too. Then the movie was over and he couldn't get his truck to start. I offered for him to take my truck but he stayed the night instead. Of course, nothing happened. I found myself thinking of Ben a lot. I should phone him and see how he's doing. I have his hockey gloves too and Belle wants to see if I left her pink runners there. So I will do that one of these nights. Maybe go smoke one? I wish we could be friends. I went to the movies last night with Tim and Barron.

Monday, Aug. 5, 2002 | 9:10am

I went out after work Friday night and I had fun. I saw Kyle out and he says he's called a lot but Belle said he hasn't. Who cares? He gave me his number again and I saw him at an afterhours party. Then a guy I work with gave me a ride home, well back to the Tap where my truck was. I think he wanted a kiss goodnight. He said, "how about a hug", so I hugged him. Then he said, "And a kiss", so I gave him a little peck and said thanks for the fun night. Then he said, "Another kiss", so I gave him a little peck again and he tried to make it more. You know the double kiss, but I didn't clue in till it was too late. He probably didn't mean anything by it. He does always like to smell my hair at work. Actually he likes all the girls' hair. So I always put a spray of perfume in my hair for him. Last night I went to Quality Beach. I went with Brooklyn, Rant-o, Mom, auntie Jane, auntie Dana, uncle Richard, aunt Callie, Debbie, Beatrice, Tyson, Rita, Tabitha, Beatrice's two Korean kids, Annie, Jordan, Al, Beemer and Warren. We had a big family BBQ for Warren's birthday. Jordan gave Warren a lucky fishing necklace. We had cake and sang Happy Birthday. Then my Dad gave me a ride home and we chanted to his chant CD almost the whole way. I also told him it was ok to feel sad and lonely. He's going through one of the most traumatic times in his life. Just remember it will pass. I think maybe it made him feel better. What to do now, my pups are sleeping? I love my little dogs so much. I should have a shower and then go to work online for the day. I think Tim and Suzanne are off today and tomorrow so maybe I'll do something with them. Life just keeps going by; I can't believe its August, where has the summer gone??

Sunday, Aug. 11, 2002 | 12:10am

My aunt and uncle from Cowgary are here for a summer visit. Tonight Uncle Richard and I got into it about Rant. Now I'm on the roof and he is walking down to Brooklyn's house (my drunken Dad is there). We've been getting into it about a boat. Rant sold Warren's third without telling Richard. The truth is maybe we were both looking for a fight and seized the conflicted conversation and dragged it out all night. I don't even know where to start, all the crazy shit he said. He is so caught up in "society's bs". It's all over a stupid boat that is still sitting in the yard. I really don't see why it's a big family issue. I wasn't going to let Richard call down my bro Rant in my house, and I was in the mood to vent on someone. Even Mom and Callie got into it a bit. But I have to work in the morning. Richard says he can't talk to Rant because Rant smokes too much weed. Well I'm the wrong person to tell that one to. I told him I could smoke two fatties to my head and challenge him to any conversation. He just thought I was wrong and I couldn't have a conversation if I was ripped. Fucking people man. Bunch of haters. Oh well Richard is going down to Brooklyn's now to talk? Part of me thinks I should be down there, but I can't always be the boss. Oh well, not my battle (although I fought it all night). My uncle Richard said a few times that I don't scare him and I finally said, "Good it doesn't scare me that you say that". But I think I do scare him because I speak the cold hard truth. I'm still a bit riled up and so I'm going to keep writing. Sometimes it just hits me (today it did). I can't believe how two-faced the world is. It amazes me how everyone says one thing to your face and one behind your back. Just a bunch of ball-less people who can't tell the truth, and they sell their friends out to agree with another person. I try not to do that. Please, don't let me be like that.

Saturday, Aug. 17, 2002 | **1:50am**

It's been a very long day! I woke up in Enumclaw at Mindy's aunt Macey's house. Mindy and I drove home from there and shopped along the way. I found some good deals. I enjoyed the three ball game stretch, Mariners/Red Sox. Cebattle won two and they were good games. The third was the best. We moved to different seats and a guy asked his girlfriend to marry him right in front of us. She was crying and she said yes! It was a close game. It was good to spend some time with Mindy, just the two of us for a long trip. Really bond you know. I got to Lafassen at 6:45 but had to catch the 10:45! A four hour wait plus a two hour ferry ride!!!! I was choked (fuming mad) when I found out. But I'm home now. I missed my dogs so much, more than I've missed anyone. I'm so happy to have them here. Belle should be home soon. I wonder when she will be. She's at work closing Pan-a-poop.

Tuesday, Aug. 27, 2002

I think I know what I'd like to do with my life as of now. I'd like to perform from now until I'm pregnant. Then while I'm at home being a mom I'll write. I'll direct my work and I'll get into producing new young talent. And I want to open women shelters around the world. There are still starving people in the world. There are so many moms who need help, so many abused women who need protection, and drug addicts who need hope. I'm so tired of the world ignoring the 3rd world countries. They need help, only a dollar a day… no seriously, who knows what the future holds… I don't know what I'm doing in the next year. Maybe our business will succeed. Maybe Brooklyn, Belle, Harry and I will become rock stars. Maybe all of the above…OK new subject. When I was young I read about Samuel Pepe's diaries and I wished my diaries would be that famous, read by school children around the world or at least in Canada. I think my diary is my sanity, everyone should have one.

Thursday, Sept. 5, 2002 | **8:15am**

I have a "discovery meeting" on Sep 23rd. Pete did call back. I called back and left message but nothing yet. As for Caiden, I ditched his phone calls because I feel like he just wants a piece and I'm not really into being used. I think that all he likes is my internet porn and he wants me because of that.

Saturday, Sept. 7, 2002 | **8:40pm**

I can't decide if I should go out tonight or not?? I work tomorrow morning at the World at 7:30am because our first volleyball game is at 10am. Tim, D.J., and Rhonda all want to go out and they want me to go. I don't feel like working online tonight so maybe I should go. I already sent the dogs off and it is Saturday night. I don't know what I'll wear, I haven't even showered and it's so late and that early rise tomorrow. I was hoping that I would figure out what I'm doing by smoking and writing. Should I go out? Should I stay home? If I'm not going to work online then I should just go. But then I spend money instead of making it and I feel like shit tomorrow. But I do love to dance… what to do… what to do??? Dad says "rest is best", and, "with going out there is doubt". Well I don't know, I guess I'll have a shower then decide. I could wear Belle's new cute dress

– not her B-day one – another one. My Dad was just at my door and my Mom yelled "shut her door, it stinks" because I'm smoking a gagger. I thought – pretty cool my parents just let me sit in my room and smoke weed. Then my Dad said out of nowhere "I love you Betty". Awww. How sweet. He's going home now. Oh mom's here now and she says "pee – u". Mom says, "If you can't decide one way or the other then stay home and keep your mother company".

So I stayed home and chatted to my Momsy all night, and now I get to sleep with Elliot because the dogs aren't here.

Tuesday, Sept. 10, 2002 | 7:48am

Today I'll go to work online. Today as I work I should write music or that film festival script. How do you find the right contest? Every day I work online or I go to work at World/tap. My nights off are all spent either with ball, friends, or my dogs. I don't have any time to do fun things and I'm usually too tired to go out. Jose still hates that dog in the mirror! It's funny I but want him to be in the movies. I want them all in the movies. Molly gets me so mad though, she attacks the dogs and me, thinking it's a game but it's not. OK, I phoned Brooklyn and she is going down to Rant's mill with him cause he got a suspension for having a cig in his mouth and Rant threw it back at him and Brooklyn wants her money or she'll go to the union hall. Anyways I guess I'm going to go to work now.

Sept. 20, 2002

I got a phone call at Mindy's house at 2:45am – Beatrice is in labor. So Jose, Kandy and I went over to Beatrice's house where she was walking around with a towel because she was still losing water. So I took Tabitha and Rita over to my house. Brooklyn and Belle went up to the hospital at 7am, and left Jordan, Annie, Rocko, Eddie, and Chip with me. The dogs all wanted to keep sleeping and so did I but the four kids didn't. They kept waking me up. So at 8am I gave up on trying to sleep. I got up, made them breakfast, fed the dogs, cleaned the kitchen, and now I'm cleaning my room. Annie is in my room making my bed. She had to fight the dogs off my bed. I'm still waiting to hear about the little Virgo horse water baby born in the hours of the snake. I think it will be a boy, but who knows. Those four kids are such a handful. Ok, I just got the phone call – BOY 10:47am. I had to phone a couple people and the kids were fighting so I separated them. I put Jordan and Rita downstairs, and Tabitha and Annie upstairs. The dogs are all out enjoying the sun. Yeah, I have a new baby nephew. Sometimes I think about quitting pot, I just never want to bad enough. As soon as my life gets better and I don't need it to cheer me up I guess… or is it me and my outlook on life that needs to get better…

Wednesday, Sept. 25, 2002

Monday was my ICBC discovery court thing. I hated it!! They asked me every question under the sun about the last two years. But I was flustered and couldn't even remember Rambo's last name. I just don't have the memory. Monday was also Mindy's sister's 20th birthday. We went to Mindy's for a little party. Belle and I took our three Chihuahuas' and they were the life of the party. It's a nice sunny morning. Brooklyn has already called and it's "time to go to work", but I had to write. I know we will be editing and painting Christmas bulbs all day today. It's a simple life, one can't complain. I see Molly going upstairs, where is she going? The little pups and I are enjoying the sunshine, but Brooklyn is right, it's time to go to work. I have to work tonight online when I get home. I will put in a good four hours and most likely make over $150, but you never know with this job. I charge $2.99/minute, but the company takes half of that, so I get paid $1.50/minute for my sexual advice. That is $90/hour, but I don't work full eight hour days so I'm not a rich or anything. I just work enough to get by and still live a full and exciting life with my friends and family. I don't know anyone that has lived as wild of a life as I have, except for a few of my friends that have done this job too. It's nice to have each other. One year we even threw a little Christmas party for ourselves. I love feeling like I have co-workers and I'm not the only one braving this job with the title of "internet porn star". I stopped caring what people think of me a long time ago. I had no choice. If I had to believe that I was just some internet slut I would hate myself. I'd rather just be the best person that I can be and trust that I am the best I can be right now. I've thought of going back to school. I have thought of lots of options but for now this job suits my life style.

Sept 27th –02

Its 2:52am Fri/Sat and Belle, her boyfriend Chester, and I are home from the bar. Belle and Chester are downstairs and I went to bed. I have to work at 9 so I need to go to bed. We went out dancing and I saw Ben and Rambo out – oh yeah. I hid from them by Jack McGuiness (I play ball with him) and his bro Junior, but I had an OK night with them. Tiffany, Jacquie, her boyfriend, Belle, and I went to Rabbitwood Karaoke first, and then dancing at the RR. Everyone loved our singing at karaoke, and the bar was the bar. Well I'm going to bed now because I work at 9. Mom still isn't home! She's out with her siblings.

Thursday, Oct. 3, 2002 | **10:03am**

There's a casting call for a new TV show coming to the island, with a twelve million dollar budget for the first season. So Brooklyn and I are going on the 19th for that. That would be cool if Brooklyn and I landed a big TV job. That would be more than cool. Everyone would tune in just to see that "internet girl". They say there's no such thing as bad publicity. I'm beginning to believe it. Wouldn't it be amazing to get a big TV job? They say they're looking for good actors – we're in!!

Tuesday, Oct. 8, 2002 | **10:15am**

I wish I could have a big paying job, buy my parents house, fix it up, keep doing big jobs, till I build up my resume enough to do artistic teaching movies, own my own big company, open women shelters around the world, and help new young artists when I'm old and rich. Not too much to ask for, is it?

Monday, Oct. 14, 2002

I played ball, worked online, and now I'm going to go to Marty & Dennis' apartment to watch a movie. I just wanted to have a quick puff before I get all pretty. I'm done ball for the year now. Soon it will be time for snowboarding!! I can't wait to get up this year because I was sick all last season.

Tuesday, Oct. 22, 2002 | **11:54pm**

I went to the movie with Lillian and we saw Tiffany, Jacquie, and Belle there. Everyone goes to cheap night. Now I'm lying in bed with Jose sitting on my shoulder and Kandy sniffing around looking for a place to lie down. Sometimes in life you feel like crying and it's nothing and everything all at once. For me right now I just feel sad, and alone. I wonder if I'll ever find love or if I have no chance ~ it's just not in my stars. My standards are too high. I want someone who I can talk to and who is willing and wanting to listen and talk to me. I know that may sound girly but I mean it. My dogs are asleep under the covers now. I hear the docks and sea lions out my window. I hear the tick of my clock and Molly's chain dragging on the ground outside. I'm getting less sad and more tired. I have lots to do tomorrow so I'd better get to sleep. Too bad I have to miss the corn maze with Jordan to work at the World.

Thursday, Oct. 24, 2002 | **11:00pm**

Belle is painting her toes on my bed, the radio is on, and all three dogs are nestled down. I have so many things to do in life but I go through phases where I don't have the motivation to do it all like my insurance deal, moving out, doing laundry, and everything in between. Belle and Chip have gone to bed now. Jose is lying on my chest. He snorts so much. I wish he could breathe better. I should look that up in Louise Hays book. I have a specialist apt tomorrow morning for my car accident injuries. I just keep being honest and hopefully my pains go away soon, or will I always have back pain. Just a part of life for tons of people I guess.

Friday, Oct. 25, 2002 | **11:04am**

All my friends are doing things – Lillian's got her dream job, her dream boy (kind of) and I think she's happy. Mindy's moving to Cityville with the man of her dreams. Judy is in love to, living in Capsville going to "make-up for movies" school and she's got jobs lined up for when she's done. And me: I'm still working the same shitty internet job, I'm twenty-three and living at home (and still broke), and I work part time at Tap (I started when I was seventeen). I need to move on. I need to start the next phase of life. I only wish that it was my going away party Monday. I'm mean I'm happy for Mindy, but when is it my turn. Well I have to go to work online for the day.

Oct. 27, 2002

I picked up two kids hitchhiking yesterday; a girl in grade nine and a boy in grade four (from Jordan's class). I could tell they don't have much. They would have had to keep hitching or catch the bus (two hours later) so I drove them into town. They had to leave their four year old sister at home crying because she couldn't walk that far. I felt like going back for the little one. The world could use more woman/children services that just even offer rides to community kids. Why don't more people see this as a problem? Not to even mention how horrible kids have it in third world countries. I need to make money in the movie industry so I can give to the poor kids. What should my organization be called? So much to do… where's my *!@&* movie deal?

Monday, Oct. 28, 2002 | **1:56pm**

Tonight is Mindy's going away party. I hope lots of people go. I'm planning on having some drinks and even taking my video camera. That reminds me, I still have to phone Kent. There will probably be a few of my ex's there. Oh well, I'll be drunk so who cares. I'm just doing laundry now – I have so many clothes to clean – it's crazy. I've got clothes drying by the fire, in the dryer, the washer and all over the laundry room floor and out the door even. For some reason I wait at least a month or more before I do a huge laundry day. I just put the music on, let the dogs run around and I dance around doing laundry + smoking weed. If you have to do laundry you may as well make a fun day of it. I worked at World today. They're getting strippers again and I might go serve there as well as weekend cash?

Friday, Nov. 1, 2002 | **2:40pm**

I'm standing at the bathroom window, looking outside. Kandy is here with me because Chip and Jose are picking on her. Chip always bullies her and Jose wants to hump her. I have to take them to the vet and put it on my m/c. Good old' charge cards, it's how most of the world lives. In debt! I'm going to settle my insurance as soon as I can. I need a new vehicle. I think I might lease a new one. Brooklyn's telling me it's the way to go. Every time I try to put Kandy with them they look like they're going to rape her! I'd better phone a vet today. I had such a bad time at the ferry. My truck wouldn't start. I need a new battery. Well I guess the best thing to do is to make a list of the things I need to do because I have so many if I want to change my life. I need a cell phone for messages, get the vet done, a new truck (4X4), and insurance money to pay off the ten grand I owe world. I'm going over to Cityville next week for the G n' R concert (well it's only Axel but he's singing all the songs).

Thursday, Nov. 7, 2002 | **7:40am**

I have a phone meeting with an astrologer at 8:30 this morning. I'm going to Guns n' Roses tonight with Tiffany, Jacquie, Brooklyn, and Rant. I have an extra ticket but I'm not sure who I will take. Maybe Harry? I hope I get paid today before we go or my trip will be on m/c. I guess I can go check for money at my other jobs. Shit – yeah, I've got lots to do today ~ really I should make a list. And I'm supposed to catch the noon ferry? I really hope my check is there and there's no problem with age verifications. I still work online and get viewers so how could they hold a check, they did say too many handle names, but wouldn't whole account be frozen not just mailing money earned?

Friday, Nov. 8, 2002

G n R got cancelled last night. Way worse was the fact that I was told last night that Kaitlyn's mom died Sunday Nov 3rd –02. I am very upset. The funeral is today. I barely have enough time to get ready and leave. I feel so bad for the family. She was like a Mom to me for years. They were my perfect family. I'm very upset over this one. Just that quiet sad feeling where you try not to think about it. I know she's in spirit now. I miss her already – I just feel awful. I haven't been there more for Kaitlyn. I would have never gone to Cityville had I known.

Sunday, Nov. 10, 2002 | **7:11pm**

We had a nice roast beef dinner tonight for Aunty Dana's 40th b-day. I love my aunty Dana. She's doing better every day that she lives away from her crazy ex-husband. I went to Kaitlyn's mom's funeral Friday and I cried very hard. It just hit me all at once in the funeral home. I lost one of my "Mom's" and I have to see the family suffer. So it's been a hard few days. I've been wanting to go back into my depression of only thinking of death, and living in fear and confusion. Instead, after the funeral I went to Stonetrees and bought a cell phone – why because I hate not getting messages. Poor Kaitlyn tried to get a hold of me all week! So life hit me and I came back up swinging. Kaitlyn is going to school in January. She's not letting this get her down and I have to be strong too. I have to live like her mom would want me to live, or try to anyways. Kaitlyn and I are going to go roller-blading tomorrow, or walk if it's raining. It's funny how death always brings people closer together. Kaitlyn and I have always talked well together, she never judges.

Nov. 13, 2002 | **8:30am**

I'm going to clean all day today with my dogs. Sounds like fun, eh. Kandy got fixed yesterday. The vet found that she had a uterus half the size of a kitten half her size. So if I did breed her I would have had complications. Two nights ago I was working at Brooklyn's and for the first half of the night Rant was sleeping. Then he woke up (apparently) with dog piss on him and he was mad because the kids poured too much of the juice he likes. So he was calling the kids "useless tits" and "fucking slobs" and throwing a fit. I couldn't tell what was said but I know that he and Brooklyn were fighting for one or two hours at least. Then all the sudden Brooklyn comes in and says, "Jose and Kandy can't stay here anymore. Rant lost it". She was crying a lot and very upset. I felt like she was saying, "Help, he's going to kill your dogs". So I stopped editing and hurried out, and said with a look of anger and concern, "where's my dogs?" And I thought while I was packing up that if he killed one of my dogs I was attacking him with my all. I was on the defense. Rant can be the biggest asshole that needs counseling for his inner anger. I know we all do, but he's damaging his kids and his wife. Annie was crying and Jordan looks up to me with his big brown eyes and says, "I did all my homework, five pages". I said, "Good boy. You kids be good and put your jammies on and crawl into bed". Rant and I fought. He yelled at me and I yelled at him. No one's treating me like that, and I left with my dogs. I ran home in the dark rain with a little shirt and no socks or shoes. I told my mom what happened and she went down to get my cell phone. She got there and saw Jordan at the window turn and yell 'Grandma's here'. Brooklyn made excuses for Rant and said the dogs pissed on him. Why was he yelling at the kids then? So Rant left to the store when Mom got there and came back crying with ice cream. "Mr. Nice". Fuck that man. I'd be saying stay the fuck out. Find a new place to live. I hope you die. But that's me – I'm more tuff love or cold hearted whatever. I just wouldn't let anyone treat my kids the way he treats her kids. How do I help the kids out of that hell? Poor little Jordan has seen enough of Rant's tirades to last a lifetime. As Lillian says - what Rant is doing is illegal; you can't talk to your kids like that. He needs help and Brooklyn is just ignoring the problem and hoping it will go away…

Nov. 17, 2002 | **9:00pm**

I start work tomorrow night serving at the World and we're getting strippers again. It should be busy and I need Christmas money. I think I'm going to go down stairs and watch a Dolly Parton Christmas special for a bit with my Mom and eat her popcorn. I'm watching Father of the Bride in my room. I feel like maybe painting a Christmas bulb or something. Suzanne's off at 10pm. Maybe she'll come over and paint. Sometimes I will work even when I have a friend over. If I get a viewer they can leave the room or stay for all I care. It's not a big deal for me to show my body to anyone. I guess I'm a bit of a nudist. I'm proud of my body. I love my body and think it's beautiful and I don't mind who sees it. It's just a human body like any other. Why are we so scared to show our naked bodies in today's world? Strippers show their bodies on stage and make a shit load of money for doing it. I make a fraction of the kind of money they make, but it's probably way different being in a room full of people then stripping in the comfort of my own bedroom as I smoke and drink tea. I am no different than anyone else. We are all just products of our environments for the most part. I know life is about choice, but sometimes you do the best you can with the hand you are dealt and you figure life out as you go. I'm sure I've made a ton of mistakes, and I'm sure a lot of people in the world don't agree with my decision to show my naked body for money. I know that I sold my soul years ago when I used to do a more explicit show. I made that choice once and went down that road. It changed me forever and I won't ever go back to the innocent girl I was before. I think of that girl and I wonder what life would be like if I never did try the internet, if I had stayed being a waitress or gone back to school or even stayed in film school.

Monday, Nov. 18, 2002 | 2:00pm

Kandy is very sick so I took her to the vet. I'm very worried. The vet took blood tests and I'll hear back tomorrow morning. He thinks her brain might be reacting with the drugs she had when she got fixed. I knew I shouldn't have fixed her. Now my little girl is sleeping and won't wake up. She wet the bed and Jose and I are both crying. I called Suzanne over. I'm very sad right now. It's so horrible not knowing what is wrong with her. She was fine this morning and now all of the sudden she's in a coma. I'm standing at the window. Suzanne just pulled in. I don't know what's wrong.

5:10pm

I am still in my room and am at the window again. My little girl is asleep in the bed. I don't know what to think. Thankfully Belle will watch her and nurse her while I'm at work tonight. I start at 8pm. Who knows if I'll like it or not? One thing I know is I'm not too happy about going to work tonight and leaving my little baby. I'm still worried I'll come home and she will have died. And I'm supposed to be happy and serve people with a smile? Life fucking bites!

Tuesday, Nov. 19, 2002 | 4:00pm

Kandy is fine today. She had nothing wrong with her in her blood tests. So the vet thinks she was relapsing from the anesthetic from when she got fixed. Mom and Brooklyn think she ate a roach. I don't think I'll tell people that though. I worked at the World last night but I didn't start. They were way over staffed and I wanted to go home. I fell down the stairs, missing the bottom step. It just felt awkward is all, but I'm sure it will get better. I'll find my groove. It's hard to go to work for someone when you don't have to. It's easy to not do the work. But I know myself well enough to not quit yet. I'm actually looking forward to Christmas staff parties. There are a lot of cute little dresses. I think I'll curl my hair tonight. And I'll work all night too. It's only an 8 –12 or 1 shift. I did see a stripper last night and I couldn't help but think that she had the way better job. She just danced around onstage, took off her clothes over three songs, and no one touched her. And all she had on me was fake tits. But I don't want to be a stripper. I strip online that's enough for me.

No Such Thing As Secrets

Friday, Nov. 22, 2002 | 3:15pm

I am sitting on my roof, and my dogs are on my bed. I should be in there with them writing on how I've quit pot. But instead I'm outside and they're in. I want to cut back on my pot. I'm going to try to keep cutting down, focus on getting my life in order, instead of getting ripped and ignoring problems. If I'm not happy with my life straight then it's up to me to change things. Marty came over last night. We had a good visit. We're always so comfortable around each other. But Lillian is a problem. So I guess we'll just keep it on the DL for now. No one needs to know and my relationships don't go public well…

Monday, Dec. 1, 2002 | 7:21am

I worked Friday and Saturday night at World and Saturday was hell! We had a group in who I had to serve free food and beer to, so maybe three guys tipped me for serving dinner. So I only made like one hundred dollars each night after tip outs and I wish I made more. Oh well though. It's busy in there and I see tons of people I know every night. Sat night (the good part) I saw Dick and a couple of his friends, they bought me Baja Rosa shots all night. I saw about seven or eight of the Barley crowd and all the Grocery Country gang after their staff party and a ton of other people. Even Belle's friend Jason Wailey (he shows up everywhere). Some old losers kept bugging me all night saying, "Can you drive my new corvette home for me, it's a 2003, you can drive me to my boat ok cutie" then pat my ass. Yeah, I couldn't believe it. Who the hell did he think he was? I don't let old ugly men touch my ass. They're lucky to see it online for US$$ and that's it! So I finally told him, NO, my boyfriend wouldn't like that. Then he stopped tipping me. Fuck wad! Slobbery ugly drunk fat asshole. Eewwww.

Saturday, Dec. 7, 2002 | 2:47am

Well another fun night out. It was Lillian's b-day night out and she wussed out at Grub co. early. But Suzanne and I went on. We went dancing at the RR. I saw lots of people out. I had fun dancing and spilling my rum and coke. Sam Giles asked me to go to Singler this week with him, all expenses paid. I get to go boarding and party with him for free. Obviously it isn't about him scoring with me, he's my friend. I think I'd have fun, free boarding but no Chihuahuas' from

Wednesday night till Sunday. But I can smoke as much as I want to, free passes to all shows and all days to myself while Shawn works. Maybe I should go, I could use a mini-vacation… it wouldn't be about sex, it would be more like he wants a fun nice date and nothing more. I could sure have a great vacation from life at Singler. Sounds like fun to me and we get to swank with all the swanks with our passes. It's a snowboard competition going on. Limo's taking us to all the parties and hotels. Then Sam's staff "Bell" (phone co) Christmas party Saturday night in Cityville down town, and then the limo takes us back to Singler. So, why wouldn't I go? I'd love to board for a few days, smoke weed, and party for free… I think I might take him up on his offer; I'm only twenty-three for a couple more weeks, fun is running out. I have nothing to lose…

Dec. 11, 2002 | **9:40am**

I have tons to do today. Laundry, internet, more laundry, bank. I might go on a date tonight. Not to Singler with Sam but to Playsville with Henry (the bartender at RR). He's the nicest guy that I used to work with and always takes my coat/purse behind the bar when I come in. He came in for dinner at the World Monday night when I was working so I went to RR after work because he was working. Tiffany was there after her Horse and Barn staff party. The RR manager and Henry were basically telling me that Sam was no good and they heard I was going to Singler with him. I said I wasn't going and that confirmed it. Henry and I were chatting and he asked me out tonight. So we'll see if he calls…

Dec. 14, 2002 | **8:15pm**

I'm standing at my room window puffing and writing with lots to do. Only eleven days until Christmas. I have a lot of painting to do of bulbs for people. I have to mail my Christmas cards with pictures of me and the dogs that I don't have yet. I've been so busy working that I barely get anything else done. I use my spirit guides help to make the night go smoother and make money. I feel them work with me; I see signs of their help. The bar life is crazy and fast pace and always entertaining. So many men hit on me and believe it or not – it's the girls grabbing my ass. For some reason when girls get drunk and they want to say hi, they grab other girls' asses. But I have kisses (I turn for cheek), hugs, and a ton of nice compliments from men. Yeah sure, they're drunk but it's still the thought that counts. Sincere compliments on something they like my eyes, my smile (number one compliment for sure), ass, abs, never boobs obviously, ha ha ha.

Tuesday Dec. 17, 2002

Last night was the Tap staff party. I had a wonderful time. I went with Tiffany, Harry, and his girlfriend. I smoked too much and drank too much, but I had a lot of fun. I even kissed someone last night. It totally surprised me. Rex kissed me. We were both drunk but it was a good kiss anyways. He asked me to go to the back with him and then he said he wondered what it would be like to kiss me. I've always thought Rex was cute but didn't think he was interested in me. I didn't want anyone to catch us kissing and be all "drunk making out" but I couldn't let the opportunity pass me by. I think he's very cute. Greatloaf played and drinks were two dollars. Some things don't change too much. I remember my first Tap party – it was '95 I think. You say too much when your drunk. I don't remember what I said to whom but Brooklyn did my hair and I wore Belle's red dress so I looked delicious. I stayed the night at Grandma's house. Good ol' Tiff stayed out late with me.

Wednesday, Dec. 18, 2002 | **4:30'ish**

I'm in the bath because I had such back pain. I've already showered. I just needed a hot bath. Rex is coming over tonight to watch a movie and hang out. So I've been trying to get the house tidy n ready. I'm really excited. He's very cute and mysterious. I want to find out more about him. I must say, I'm very surprised still that he's interested. The place was packed last night for opening night. I looked good last night. Curly hair, hot outfit, and a "southern smile" (I heard someone say that). The funniest comment of the night was that I'm a "breast of fresh air". I always start my night not wanting to go to work but then by the end I'm happy to be there and I really like the staff and atmosphere. But the weird thing is I work in a Hells Angels hang out and all the "boys" talk to me all night. I even see Doe Javidson, the supposed murderer of my cousin Brent. He can't look at me as if he knows who I am. Then he leaves or at least I don't see him. One day I will tell the world what he did…

Thursday, Dec. 19, 2002 | **3:45am**

WOW! I had to write I'm too excited to sleep. I just had the best date of my life. Rex came over and we talked for hours and it flew by like it was a half hour. I hope he feels the chemistry too. Wow though, we didn't even kiss, I think we like each other that much? I just wanted to hear about him and we talked about me too, even about my dead friends. He talked to me about his Mom who has passed and just everything. It's so good to be true. I keep waiting for something to happen but maybe this time, just maybe, I'll have a decent relationship. But I'm going to just enjoy the moment. Wow, I really like him. All these series of events, it seems so weird.

Dec. 20, 2002 | **4:34am**

I'm home from Suzanne's. I had a fun time. I think everyone enjoyed themselves. I had some good talks with all my friends. Suzanne gave me a pillow she sewed that had a green Canadian pot leaf (super cool), a magic ball, and make-up kit. We had so much fun. I got another email from Rex. I tried to check again when I got home but my Shaw mail is down. So I'll go to someone's house tomorrow morning. I emailed him from Suzanne's this evening. I've thought about him all day, more than anything else. I'm pretty drunk and smoking one last one before bed. I wonder why I'm thinking of Rex so much. It's a good thing I guess...

Wednesday, Dec. 25, 2002 | **11am'ish**

Wow, today has been the best Christmas so far, and we haven't even opened presents. We're still waiting for Beatrice, Brooklyn, and co.'s. I saw Rex last night, I really like him. He makes me feel so happy and he always says the nicest things to me. We just lay in each others arms and talk for hours all night, even though we should be sleeping. He's always saying how pretty I am and makes me feel so good about myself. We smoke weed out his window and lie on his bed and look out at the stars.

Dec. 27, 2002 | **11:48pm**

Rex was the sweetest boyfriend on my birthday. I'm so happy to be with a nice boy for once. Most men are just dicks. But Rex is a little mushy sweetheart and I love it. And we have great sex. Not to be graphic but he loves to eat box and that makes me feel super sexy and it's all about how a person makes you feel. He calls me a goddess all the time. And he's not even legal in the states so I feel like "the man" for landing the young hottie. He met me at the Kings and he was so cool with all of my friends, which is a first for me. He seemed to fit in. My birthday was good. I saw Rex at 12:09 and he kissed me and said happy birthday honey. Then we had good sex, slept till noon then laid together. I had dinner with my whole family and they all sang happy birthday as Suzanne walked in and joined in. Tim, Barron, and Suzanne's boyfriend Buck came over and we all drank before my Mom drove us down town. Then Uncle Richard and Dad came to the World. Lee, Kent, Stinky, and Ben were all there and everyone bought me drinks. Tiffany, Belle, Jacqui and her boyfriend (his birthday too) were there too. I saw tons of people out. Then we went to the Kings where I met up with Lillian and Rex. Everyone goes out Boxing Day. My dad fell down dancing but I kept dancing away. After I wondered if I should have helped him up. Anyways I had fun, and took pictures to prove it. Tonight at work – it was dirty. A stripper pulled a girl on stage, stripped her down to her shoes, socks, and g-string, and then started biting her crotch. The girl was so drunk. I talked to Roland about cutting her off. They put on quite the show and grossed us sober workers out. I'm going to get ready for Rex now.

Dec. 30, 2002

Tiffany & I hit the slopes today snowboarding. The sun was shining and there was fresh powder from last night. It was a little heavy but it was a real nice snow day. I had to crash for a nap when I got home. I feel great now after that power nap. Now I'm just waiting for Rex to get off work. I'm going to keep cleaning my room till then. I'm so busy I never clean my room. Now the dirty laundry is piling over into the spare room (my big nasty closet).

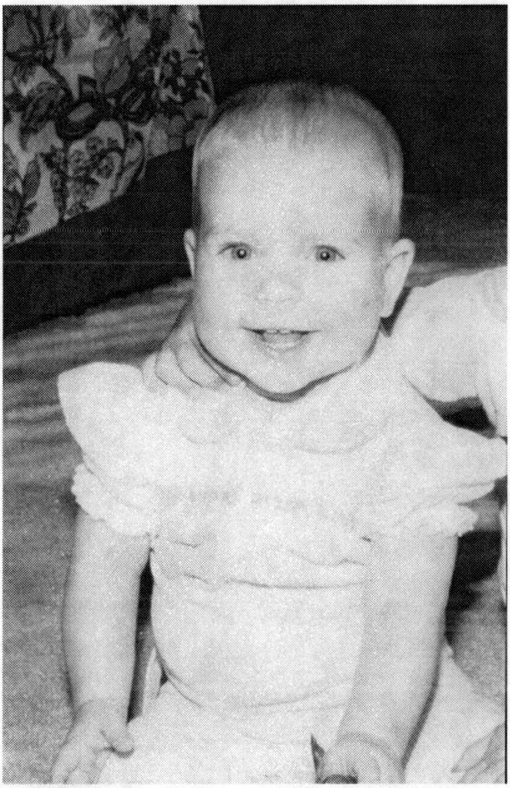

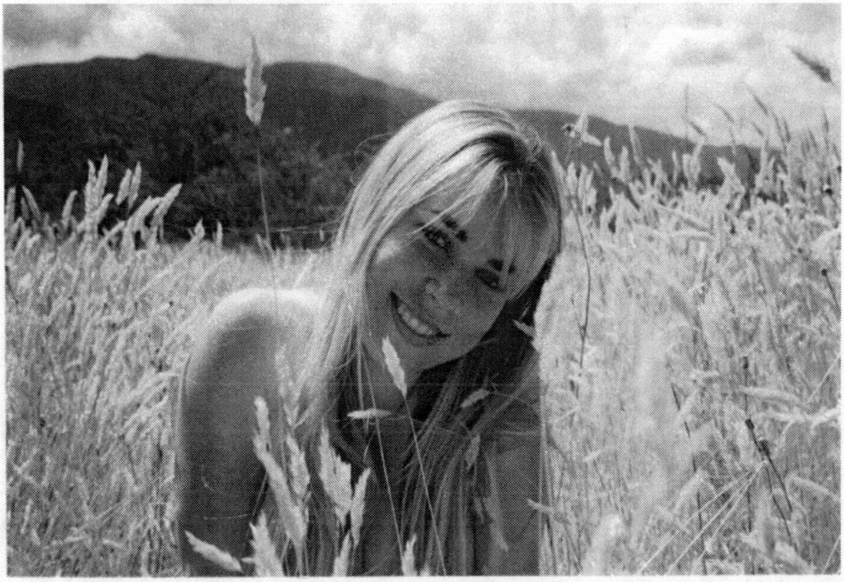

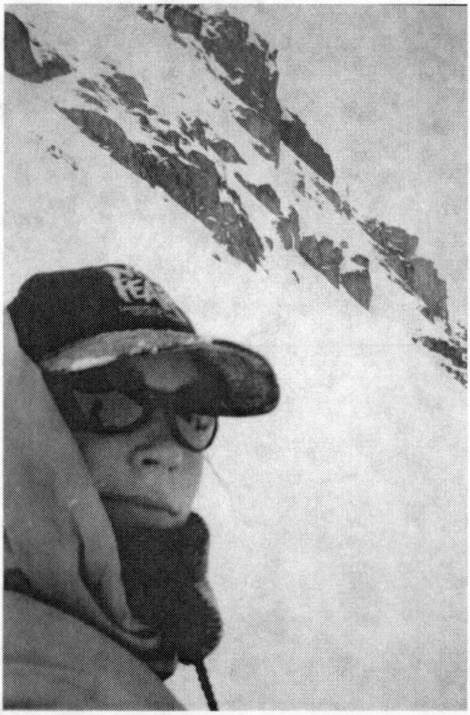

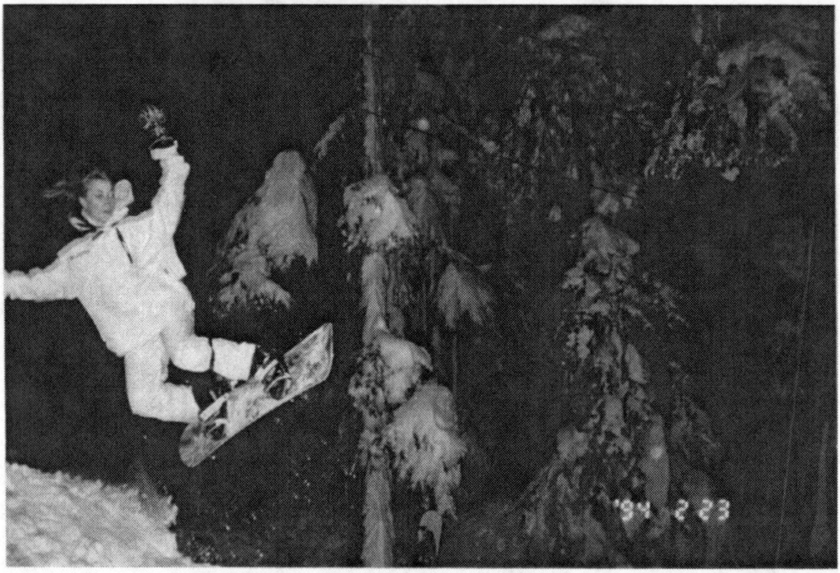
'94 2 23

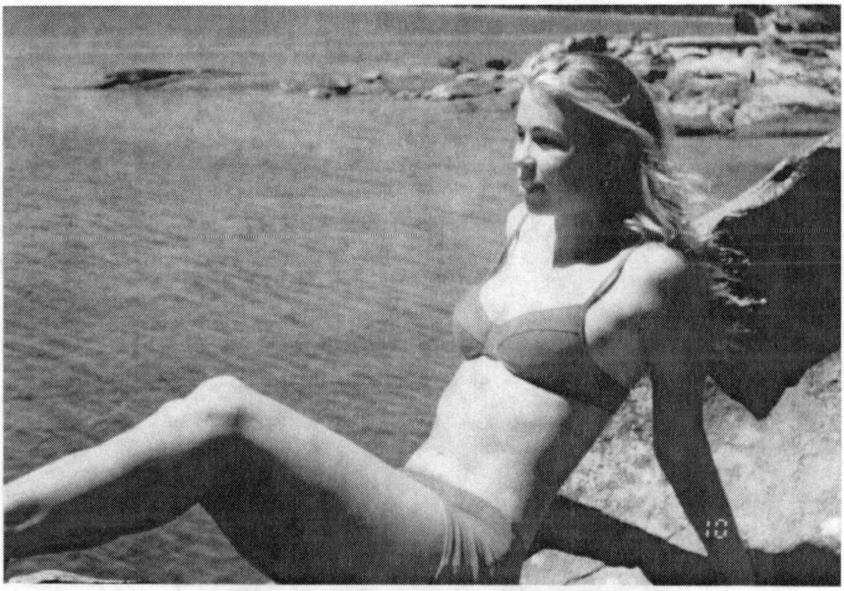

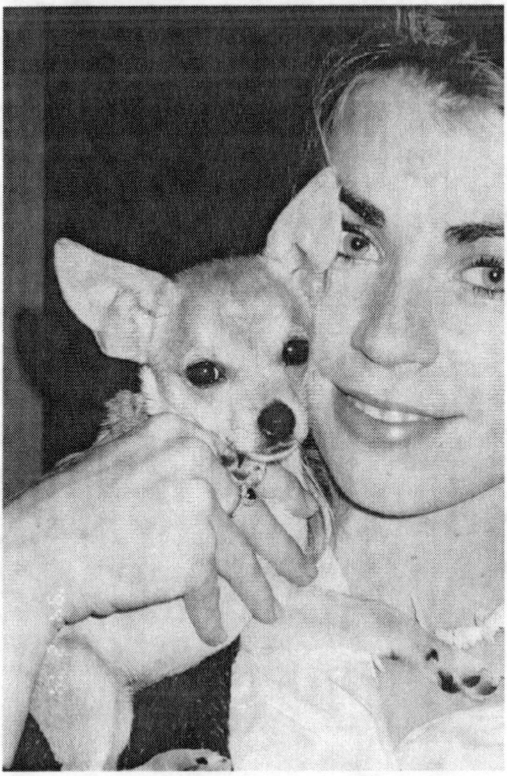

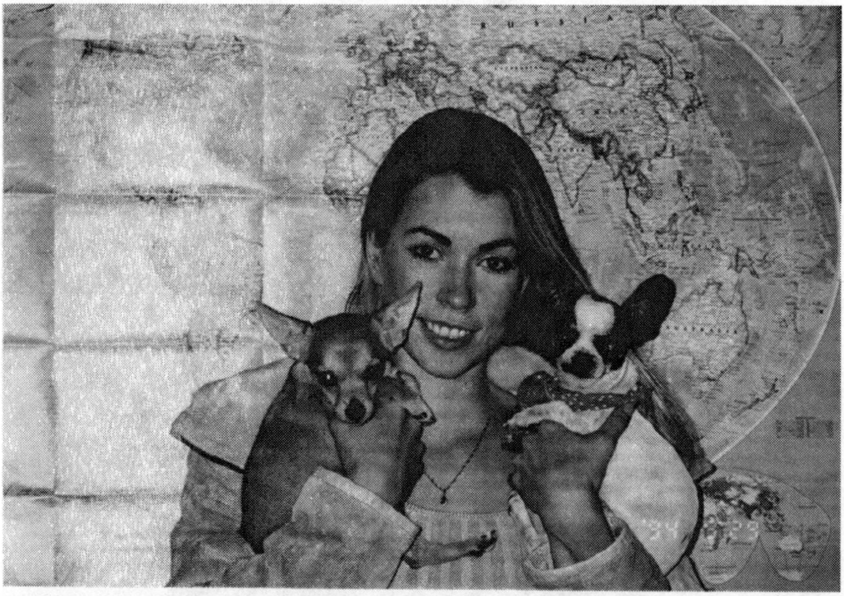

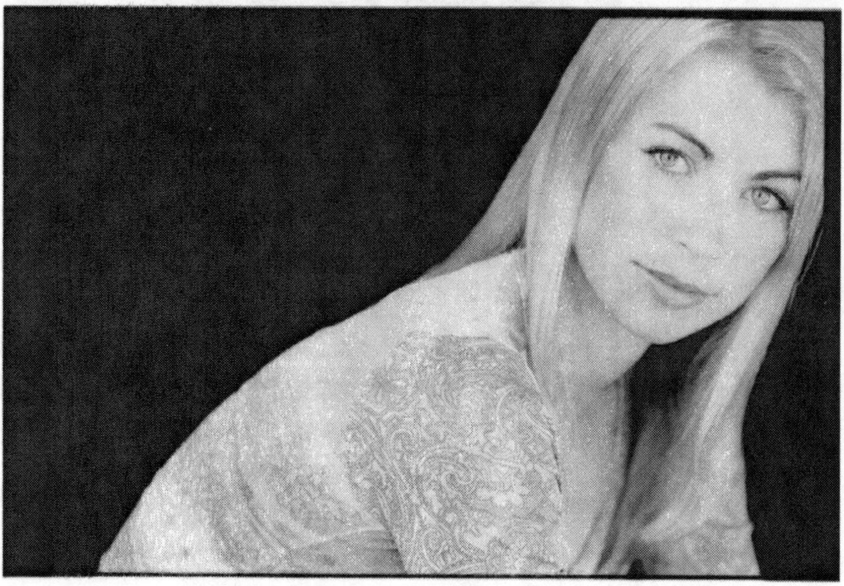

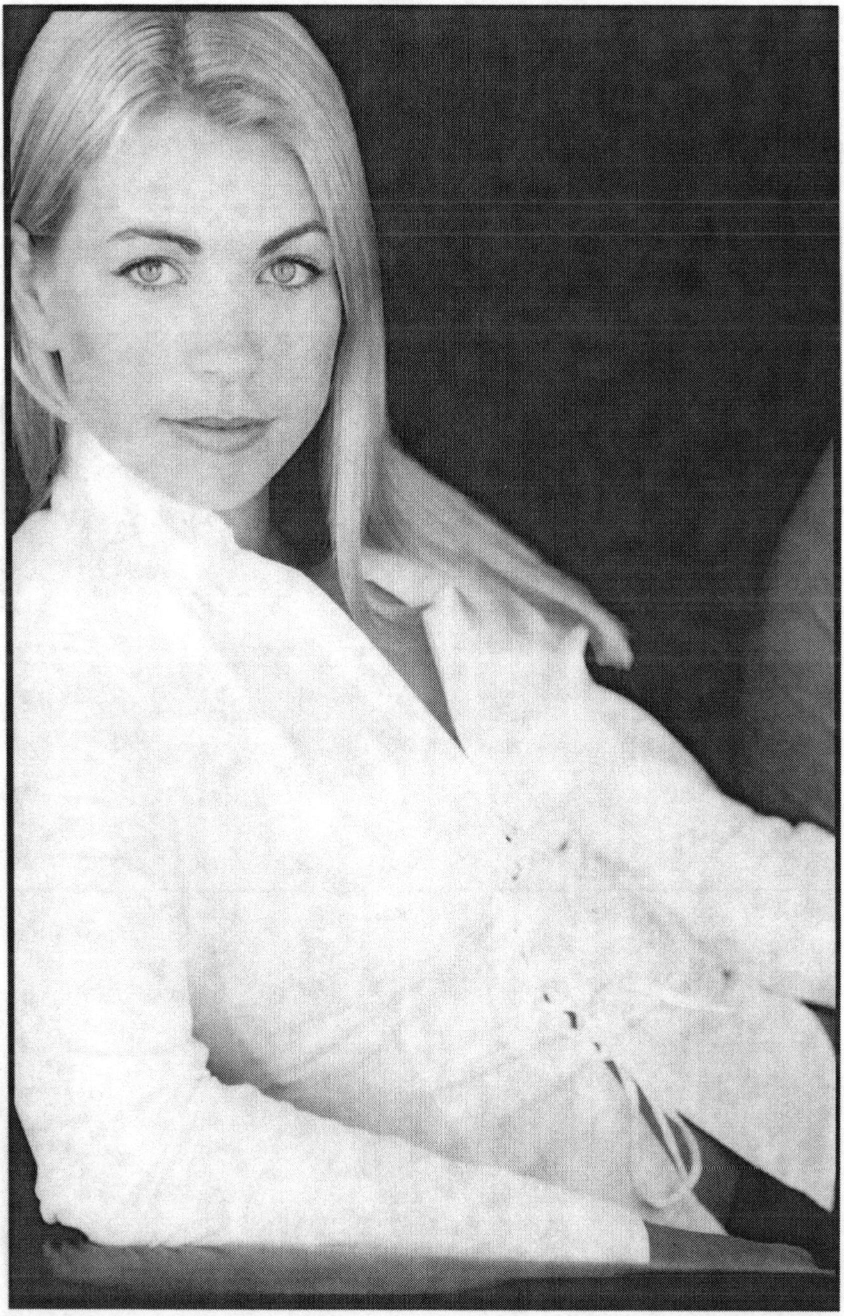

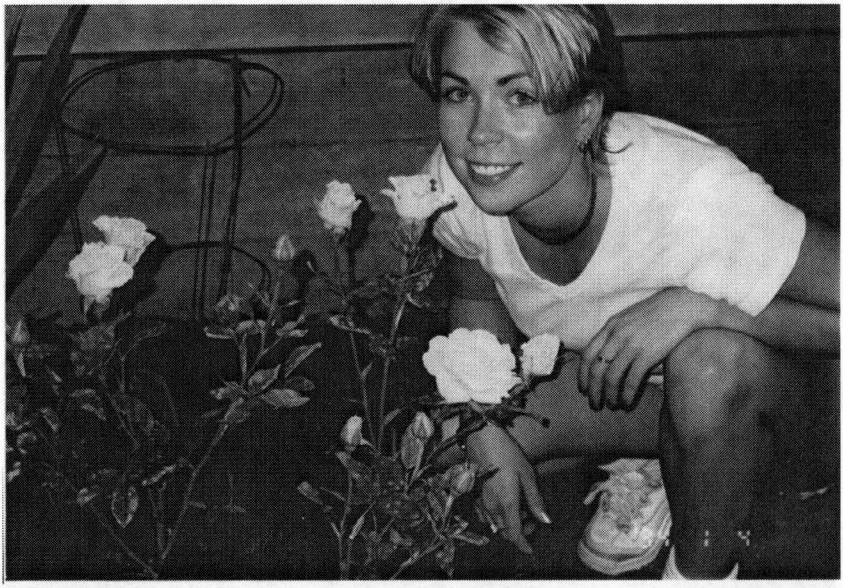

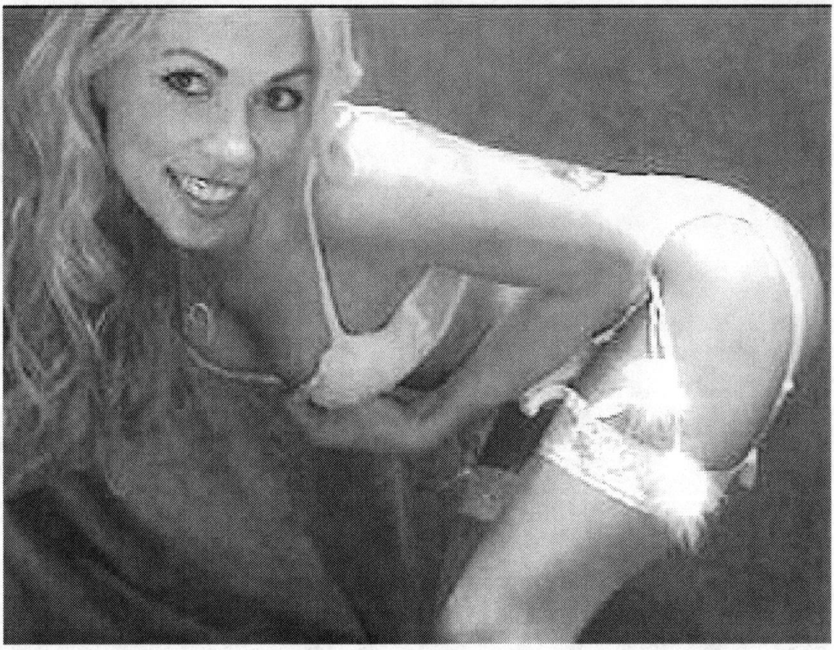

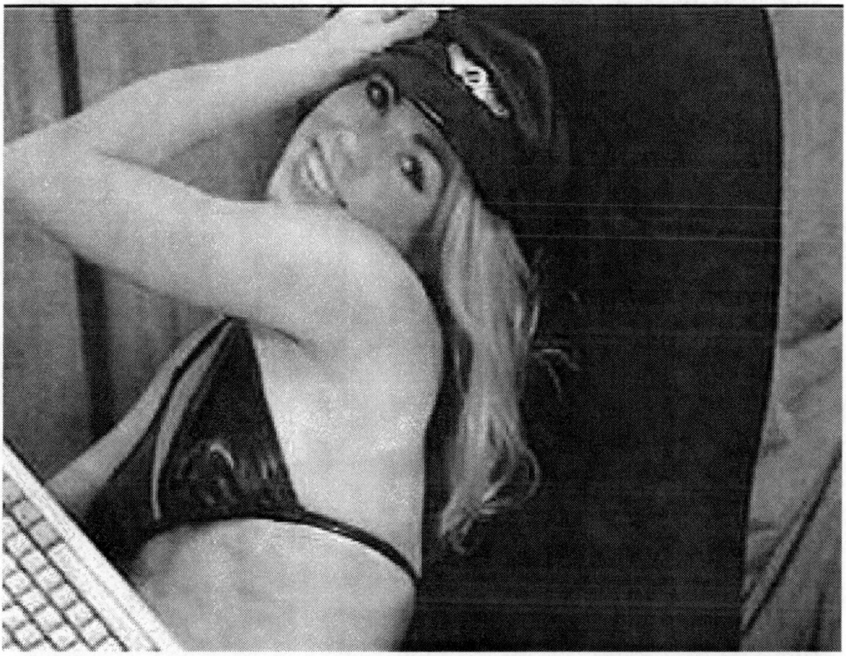

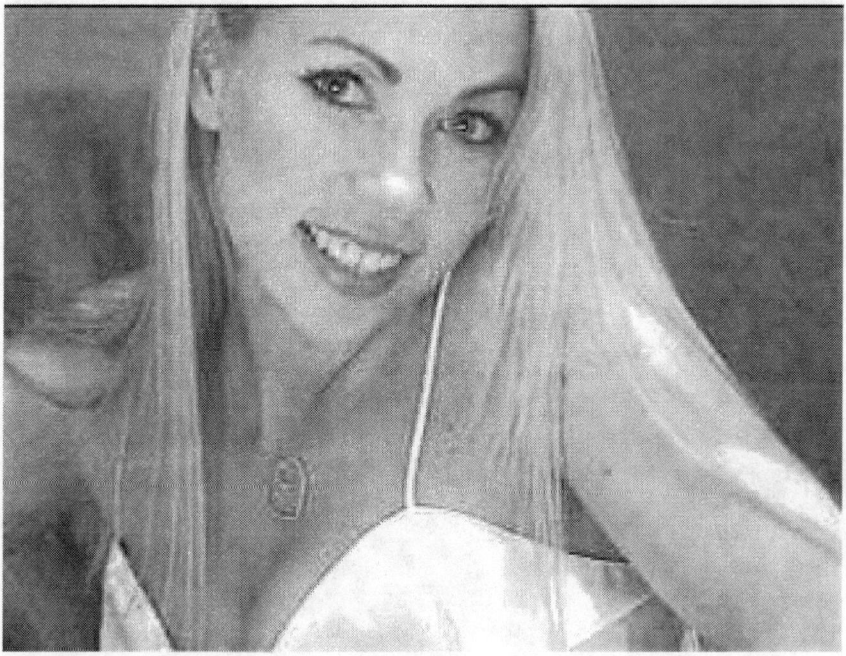

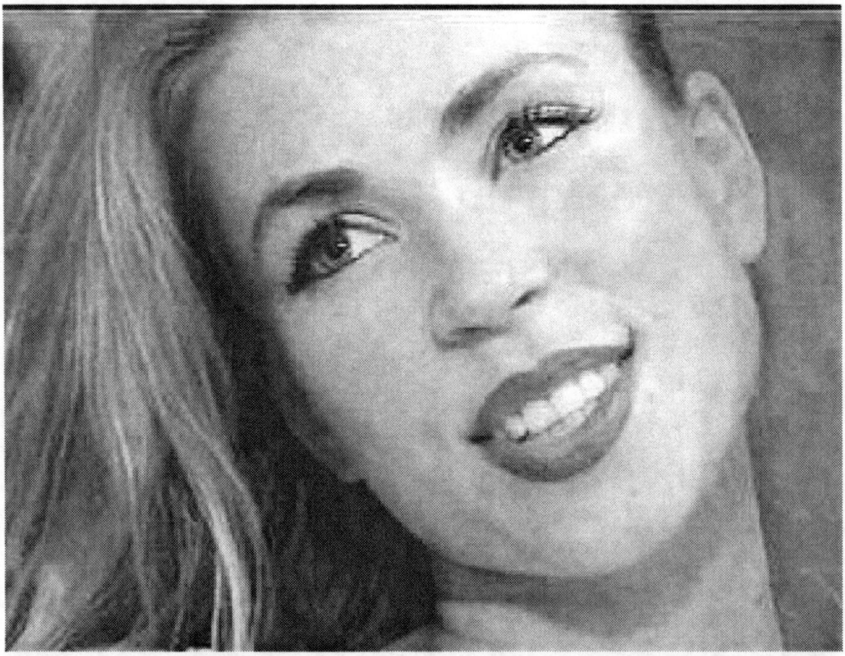

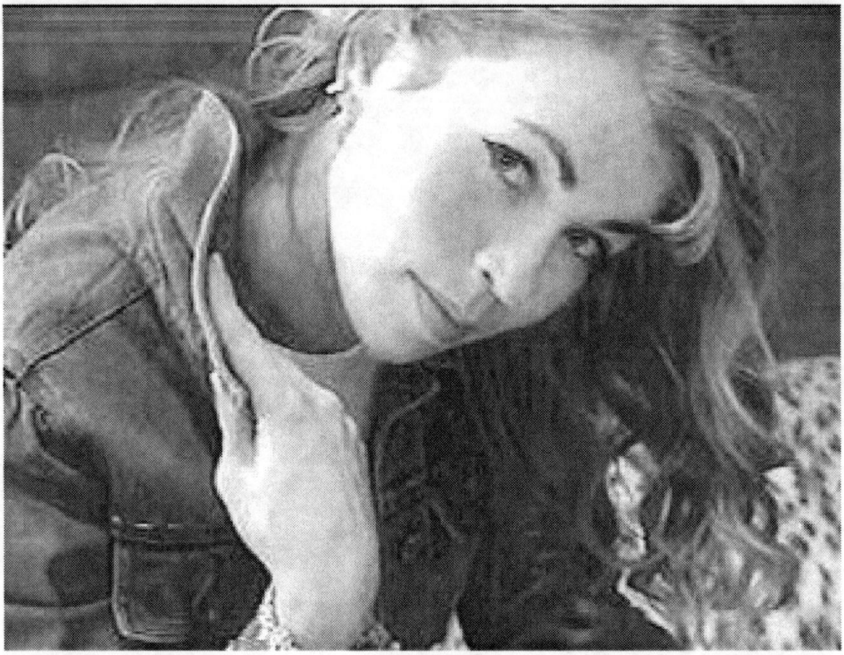

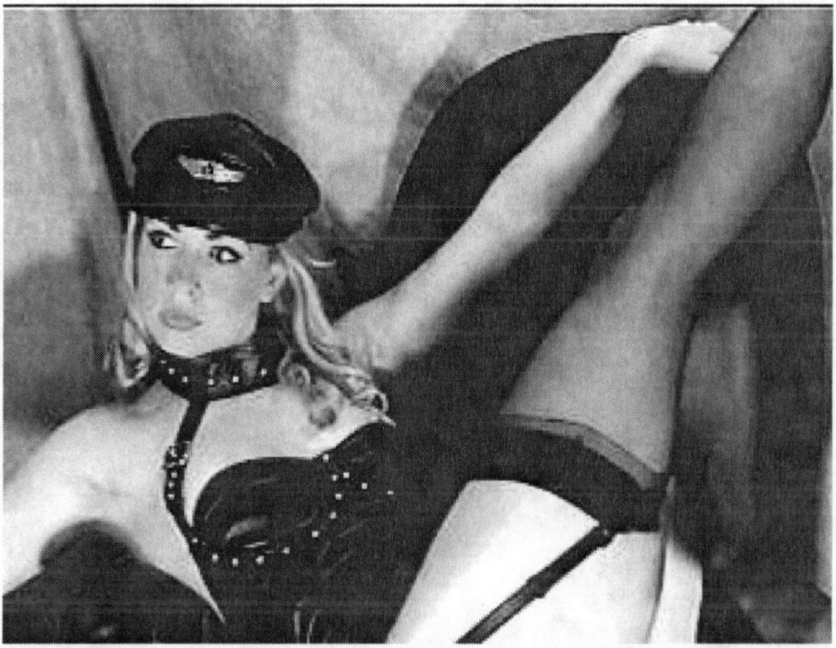

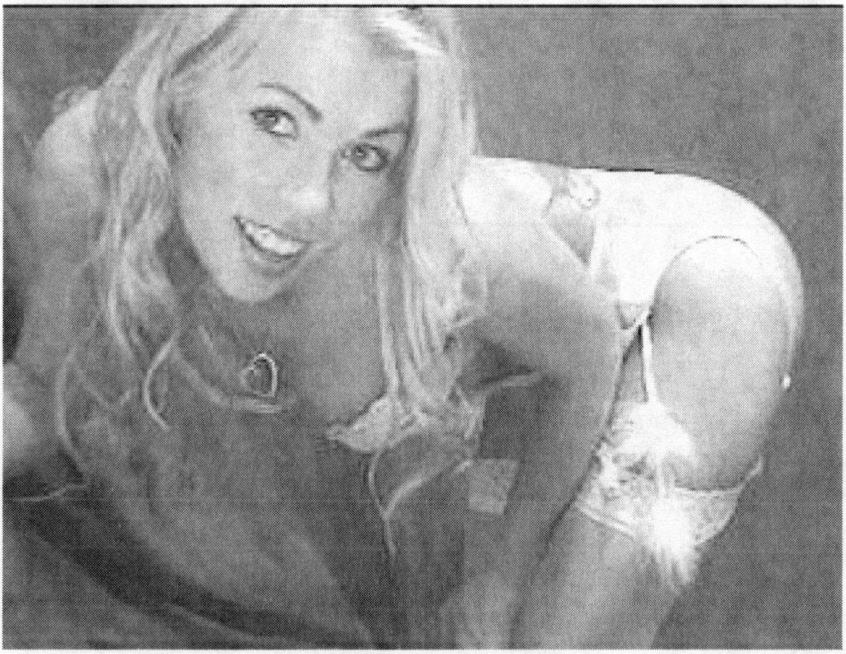

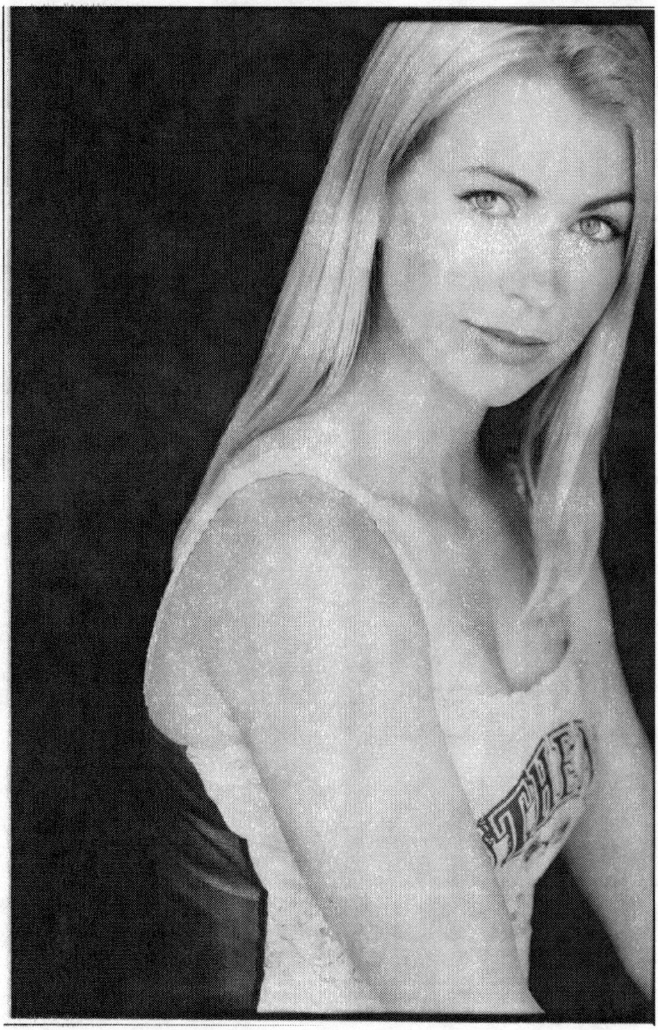

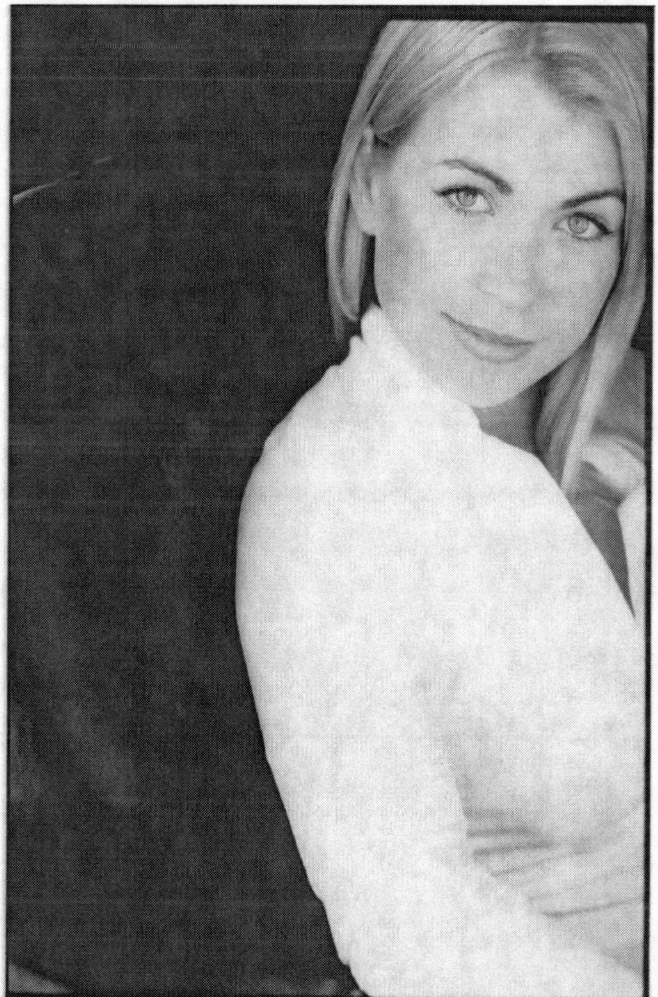

CHAPTER FIVE

Jan. 2, 2003 | **7:52am**

Well Brooklyn got married to Rant yesterday. So it's official. I must say that I feel really different about it. I think that Rant won't quit his speed and other harsh drugs, he'll continue to be verbally abusive to Brooklyn and the kids, and he'll continue to hate himself for it. Only I'm not going to be around to make jokes and lighten the mood. That's their life and I'm washing my hands of it. If she wants to be abused she'll have to do it without me. And the day the kids want out I'll take them. I'm not scared of him. I'm crazy too when it comes down to it. I have Brooklyn and Brenda (Rant's sister) making me think Rant can change and I have my mom and Beatrice, Tiffany, Belle, Dad, saying Rant's an asshole and won't change. I feel very much in the middle. So fuck it – I'm walking away. I've decided that when Brooklyn and Rant put me into the middle of their fights I don't have to live like that. I don't care if she stays. That's her choice and she's a big girl. But I'm not going to pretend nothing is wrong or hang around them when the mood is off. She may like all the BS that Rant gives her, but I wasn't born to help Rant. Rant swears that the other night was the last time and he'll get help. But he thinks he needs help to prove something to my Mom when he should admit he has a problem. It's so text book, but Brooklyn can't see it. All I know is that I will never live like that. He's so verbally abusive to that family when

No Such Thing As Secrets

I am there. Imagine when I'm not. Rant told Brooklyn about all the speed houses, but here's the part that gets me mad at them both. The other night when the big blow up happened and I had to get Jordan from home because they (Mom and Brooklyn) didn't know if Rant would target him and I'm the strongest and meanest. So I go get him and try to talk to Rant, but Rant has lost all sanity – not a word of a lie – lost it. I tried to talk to him but couldn't. He thought I was lying and Brooklyn was going to leave him and was always cheating on him. He wouldn't let me answer the phone and he had me cornered. He was crying and making no sense. He finally told me to take Jordan and leave because he was "snapping". He only had to tell me once. Jordan was sleeping nude, so I grabbed him in his blanket and left. As I was leaving Rant was shaking the trailer as he threw things and kicked around yelling in the bedroom. Mom pulled up then behind me so I got in her car with Jordan and she went inside only to come out again shortly after. She was shaking her head walking quickly back to the car saying, "He's lost it". We both noticed that he had gone off the deep end and was in a bad headspace. We came back here to Brooklyn and Annie already tucked into Grandma's bed. Jordan went to Belle's bed with Chip, Kandy, and Jose. The phone kept ringing and mom wouldn't let Rant talk to Brooklyn. I told Brooklyn as plain as day what I saw and what I thought of the whole big fight that lasted from 10pm – 2am. The fight started days earlier and who knows if it ended. Rant has a great way of making people feel sorry for him. He doesn't even know he does it. He needs some serious counseling. He blames everyone else for his problems. But she went back to him. I left my house and went to Rex's and she went back to him at 3:30am or something. And yesterday she married him. I have to take Jordan to hockey today. Rant took my truck to the wedding and I went with Brooklyn. Then after the wedding I was on my way home and he caught up to me and said I had all his weed. And there was a weird knife in my door so I gave it to him and he said, "oh yeah I never sleep without it". Now I'm tripping out worrying that he killed her with it last night because he's fucked in the head. But I just keep telling myself that I'm tripping, she'll be at hockey. He hasn't killed her yet.

Friday, Jan. 3, 2003

The stupid internet is down so I can't work. And I need money. I'm hoping that it will mysteriously start working again the way it mysteriously stopped. Brooklyn and Rant made it to hockey, but they were late so I was really tripping out worrying about what had happened. So I'm glad I was wrong and they had a wonderful dinner out. Last night while I was at work (9pm – 2am) my truck got smashed into and they took my overnight Nike back pack, purse, clothes, make-up, and stereo (they barely touched the dash and snipped wires), but they left a rolled doobie, ski goggles, unscratched scratch n win, cd's, and speakers that were all easy to take. Why take my clothes and make-up, and not weed n cd's? It creeps me out. I think they took the stereo to make it look good but they were considerate enough to break the passenger window. They didn't even go into the driver's door but knew my wallet was under my seat. When I cancelled my credit card, nothing was charged to it. Oh no! What if any of my internet shit was in there?! My street address is on my license. Now they'll know where I live. I feel like whoever it was took my personal things but not my valuables. I feel watched, like they knew my wallet was where I always put it. They didn't destroy my truck, but they smashed the window and took the stereo but not the cd's to make it look like theft. I can think of a number of guys who come in to see me that it could be. Some of which are not the kind you want after you. I wonder if I should work there anymore. I don't know what to do with my life anymore. I'm tired of it all, and no wheels anymore.

Monday, Jan. 6, 2003

Today Rex's mom would have been forty. Poor boy tossed and turned all night and I know today is a hard day. He's got too much stress because he pays way too much money/month on his race car. I'm going to work online today. Rex is going to do some bill stuff, drive his roommate to work and I bet go to departure bay and drive around in his car. I tried to give him some weed but he didn't want any?? Maybe he should deal with the day straight anyways. He and I are really good together. We keep our own space but we are very open hearted to each other. He's never had a long term girlfriend, so he's never fallen in love then I'm thinking. And there's nothing like your first love. This could actually work for a while. And I tell myself not to think of how long it will last. Just enjoy the moment Betty – I say. I'm really secure in my head that if something does bother me I'm going to say something. That's how I screwed up before. I'm always trying to be myself around Rex. Because if he doesn't like who I am I need to know now. Before I always changed myself to be the perfect girlfriend. But I need someone who loves me for me, so I must be as me as I can be.

Wednesday, Jan. 8, 2003

I'm working online, watching much music, reading the Enquirer, and writing in my diary. This viewer has a vibrator, oil, hand cream, candles, and so I said ice? It's Nez, an old time regular/slave of mine. I've made $109 US in two hours so that's $155 CAN. Now you see why I like this job. It's not exactly hard to sit in my pretty panties and tell slaves what to do for my amusement. Sometimes I feel like being nice, and sometimes I feel like being naughty. I control the slaves. That's why they come to me. When I tell them to put on ladies lingerie and fuck their ass with a vibe, it's more acceptable in their minds by society's standards because I'm a pretty girl telling them to do homosexual things. Yeah, it's me that wants you to dress up like a woman and fuck your ass like a little bitch. I'm actually not into the whole dominatrix (dom) thing in real life. I'm honestly more submissive, but I can get into the role of dom. I like to do the cock and ball torture just for the fun of it. Knowing that I am making a man squirm around in pain from the comfort of my bedroom, and the fact he's paying me to do it makes it all acceptable. Old Nez has been seeing me for years. He's even been getting me to even tell his real life Mistress how to dominate him. I think he is probably married and having an affair with this woman which makes it all the more exciting for them. They will anxiously wait for my every command and both pay to have me be a part of there sexual games. Even though I'm just in my room typing words, I liven up any sexual encounter! I have answered more questions about sex than anyone I know. I read up on things but mostly just make it up and use my common sense. I went to acupuncture today with Brooklyn and it took three hours. It's relaxing but that's just too long (1:30 –4:30)! My Mom has been on my case about money and everything and anything else she can think of. It makes me not want to live with her. I'm just too old to live at home with rules and questions etc.

Thursday Jan. 9, 2003

Today I finally phoned the Tap office manager about the whole weekend cash confusion. I told her how I went to do the cash Dec 21st and the other girl was there. The manager was informed that I didn't want to work as much due to the World work. So I basically told how I feel about that bitchy manager Micole and her thieving husband Moe. Then a few hours later I get a message on my cell from Micole. I haven't called her back yet. Lillian told me some good things to say. I really should phone her. Fuck, like I don't have enough shit to deal with. What does she even want from me? Just another thing to do on my never ending list. My reward is that someone above is watching. Someone sees how much I do in a day. Someone watches as I make my choices and sees other people's motivations.

Sunday, Jan. 12, 2003 | **11:45pm**

Today I went snowboarding with Jordan, Rita, and Tyson. We had an amazingly great day (10 – 11 degrees, powder from last night, fun crew, beautiful blue clear skies). It was perfect. Until I dropped Jordan off at home and I was reminded of reality. Lately whenever I want to see if Brooklyn wants to hang out Rant makes me feel all – what are you two up to – where have you been and Brooklyn always wants to hurry home or not go with me anywhere anymore. It just pisses me off that they live like that now.

Monday, Jan. 13, 2003

I have to leave to drive Belle to work and then go to the Dr.'s. I'm out of weed and I have no money for medication. I think I'm going to borrow money off my Dad because I need three hundred dollars to get my window fixed? I have money coming in but not until next week. Or this Friday is World pay day. As time goes on the only thing for me to do is watch human behavior. And humans are for the most part greedy. I understand why greed is a sin and I wonder if there will always be those "takers". They think the world owes them so they take everything they can. I always tip out way more than I should, and I'm everyone's favorite for it. I'm Happy about who I am. I fall asleep easy at night. I'm not intentionally mean to people. I do flaw often but I'm trying. I'm always trying to make me happy first, make others happy second, and try not to get sucked into the show. Life is only a movie – not to be taken so seriously ~ just enjoyed. Like spending all of your money snowboarding and not worrying about the next day. Time to ask Dad for money.

No Such Thing As Secrets

Tuesday Jan. 14, 2003 | **2:23pm**

Rex brought me flowers last night but he didn't stay long. He doesn't sleep well here I think. I've been thinking lots about quitting World just because I like internet more. I like being my own boss.

Thursday, Jan. 16, 2003 | **11:32pm**

I did nothing tonight. I had a lazy night on my bed watching much music and tuning out my mom's nags. The house is too hot (at least I kept the fire going all day and it wasn't easy), the kitchens not clean (trust me I'm the only one who cleans it), and I let the dogs in her room and one of them shit on her blanket (yes a big glitch but how many times does she have to tell me). Rocko ran down here and Brooklyn found me on my bed, depressed. She thinks I'd really like living on my own. I think I would too. It would be about $1000 more than I'm paying now. Oh to live on my own, now that would be heaven. My very own place that no one else can say anything about. Only clean up after me and no yelling at myself. There's a two bedroom cottage on the water for $450 in Greenpoint. I'm ready for my own place. No roommates except Jose and Kandy. And on the water sounds too good to be true. Think of the photography. All my stuff set up nice in my place. Not crowded in my room. I have a lot of things all ready; I wouldn't even really need too much. I have the basics (bedroom suite, TV, computer, Mindy's old futon, some chairs). I would like my own place a lot. I need some big changes in my life. I need out on my own. For the little money a roommate contributes and way more stress they cause – I don't want one. What I need to do is get my insurance claim done. I'd absolutely love to move out February. Hey, that's one year after I came home. I do love all the nurturing my Momsy gives me – but I need to grow as an adult and not a kid. I need to feel more in control of my life. I need a home where I feel at home so I'm going to look for a new place. I'm going to work Monday-Friday, I'll have my friends over, and I'll invite people over for dinner. I could walk on the beach and work in my living room if I wanted. I could have the kids overnight or boys for that matter. Rex and I haven't been seeing that much of each other and I must say it's him. And now I don't know if I want to be with him anymore. I think he's looking for someone to take care of him, nurture him, and although I would love to do that with him I don't have the time or energy. I need to focus on my music and my new place. Although he doesn't take a lot of TLC I just don't want a boyfriend right now. And I don't know why even. The thought of spending a few months or years with someone scares me right now. It's 12:02am. My truck insurance just ran out at midnight… zero moola.

Sunday, Jan. 19, 2003 | **12:22pm**

I have an ICBC appt I'm going to have to cancel tomorrow morning because I don't have $300 for deductable on my window and I don't have insurance on my truck and mostly because my fuck up father won't lend me money. All I want is $300 to fix my truck. He has been talking to Mom and Brooklyn about lending me money (or not) because he doesn't think I'll learn if he lends me money. I've learned to hate him with every drop of blood in me. He never has been a father. Why would he start now? The man is a useless piece of shit who has done nothing for me. He only thinks about himself. I still just can't believe he won't lend me money. I feel like spitting in his face. He is a disgrace to the name Dad. All my friends have dads that lend them money and vehicles and give them money! But not me, my dad only does things that will benefit him in some way. The only thought that makes me feel better is planning to move out where he can't find me. I won't ask him for another thing for as long as I live. Including spending any of my valuable time with him. I really don't want to stress so much about all this truck stuff because he's teaching me a lesson? No, he just cares more about $300 then me. Sad but true and that's why I hate him. I hate how he's never been a father and still isn't. He's more like a mean older brother. Mom doesn't even want him here for her birthday dinner, but he'll show up and I'm going to stay up in my room working. I have to move away from them. I'm tired of being the bad daughter. I'm the one who stays and takes it. I let them make me feel bad about myself. I am a good person. Then why do I try so hard to be "good". Is it cause they've made me feel bad about my pot, jobs, financial state, messy room, shitty/pissy dogs, and now I need a vehicle to borrow because they've taken that too. I get more help from strangers, more compliments from co-workers, and more respect from my boss than I get from my family. I just saw me for who I am right now to them; I'm the black sheep who is so confused in life that she's always too ripped to talk to. That's why I need my independence. I need my own place for just me and my doggies and only the nice will be allowed to visit – if they phone first. It's time to put me before my family as they do with me. It's my life and I'm the only one who can build it up. I'm the only one who can make me happy.

Tuesday, Jan. 21, 2003 | 8:15am

I need someone to go in on a bag with me. Brooklyn has no money and has been smoking smagma. Lillian got weed last week and won't need any. I can try Tiffany but she probably won't need any or have any moola. And I don't have enough for a whole one. I'm sure I can go pick up a half but that's a bit of a waste of time. I should spend as much time and energy working as I do getting ripped. I keep writing so it's never like I'm doing nothing. I guess I'd better go and buy a new diary soon. I need someone to go in on a bag with me. Someone with seventy-five dollars who smokes weed is hard to find though. But it seems wrong to be spending the last of my money on weed. But with weed I can't help it. It's like it's all I can think of unless I just smoked one. Even after I just smoke though I could always smoke more. Look at how much energy it uses of mine. But I also feel more motivated after I smoke. I don't feel so "I hate my life and surroundings". I need to settle my claim and get on with my life and out of my surroundings. I love the staff at the World but I'm tired of the job and I'm tired of the atmosphere. Not that internet is much better but at least I get a lot of respect online. With waitressing some guys are rude to me and they don't even tip and I'm a Mistress and Goddess online. I know I have to work; it's just a matter of having a good job and a life I'm happy about. I know I'm not too happy right now – and why? I guess I feel like no matter how much I try I'll never have enough money to live life on top rather than trying to get by. Unless there is some miracle. Yep, I'm in need of a miracle. What I want is to be a rock/movie star. Travel around with my dogs in my motor home with some friends, writing music and performing on stage, making money. Brooklyn in her motor home and Belle in hers. And it would be wonderful – free. Free from the boring life society wants me to live. Free from the money problems that affect everyone I know. Free to send love as me and buying whatever unique clothes I find and wearing wigs n glasses and going to parties all around the world. Who knows who I'll marry but I bet it's already planned out so I shouldn't worry about it. So what does this all mean about Rex? I guess I don't know if I want to be with him anymore. So I just have to gather up the courage to tell him. I hate breaking up with people. That's the one reason I hate going out with people. I wish it could go back to the days you would call your best friend and get them to do it for you. So I need my life back. I need no World, no Rex, not living here, and no broken truck. Yes to a new truck, new place, and new job. Please give me these things now; my dad says we're supposed to say 'now'.

Jan. 23, 2003

Well I might get my life back in order a bit today. I found my mail key in Brooklyn's car (where I told her to check three days ago). So I made a payment on m/c, changed my cell phone billing to a new card, I'm going to get my birth certificate and driver's license replaced today, hopefully replace my truck insurance, and go to ICBC today with Mom at 5pm. So we'll see how much actually gets done. I want to move out so bad. I have an apt to see my lawyer in early February and I'm going to say settle me out, and he's not talking me out of it. I'm just going to say how or what do I need to do to settle. I also will break up with Rex. He's too nice (fake nice) and only calls me Honey and never Betty. Now I should go to work online, or go to the shopping centre and buy a new diary. I work tonight too. There's too much to do today!

Jan. 23, 2003 | **9:40pm**

I'm in my room. Rex should be coming over in about an hour after he gets off work. I don't know what we will say to each other? Why does life stay so interesting? I figured out that life isn't about what society says is right or wrong, but life is about what makes you personally happy. What makes you feel good about yourself? What makes you feel like a good person? What brings a smile to your face? What meditates you personally? For me I enjoy music, smoking weed, snowboarding, base ball, horses, movies, good theatre, romance, writing, jokes, babies, puppies, teaching and helping others.

Friday, Jan. 24, 2003 | **9:28am**

Starting a new diary is always exciting. Where will I travel with this? I hope I travel a lot, and with my dogs of course. I just keep trying and I think that's all I can do. Amex sent me a credit card application. They want to give me a platinum card with $5000 limit. Now this will be a test. Can I have a card and not use it? My m/c is up to $2800! Needless to say I must work all day. After I'm done this entry and my doobie I'll get ready for work. I guess I should do my chores first. Then after work I'll go to the gym with Belle. Belle has the day off. Oh that reminds me, Lillian and Suzanne want to hang out today. Maybe I should go to the gym now and work later. I have tons of laundry to do too, and I mean heaps and heaps and heaps. I'm going to go to Lillian's, then the gym, and then home to work. I can do it all.

Jan. 25, 2003 | **12:22am**

I'm in my room with Lillian. She's breaking up with her boyfriend and very sad. We're watching a Dirk Manly movie. The dogs are all asleep. Lillian and I had a few drinks. So I'm a bit tipsy. But I'm not going to fall out of bed or anything. I don't have anything to write about. A new diary – a new beginning.

Jan. 26, 2003 | **3:31am**

Oh my God. Noel just gave me a lecture about "laying off the chron and getting my life together". And meanwhile I have puffy eyes because I've been crying. I was thinking of Wonder and Dean, my friends. It makes me sad that I can't see them. Right now I'm in my room watching Dirk Manly again. Noel said if I needed to borrow money then he'd lend me bucks. Kept making me look at him and I wouldn't. I also said don't worry my mom has me covered and my credit card was stolen. I was waiting for a new one in the mail. I got it a couple of days ago. I tell you what I need – I need to get away from anyone and every-one who makes me feel bad about myself. That means changing my friends' big time. Lillian and Suzanne want to move out with me and I don't think it would be wise. You should never mix business with pleasure. I want to move out from two girls. I don't need to move in with two different girls. I want to live alone. I'm losing my mind. I feel very alone in the world. Like no one believes in the things I do. No one knows how to love. I basically ignored Rex after he called tonight. I feel really bad about it but I can't help it. I just don't want to phone because then I'll have to deal with it. That's how bad it's gotten now. Tonight I had to drop off weed for a DJ from work and I didn't feel like calling Rex because I don't want to see him. Sometimes misery likes to be alone. I had a lot to drink and I smoked two joints on the way home (I took the long way). For people to say fix my life, who's to say my way of living isn't right? Just woke up – I guess I dozed off. I still feel bad about not talking to Rex. What is wrong with me? Seriously what is wrong with me? I can't stand it.

Monday, Jan. 27, 2003

Last night Rex came over. I really like him but I just don't want something serious. I didn't have the courage to tell him this. I need to tell him. It's never good to procrastinate with breaking up. If I did it one or two weeks ago (like I've been thinking) then I wouldn't be here now. I think I hate breaking up with boys more than anything. I wish they would be the one to say something. All Rex talks about is how beautiful I am and how lucky he is to be with me. It's hard to go from that to break up. I wonder what Brooklyn is up to these days. I never see her now that she's married. I don't know how she lives in hell like that. I go down to smoke one with them once in a while but she could come here. I'm going to try to clean my… Belle hates when her socks go missing. She's getting ready to go work at her waitress job. She's petting Chip now and hating life. I must clean my room. All I want is to be famous entertaining the world. I want my work computer in another room and just my iMac in here.

Tuesday Jan. 28, 2003

I'm very sad right now and I have no clue why I broke up with Rex yesterday. I miss him today. I'm worried I made a mistake. My room is actually clean and rather than feeling good I just keep thinking about Rex and the World. Maybe I just want the internet and Rex instead. I have no clue if I made the right/wrong choice. But I don't really feel like going to work at the World. I'd much rather work online. I don't even want to work another shift there. I phoned Rex and left a message but he hasn't called back. I'd much rather be going to the movies with him or something. Not going to sling beer.

Wednesday, Jan. 29, 2003 | **8:45am**

I'm hung over because I worked last night. After work I went to the Kings with a couple guys from work. So we go to the Kings because I've had a long hard day, crying and sorting socks. We get to the Kings (Kip and Renold were playing) and

Stanley and Dez were there. So we sat with them had some drinks and watched the show. We drank a few then the place closed and all the non-industry people were kicked out. I've been waitressing downtown so long everyone knows me. There's not too many Betty's either. Dez, Stanley, and I went back to Stanley`s place to have some beer. Dez leaves and Stanley and I are chatting away when he leans in and kisses me. I pulled away and said I wasn't expecting that. I was just dating Rex. He said knew and understood. So we kept talking about me and him, my closet, and I even told him about my other "online dominatrix" job. We were both drunk so all of this was easy to talk about. I even told him about my weird feelings throughout the night. He wanted me to stay the night and just lie there with him, but I had my mom's car and I most certainly didn't want rumors flying because my car was parked there over night. So I left after not too long and said I'd talk to him today.

Friday, Jan. 31, 2003

Well I was going to work last night but we lost power. So now it's Friday and I've made no money online this week. But I did write a couple songs so that's good.

Tuesday, Feb. 4, 2003 | **8:35am**

Sunday I got up early and went snowboarding by myself. I had a wonderful day. Very selfish. I hit the hills hard and worked on my form and endurance. I only stopped to smoke one (I usually smoke more), change CD's once, and eat a hot dog outside at a stand. I headed straight home, got ready for our staff party, went and hooked up with my date (Tiffany), and we went to the Tap for our staff party. Rex was working and I went to say hi and he was all weird. But I was drinking so I didn't mind. It was fun and everyone was loaded. We even had some pot brownies (other people did mushrooms) and then we all went to Kings. They paid for our drinks there too, so I got really drunk. I was wobbly and had to dance because I was feeling sick standing still. I was dancing up a storm and I didn't care who watched. Truth is I felt the whole bar watch my hips as I swayed and trotted around. Dez Thompson danced with me and he was a great dance partner. We even got the other people to dance because we looked like we were having so much fun. So we closed the place down and then we headed to Chevy's place. I went with Stanley and we stopped at his place. I was feeling really burnt, drunk, tired, and comfy, and I didn't feel like going upstairs. Then all of the sudden I was having sex with Stanley. I couldn't believe it. I stopped because I was drunk and then he went upstairs and I stayed in his bed. I woke up at 6:30 to Liam and another co-worker talking out in his living room. I hated being in his bed and I wanted to go home. I was looking all over in the dark, rummaging through his dirty laundry on the floor because I was missing some parts of my outfit. I kept looking until I found a pair of girl's g strings that weren't mine! Then I felt gross. I couldn't believe it. I was just wondering whose they were and how fresh they were. I didn't know what to think. I felt awful and we weren't alone in the apartment. So at that point I quietly closed the door and put on the light. I found everything but my underwear and was still looking for them when Stanley walked in. I found my panties but first he found those other ones and said here you go. And I said those aren't mine with a smile. He claimed that he hadn't been with anyone for months and he didn't know whose they were. And who knows, maybe he was telling the truth. Or he lied and I hate liars. So I didn't know what to do or think all day Monday. I took a cab to Grandma's and got my truck and drove home the long way. I smoked a couple doobs listened to my disc man and thought about driving as fast as I could off the road into a big tree just because I can't take it anymore. Life keeps getting more and more hectic and I want it to get better. I was going to go for a run when I got home but Brooklyn phoned as soon as I got there (she saw me drive by). She came over for tea and we did our Russian cards. Then I remembered I had a lawyer's appointment at ten and it was 9:45. There was no time for a shower so I flew to town. I apologized for my appearance when I got there and talked about settling my claim. So mediation is set for two months away and I must get all my stuff ready for then. So I think I must stay at World till then or it will raise too many questions. Besides, it's entertaining there. Actually, I should do a TV show on a strip club one day. I bet it would be so funny that everyone would watch it. Making fun of the drunken clientele, and showing all the funny things that happen. We would have wars with other strip clubs and show all the drugs and old ugly men hitting on hot waitresses and the dancers. Show the dancers too and all about them. Why they do it and who they are. I guess I can look at work as research.

Friday, Feb. 7, 2003

On Wednesday I went for a jog down Rope Bay Trail and got lost coming back. They've done so much logging in there that I didn't know where I was. I also went for a walk with Stanley along Leaving Bay. It was nice, very casual. Yesterday I bought a new outfit to wear to work tonight. I have to do beer tub tonight. And how that works is the hotter you look, the more beer you sell. So I bought this little jean skirt and jacket and some nice boots on sale to match. I'm going to curl my hair and more than anything have fun. Who knows, maybe I'll like it? I worked online last night and got $109 US off one guy. This guy was an extremist. I couldn't do harsh enough cock and ball torture (CBT) to him. He told me to go harder on him next time and I don't know what that would be? So I have to grow as a Mistress and step it up a notch. I even actually got him (with a clean unopened needle) to pierce himself between his ball sack and asshole. He said it hurt, but still wanted more punishment! I had a big candle lit up in his ass, dripping wax all over his ass and sack and still he wanted more! He even had a medical kit to stick rods up his urethra! I guess that's what I'll do next time. I'll have to do some research I guess. Actually, he wants to know how to stretch his asshole so he can fist it someday. So I said I would talk to my doom friends and do some research and email him some tasks. And I will do just that because he's got money and I don't mind the CBT. The men know their place, on the floor at my feet.

Monday, Feb. 10, 2003 | 7:50pm

I'm in my spare room, working online. I don't know why I sit here and waste time in hopes of making money. I should be out there making huge coin on movie deals/TV shows/modeling/singing ~ entertaining. I'm watching Couples Fear Factor. They ate a roach for $1000.00. I wouldn't I don't think, ewe.

Wednesday, Feb. 12, 2003 | 7:30am

I have to do cash today. I'm not looking forward to tomorrow. I've been thinking about "Thursday 13th" all week. I can't believe they've been gone two years already. I already don't want to see anyone tomorrow and I have to do cash, and go to ICBC tomorrow for my truck stereo at 5:30pm. I wanted to go boarding for the day, stop in Pintnay at the crash site, and make a day of it. But I'm not sure because of stupid cash. I always set off the alarm and I don't feel like doing that at 6am! I guess I'll talk to the owners today about it. See what they say. I don't know what I'll say, just that I want to go up to Mt.Laundryton. I hate explaining myself. I have very nice boss' though – as far as boss' go – they're all cool and friendly. I hung out with Stanley yesterday. We went rollerblading. Then we drove around and I showed him Hemlock. I showed him my messy house. I read his fortune and we had tea. He's very quiet. He's entertaining and harder to read than most people. And you know me, I love a challenge. I like that he's not predictable.

Thursday, Feb. 13, 2003

This working for a living bites the big one. My friends Dean and Wonder have been gone two years today. I miss them all year but today even more so. I just think of the death and the unfairness of it, then my brain rationalizes and I say they're still here. Even though you can't see them you'll be together again when you die. Then I think of meeting them in the white light. I know I have a full life ahead of me, but I'm not scared of dying. I have to do cash but I took the day off from serving. I don't feel like being nice today. I think I will drive up to Pintnay today just get out of town. Maybe take some flowers up? Well I'd better jump in the shower soon…

CHAPTER SIX

Friday, Feb. 14, 2003

It's Valentine's Day and I work all day just the way I like it. No time for "love". I made Valentines cupcakes and took them to work when I did cash. Then after cash I bought a new outfit to wear to work tonight. A red tank top with a heart and grey pants and a red fleece sweater because it's always cold at work! You would think with having naked ladies on stage they would be warmer. But no, it's always freezing there. I've started curling my hair, while I watch my computer screen hoping someone will come in and pay me money… still no one. I can't wait to get dressed in my new outfit. It's funny how I make money by looking good. I just got tired of all the other girls dressing up and being all that while I sit back with no attention. Now I'm in the spot light. All the attention of all the boys ~ living the life… but I miss my dogs, the attention isn't so great and my career is being sacrificed.

Monday, Feb. 17, 2003

Last week was long and full of work. I need my career, and I know it all starts with who you are. I think you need the confidence that your style is good. You can't judge because your only saying what you don't like about yourself. Then change what you don't like. Make yourself into the person you wish to be. No one can make me hold my temper, think before I speak, think nice (not evil) thoughts about others; except me. It is still a work in progress. I make the choices every day to be a better person it gets easier. It's hard not to get wrapped up in all the BS of life and what others say and think of you. But life is what you make of it. Just smile and trust the movie will have a happy ending. Trust the universe will provide and teach you. But at the same time you can't wait for things. You've got to go get it yourself. You have to make them want to come to you. I almost feel like a celebrity in this little town already. When I work at a hot club and I dress hot and I go out I feel the whole clubs eyes on me. I know all the people in town, just because I've served here for years. They all know "Betty" the waitress, who is a "porn star". That's probably what they say. I just care what I think of me and how I sleep at night? I respect myself more when I've been a nice person, doing kind things all day. I make time for people more. Slowly I am becoming all I can be, and it feels good. It's hard working out, working jobs, working mind power too – but I do it, with a little help from my angels.

Tuesday, Feb. 18, 2003 | 12:40am

I lost my temper today. I hate when I embarrass myself like that. It started last night when Rant sent the kids down to me in the dark to go to Beatrice's hot tub "girl's b-day party" for Brooklyn. I wasn't about to send them back to him, no telling where his mind is. So that annoys me to see abuse obviously still going on. Then today the kids came down because I was taking them swimming because Brooklyn and Rant were fighting. They had a twoonie each that they wanted to keep "to remember" their Dad. So I of course did damage control for the kids and it was OK until I had too many kids in the pool. Annie and Tabitha both needed my attention every second and Tabitha was running around. The life guard even had to tell her because he saw she wasn't listening to me. One man said to me, "Are all three yours?" No, none of them, I'm just Aunty Betty. And it maybe was the look on his face that made me wonder how I agreed to take them all swimming. So I was irritated and the girls were crying. Jordan only had jean shorts on because he had no clean swim trunks and that pissed me off. I'm sick of Brooklyn drowning in the parenting work while Rant does speed and sleeps. So we go to McDonalds and my muffler falls off driving home. Of course my cell wasn't with me so I had to walk to the pay phone. I phoned

Brooklyn, Beatrice, and Mom (I got all machines) and they all got not so nice Betty messages. I was mad because I felt like all Beatrice cared about was her stupid yuppie girl club meeting. I phoned Dad and got through to him, and it wasn't pretty, nice, or polite. I got out of all my "you drive a nicer truck than me" and "you don't care about me and my life or that I'm on the side of the road". Jordan and Annie actually had their McDonalds on the side of the highway. But I got it all out. He started to say he couldn't come and get me. He said "what does everyone else say"? Who cares? Are you not my father? I said never mind I have a pocket full of quarters I'll keep trying people. Then he changed his tune and he came with wire and tied my muffler. Of course he didn't have time to take it for a drive. "Why is it good enough for me but not you Dad?" I said it all! Really I did. I even actually phoned and apologized later. I said "sorry I was short". I also said it's no wonder I have no use for men with him and Rant around. They don't care about me or that I'm on the side of the road. Yep, I went off. But I was honest. I felt like I had Brooklyn's kids and who knows where her and Rant are. So now my truck is a waste of fucking insurance. I need money so I can get a new truck and get a new place to live. Get a job that lets me sleep at night. Get a life. Will I ever be able to stop making money on my body and start making money on my mind and my pen?

Thursday, Feb. 20, 2003

I think I'm going to move iMac into spare room so I can edit while I work online. I will do that today – but I already know that I don't know where my fire wire cord is. I'm going to go down to Brooklyn's to get the mail. It's always weird down there but I'm usually ripped and can ignore it. All I want is for all of them to be happy. Right now none of them are happy. In fact I think they all are hurt and tired of the struggle. I can't believe Rant has done the damage he has. I can't believe the looks of sadness in her kid's eyes. It gets to me, makes me angry. Why can't he just grow up and be nice? Only he can change his attitude…

Wednesday, Feb. 26, 2003 | **8:50am**

My life seems out of control these days. Most of the time, rather than doing what I should do, I do fun things instead. Last night I wanted to work online but I had no energy to do it. Is it because I smoke too much weed? I know what

I want to do but it seems impossible. I want to be a rock star on tour and do movies and maybe be the host of a reality TV show with my partner in crime, Brooklyn. So then I look around me and I think how do I get from here to there? I don't know or I'd be there I guess. There's so much for me to do in a day. I guess I'll make money online and do laundry at the same time.

Wednesday, Feb. 26, 2003 | 7:42pm

Well Belle, Jacquie, and I did mushrooms today. They want to go to the late show but I'm high already and my dogs need me. They want to do more mushies, but I'm worried Kandy ate some mushrooms. She ate my burger and it didn't look like the mushies but what if she did and she's high too. They don't think Kandy is high. They think I'm tripping and I don't know if I should go with them or not. They want to do more mushies but I'm high. So I don't want to go, but I should make sure they're ok. I wish I knew if Kandy was high or not.

Saturday, Mar. 1, 2003

I have this problem where I fall asleep early in the night and I can't help it. Then I wake up so early the next morning. It's 6:10am now and I'm wide awake. It sucks when my sleep pattern gets out of whack. I went boarding yesterday but it was so foggy that I came home early. A lot of people left early. I was so tired after boarding I did nothing last night. I hate doing nothing – I like to feel like I accomplish things in a day. None of this falling asleep at 7:30pm anymore. Seriously, I'd rather die than waste another day. Life is too short to be sleeping depressed. That's why I figure I get so tired here. I don't like living here, it depresses me?

Mar. 2, 2003 | 3:21am

I'm at home. I worked all day then went to Barron's going away party. Now I'm home alone thinking of someone I shouldn't be. That's all I can say. I can't even write down more. I believe in fate and whatever will be, will be. I had fun at Barron's house. There were a lot of people there that I haven't seen in a while. I even talked about the someone I shouldn't say with someone else there tonight. The truly horrible thing is how much I think about this person. I shouldn't be thinking of this person. Today I talked to "him" and I felt like a nervous school girl, not knowing what to say to her crush. That's not like me. I'm quick witted. I really haven't felt this way in years. I haven't told a soul. I wonder how he feels about me more than anything. I know I can read vibrations and energies – but am I right? It was fun at first but now I worry how I look talking to him. Can anyone tell? I can't control the movie – I can only watch it – try to enjoy the show and have a good time. But I must say I'm curious to know if even in a few decades anything would happen with that person. Now that would be a high point.

Monday, Mar. 3, 2003

It's 4:02pm and I'm in my computer room. My online account just got shut down for discussing "fisting" when I wasn't even. Fuckers, like I don't have enough on my mind. Now I can't work. I guess I could edit tapes. How dare they suspend me? Fuckers! So now I have to email them and see what is up. There's always someone holding a hoop, wanting me to jump. Stupid online made me mad. I had no idea that talking about fisting was illegal online. I guess it's considered obscene. Anything that you can't find in a porno magazine that you can buy at a grocery store is considered obscene. Even though I hear so many people joke about "fisting" all the time, it's too obscene for me to talk about. I can discuss cock and ball torture and get them to stick a candle up there butt, or any vegetable or fruit for that matter, but not their fist! It makes no sense sometimes the boundaries our society tries to put on sex. Everyone has sex, and everyone goes on the computer and looks up porn; but because I talk freely about it, I'm the obscene one. Maybe I'm just the honest one. Do you know that almost every client I have is married and tells me that they could never talk to their wife about the stuff they confide to me? I always try to get them to open up to their partners and not turn to someone else. Just tell them you want to try getting a toy in your ass. Maybe your wife will be more understanding than you think. Or tell your wife you want to go online and try adding that extra element to your bedroom play, don't hide it and build up walls. Sometimes I try to get them caught by their wives or neighbours. I tell the slaves to dress up in the lingerie (most often their wives) and stand over their wife who is sleeping in bed and whack off until they cum. Or I tell them to dress up and go out into the middle of the back yard and whack off. They know and I know that they might get caught, but that is what makes it more fun for both of us. I laugh when I think of these men dressed up and just pray the wife wakes up.

Friday Mar. 7, 2003 | 7:15am

Well yesterday was Tiff's b-day. I was lame and stayed home. I'm still fighting this cold. I wanted to go out and party, but Tiff understood. She had to go on antibiotics to get over her cold. She thinks I'll have to too. I just couldn't find the energy to get out. And when you make yourself usually you have a bad time. Tonight is Barron's going away dinner @ Chicken Palace. Tim's brother will serve us dollar highballs. I knew I wanted to go out tonight and I have the gym at 10am. I'm starting to enjoy going to the gym though. Looking buff feels good. I wish more people would work out and feel good about themselves. That model search is in Cityville next weekend. I can't believe how soon it is. We have so much preparing to do and it's only one week away! Somehow (we don't know how yet) we will get everything together, hear what they say, and who knows, maybe an agent will find Jordan. I'm not holding my breath though. Jordan won out of two hundred kids and we owe it to him to go.

Friday, Mar. 7, 2003 | 1:15pm

I'm back from the gym, thinking of that same old person. I talked to Stanley on the phone and he said he talked to that same person for a while this morning (he never has before) and I can't help but wonder if maybe he talked to him to see who I was dating. He asked why I don't work more. Stanley being smart said I couldn't because of my back injury. I tried not to ask Stanley too many questions. I had to hold back and pretend not to care. When the truth is I think about him all day. I just want what I can't have. It's just a crush, nothing serious. Keep telling myself that.

Sunday, Mar. 9, 2003 | 2:15am

I worked tonight, seemed like forever. But there's always something exciting going on. One waitress called in sick because she "took too many perks and crashed her truck". Cool, I just laugh because we all have to be a bit crazy to work there. I'm getting good at answering drunk men asking, "when are you going to get up there?" I smile, pause, and look at them then say "in your dreams".

Eyes that shine blue
A body nice n' tight
A soothing persona, rare and true
Could it be my Mr. Right?

The way he says my name
It's like he's said it forever
I think about him so much I think I'm insane
Why can't I get you out of my head Mr. _____?

I'm not permitted to think these thoughts of you
Because you belong to another
But I can't help what I do
My heart feels the way it does regardless of her

It's my mind that keeps me away
I would never chase a married man
This moral I just can't sway
I can tell you understand

Why is it I can't get you outta my head
All I can wonder is your true thought on me
Do you feel the heat, do you see my face go red
Oh merciless thoughts please let me be

No wait come back, I changed my mind
I'd rather have these thoughts than nothing
    In my thoughts your one of a kind
And in this cold world it gives me something

A person to be attracted to
In this world full of fools
(Betty Benson)

No Such Thing As Secrets

Tuesday, Mar. 11, 2003

I get to "shine" at work tonight. What should I wear? I should work now online, build a fire, keep it going, do laundry all day, and then work at five.

Friday, Mar. 14, 2003

I love my dogs. I'm going to miss them until Sunday when I return from Cityville. I still don't know how we're going to do it. I don't know if Brooklyn even has enough money for Jordan's registration. I made good money at work last night; men were throwing it at me. Some nights they are throwing bills and other nights they're keeping quarters. Some drunks say the rudest things. One guy said he wanted to lick my breast and he was licking my hand. He was harassing the whole bar. But I can never get mad at people. I just laugh at their behavior and make fun of them. That same drunk guy asked me last night "if you and I were on an island together, what could we do then?" I said, "I'd tell you both what to do and run the island". He said "who would have to do more work?" I said "I'd change it all the time. One day I'd tell you to do this, this, and this, and you do that. Then the next day you do this, this, and this, and you do that. And you could get a big leaf and fan me." And he said "Every island needs a queen, pick an island." They liked the idea of being my slaves. Little do they know how evil of queen I would be. They would be there for my mere amusement, kind of like men are to me now. When everyone wants you and says "you're beautiful, will you marry me?" they want your body, not your soul. Jealous, aging, and insecure women hate me and hate that everyone loves me. But women who are confident and have attitude like me and all the men (except gay guys) love me. I know all the cool people in town. I work in the hottest club in town and there are rumors I'm an internet porn star. I'm going to the gym and I look buff. It's weird but the world likes a pretty girl more than a smart one. I'm no better. I always like the hotties.

Monday, Mar. 17, 2003

I'm back from Cityville. Jordan had a good time. I enjoyed the "rest" of it. I didn't do much. It made me realize that I just have to get myself out there. Having the acting experience I have is a bonus. But also I realize that there are a million pretty faces out there, but not many of them can write! Brooklyn and I don't need music to our songs; we can just send them off as is. So Brooklyn wants me to talk to the DJ's at work about recording our songs. We've picked four songs to send out. I'll need my insurance money before we can afford to record. Then a record company can help us do our first album as "BLUNT", and all I need is to get Belle in. She never wants to practice and thinks it's an impossible dream. Should we just not bother recording with her? She has such an amazing voice and such beautiful face, but no confidence. I just can't leave her. She'd hate Brooklyn and I in a band without her. I'm watching much more music and thinking how that should be me, our songs, our videos, our magazine cover, us on TV, late show interviews, and our fans. I want a calendar of BLUNT. "Beautiful, Hope, Faith" – our stage names and middle names. And I want Jordan to have his movie career. They love how small he is at his age. They think he could easily pass for a six year old. So we need to get him an agent in Cityville and get some experience under his belt ASAP. The agent from ACME gave Brooklyn his number. I saw that I would get more respect for my writing then for my looks. I love that I have the power to write and I feel it's something I do well. It just comes naturally to me. I just want to focus on my career.

Thursday, Mar. 20, 2003 | **4:05pm**

I'm wearing the cutest new pair of pink panties, working online. They've already paid for themselves. I love to go shopping and buy new lingerie (panties and bra sets). I always give myself the excuse that it is for my online work. I love to take the profile pictures of myself and see how pretty I look in my lingerie or knee high lace up boots. I love looking hot and feeling like such a Goddess. I tell my slaves to call me Goddess or Mistress, but I prefer Goddess. I even have a t-shirt that says "Goddess". It has a little cat on it so I call it my "pussy Goddess" shirt because I am the ultimate Pussy Goddess. I have had slaves bow at my feet, lick my feet, and do whatever I want for too long. It makes me really feel like a Goddess and not like an average girl at all. I have two sides to me. One is the nice and sweet girl that all my friends and family know, and the other side of me is a diva, a Goddess, and a superstar waiting to erupt. I am meant for so much more than just serving beer to people. I am meant to be a Goddess.

Saturday, Mar. 22, 2003 | 3:50pm

I'm working online. I have a book that I keep notes in to try to keep the clients and their fetishes straight. I write down what props or toys they have (candle, cock ring, vibe, ice, lingerie, whatever). I always think of what they have and what they might want to add to their kit to match where their fetish is going. It is my job to figure out a mans fetish and fast, so I can make money off it. I can look at any man on the street and figure out his fetish pretty fast in real life. I know who likes the little school girl outfit and I know who likes the ball and gag. I play the role they need in order to get them back and make them spend that money. It's all business for me, and knowing how to please a man sexually is a gift I have. I know what men like, how they differ, and I know how to get into the role they need me to be. It's all just work for me but it's making me look at all men like they are just here for my amusement. I play the role of a Mistress so often that I really do feel like I know way more about sex than any man. I have heard everything you could imagine, and have seen things that you couldn't imagine. I've seen things like men piercing their urethra with different size rods, to men in lingerie with a carrot up their butt dancing around to sexual pop music. I did cash this morning, and I serve tonight at 9pm. Busy girl, I'm watching another diva bio on much… chatting with chatters – oh a viewer.

Mar. 24, 2003 | 2:30pm

Ok, I was pretty hammered last night. I had too many ciders. I shouldn't have driven home. But I did. I worked online and watched the beginning of Oscars. I went to Rabbitwood Pub to hang out with some people from work. We played crib and pool and music in the jupe box. Then a few of us went down to the Kings where I was dancing by myself on the dance floor by the end of the night. When I sat down again Stanley said "what are you doing in this town, you're too good for Newsville". I thought that was a nice thing to say to me. He's a cool guy. Oh my gosh – I was so sick today. I puked about six or seven times from 9:30am until 1:30. I last puked up a few mouthfuls of water. I couldn't keep a sip of juice down. Yuck! Then I just lied in my blanket on the floor all over downstairs, puking every 30 – 60 minutes. Thank God I'm not still crouched over the toilet! On Saturday night at work I saw the guy and when I first saw him and said hi, he asked about my dogs, and then I feel nervous and dumb for a few minutes.

And while I'm feeling this way – I'm pretending that everything is normal. Then I thought… Mom interrupted me. I'll go back to that happy thought after I vent for a bit. She just chewed me out for like 10 – 20 minutes about money and the fact that my credit card is maxed… I kept my cool though. Ahhh, she gets me so mad. I hate being under her power. I need to settle my insurance claim and pay everyone off. I must move out for my sanity's sake. She just wanted to get mad at me and I could see in her eyes she thought I was oblivious to what she was saying, but she wasn't listening to me. Of course I work on getting my life in order every day. Of course I care my cc is maxed. I'm working on it! She has way too much control of my life and happiness. All she ever does is bitch, nothing nice to say about anyone ever. Everyone is doing horrible, she's a hater, and no wonder I don't like living here. It's always so gloomy. She's always bitching about Rant, Tiffany, Dee, Brownies/Sparks, Belle partying, Dad or my money, and pot. Oh I'm so bad, I smoke pot. She doesn't even realize what a good person I am. What a smart girl I am. She just sees a burnout who is lost and doing horrible and she's "so worried about" me. I didn't think I was doing so badly. Everyone at work likes me, thinks I'm responsible and a good hard worker with a great personality. And they smoke weed too – so mom would just think they're all lost too. I need to move out really bad. Maybe I wouldn't be driving around so much if I liked my home more. I just can't stand the stress of this place anymore. I phone Brooklyn and Rant thinks we're up to something. She's looking sadder than ever. I almost think she's had it. OK I'm feeling better now; even when I'm mad that she stays I still love her with all my heart. OK back to my heart… At one point Saturday night I thought, okay, I'm going to look into his eyes. Then I was walking from the back, past him and didn't think he'd notice but he was looking out of the corner of his eye and it was crazy, like a movie or something. But we both caught each other looking and knew it. Then both looked away or I did anyway and felt Oh my god! It was a moment. I just wonder why? Does he have a crush on me too? I don't know what to think. I'm really attracted to him, his eyes are amazing. So blue and I imagine he's smart. It's like Romeo and Juliet in a way. We're just at two different points in our life. I wouldn't want him to ever come over here or go to his house for that matter. He's just too hard to resist, I can't get him out of my mind. Then I'll stop a little bit but then I'll see him at work and there it goes again. Butterflies, nervous, a crush…

No Such Thing As Secrets

Tuesday, Mar. 25, 2003 | **3:00pm**

Last night I went to Brooklyn and Rant's. They've stopped fighting. Rant says it's the speed and he thought all these strange paranoid thoughts. He was crying the whole time, telling us everything. How he wanted to kill himself. Drugs are bad… as I smoke my pot. Brooklyn had to hit him to stop him from killing himself. She bruised her hand. But he's starting to trust Brooklyn over the drug so I hope he really never will do it again. He's really sorry to everyone and he wants to change. Brooklyn said he got up, had a shower, dressed nicer, and took a pen and paper to work, no doobs. Good for him. I prey to everyone who can help him and anyone on speed trying to get off it. I wish them help. It doesn't look like a good situation to go through. I just hope I make enough money to pay my loan payment tomorrow. I'm one hundred dollars short. I hope my tips get over that much. I decided to cancel that other credit card. I don't need it, and it would be dumb of me really. I need to spend less on clothes too, do more working online and less shopping. And mind my own business, just write and stay out of trouble. I'm tired of trouble finding me. It's time to live the good life. So no more drinking nights and next day's wasted on hangovers. Time to grow up I guess. Time to take care of my shit. Stop all these pushy mother fuckers who are pushing me down and stand up for me. Take my life and reputation back.

CHAPTER SEVEN

Sunday, Mar. 30, 2003

I feel overwhelmed sometimes when I'm out at work or in a club after work and I feel all eyes on me. I know they all talk about me and like I say, it's a bit overwhelming. I feel like they all want me for the wrong reasons. I want to find someone special. Actually last night I met someone. I'm sure I've met him before. Dick and Stewart were out drinking and needed a ride home. Dick was hammered and I had six guys to drive in my little truck. So we were going to get Stewart's truck because it was bigger while I took Bill and Stewart to Bill's house. Dick waited with D.J. and another guy at Mucko's Pizza for me to return with booze for the after parties and wheels. So we get to Bill's house and he wanted to check on his dog. He loves his dog, he rides dirt bikes (I was on one at 4:30am but I'll get to that), he snowboards, and he's even learning guitar. So I played his guitar and we lost track of time. Then Dick called and wanted a ride. So I get there and there are two extra girls, so the guys jumped in the back and off we went back to Bill's. So we get there (I smoke and everyone else drinks) and Dick, Bill, and I went on a little fifty ride. Bill doubled me so I had to hug him and be close. I like guys who ride bikes as much as I think it's dangerous. I love the way they don't care about danger – it's sexy. Not so much on a fifty, but still cute. So anyways I wonder when I'll see him again. I might go on a bottle drive tonight over to Dick and Stewart's for Jordan's class. I planned it last night. Then I could ask Dick about Bill. Back to last night though, it was crazy to be me, 'live as Betty Benson'. Everyone wants me only because I'm hot, funny, and know how to have fun. They think I'm this person that I try to keep up with. Try to be as great and perfect as they want a dream girl to be.

Friday, Apr. 4, 2003 | **10:45am**

I am sitting in my work room, online, and waiting. Last night I had my first ball practice, and Lillian and I went roller-blading down at the seawall with some mud slides and doobies. It's a lot of fun but my blades were giving me a blister so we had to stop. We drove out to the beach we went to when the boys died. We cheers' them and went to my house to get my dogs and drive her home. I'm working making a bit of money and enjoying life. I'm actually enjoying being me; telling jokes, living the life, going out on the weekends, and being a Mistress online even. It's a life I'll think back to and remember the freedom.

8:00pm

Today I went to Melissa's house and curled her hair for a job interview. Suzanne came with me. Then we went to Chicken King in Girlsville and then we stopped at the Hemlock grave yard. I always blow two kisses their way but never go in. Someone looked them up and Wonder was cremated there but they don't know what was done with his ashes. But Dean was buried there. So we saw his tombstone and it was very sad. I really wish I could go back in time and talk to them. I was very sad all day just picturing that tomb. It had a motor bike and yin yang. It was sad. 1978 – 2001 Dean Harry Bossley I think of him a lot. I think of them both all the time. But I always feel like a part of me died. I'll never have that carefree smile again. Their memory will always be sad. But if I ever need to cry in a movie I could. Just look at the picture of them and think of how they are gone. How I really won't see them until my life is over. Seeing his tomb made me think that is just his body now. He is gone forever, never again will he be. So when will I get over it? Maybe that's what people like about me – my inner silence, that unspoken pain you see but don't know what it is. Why is she so sad? Who hurt her so bad? The worst kind of pain, only in her heart and memory and imagination… I guess I needed to learn to be alone this life. I needed my independence and I do have two very strong angels watching over me all the time. Making sure life isn't too horrible for me. I know their soul still exists and they are here always. But I won't ever hold them again. Good thing they are still here as souls. Who knows why their time came so soon, why they had to die so soon. An eagle flew over us at the grave yard. It was nice. I can go back and see him on my own now. It's no fun burying someone you care about or looking at their grave. On a good note I'm going to Larry Harry with Lillian on 14th in ten days. I can't wait.

Saturday, Apr. 5, 2003 | **6:35pm**

I have to work at the World tonight. Last night I went and hung out with Suzanne at her new place that she and Buck are moving into. At around 1:30am I drove home and took the long way. I've been sad all day today and I actually slept because I feel a flu coming on. I slept from 1:30 – 6:30. Wow, that's five hours. No wonder I feel better now. I worry that a man will hurt me or I'll hurt him. It's way easier to be a hermit and not share myself. I just hate feeling vulnerable to people. I like it when they can't touch me or get me. I'm just one of those untouchable girls. I think men like this, but not as many girls. Most people need someone, one after another. Others are way happier alone. It's just all about me right now.

Monday, Apr. 7, 2003 | **11:00am**

Last night I was just sitting at home, chilling, when Dick phoned me up. He was at Bill's house. They were going on a ride and wondered if I wanted to go too. They said they would wait for me. Two girls went with Bill's roommate on his quad, Dick took the drinks on his fifty, and Bill doubled me on his little fifty. And sometimes when we would stop he would wrap his arms around me, claiming to be cold. I didn't mind. It felt nice actually. The only thing is he's born in the year of the snake, and I vowed not to date snakes again. But he's cute. He has a race this weekend on his bigger bike. I wonder what I should do. I'm going to have to phone Dick and tell him my dilemma. He'll be able to figure it out. I was going to mention something last night but he's such a loud drunk and I was worried he would ruin it for me by saying something loud and embarrassing. I keep thinking of that other guy. But I thought I didn't want a boyfriend because of my online work. It's so hard explaining that one to guys. Mind you, my slaves would love it if I could find a man that would perform with me. I'd like to watch him race this weekend. It's funny phoning Dick and not his sister Janelle. I would know so much more about Buck if I asked Janelle. He has a dog, so he can't be that bad. He really loves his dog, like I love mine. Well I don't know if anyone can do that.

Tuesday, Apr. 8, 2003

I'm waiting for my tea before I have to drive Grandma to the doctors. I phoned Dick yesterday and told him I want to get to know Bill. He says Bill hasn't dated anyone for a few months. I keep thinking about him, he's pretty cute… I wonder when I'll see him again. I have to work tonight and I'm supposed to rollerblade with Suzanne and Lillian tomorrow night. And wait, Thursday night I'm supposed to go to Aunty Alice's and sing, and then I work Friday and Saturday. I really am too busy to fit a boy in. I should just concentrate on my career. I have to bartend Friday night because it's the regular bartender's b-day so all the boys are going out. I like bartending. You get a little bit more respect than the waitress gets. Well I really should go drive Grandma now.

Wednesday, Apr. 9, 2003 | **9:15am**

I'm tired. I got home from work at 2:30am and then the dogs needed out for a pee too early. But I'm up now and I have lots to do. We're having some real-estate man in at 4pm so I need to get the place clean and ready. So I worked last night (a long eight hours), 5pm – 1am. All the men saying I was the best one in there and they tipped me well. I guess they like my energy. At one point the DJ paged me (Hollywood) to the DJ booth. They needed drinks up there. Actually I can still remember – four red headed sluts (shooters ½ jagger ¼ red sour puss ¼ peach schnapps) three MGD and a vodka seven with cranberry and a little OJ. It came to $38.75. Not a bad memory for a burn out eh. I'm starting to categorize the men clientele. Some are business men, after work in their suits. These guys sometimes drink coolers, ciders, MGD, or Corona beer. Then one guy will buy a round and flash out his big bundle of bills that I know he wants me to see. They always sit in gyno row and don't eat. I don't think they would eat in a "strip club" unless they were really drunk and ordered nachos for all. The next group is the generation family affair. This is where Dad, son, uncle and even Grandpa come down. And they drink hard. They're a lot of fun. The son is always a little embarrassed as the Dad says "my son thinks your cute", and I look at the son with sympathy as if to say don't worry I know you'd never hit on me so cheesily. But then they keep drinking and the son likes that his dad got him an in. And they stay a while. These groups usually get an appy to share earlier on. The dad, son, and uncle drink beer, all their own preferred brand (Kokanee, Bud, Canadian) but they don't like draft. The Grandpa and all old men like good scotch on the rocks (Glenfiddich, Glenlivit) and they sip them. They like English cider or Irish crème ale (Strongbow and Kilkenny). The older the man is the more forward they are about hitting on me, or just saying how my smile is nice, or "if I was 20 years younger". The oldest man in there last night was smacking my butt with a poster. Another old guy (scotch again) said he was a photographer who likes to take pictures of natural beauty and gave me his card. He says he's known in Europe and yadda yadda. And then there are my Saturday day oldies that I don't see now because I work nights. The old men don't sit in gyno row unless they have a buddy to sit with or the stripper calls them forward. Then they go back to the table if they're alone. They do like gyno if they're encouraged. Then there's the mid-age friends that meet there and end up getting really drunk for some reason. They drink Pale Ale and Honey Brown on tap, and cocktails like Caesars or Seabreezes. I can usually talk them into a double. These guys get drunk, they sit in gyno row, they spill beer and drinks when they're drunk enough, they hoot n' holler and sing, and make us laugh the most because you can tell that they don't usually go out and they are hammered. They like to run tabs, ordering round after round. Seldom do they pay as they go; it's usually on their visas. Then we have the bikers. They stand and walk around and are what I like to call "coke snobs". Yes they have money but the dealers tip more than the bikers. They think they run the room. You'd be surprised but some bikers don't tip well at all. The big ones that have lunch tabs do, but the groupie or weird ones don't. Some of my friends tip me well, some quarter me. My friends fit into the "whatever's popular in town weekend night crowd", drinking crown n' coke, gin n' tonic, double highballs, and right now we're the place to go on weekend nights. And then there are the college kids on spring break drinking pitchers of beer. These are the nineteen year olds in town and some know to tip – some don't. The odd one (the funny looking one) drinks a gin or some double highball. After work the PR manager wanted me to stop by and say hi and my customers wanted me to go to Kings. And I totally could have gone but I was hungry so I picked up a teen burger, onion rings, and coke, and tipped the drive thru girl. She was so happy over a measly five dollars. Then I smoked, the long way home and shared my food with Molly, Jose, and Kandy.

Thursday, Apr. 10, 2003 | **12:40am**

Where to start tonight? I feel like writing. I've had a few mudslides and I'm going to spark one or three. I was blading on my brand new blades today – K2 – so cool n' comfy. I was drinking, smoking, and chatting with Lillian, and then we met up with Suzanne, Lillian's boyfriend Wilky, and his boss at Wilky's. It was OK for me because I was drinking. Suzanne drove me back to my truck and we talked about it. Lillian doesn't seem happy or herself. But I had my drinks and my weed and I'm sociable with everyone. Actually I held the party together. I made a cd but it won't work. I swear ghosts can control music. I had to restart my cd. I think there should be a TV show that taped me 24/7. So right now there would be cameras I'd be on channel? I'm in panties and a camisole. Anytime I see that guy (the one I can't say) I think of him for days after. And I always wonder what he thinks of me? I realize that no matter how much I fuck up I'll make it to the next phase in life. I even see glimpses of it. I think everyone does. I had to get a tick out of Molly tonight… on her eyebrow, so she felt it and fought it. But I rubbed her nose to calm her and then give her treat after. I still think of Wonder and Dean every day. Most of the time I can reconcile with it and say it's ok they're dead, but then I think, no, fuck no, it's not right, it's not ok, and it's not fare, now what? And that lump in my throat carries to my eyes and I get dry socket pain as I fight back the pain and tears. My cd stopped again. I guess it's time for sleep.

Friday, Apr. 11, 2003 | **3:12pm**

I am working online, waiting for viewers, waiting and waiting. It's not hard to sit and wait. I will do laundry, arts and crafts, watch TV, listen to music; anything I want to pass the time. I just smoke as much as I want to smoke and hide in my room from the outside world. I meet people or see people I know all the time, but I don't really let people get too close to me. I have been judged so much for my choice to work online that it makes me not want to get to know anyone. I know that everyone talks about me. I just choose to ignore it. I can care what they think, or instead I can care what I think of myself. I know I am a good person. I know that I always try to do good things and be a positive influence in the world. I know that it's only money online and it doesn't make me less of a woman. I know that I am still the sweetest girl around. I just don't really want to let anyone in and have them judge me, and not see the sweet girl that I really am. I just want someone that see's the sweet side of me and who ignores all the rumours. We all have sex, I just happen to make money by talking about it. When I am with a man I am loyal and I would never talk to anyone about our sex life; but I can see why guys wouldn't guess that about me given all the rumours.

Saturday, Apr. 12, 2003

I am very tired and sad, exhausted and teary eyed. I saw Dick, Stewart, and Bill tonight. I gave Dick and Stewart a ride home. We smoked a doob at Stewart's and Dick mentioned (he was drunk) "is it true about the internet porn?" I didn't know what to say. I looked at Stewart and it seemed like he didn't hear Dick and I ignored it, but it bugged me. I wanted another shot and a beer. I just kept doodling and thinking about the whole thing. I drove Dick home and we talked more. I laid it out for him and ended it with "it's easier to be alone anyways". I don't think it would work with Bill because as Dick says "he's worried about the porn thing". I say fuck the world, especially him! So be it. I'm not "good" enough for him, too "naughty" (my words). Well grow up and see past that I say. See the real me. He's obviously not enlightened enough for me. And they want me to go to Cityville on Thursday for Janelle's birthday. Why so you can all talk about me more. Judge me more. Be fake with me more. No thanks. I was so upset when I left Dick's that I really wanted to die. I wished so much to leave this world and be with Wonder and Dean. Have them understand and just leave this body. The world is too hard on the pretty girl. I even have a tree all picked out to drive into. I was very upset after Dick's unknowing drunken belittling. I was crying and not even smoking, thinking tonight I'm doing it, I'm going do it; I'll see Wonder and Dean. I'll do it. Won't that be a surprise to the town – I'm dead. Always wondering if it was on purpose or an accident, and why was she driving way out there. I'd like them to talk about that. She's dead. Society killed her. They made her what she was and then killed her by judgment on what she was, and not who she was. I came home still crying, hugged all my dogs and cat, played guitar, and came to bed to write my sorrow away and hope tomorrow is a brighter day.

Monday Apr. 14, 2003

Yesterday Bill phoned me and we hung out last night. He had a few people over having drinks so I took some mudslides and doobies and chilled with them. Finally everyone was gone and it was just Bill & I. We talked for a while, and then we kissed (instigated by him of course). We talked about this and that, and I still think he looks familiar – but I don't know where from. I did find out that he was friends with and neighbors to my cousin Warren for years. Small town. I didn't bring up the net, I didn't want to ruin the mood… and make it all serious. Obviously that's a big subject, very big, and one that only I choose who I talk to about it. Maybe it would be nice to have someone to talk to about it… but we'll see if he can handle it. Or is he a prisoner of society? It was nice kissing him. His skin is smooth, he's got a nice body and cute face, and he has green eyes like me. You don't find too many green eyes. You know the net job is a good tester for men, because if they can't see past that, they could never handle my fame or movie love scenes. The whole town knows of me, "Betty the cute waitress/porn star". Like those jobs describe who I am. I'd rather be known as a writer/artist, but oh well. People will be people and choose to pass on juicy info on anyone they can. Why, because its fun, and they don't feel judged when they're judging others (like me and my porn). But ironically, what they say about me is what they feel about themselves.

Wednesday, Apr. 16, 2003

Last night I had ball and batted 550. First day out felt good. Then we went to the World for a beer. Later I phoned Bill and went to watch a movie. After the movie we were watching TV and chatting and I felt like he wanted to ask me about internet. We channel surfed to a 'chat phone sexy girls in bikini's' and he said, "Oh there you go, the internet", then he froze. I said phone and meet people and saved him but my face went red and I thought, "You dumb ass. Really smooth buddy". I thought "what should I say, should I say something?" Then there was a computer commercial or something and I said, "I have two computers", almost toying with it. I told him all about my iMac, avoiding the internet on purpose to make him think I was avoiding it, and then I said, "My other is for work". Pause (I do have my fun). He said, "work?" "Yeah, I do online dominatrix." I tried to explain it as best I could, which isn't easy, especially when he was so quiet. Not everyone can handle me. I wouldn't be too surprised if he doesn't call again. I very well could be too much for him. We chatted and kissed a little, but I felt him pull away a bit and think "wow, who is this chick?" I'm only human. So what if I exhibit my beautiful body, I'm just being resourceful. I'm going to Suzanne's house now to unpack her stuff with her and drink and smoke.

Thursday, Apr. 17, 2003 | **2:40pm**

I went to Suzanne and Buck's and I stayed for a bit. I had six mudslides, smoked some weed, and at one point I went to check my cell (charging in the car) and I saw that he had called and left voice message. I called him back and we chatted for a bit, and I said I'd call later. I phoned on my way home and we talked for a while. I had a few so I was chatty Cathy. We're going to hang out after singing tonight. Last time I saw him after ball I didn't look good and I laid the entire internet thing on him … so tonight should be much more fun. All the hard stuff is out of the way. Now we can just chill. Singing should be fun tonight. Aunty Alice works us hard, but that's good we need some discipline. We need to focus. Put all of our energy into making a demo cd and get it ready to send off. I can't wait to have our cd done, so we can hear it, play it, and give out the finished product one day to whoever I want. Have a record company even. I'm looking forward to seeing Bill tonight and not feeling that "when should I tell him" feeling. It's all out in the open now. It should just be normal tonight. We can get to know each other more. It should be fun. It is fun to date, as long as you are being honest, you won't go wrong. Sometimes the hardest thing is the right thing. It's hard to open up to a man, but I think I can?

Friday, Apr. 18, 2003

Last night I slept with Bill. I totally wasn't planning on it. I was just happy to go and hang out. But we enjoyed kissing for hours and just couldn't really stop. I actually really like him so far. I go out with so many guys that I don't like, but am bored so I date them. This one is different. I want him to like me. I actually want him, not just him wanting me. He doesn't say much, but he seems honest. He seems like a hard worker. A big part of this going better is me trying to be open and not be scared. I stayed at his house and we spooned all night. He had his arms around me and he does this thing where he puts his hand on my head as I'm on his armpit. He's coming to Suzanne and Buck's with me and Jordan tonight. Brooklyn and Rant are going for dinner and Annie's going for a girl's night at Auntie Alice's. I'm going to ask him over for dinner with Jordan and I. Work is dead. I wish I could just make money and sign out now! I hope the universe gives me money! NOW!

Saturday, Apr. 19, 2003

I'm watching a Shania Twain biography. It's always good to watch music TV. It makes me see that real people slowly become stars, not over night. They write for years first just as I am doing. And the writers make it much further. Keeping it real with your writing always sells. They write from the heart, hoping people like it, but not caring about others opinions more than their own. Now I'm watching Tom Hanks win a national achievement award. Wow, I can't wait to get back into acting. I love acting. It's an escape from your life. A better escape than drugs can give. You are in the moment on stage and all eyes are on you. Steve Martin is giving a great speech. It's funny. Last night Bill and I went to Suzanne's house and I got drunk. I haven't wanted a man around, but I like those arms around me. I feel calm and like I can be myself around him. I feel like he listens to what I say and is honest. I know I've only known him for a short time, but I can tell this could last a while. As long as he keeps being cool. I'm so worried he'll turn into "Clint" or "Rambo" and be a jerk to me once we get close.

Apr. 21, 2003

I'm working online (bored because it's dead) and importing some party videos into my Mac. I wish I had a brand new Mac. This video will be a good one (mushrooms with Belle and Jacquie and Suzanne's housewarming party tonight). Good videos. It's fun video editing. Holy Fuck – online is dead. Music is my way out of this job. Well I had a viewer (Eddie). He paid me $139. Yeah, I love money. I love to shop with all my money.

Wednesday, Apr. 22, 2003 | 12:52am

I'm at home from the bar… drinking after our ball games. I'm always drinking these days… I should mellow out a bit. I'll admit I'm destined to feel alone for various reasons and it gets to a person. I think I should go to bed…

Thursday, Apr. 24, 2003

I had to move my work computer back into my room because Kandy chewed the cord that ran to the other room. That's okay though, I kind of missed having the computer in here. I can do laundry this way. I spent the night at Bill's last night. Everything has been great so far. Not too fast and lots of fun. I'm just waiting for something to happen but I guess it might not. Maybe he won't get weird? Or better yet, maybe I won't get weird.

Sunday, Apr. 27, 2003

I'm on my roof, puffin before Bill comes over. Last night I had a bad night with Bill. I met up with him at RR and I felt like he was showing me off. Making me (and I mean making me) kiss him around the bar, in front of different groups as if to say "she's mine". I would talk to people and I felt like he was being weird about that, and then he'd quickly go and put his hand on my back. I can't be your "gold bracelet" man. I fucking hate that so much. He was drunk and I was sober – bad combo. I don't need a guy telling me what to wear or how to do my hair, or all that goes along with dating someone. I felt like he wanted to own me, as cliché as that sounds. Brooklyn says I'll have that problem no matter who I'm with. I think I just need to find the right person. But now what do I do? Cut him loose now (saving heartache) later (when I can't stand to be with him). One day at a time I guess. Today I'll go for a walk with Bill and see how it goes.

Monday, Apr. 28, 2003 | 1:01am

I went to Suzanne's for dinner and had some drinks. Melissa was there and so was Suzanne's mom Bitsy. We had a great time. We ate soft tacos, and read Russian Gypsy cards for everyone (even Suzanne's landlord and Buck). I drank seven mudslides – yum. Now #8 sits beside me waiting to be opened. I went for a walk with Bill and Jordan and I found that Bill was too controlling with his dog. It's an example of how he is in relationships. "You have to hold her tight so she won't run" and making her come over and heel constantly when no one is around. Poor dog. He kept testing her, making her obey, and Betty don't play dat! Molly ran free and came happily if I called. Okay, but as for big reason I'm writing… I cannot get Mr._____ out of my head. Especially when I see him and we make eye contact. It's crazy how we can have this secret energy for each other. I totally get the vibe that his girlfriend doesn't like me (rightfully so). I have feelings for her boyfriend but she can't prove it. He said his birthday was coming so I found out how old he would be and when, (sneaky, sneaky). That tells me tons about him. Oh… I wish he was single. I guess whatever is meant to be will be. Could you imagine us actually being able to talk for just a couple of minutes? I wonder if he's happy. They don't seem in love. They seem like they love each other but don't have that passionate drive. I saw him Saturday night when I had to run out and get info from him. He handed a piece of paper to me but we both weren't looking at the paper, but in each other's eyes… then he came in later and whenever I glanced he was glancing too.. Now I'm thinking about it and thinking fuck, how can he be looking at me. What is he doing – he's not single! I feel like she doesn't like me and perhaps has questioned him about me even. There's a picture of him and her up at work and I always try to non-noticeably glance at it.

Apr. 29, 2003

I worked last night and guess who came in for dinner, the owners. I actually was going out for a doobie break and then I saw the hummer – so oops – no break now. So I served them dinner and gave top service of course. At one point his wife was down chatting with Eddie and I took up some table settings and we started talking. It seems like we do this whenever we think no one is really around. He asked me what other sports I play and that shows interest. Do you know how few guys actually ask me about myself? They usually don't care, only how I look. Then he said he almost died at twenty-one from a car accident (I gather). I'm always sure to walk away and look busy, but I could talk and talk to him. And I always feel his girlfriend's dislike for me, but she's smiling. Her insecurities are coming out. She really looks like she has trouble smiling at me, so I try to shoot her some love and that seems to help her relax. But her intuition is right. I am attracted to her man. I want to ask him what sports he plays. He is always trying to be loyal. He'll bring her name up (maybe to remind himself he's with her) and say nice things about her, like ____ played ball for years, she's really good (ok I'm the best girl ball player period). But I let them tell me about her ball career as a kid, meanwhile I play every year. But I wanted to talk to him, but can't because it's just not allowed. But we did look into each other's eyes a lot. And maybe I'm crazy, but I swear there's something there. Yeah, I'm crazy. I probably just want what I can't have. I was having weird dreams. I dreamt I was at work, sitting down with customers, and Dean walked in. I saw him so clearly and I was going to go see him like nothing was different, but the dream changed. He leaned in to talk into my ear because it was loud and asked what I was doing Valentine's Day, and kissed my cheek. Weird dreams eh. As for Bill, well who knows what happened there. It's me seriously though – it's me. I can't commit. Brooklyn says I just haven't found the right one yet.

Thursday, May 1, 2003 | 5:52pm

I don't know what's wrong with me! I went to Bill's last night and watched a movie. Then I went home because I was all stuffed up. I'm sure we should do something tonight but I haven't worked all week and its Thursday. I don't think he likes the internet, and just hasn't said anything yet. Also, I just want a guy who smokes green with me. I feel like I have to be perfect around him and I can't work enough online when I date someone. I feel too judged and guilty for not spending enough time with them.

May 3, 2003

It's Saturday and I need to call Bill. Tell him what's up. The problem is I don't know what that is. I'm just not ready to get into a serious relationship. I'm only looking for casual sex on the down low because I think you're a bit too jealous for the long-term troubles. I can also feel myself not being myself… I guess I'll try a little bit longer with him. No chatters even online. I have never been able to balance the whole online work with a boyfriend. Maybe it's me or maybe it's them. I get to have very real conversations with the men online, and when I try to be real with any boyfriend it's like, no you can't talk like that. You are supposed to talk about make-up and puppies and weddings. I am so used to being single and doing whatever I want every day it's hard to be in a relationship and feel like someone wants me to change and become a perfect little housewife. I should just sign out and clean and phone Suzanne. And bake a cake.

Thursday, May 8, 2003 | **4:32pm**

I've been a busy, busy girl. Too, too much on the go. It's busy online now. I'm looking heavier in the face n' boobies so I'm looking good these days. I've been doing cash in the mornings. Lillian and I are going to hang out and go to her dad's and discuss her sister's wedding. I want to go to the gym with her but I also want to go roller blading… its fun chatting online with folks from around the world…

9:39pm

I'm getting ready to go to Bill's house in a hurry. He was late in Duncan anyways at his Aunts birthday. I was at Lillian's Dads house. Having drinks and talking about the wedding. It will be nice to stay with Bill tonight. I miss my dogs when I go. Lillian and I went to Dean's grave today. It was easier this time, but we had been drinking and smoking so life was good. But it's hard. I miss them both.

Friday, May 9, 2003 | **2:45pm**

What a day from hell today has been. It started last night close to midnight. I got a migraine at Bill's. And I felt weird at Bill's because when I got there he was tired and we just went to bed. I was like, no sex? It was pain until I fell asleep and didn't really wake up till morning. In the morning Bill said thanks for coming over and sleeping with me, but I just felt weird and left. Then on my way to World I got another migraine and had to go home. It was a bad one, killer… just killer. I have a doctor apt at 3:20 today. Then at work my boss Lynn told me about a pay cut. Say what? The look on my face must have been like 'what the fuck?' Are you serious? As if I didn't get paid little enough! Now it's just $10/hr! So that's not even worth my day! By the time I get there and then go to the bank, it's such a pain in the ass for $20 minus taxes. Fuck you bitch! I'd love to tell her I don't want it anymore because it's not worth my time… too little pay for this girl. But I can't because my insurance isn't over yet and I have to think about my moves more carefully. Soon, soon I will tell her to keep her job and the twenty dollars pay and I'll work online instead, and do anything I want with my weekends. Soon enough I'll get all my days back. Waitressing at the World is costing me money, not to mention the drinking! The party lifestyle, the measly pay, late nights, bad bosses, and crummy people drinking and being rude. More cons than pros.

6:55pm

I'm in my room and have made zero dollars online, but I've been watching TV with my dogs. I've been doing a lot of thinking and I want to make my life happy. That's easier said than done. But I've been drinking too much, smoking too much, eating bad, and being too busy. Taking my health for granted. I need to like my life enough to only smoke once a day. Get baked once rather than all day long. Lillian just stopped by and dropped off my purse. She thinks the weekend cash isn't worth my time either! That job isn't worth my time or energy. I don't know why it's taken me so long to realize it. I need to settle my claim and retreat to the country!!

Saturday, May 10, 2003 | 9:15am

I went to work and on my way I got a migraine attack. I took two Advil and checked the time on my cell phone. Fifteen minutes later I was at work with the noise and lights. When I first got there Scooter told me that everyone thought one of the cooks got fired for sexually assaulting me. Oh my God! No, he just stole money from the ATM! I went upstairs to the office and I took a magic $10 pill for migraines. It started to relieve the pressure fast and I started to read the pamphlet. Then I got nervous because it looked like a potent pill. So I told the DJ what was going on and he agreed I should go home. I went home with a migraine and I bet the rumors are flying now that I was too upset to work. LOL. It's so funny because it's completely not true. Anyways those pills I took were good. They took the migraine away, and after a bit, even the slight headache I had was gone too. They also got me very high. I won't try to leave the house on those pills. I won't work or drive on them after how dopey I was last night. I was high. Now I'm scared I'll get up and get another headache like in the last few days. I only have one magic pill left. I'm going to go back to the doctors and get a prescription for them, because Tylenol and Advil don't work.

Saturday, May 10, 2003 | **10:20pm**

Day from Hell #2. Today I told the mean office lady that I didn't want to do cash anymore. It wasn't worth my time and extra headache – literally. Then I got a migraine on my way in to Grandma's to meet Jacquie. And it was a very bad one. I was in tears and pain, and was moaning. The Advil didn't work so I took my magic pill. Finally over time it slowly released the pressure. Jacquie had to drive me home and I was going to be fine until I heard Dad had Chip on a walk. I knew he couldn't be trusted. Sure enough, he came home without Chip! He left him to die saying to Brooklyn, "one less dog to worry about", "he's lucky I didn't find him, I would have rung his neck", and "he ruined enough of my day, I've put in my time looking". Of course that got me fired up! It's bad enough he's a bad father and partner, but now a dog killer. He left Chip, not caring if the dog made it home. Belle and Jordan took off on bikes, Brooklyn and I on foot, and Rant on the 50. We looked everywhere, calling and calling, and whistling for him. I was so scared that he was a goner. I was very upset. Dad didn't help look of course. So after an hour or so we wound up back at the start of the trail. I needed pants, cell phone, and a flashlight (it was going to get dark). Brooklyn and I ended up where Belle and Jordan were so we all went home. Then Chip followed us two minutes later. We think he heard us and followed our tracks out. So thank God Chip is ok. I got home before I heard the news that Chip was back, and I laid into Dad again. "How could you be so heartless to leave a little dog out there to die"? Then I was in the middle of saying "he'll probably die out there" and Chip, Jordan, and Belle walked in. Oh Chippy! I was so happy to see him. Then I said to Dad as he sneered at us all, "you're just mad because we love the dogs more than you". I looked him in the eyes with a matter of fact look. I was so mad I couldn't think of anything civil to say. It's bad enough he's good for nothing. Does he have to ruin our lives too? Can't he just grow up? Why am I more mature than my father? I just don't know what to do with him anymore. Everyone is so scared to say what an asshole he is because he's so "depressed" and "a lonely old man" and "he's really doing bad". FUCK. The man's been there my whole life. Yes he needs help. I think he's definitely psycho. What sane father would try to harm his daughter's beloved pet, a five and a half pound cute puppy? Chip was running from him because he's an asshole, not because Chip's a bad dog. I bet my father would have killed Chip if he got him. He loses his temper and doesn't think. He's killed so many dogs over the years. I don't know where he gets off living so ignorantly. The man is crazy in some degree, I swear! So I get home close to eight and call Bill. To make a long story short there, he didn't want to come over because he was tired. And it just pissed me off. I had a really bad day and I wanted to tell someone about it. I want someone to hold me but where are all the men now. They love me when I'm dressed up and have make-up on, but no makeup, grumpy Betty, stay the fuck away man. Now who is listening to my day? Who is comforting me, my diary is that's who. Who knows, maybe one day someone will read this and they will feel for me. I'll sleep on it and feel better in morning I hope.

Tuesday, May 13, 2003

I've had migraines every day. I've taken six zomigs including one today. I went to the chiropractors today ($40), acupuncture is tomorrow ($60), and then I have the chiropractor again (Thurs, Tues, Thurs). I go back to the doctor on Friday. I've taken tons of Advil trying to keep the headaches at bay. It's been hell I tell you. My whole life has been put on hold for these things. It's depressing when you don't have enough energy in the day. I'm lying on my bed now zomig'd up, lying on neck balls to keep my neck straight. I can't go to the gym with this medication. My life is on hold. I'd love to go to the gym for a light workout. I actually miss the gym. I don't think I could even write music on these pills. I'm just scattered brain.

Friday, May 16, 2003 | 5:15pm

What a busy day I've had. I went to the World to do cash and then hurried home for an online appointment with subbie039. A true slave! He has spent a lot and only wants abuse in return. He doesn't think he deserves to see my naked body so I am always dressed in black leather lingerie and a strap-on cock mostly. I don't think I look overly hot with a strap-on but I guess it really does the trick for some men. Some men want to be fucked up the ass but they want a woman to do it so they don't feel gay. It's easy for me to do the fucking motion and tell them to "take it bitch, take it and like it". The dominatrix work brings out a different side of me that is very tough and mean. I like to call them little bitches and tell them to jump up and down on the chair with that vibe up their butt. They love my abuse and name calling. It's all very amusing and surreal. Then I had to fly to the doctors to discuss my migraines with him. I came home, cleaned, ate, and edited a bit. Now I'm in the bath. I have some editing with Brooklyn tonight at 6pm, and Suzanne's parent's 25th wedding anniversary party is tonight starting now, but I'm sure I will go late. I'd love to have some drinks tonight. I haven't taken a zomig since yesterday at 12:45pm. Lillian's sister's stagette is Saturday night. I don't have the cash for it all. I don't get money until Tuesdays internet check. Sadly Mr. X has moved out of town. Who knows when or if I'll see him again? I'd like to meet him again. But I'll leave it up to the movie Gods.

Tuesday, May 20, 2003

I'm in the bath tub. I made it too cold so straight hot is on now. And tonight the hot is working – yeah. I played ball tonight. We won both games. I can't wait to play the 'Sinkers n' Drinkers' (old Barley team). They're the team to beat right now. I like being the best. Bill went to Fun Island with me on Sunday night. Suzanne, Buck, Tim, Melissa and Buck's brother went too. It was so much fun. I didn't drink too much because I didn't want to overdo it. Today when the stress of life came back I got a migraine, sadly. I had to take a zomig but I'm getting better at functioning on them. In the Louise Hays book it's (migraines) from feeling bad about your sexuality and one should masturbate more. I guess that makes sense with my work and me feeling like less of a girlfriend if I use toys online. I've gone out with some guys who think of it like I do (like Marty) and some who just can't handle it (like fucking Rambo). I'm trying not to paint Bill with the same brush as the others though. Let him say something wrong or do something wrong before leaving. Maybe he's not so bad. I know these migraines are a physical injury from that car accident. If only I could live a normal life again, like I did before the crash. I've been crazy since then. All my weed smoking started then, and I couldn't do school. The head injury changed me for life. I used to be something… now I can't concentrate.

Thursday, May 22, 2003

Lillian's sister's wedding is today. The wedding should be fun, providing it doesn't rain. Cross our fingers. Bill got a new bike yesterday so he's going to be busy again. This is a good thing. I like my men always on the go. He's going to come to the reception after work, although he didn't look like he wanted to. I'm old enough to ask things of my boys. Lillian's Dad wants to meet him and I'm sure he'll like him. All my friends seem to like him. And I like him too. This bath feels so good. I could go back to bed, but no time for that. I have so many things on the go. The plumbing video is on my mind, and now that Rant is off speed maybe we can get our life back. It would be so nice to have our studio back, we were doing so well. Rant seems to be doing better. A lot of this town is on speed. It's cheap and it gets you high, but worst of all the drug begins to own you and make you believe the paranoid illusions. Apparently Rant's uncle Pedro is close to suicide, hooked on speed still. I've heard Mindy's sister Emily is into it, the list goes on. That's the drug to try right now, not that I will. I'll stick to my BC Bud ~ thank you very much. I'll only ever do mushies, alcohol, and weed. No more chemicals! My body has enough toxins from my E days. I wish Brooklyn's computer editing would work by the wedding video. I can't keep going into debt! Having to take so much time off for migraines has really put me behind. My main goal though is music. To quote Eminem, "Music is the only mother fucking option, failures not…"

Friday, May 23, 2003 | 7:15pm

I've had a bad day because I've been thinking about last night. We had a great wedding with a good party after. Bill was great with all Lillian's family and Lillian's Dad liked him. I had a few drinks and so Bill had to drive me to his house (we left my truck). On the way to Bill's I said, "I don't have any condoms so you'll have to stop at Mohawk". I didn't have any money, it was midnight, and I'd been drinking so I wasn't going to go in and buy condoms (mainly because I had no money). He wanted me to go in so I said, "I'm not going in. You go get them, you're the man", but what kind of man would ask a lady to buy condoms at midnight from a gas station? I just basically said I'm not going in there so you may as well go home and he did. He didn't get condoms! He drove home and I went to bed right away. I barely slept through the night and I was mad. I feel disrespected.

Why am I not worth the condoms? We've been dating six weeks and he hasn't bought condoms. That's no man. I'll tell you that I don't find that appealing. I've brought how many condoms to his stinking house. Fuck him. I just don't like being treated like some whore sent to do the dirty deed of buying condoms. Now maybe he didn't have his wallet, but why would you leave home without it? I think he was trying to control me (command me) and not do what I said, but rather break me and win by driving home. Well you win buddy. You get the prize behind door #1. Oh wait, better luck next time. Game over. Betty don't play dat. What kind of man doesn't buy condoms in six weeks? We've barely had sex and the last time we did he finished first then went to sleep saying, "I owe you one". Ok, um, I'm twenty-four not one hundred and four, let's get serious. I can't be with someone who makes me feel like a horny pig because I'm horny. I mean sex is normal. He should want to have sex with me. And not buying condoms – ugh. The more I think of our sex life, the more I want to end it. I mean I'm good, I'm the best even, but you're only as good as your partner. I guess I didn't feel comfortable saying I'm broke and I can't afford condoms because I feel he's judging like all snakes (Rambo, Clint, Bill) They're all the same those fuckers!

Thursday, May 29, 2003

It's been a busy day. I've worked on the wedding video, went to the gym, worked online, and now I'm contemplating on either more wedding video or cleaning my room, so of course I decided to write in my diary instead. I've been thinking a lot about Bill and trying to figure it out. I guess it's natural to be scared of being alone, scared Mr. Right is the one I think is wrong and I'm making a huge mistake. But I don't believe my head. I believe my heart

May 30, 2003 | **1:07am**

I'm home and what a long day and night I've had. I went to Mindy's b-day and at I first didn't know what to do about Bill. So I didn't break up with him. And while I was there, Marty was there and I just didn't want Bill there. Him, Dick, and another friend were going to stop by and I didn't feel like going through it, so when he called my cell I didn't answer (sad I know), but I didn't want to spend the night with him. He sounded like he had been drinking and was in a mood because I was being a bitch all week and then on the night we were supposed to have a good night together Cindy's party happens. Cindy made me stay and drink, and at 10pm I was going to get a ride home (or to Bill's even) with Belle, but Cindy and Suzanne made me stay. And so I tried to drink but my stomach was upset from worry. Cindy, Suzanne, and I were on the deck talking and they were saying that I always put off breaking up with guys. Belle said that too. I guess I could be wrong but my relationships don't last more than a month and a half… I'd say I'm quick to break up. In fact Suzanne drove me home and I broke up with Bill. I hate being a bitch. Joy's my middle name for Pete's sake. I just want to enjoy life or 'Anne Joy' life. I just want my life back, my busy social life back. I'm Hollywood and lately I've been lame sick Betty and I swear my body reacts to the men. I can't eat, I get migraines, and I don't see friends enough. It's a sign. I haven't seen Mr. X in probably a month. I wonder if he thinks of me. I wonder when our paths will cross again. I think I might go to Cityville with Min-dawn tomorrow for the night and then I can look for an agent like planned. I want to audition for commercials.

Saturday, May 31, 2003 | **12:19pm**

I'm exporting the wedding. Yeah. I'm single again too. Does everyone have as much trouble as me at dating? Or am I just really bad at it? Oh well, I'm getting a lot done. Bill said some hurtful things but I've heard worse. I think that as soon as you know it's not the one you should move on right then. And I think Bill had the same mean streak in him as Clint. That fuck you I'm a little man syndrome. And that won't due. I'm sure he looked down on the internet too because he said I would never do that and had a funny look when I talked about work. But I can tell other people about the internet and still feel good about myself. More mature people see it like me, it's harmless. I hope Lillian's sister likes the video. I'm almost going to watch it and record it to VHS. It's one last watch for errors. I can turn up the first song a bit because I can't hear it when Lillian's in cooler. I can turn up that laugh when her Dad's talking on porch before the ceremony. The ceremony is boring, especially after watching it ten times. I couldn't get a good shot at the ceremony so it's a bit painful to watch me move around. It looks better on the big TV vs. the iMac. Oh shit, I need music to start sooner after the ceremony.

CHAPTER EIGHT

Wednesday, June 4, 2003 | **1:50pm**

I'm in my room puffing a puffer and working online. I'm hoping to get money and a viewer ASAP so I can go out on Suzanne's boat with her when she's off work from the Horse at 4pm. So puff, puff and pray for money. I went up to Pintnay yesterday with Jacquie. I wanted to switch that poem I wrote for the old one I put up that was too personal for public. So we finally found the place and my old one was smashed and on the ground and I can't help but suspect foul play. I had it taped up really well and it had nothing to smash on (just soft broom brush). Jacquie says don't think like that, the wind and snow got it. I say foul play. Oh well, the new one is up, like I wanted. That's one less thing on my list of things to do. I think I might just throw out the old picture because it's so dirty and now it's just ugly and all smashed. I don't need to carry that around with me. I have a copy of what I wrote somewhere. That will have to do, especially because the old one is so weathered all you can see is the faded pictures I put in. Somehow life goes on, days go by, and time keeps ticking away. Here I am twenty-four, living at home, and still dating Mr. Wrongs. For a long time I was hoping to magically get happy and get all my dreams. But the truth is, it takes effort, a lot of effort. I should go to the gym but I need to make money online. There really aren't enough hours in the day to do it all. I worked on Monday night and a couple of my co-workers wanted me to go out. We went had a couple of drinks and my cousin Braiden's killer was there. I'm putting it all together. I don't want to write names but I know so much about him and he knows nothing of me, or so I hope. I just play it dumb around them but I'm all ears. I know the killer doesn't even like going out because "he thinks it's heaty" because they move a lot of blow and why be seen? The killer lives next to Mindy's mom now. I have to shake his hand and keep my mouth shut. He has no interest in me, not knowing that I will be his undoing. His partner who he owns a bike shop with wants to take me out to dinner to talk because his life's a mess and he's going through divorce, and I just think I'm getting in way over my head and it's not worth it. It would take too long to find anything out and I don't want to get close to anyone. I hate being close to people and have them enter my life, and these people are proven to be bad. They need to grow up and stop killing people, and I'm sure they beat people up too. The whole bar industry is just bad. I'm tired of it. Its fun, and a lot of fun at that, but dangerous. It's a party scene all the time. Even Monday nights. But it's good to socialize. I wish I could get Brooklyn out more. Rant came home from work today. Why? Because "Brooklyn was giving him a hard time" – lies Rant lies. She thinks he's on speed again. What a looser. She has tried everything. He won't help himself and admit he needs professional help and she's letting him destroy her. It's killing her. She says he's looking bad in the face again. I don't know how to help. Or if I even can. What can I do? It's her battle. I've given her advice for years and this time it's up to her. I give up on telling her 'he won't change'! So I say nothing and watch.

Friday, June 6, 2003 | 2:57pm

I'm in my room, working online. I work tonight at 7pm – close. I'm feeling guilty because I should have gone to the gym this morning. I should still go today. I did work out a little in the garage while Molly, Chip, Jose, Kandy, and Elliot all watched me. I could have met up with Suzanne and Maryanne at the river, but I stayed home with my dogs instead, washed dishes, did laundry, and am working online till tonight's shift. My mom is making Dana's chicken salad for dinner, yum. With some good luck I'll make some coin now and tonight. Because I want to have a lot of fun this summer, and that takes cash. Everyone wants to party all summer because there's no school. I'm sitting in my room, listening to music, smoking, and waiting for slave to use and abuse, and writing about my life. It's good to write. I always understand myself and any situation when I'm forced to actually explain my feelings and write out what happened. I wonder what to wear to work tonight? I'd like to wear a skirt, but I don't have any cute skirts that aren't jean. I need money to go shopping too. Basically the hotter I look the more money I make (at both my jobs). Hmmm, what look should I do tonight? OK, I think hair pinned up and country bumpkin look… sweet and good for tips.

Thursday, June 12, 2003

Last night was fun but I got way too drunk. We started drinking at Melissa's and then ate at the Barley. Then we went over to Suzanne's house for more drinks. All of the sudden I was too drunk. So Tiffany, Tim, and I got a ride to my house with Lillian. Tiffany had to work in the morning and Tim wanted to see "Spring 2003". After I got sick in the bathroom and put on jammies, I watched the movie with Tim. Next thing I know, he's all over me. And he has a girlfriend! His girlfriend has only been gone a week. I just don't know what to think of all this. I mean I've been with D.J. and Ben. I couldn't go out with Tim. And he has a girlfriend. I can't be "another woman". What was he thinking? I stopped him right away and told him to go to bed. We didn't say anything and I dropped him at his car later, but Brooklyn was with me so what could be said. Then today I was on my way to the gym with Jacquie and Tim phoned and asked if we could talk. I said ok and he's going call me when he's off work at 11pm. Part of me thinks we should just talk on the phone. Today I was talking to Suzanne and she said how just last night Tim said that he was probably going to be the next to get married (with his girlfriend next summer). So he says that and then kisses me. I don't even want to deal with this. I think that Tim I are good friends but one, I don't want a boyfriend, and two; he has a girlfriend "he wants to marry". I wish that none of this was happening.

Friday, June 13, 2003 | **7:49pm**

I'm in my room working online and I have a sick dog. Kandy has been puking. Last night I was going to meet up with Tim, but I just wanted to stay home. So I "missed" his call. I called him this morning and we talked. And I told him I never want anyone to know because I don't want to be seen as like that. But as a friend he should look at that. He owes it to himself and to her. He made it sound like he was so drunk that he barely remembers. Yeah right!! It was all him. I was the one who stopped it, not him. He's obviously thought about it before. Suzanne brought me pictures and there's one of us all at the Barley and he has his arm is around me, and it makes me think it was premeditated. But he said he'd never confess to anyone and he was going to her parents to baby-sit her little brother. And she's a good girl and he still wants to be with her. Viewer… $43.36. So anyways I handled it cool, but I can't help but feel a bit used by Tim. He's just a cheater staying with her! But on a good note I went to see an agent that lives in Hemlock but is hugely qualified. So there are some classes I can take and I can go audition in Cityville for commercials. So I'm really happy about it. She seems very dedicated to her people. I'm going to go back into acting and still sing and get this life started. I'm ready to act, I'm ready to sing, and on this lucky Friday the 13th I learned that all men are more interested in my body, so I may as well market myself and make some money. I'm ready to go into the world. I can't be an online porn dominatrix forever can? I have learned so much from this line of work and I'm good at it, one of the best for sure. But I'm bored with this town and all the same people. All the same bullshit that has been here since I left college. This was a phase in my life, the burn out porn phase, but I'm ready to act. I'm ready to work hard and make money. I just can't stand being me in this town any more. I'm ready for a change.

Saturday, June 14, 2003

I'm in the bath right now. I've been doing some thinking today. Well I did get two-three ladies massaging me today being aunty Dee's guinea pig for aromatherapy advanced. It was heaven! I took the long way home and was thinking about the whole Tim thing. I feel played by my own friend. If he wasn't serious about leaving her for me, why go there, why risk our friendship? Why play me like that? I'm no one night stand whore, and that's why I, yes I, stopped the whole thing. Then he says he was drunk and didn't mean it. This has really upset me. Now I have no guy friends, just a bunch of guys that want to sleep with me. I hate feeling like Tim's dirty secret. That fucker. I think I have the right to be mad. He totally one hundred percent did it all, even though I had already puked and was hammered. But I stopped it and he "was drunk". No, he was horny and all over me actually. I had to wake up to him groping me. Yeah I'm mad. He used me and I'm really mad because he's not being honest now. I'm tired of all these pigs trying to get with me. I don't think I'll ever be able to see Tim the same way. He used me and that's no friend. This life is fucked. What the hell will happen next? I'm going to see if I can get Monday off work for acting. That would be fun. I'm nervous about it because it's been a while since I've done improve., but I'm sure I'll get into it and have fun. More fun than dating boys that's for sure.

Sunday, Jun 15, 2003

I'm in my room, working online. I want my career and that means putting all my extra time, money, and energy into it. I wanted to go to Fun Island today but I only have enough money for acting tomorrow night and some gas in my truck. No mudslides tonight. I'll see if Jacquie wants to go either roller-blading tonight or for a walk/jog down cable bay. But no money spending. I don't know how busy work will be, being Fathers day and all. Most of the pig men are with their families pretending they're not pigs. But they are! They all are, even Tim. I'm tired of being like this. Everyone wants to fuck me but not be my boyfriend. Oh well, screw them all, I'll stick to myself. Make my money, write my music, do my acting, work, gym, career, work, gym, career. No time for booze and parties. I need to get serious about getting out of home and getting a life of my own. I'm ready to grow up and move on. I've lived off mom long enough. I'm twenty-four and a half! I had lots of motivation after college. What happened? Where did the years go?

Monday, June 16, 2003

I must clean my room today. It's a mess. Our washing machine is still broken and the clothes are piling up. I have improv tonight from 6 – 8pm. I guess I'd better sign in online, clean my room, work all day until acting tonight. It's funny how I have just the right amount of money to go to acting, not a dollar more or less. I made the amount Saturday plus twenty dollars for gas after a twenty-five dollar tip out. I actually made seventy-two dollars. I got a few five dollar tips. Now Brooklyn wants to go return the camera to the store because it won't work. I wanted to try putting a tape in it first. See if it was safety feature where it turns black instead of on if there's no tape in it? So she wants to return the cam and start editing for money! Well halleluiah! Finally she wants to do the business again. Rant is doing work on his boat and truck with Tyson and another friend.

No Such Thing As Secrets

11:15pm

Acting class went great. I had a lot of fun and the other actors were great. I didn't want to be ripped so didn't smoke any after I got back from town with Brooklyn. I was nervous about the night, but I went there and I think I did well. I think I impressed them and gained some respect. And they were a fun group. It's always a bit weird meeting a new group. I think already I felt a connection. So class ended and they already had scripts and she photocopied one for me for next class to do on camera. I'm nervous but ready. Then at eleven I had to pee and take the dogs for a pee. So I was downstairs, I made tea, the dogs were out and about, and I sat on the hood of moms car for a bit and I thought, I don't need to smoke pot to sit out here and enjoy the fresh air. I came upstairs with a new tea, changed into my phi's, and said oh let's give it (the script) a read. I began to read the first line out loud. It's a medical examiner sparking and it says "Caucasian male around 15 years of age kill__". I froze. I could read it but not say the words. I can't believe out of all the scripts in the world I get this. I whisper the words and get tears in my eyes. "Killed in a car accident…" I put it down. So I grab my diary and start writing. I have a few puffs and slowly relax. Then I read further. "This boy broke a lot of bones, mostly in his face, hands, and torso." I threw it down and said, "You must do this, you are an actor, its acting, the ultimate test". I think of Wonder`s coffin as I read more of the script. I picture his wood coffin, lid open, him in it. I write in my diary, puff the roach, watch TV, and stare at the script. I'm glad I got a copy of it now so I didn't get surprised next week. I got to deal with it now and move on. I have a week to prepare as if it's an audition. I'll beat it. I just read it once through like a medical examiner. It's not so hard, just like any other script. I guess this is the next part of my life. I can see that I'll audition more and more until I get parts. Today was special, it's a new start. It's going to work. Now I wish for energy. I wish for more than enough energy to work and do these classes and work more to afford it. Partly less and less so I can look better for my new agent. I just want to act for a living. I want to sing and write music and make movies. And even direct one day. That's what I want most in the world as my career. I want to be a star to entertain and bring joy to the world, but first it starts with acting class. I learned a lot tonight and look forward to more. I'm proud of myself, it was a hell day but I did it. Even if I was in bed and didn't eat all day. I went full of energy and I spent my money on the right thing.

Friday, June 20, 2003

Tuesday night was ball and I think I'm getting a little crush on Bernie. He's the short-stop. I like a man that can play good ball. But I actually keep thinking of Mr.X. People mention his name from time to time and I wonder if he thinks about me. Tonight Zarren called to hang out with the grocery country gang, Jacquie being one of them. Zarren's been going through a bit of a crisis breaking up with his girlfriend and moving in with Zeus and Melissa. So that will be fun, hanging out with Tate, Zarren, and Jacquie. I'm supposed to go to Capsville on Tuesday for an extra shoot with Brooklyn and Belle. It will be fun to do together. I'll call her tomorrow and I can ask her more about it then. Monday night I have acting 6-9. I have to see my lawyer beforehand and afterwards it's Tim's birthday. Capsville is Tuesday and I have ball Tuesday night (which I'll be late for). Busy as a bee, or social butterfly, but I'm happy. I feel like acting is the right path. It's been smooth so far. I like my agent; I think she'll get me places. She is full of energy. She was just in the paper for helping one of her students on a film with a famous actress in NY. She can tell me where to go next, each step. I feel like I'm going in the right direction and I laughed a lot at acting. I want to tell Mick about these classes, and other actors I know too. I want to get more comfortable with the group first though.

Tuesday, June 24, 2003

Stupid old Clint was in on Saturday. I said hi, yadda yadda. And he told me he might build near my sister Beatrice and that's where Mom and I might build! Wouldn't that be crazy! So we can see what each other does every day, what a joke! All three of us wouldn't build would we? I think he wants to be in my life more, but Beatrice thinks he is just after a good deal. Well neighbor or not, I don't have to be nice to him. I hate thinking about him. I'm sure he's probably still with his girlfriend. Still cheating on her and abusing her verbally and mentally. The man is sick. But at least I saw Bernie Saturday night to make up for it. I told Bernie I couldn't be at ball tonight because I had to go to Capsville. Brooklyn and I`s call time is 3:00, so we should be there early and bring a book. I told my agent last night that Belle wasn't going. She wasn't happy about the short notice. She wanted three sisters on the set. She thought it would have been cute. But now there are two sisters. And I wonder if someone will say, "Are you two twins?" Every day we get it.

Wednesday, July 2, 2003

Well I'm going to do my day without weed. I could just spend the day organizing my life. I still want to smoke weed today but I just can't afford to until later today. I need the house clean for this weekend. It's the annual industry slow pitch tournament. It's on Sunday and I'm guessing maybe someone or a few will want to go to my house at some point because the tourney is in Hemlock.

Sunday, July 6, 2003

Today was a big day for me. I was tested and I failed – Big Time. I was the coach for the World strip club I was the leader and I was way too competitive and hard on the team. I yelled way too much and I never want to coach again. No one likes to be yelled at, especially by me. I was a real jack ass. I would have had a better day and the whole team would have if I made it more fun. I was there leader and I yelled at them. I have failed as a leader. And I just looked like a loud mouth, cocky, arrogant prick. I could have been hot and nice but instead I was a good ball player that must lose it all the time. So who wants to play with me? No one does, especially me. I'm never going to embarrass myself like that again.

Saturday, July 12, 2003

Looks like the last entry for this diary. I've been spending a lot of time with Marty, of course Lillian doesn't know, and I always wonder what to do. I get along with him great. But I love Lillian and don't want to hurt her over someone whom I may not even marry. One day at a time.

July 20, 2003 | **12:22am**

Tonight was Melissa's wedding to Zeus. It was great but Tim got all drunk and decided to have a heart to heart with me. I told him "I'm not a talker" and I didn't want to talk. We walked over to Wonder's grave and when I said we should go to the other one they all didn't want to. Tim sat there crying and I thought I'm not crying in front of you all, so I did on the way home. Everyone's going to the bar but I came home to bed. I'm not going out with Tim and D.J. I don't particularly like either of them right now. We have this fake niceness for parties and there are all sorts of unsaid stuff, because I never talk. Really, I'm mad at Tim, he used me. He says he doesn't want me to hate him. I may be disappointed beyond repair, but I don't hate him. I need a new web site to work on. I need money. I need more acting and less negative World environment. Then out of public down town eye. Give me all I dream of now, for I am ready. Wherever this road will take me, I will not be afraid. I welcome all new life. I welcome happiness and pure joy. I welcome being proud of who I am and I welcome all the joy in the universe. I'm getting older and I'm seeing life differently. I don't need babies yet and I don't see any fathers in sight. All I see is dirty, sleazy men. I see too many guys sitting in gyno row, staring. They love pussy so much, is that all they think about?

July 20, 2003 | **5:00pm**

I didn't go to the gift opening. I just didn't feel like it. I was looking into other online sites to work for and signed up to a couple more. We'll see if either of them works out.

Friday, July 25, 2003

I really need money these days with my internet being tits up. Part of me just wants to let it die. I'll just waitress full time, as strenuous as it is. Brooklyn's finding out a lot at school. She's already planning out where we can take our resumes. We'll just keep at it. She says I have enough to become a PA now. You work really long hours (15hr days) but you make 70G/yr. Yeah, I don't believe it, or I will when I do my taxes for that year. But even half of that would be good. I do enjoy my serving, but sometimes I just wonder how much longer I'll still be serving tables, pouring drinks?

Saturday, July 26, 2003

Its bathtub weekend and the clubs are packed. I worked last night and then work day shift today. Then The Real Room tonight for the time. Hope I like it.

Could be too long of a drive. Sometimes I still hate my life. I hate my place in society. No money for all of my efforts. I can spend an hour and a half getting ready, then all the men hit on me and I'm only making twenty to thirty dollars after tip out. That is shit money.

Tuesday, July 29, 2003 | 12:20am

Sitting outside on the back writing in hopes I will sleep better, as I can't seem to right now. I watched Gangs of New York tonight with Belle and Marty. They both fell asleep and I watched it and thought of acting. The actors, me as an actor (the tear scenes were about death), and I could relate. I could use my death sadness and say the lines with more conviction. On Monday after acting class my agent told me she wants me out there auditioning. So I need my headshots done. She also said I was the most talented in the class and filled my ego on how good and natural I am. I was shocked to say the least. And she invited me to a party Saturday night that no one else is invited to. So I'll go audition. I can't wait to get out there. You really never know. Any audition could be the lucky one.

Thursday, July 31, 2003 | 10:25am

I need my pictures done for my portfolio ASAP. So I had to die my hair, wax my brows, etc. I think the blonde hair, along with my ratty split ends cut off makes my look younger. I say seventeen, but Belle says nineteen. Not bad for twenty-four and a half. In fact I bet my body is in better shape now then it was at seventeen. I'm going to wear something hot to work tonight, to match my hot new hairdo. Dad hasn't lived with anyone in a few years. This will be weird. They keep fighting over the littlest amount of money. They shouldn't have gotten married. They bring out the worst in each other. They can both be so wonderful for very different ways, but I now see how evil and nasty divorce gets. People change. They now fight over who has to help me, lend me money. They both should want to, not try to pawn me off. Right now my mom is winning by a landslide. She will get the nice condo in Hawaii and Dad gets "Helga" the nurse in his old age home. No, I would never do that. I may joke all the time to him that that's where he's going but I never would. Marty stayed the night last night. He's at work now, working at a grocery store downtown. I work at the Real

Room with Kip who lives upstairs to Lillian. It's a matter of time before she finds out about Marty!

Tuesday, Aug. 5, 2003

We had our slow pitch finals on Saturday and we won. It was double knockout. We lost our first game but then won three and took the title. The last game was 13 – 11 in the 9th. I have a huge bruise on my inner thigh from an over throw that hit me running home. Suzanne is on the phone. Brooklyn went fishing at the same spot as a big derby and she caught the biggest fish, but she didn't enter the derby so she didn't win the $5000.00! She's back in school today. Lillian just called. We're going to go to the gym. Marty's basketball finals are tonight and I want to go. I wish Lillian could go with me… like that would happen. Maybe I'll talk to her today about it. It's a tough situation. Brooklyn and Rant are another weird situation. Brooklyn found speed again in his wallet. He says he "hasn't done it in six weeks". I say maybe six hours. I just don't like the whole situation there. And what kind of life is that for a family? A drug addict Dad, who doesn't work and provide for his family. He lets his wife do everything, he yells, and has harsh mood swings; from Mr. Can I make you a tea, to Mr. Fuckhead getting physical with her. I don't feel sorry for him. He's ruining my sister's life, and worse, I fear he'll never change. I can't ever spend time alone with her. So I don't even know what she's thinking. He's very good at isolating her from us, and he is such a manipulator. He needs to get a job and provide for them, like Tyson does for Beatrice. He doesn't help her, he holds her back and he lives the life he wants, which is getting high on speed like a fuck up! How on earth can she be attracted to him, so skinny and weasley? Just like his uncles, he treats poor Brooklyn about the same as they treated women.

Sunday, Aug. 10, 2003

I'm going to go blueberry picking with my mom. She won't let me smoke (even though I said let's take my truck) on the way there. She said you can't have a couple shots before we go. So of course I got the drug lecture too. But only because she sees me as "so much more than a pot head". She has her sun visor on and is ready to go picking. Brooklyn was going to go with me but chickened out. She stays at home most of the time.

Wednesday, Aug. 13, 2003

Jordan and Annie are bugging me to go to ball. No adults ever want to watch me play. Nothing has changed when it comes to my family. They never want to watch me play ball. I play on a good team and I'm always one of the best players. Less and less I care about things like that though, and more and more I care deeper for my little family with my dogs. We are a very happy little family. We play together, snuggle and keep close all night and we miss each other when we're away. The kids mean more in my life all the time too. All summer they come over and talk my ear off and ask me to do anything, just take them anywhere; the store, the river, movies, or stay the night. Or if I see them at Brooklyn's they say can we go with you please. Just like all kids, bored at home on summer holidays. Fall ball starts tonight.

Thursday, Aug. 14, 2003

Last night's ball game sucked. Marty was being a jerk because he "had to ump" but I knew it was because I broke up with him. He couldn't handle me teasing him. He was throwing a fit and he said "fuck off Betty", and he threatened to "toss me on my head over the fence" I was sitting on. Fuck, way to ruin my ball game. Stupid men. I think all men and women hate each other because of our differences. Well I hope Marty and Bernie had a good time last night. I saw stupid Tim today. I had to meet Rant at a gas station that Tim works at. Tim showed up at the gas station for work. The other day I saw him and his girlfriend riding their bikes around Hemlock. I can never look her in the face. I don't want to see either of them ever again right now. I feel used and like that's no way to treat a friend.

Sunday, Aug. 17, 2003

I'm on the 10:15 ferry to Cityville to see Mindy and get my pictures. I can't wait to see them. I hope they turn out great, but I'm bracing myself for anything. It is ten dollars to get on the boat now. A rule of thumb is to not smoke weed until after you leave because they can't kick you off out in the water. So I'll wait until we take off. Weed is such a waste of money I should just quit. Learn to eat without it again. A real good diamond sea out there, the sun is so bright I should have brought my shorts. Oh well, I may have to go shopping. Maybe I could find some good deals. Mindy hates shopping. I sold a guy from ball one of the bags that Jason gave me on my way to Playsville last night. I don't like selling weed. It's a heat score waiting to happen. It's not where I want to put my energy.

Aug. 18, 2003

I spent the night at Mindy's and now I'm waiting for the bus again, back to the ferry, and back to Newsville life. The bus is taking a while. I chatted with a girl from Taiwan. She was very friendly and hopes to see me on the big screen one day. She's becoming an accountant so I said hopefully I'll need one of those and you can be my accountant. We laughed and she liked that idea. Her family is sending her to Philadelphia to school and she said accounting didn't even interest her. She likes Cityville and the entertainment. I looked through my pictures and picked out a few of my favorites. Now I need to buy a photo album to put the pictures in before I show people and they get finger prints all over them. I don't know who I will or won`t show. I don't want people to think of me as some beauty queen. And I don't want girls to think I'm some attention seeking girl showing off my "sexy" pictures to all the guys. That's what I like about the World. I fit in there. There are a lot of pretty girls who "do it up" and wear less than I do, and look really good. I don't feel guilty because it's not that I want to take home a bunch of guys, it's just who I am. I love to look good. It feels good and I want everyone to look and feel their best like I do. Today I'm not, but when I go to work it's my job to look good. Not just good, but one of the best in town. Or else you don't work there.

Aug. 21, 2003

I'm upset. I heard that Marty was spreading shit around the grocery store he works at, about me and the internet, until Zarren said "there'll be no talking about that". So yeah for Zarren and a 'fuck you asshole' to Marty. Why didn't I see it sooner? He's a womanizer and apparently he tries to get Zarren to watch video tapes of him and girls having sex. I hate him right now. He's so gross and he's doing coke with Bernie. And they smoke my weed for free. Fuckers, they need to leave me alone. I want to switch teams. I hate Marty that much. I'd rather play on Erin's team, and say fuck it, I don't care. I'd play with a different team where no one knows me and I don't know them, and we practice more and play better. Marty just pissed me off.

Wednesday, Aug. 27, 2003

It was all hell here on Sunday. I woke up to Annie crying that her mom had a bleeding mouth from her dad. I took the time to say does your dad do this to your mom? She sobbed, yes. I put on a proper t-shirt in case of a fight, I didn't want my pj's to unbutton, and I went down there ready to kill. I put Annie in my bed to watch cartoons and told her to stay there until I returned. I saw Jordan in the swamp and told him to get to my house and I stormed up to a pale Rant sitting on the deck. "What the fuck Rant", I asked? "I got to tell you my side, my story", he said. "Well it had better be a good fucking story because I don't like what I'm hearing". Then the little fuck started crying like a baby, oh woe is me, boo hoo. He had scratches all over his face and was claiming she beats him. I said," well she's never attacked me. What did you do?" I calmed down and I gave him advice, and said that the kids can't grow up with fighting like that because they'll think it's normal. We talked for a while, and then Brooklyn came in and started to tell the truth. She was mad and she let it all out. He told me one story and she said another. Of course I believe her. She called him a woman beater piece of shit. She said get the fuck out, I don't ever want to see you again. He had her up against the wall and when she went running away he leveled her. He denies it but Brooklyn has no reason to lie. Keep telling yourself that asshole. Then he went on the deck and she told me more. He slapped her so hard across her face that I could see four fingerprints. And he tackled her. Now she has a purple mark on her lip. I think it must be from a tooth. Her poor little crooked teeth. I asked if the slap happened before or after the tackle, she couldn't remember. I didn't want her going back to him so rather than party all night for the Real Room staff party, I stayed home. She and I went to get ice cream bars. We talked alone at last. Then she stayed at my house. Jordan, Brooklyn, and I slept in my bed. Jordan woke up crying. He's not taking this too well. He knows you're not supposed to hit girls and he knows his dad is wrong. Brooklyn had a field trip to Capsville the next day so I packed her a lunch and she stayed over. But then she went back to him Monday night because you guessed it, she's going to take it one day at a time. I got home from acting and I talked a bit of sense into her but she went home to him anyways. I said make him sleep in the travel trailer. I told her that something has got to change. You've got to do something different. Jordan was already down there and she went home to him. Annie wanted to stay with us so she slept with Belle. Then Rant came over to talk to me the next morning. He apologized for slamming the gate on me. He said he was trying to work it out with Brooklyn and I told him that he had crossed a line that I couldn't forgive. He then said well I guess you and I will always be enemies then. He started saying that I had no compassion and that I didn't know how to make a relationship last. Yeah maybe, or maybe I'll be happily married. It was a long fight. I said he was trying to draw on my insecurities but it wouldn't work. And anyways, we're supposed to be talking about the environment that is down there for your kids. You fight all the time and I don't think you should live there. I'd rather see the kids live here than down there with you guys fighting. Kids shouldn't have to live like that, it's wrong and I won't have it. My sister's a good person and she doesn't deserve to live in hell anymore. He said your right Betty, that's why I'm moving out… Well he never did move out and I hope she's not forgiving him. His abuse has gone too far.

Thursday, Aug. 28, 2003

Yesterday was a hard day for me. When you're in hell, you deal with it, but when you're out of hell in your safe zone, it all kind of hits you. I was at work and I wanted to talk about it all so badly and I couldn't. You can't talk about your sister's husband beating her, all you've done, and all he continues to do to her. He's nothing to me now. I guess I just see it for what it is, control, abuse, drugs, violence, name calling, etc. It's all fucked. He's fucked. Annie wants to live here and she wants her mom to leave. Her Dad hits her mom and name calls all the time, and she doesn't want to live there. How could I, as an adult, make her go home and pretend that nothing happened like Jordan and Brooklyn? She doesn't want to live there and do all the mountains of laundry while her Dad sleeps. If he's sleeping, he's using. I know it. I hate all the pain he's caused my loved ones. I really don't care if it kills him to go, better him than her. Annie sees it. I asked if he smacks her a lot and she said he jumped off the deck onto her when she was running away. I said I know about that one, but other times. And she said yes. Now sometimes kids say what you want to hear, but I asked a couple of different ways and the fact is that she's scared to go back down there, not even for underwear. She has seen enough of her Dad hitting her Mom and calling them all names. I think I have to do something. I think we need a meeting with Mom, Dana, Beatrice, Belle, Tiffany, Jacquie, and I'd like to hear what Dee has to say about it. Annie wants to jump in our bathing suits on the trampoline with water balloons and blow bubbles. I said yeah, I could use the tan, so I'm going to enjoy the sunshine with Annie while it's here.

Later that day

Of course I keep thinking of Mr.X. I see him once and I can't stop thinking of him. Rant has another appointment this morning all the sudden. Yeah right you speed freak, sure you have an appointment. So Jacquie will have the kids all day and night because Brooklyn's busy with a wedding tonight and I work all day. Funny how Brooklyn didn't talk to Jacquie about Rants "appointment" this morning, only the wedding stuff. So I conclude that he just wants to go do speed, like a fuck head. The shit Brooklyn puts up with, and denies seeing. Now she's getting hit and called a "cunt-cow" who does nothing. I hate Rant! He is such a fuck up. He only ruins the lives of people I love. He only thinks of himself like an addict does. And who cleans up his mess, finds babysitters, feeds and clothes his kids, consoles his wife? Me, and my family, that's who. It's affecting me. Last night at work I got there stressed to the max and the new boss calls me to the office to say the office cunt (bitch from hell) said I needed to put my name on my sheet and I basically started to cry. I said how she needs some people skills. She saw me do my cash out and there are greater tragedies in the world. I'm always doing favors for her and she is always mean. He agreed that she was over reacting because of all the other problems going on, and then he told me he understands. I want to have fun at work and he talked of how he lost custody of his kids and he couldn't bare it. He got misty eyed and buried himself in his work. But we had a good moment. He asked me what he could do to help me get over it so I could work. Actually, he's got great people skills.

Saturday, Aug. 30, 2003 | **7:38am**

Last night Zarren and Jacquie were over. Zarren and I had a great talk. But we were up until one talking about life and karma and stuff. Now I have a 9am ball game so I've got to get going.

Saturday, Sept. 6, 2003 | **9:00pm**

I have to work at 10:30 in Playsville. I worked five days in a row at the World and now tonight too. I've been doing cash too. It's hard working all week. I like day shifts though. Better than nights. I need money to live and to get ahead in life, and I need money to do all the fun things in life, so I work hard to get the money, no matter how tired I am. I work hard and party hard.

Sunday, Sept. 7, 2003

I wonder if when you're thinking of someone it means they're thinking of you too. My agent says there's an audition on Tuesday in Capsville. Do I want to go… um yes! I have acting class tomorrow night and on Saturday. So acting is taking off if I like it or not, and now that I settled my claim I have enough money to do it. It costs money. No wonder my parents jammed on me. It's expensive for lessons.

Friday, Sept. 12, 2003

I work, work, work. Oh well, the money is nice. I have to work day shift today. I don't mind day shift because it goes by real quick. I just bartend and another girl takes the floor and gives me the tiniest tip out. When that is me I split my tips with the bartender and make it fun for all. That's why everyone wants to work with me and no one else. I'm the fun one who tips big and smokes everyone up. I'm learning that life doesn't change, only your perception on it. It's up to you if you are happy watching the movie or sad.

Saturday, Sept. 13, 2003

Johnny Cash died yesterday. John Ritter died on the 11th. Time keeps going by and life keeps changing uncontrollably. The more I think about it, I think I want to teach snowboarding up the mountain. I would meet lots of people. I'd get out of this town where everyone knows me and talks about me. I would still go to my acting classes and still go to Real Room on Saturday night, but I'd probably leave the World. It would be a big change in life. But that wouldn't be until December. And I'm not totally sure… but I think I'd like spending the winter on the mountain teaching kids to snowboard and get paid. Sounds like a dream job. I can't resist it.

Sunday, Sept. 14, 2003

I met a boy last night. Of course he is young (twenty-one). He kept pestering me for my number and I thought, oh Betty, you never have any fun… so I gave him my cell number. I talked to him briefly last night and today and he'll call me back. He was too cute to resist. This is the first time that I ever gave my number out. Well, I must drive Annie home and wait for my phone call. I'm too tired to do much.

Wednesday, Sept. 17, 2003

Well now I remember why I never give my number out! That kid had a girlfriend, but at least he was honest and told me. But what an ass for conning my number out of me. Fuck you – you drunk! Fucking drunks! So horny and full of shit. Like tonight after ball Marty kept saying why aren't we together, you know how I feel about you, yadda, yadda. He wouldn't shut up! People were getting up from our table and moving away. Can you say drama queen? I can't even begin. He went off and I tried to be straight up with him and he was just so over the top, I wonder if he was high on coke? Well who knows and who cares. I only care about my life, my career. My acting career. The one thing going smoothly (knock on wood). I sent away for enlargements of my pictures, then I'll send away to get more of my favorites. I just wonder if I'll ever find the right man? Time goes by quicker when you're happily in love. Every single person longs for their perfect partner. Love is this huge part of our world but we don't even see it. Love is what brings joy to us. There are few things like it. Another gift is laughter. I appreciate a laugh so much more than I used to, because they're harder to come by.

Thursday, Sept. 18, 2003

I'm a little slow getting up today. I had a lot of fun, except for Marty going off and embarrassing me. I feel like phoning him and saying, "what do you want? I'm tired of you getting all territorial with me whenever you drink and we're out together. You embarrassed me and let's just get it all out now over the phone so this doesn't keep happening". That's twice he's done that now, ruined my night. How am I going to meet someone with him always looking like this big ex in my life? He needs to move on and just accept that we are friends. I'm going to phone him. I don't want to embarrass him but I need to tell him so it won't happen again. What do you say to someone? I told him last night he was being a bitch and he needed to calm down. I see right through him. He's such a liar. And he's not even a good friend, because friends don't talk behind each other's back like he did at his grocery store, etc. I think I might quit drinking, or quit drinking in excess. I talk too much, drive too often, and then the next day I think of way better ways of handling myself when I'm straight and sober. So why spend the money to look like an ass. Why not just sip, save money, and look better. The odd time at Fun Island I can get gooned, but I should cut back for sure. I need to concentrate and work hard on my acting career. Going to the gym and think about cutting down on weed for my appearance and overall health. I need to get a vehicle too, sell my truck. The more I think about it, the more I want to work up the mountain.

Saturday, Sept. 20, 2003

At class today (11-2) there's going to be a casting director from Cityville. My co-worker was helping me work on a scene last night. He's such a good friend of mine. Then I came home and worked on my Christmas crafts. After I'm done this diary I'm going to go over my lines again. And I have to put the golf video on VHS for a BBQ at Roland's house after class. This casting guy could be good though. He likes new talent apparently.

Monday, Sept. 22, 2003 | **11:00pm**

I was at Melissa and Zeus' house for Barron's welcome home dinner. It was a nice dinner. I had to see Tim and his girlfriend for the first time. It was weird. I totally don't feel good around her. I still don't know how Tim could do that to me. As I watch TV, I see all the roles people are getting paid for, it's all possible. The weeks keep going by and I'm still in Newsville, I'm still not famous, not out of here, but I'm getting closer. I keep going to class and I keep paying my money for pictures and everything else. It's a lot of money, but I don't see another way. I mean I've already written Dirk Manly, what more can I do, lol. I don't know, I just try to pay the bills and find a place to live now. Belle won't live with Dad alone, I'm going to sleep.

Tuesday, Sept. 23, 2003 | **7:00pm**

I'm in my room, enjoying my day off. I had to get Jacquie's car from Playsville with her, and then we went to the gym. Lillian is coming over tonight. That was just her on the phone now. She wants to get drunk with hot men, funny how I'm the mellow but single one. Last night in Playsville at the Real Room I sang three songs for karaoke. This guy paid for my drink tab and I didn't want him to. He has a huge crush and he's not at all my type. He's nice, but has no chance. He does way too much coke for one.

Wednesday, Sept. 24, 2003 | **10:40am**

I am waiting for Jacquie to come over. We're going for a run down Rope Bay. I work 2 – 6 and have ball tonight. Last night Lillian and I hung out. We went to her Dad's and watched a DVD of my acting pictures put to music. We did some Christmas crafts and then we went to Lillian and Wilky's house where we saw Wilky and his friend Trent Smalls. Trent is still looking good. Actually, I used to have a crush on him years ago so it was good to see him again. I feel crazy setting myself up for heart troubles. I hate dating men, but I can't stay away from them. There's a rush you get out of crushing on someone. I wonder if he'd like to go to the movies with me? I guess there's only one way to find out.

Saturday, Sept. 27, 2003

Trent came over Thursday night and I met him after ball on Friday night. I've known him for years. I read over an old entry and I didn't remember that I had given him my number and email and he never contacted me. But it also said he broke up with his ex of seven years, but now I know he went out with her for nine years, so that must have been why. Timing is everything I guess.

CHAPTER NINE

Monday, Sept. 29, 2003

Today Trent and I talked about some shit. He insinuated that he'd heard bad rumours about me, although he didn't tell me exactly what. I'm still upset because it made me look inside and realize how scared my brain is. My heart isn't, but my brain is. It's hard to explain. Anyways, he said, "I'm sure you've heard things about me", which I have, only from Lillian. No one has said that much, but I can imagine how many talk about me and the shit they say. We ate at Smithy's and I felt like crying because I felt uncomfortable about what was said. Then he said how he's heard good things about me too. I said "yeah" as I stared at the menu and fought the tears. It hurt, I was embarrassed, and we were in public so I couldn't even explain myself. I didn't know what to say, he didn't know what to say, I thought about excusing myself to collect my thoughts in the bathroom but I thought it would look like I was upset. And I hate people to see me upset. I don't like to cry in front of people. I'd much rather not talk about it. No need to talk about sad things. Anyways, then it came up about his ex and I asked how long ago were you with her? He said one month ago. What, one month ago? Holy Fuck! We've been hanging out for a week so that's only three weeks in between. He asked me if that scared me and I said well don't you want to be single? I told him I was a rebound and yeah it did scare me. Is there any way possible that this could ever work? I mean so what if he rejects me or calls me names or talks about me, it's not like the whole town doesn't talk now. Even my own so called friends talk about me. I have few people I trust, very few people I love, and I'm careful who I let in. And 1 month! I'm setting myself up for heartache I think…

Life is like a movie
Better than any author writes
You may see the life of a floozy
Or be born to fight those inner fights

You may be born pretty
Or you may even be shown ugly
You may see the movie in the city
Or be out in the country

But all of you are the same
In that you can't control the show
You can only try to keep sane
And roll with the punches as you go

It's a test to see how you behave
In even the hardest of times
See if you crumble and if you cave
Or make a margarita with your limes
(Betty Benson)

Tuesday, Sept. 30, 2003

Everything is going good so far with Trent. I like him. I'm very attracted to him, where as usually there is something that isn't perfect. He's very nice. I can tell if someone is an asshole or not and I don't think he is. He doesn't seem to judge me even though everyone talks shit about me and I'm always very cautious about that one. I am very aware of every comment that comes out and at the first sign of being judged I usually bolt. We're still getting to know each other and talking now. And it's been one week since I went over to Lillian's house and saw him. He's very sweet but he also seems to have quite low self esteem, but why?

Sunday, Oct. 5, 2003

I am sitting in the tub after a long day of four ball games. There were no subs, I slid and froze in shorts (my pants got dirty I had to play in shorts), and right now I'm resting large raspberry on my upper thigh. Our team got second, so that's good. The team that won, were the winners of the nationals last year! They're good. We beat a lot of good teams to get second. Now I need to relax. I still like Trent, which is odd for me. He's not too clingy like so many guys are, and he's always doing things with his friends. I should take a picture of this leg. It's puffy and a large section is red. There are various reds down to my thigh and shin. If I had sliding shorts like I was going buy… next year. I wonder where I'll be playing next year.

Wednesday, Oct. 8, 2003 | **4:00pm**

I have to go to Capsville tonight with Tiffany, Jacquie, and Belle. I wish I could say for pleasure, but its business. We're going to be extras in a much music thing. I'm not too sure yet what it's all about. I guess all of these shoots will be slightly different, yet the same. Now I've gotten sidetracked. I want to know my IQ, yes that may be shallow of me, but I'd really like to know. Because I've done some IQ tests, and scored high, so I emailed Mensa for them to send me a home test for ten dollars and they send you the results. Well that was fun, I found a free one. I got 148. Problem is – I don't know if that's good or not. Wow time is flying by. I should start getting ready soon. I had to go to the doctor yesterday because my leg was infected. She scrubbed it and bandaged it up, and even gave me a testis shot. What a bad doctor trip that was, but she was very nice. I would switch to her if I thought my doctor wouldn't mind.

Thursday, Oct. 9, 2003 | **6:20am**

Well that was freezing! Oh so cold. For the shoot we were at a Swollen Members concert. It was the same song over and over in between standing in the rain. It was cold, so we ended up jetting early because it was too long. It was 4:30am and we made a run for it. A girl from class booked it with us, so if I'm in trouble at least I have a partner in crime. We're going to say that some lady gave us permission, but no one did. Oh and Jack Peestly was in the movie. I used to have the hugest crush on him. He's just a guy who took his acting career seriously and got a big break on a big TV show, just like I could get my big break on some lucky audition. It shows that I'm doing OK if I saw Jack Peestly tonight. I'll keep going with acting and see how far I can go. I may even be good at it. I think after tonight, I've decided I don't want to do any more extra work. It's just not my thing, although I have a great amount of respect for those who do it. I need to be the actress on stage or the singer. I want to audition now. I want my agent to send me out already.

3:15pm

I'm in the tub now, soaking my leg. It gets it cleaner than having a shower. Tattoo tonight can't hurt more than this blasted leg. My mom said she would drive me, but I kind of want to smoke on the way there. Should I go with Brooklyn? Poor Brooklyn, what hell she lives in. Never knowing what love can be, only knowing her misery. I wonder if I should have made those girls stay longer last night? I worry about authority getting mad at me too much. Who cares, I wanted to leave. Well they all really wanted to leave and I used my brain to get us out. The rain delayed the whole shoot so much. We could end up not getting paid – but oh well. At least we got out of there early. I'm calling Suzanne. Maybe I'll catch a ride with her. I don't want to get out of my bath yet. It's nice to just sit in the water. They say that the spirits can communicate better through water. I don't know what Lillian's doing? I could go with her for my tattoo? You can buy some numbing cream or I could just take it like Belle did, brave little mouse. I feel like taking this bandage off, but I'm not allowed to for another day. I hope when I take it off, it's all better.

Friday, Oct. 10, 2003 | 1:50am

I think I missed Trent's call at 10:59. I was in between the Horse and the Barley, and because he doesn't have a phone and I can't call him so who knows where he is. My stupid phone makes it hard to know who calls and so I missed his one call. I'm near my phone 100% of the time and there's no number to call back. I just have one chance to get the call or talk to him the next day. I can feel the power of my unicorn tatty already. I take no shit, I'm strong, and I'm happy. Yes I've been drinking, but I'm happy. I missed Trent's call and I'm still ok, usually I trip out over anything, but not now. I wished it all away in my tatty, all my pain and depression, and all my tears and anger are gone. It hurt, yes it hurt, but 1hr 40 min later I was done. It was $160 and worth every penny of happiness it will bring me.

Saturday, Oct. 11, 2003

I just can't keep up these days. So I need the perfect place to live created for me and Jacquie, not too expensive, not too sleazy. I have to work tonight (every Saturday night). But money is a good thing. I love money because it gets you things, but I hate how money can make people so sad. We don't give the underdog a chance. It's like no one cares, it's just a dog eat dog world. Now I lucked out because people want what they can't have and you can't buy a pretty face. Well you can buy someone with a pretty face but you can't make yourself beautiful. It's like you don't have a choice on anything important in life, only small things. You can't choose your dress size, you can't choose your parents, and you can't choose your health. You can choose what flavor of ice cream you want, or if you go tanning or not. And you can choose if you are happy and a good person or if you are miserable and ruin everyone's lives. Well I have to get ready for work now.

Sunday, Oct. 12, 2003

Trent just called my cell and woke me up. It's Sunday and I kept sleeping and sleeping. That was Harry on the phone. He's coming over to burn one and then he's out of town to his mom`s working for the week. My darn room is always messy. Not big enough I guess. Well I guess I should jump in the shower before Harry gets here. I wonder what he needs. It's weird, he never wants to talk in person, but he didn't want to talk over the phone. Maybe he just wants a bit of bud to take with him or something. I hope nothing serious. Chip is funny digging under the covers to find a place to nap.

No Such Thing As Secrets

Wednesday, Oct. 15, 2003

I'm not sure if I'm worried or mad. Trent was supposed to pick me up from Lillian's house last night. He phoned at 1am to say he was on his way but at 2:30am, I gave up and Lillian drove me home. He had a few drinks, what if he got into a car accident? I'll be happier once I hear from him, but what the hell went on last night? Is this normal behavior, or what happened? So we didn't see any mangled cars on the drive home. I cried myself to sleep because I found the whole thing upsetting. I waited and waited and waited and waited. I just wanted to get home to my dogs. I was tired, and very fearful that Trent was dead, because I still have that fear of death taking anyone. I tried not to imagine him dead, he has a bad head and even one hit could kill him. Why would he not come get me? Why would he phone and say he's on his way, then never show up? Aren't I worth coming to get or even a courtesy phone call. I mean I'm a bit mad that he left me there, but maybe he got pulled over by the cops or who knows. I'm tired of happiness being a struggle. Life just shouldn't be like this. On a good note, I found a place to live yesterday. I paid damage deposit already and I move in Nov 1st. It's on First Street, but the far south side, in the basement of a 110year old house. But $350 for everything is a great deal and they've never had a break in. It's kind of tucked out of the way. And Mindy can stay the night and walk to her Dad's from my place. It's just one big kitchen and one big bed room, no living room. I'll make it work, the main thing is that I have my dogs and I bet I could even take Elliot in time. I'm so tempted to drive by Trent's to see if his car is there, but how degrading is that? Why would he forget me and ditch me? It's going to bug me all day until I know what happened. Every time I feel mad I think what if he crashed. So I guess I'll try not to think about it. Oh well at least I found a place to live for cheap. Jacquie kept being wishy-washy on me and finally yesterday she admitted she can't afford it. So I'm on my own, but this is my starting out pad. The owner said that it always goes the first day in the paper. The guy loves dogs and can put up chicken wire around the bottom of the fence. I will make it into a nice little place and I can let the dogs out no problem. I can put a little Christmas tree up in my room and decorations in the window. It will be so cool. I'll have my own wrapping paper, and mom and Belle might stay the night Christmas Eve. I can't wait to get in there and decorate. Now I'm going to get up, go to Jason n Lana's, and then go to work 2 – 6, and hopefully I've heard Trent's voice by then.

Friday, Oct. 17, 2003

I ended up hearing from Lillian and Trent. And Trent wasn't there because he did coke, thinking he could hide it from me but once he got to Lillian and Wilky's he chickened out and went to a friend's house (he partied and crashed there). Lillian said to dump him and he and I had some talks. I guess I believe him this time but I'm taking a big leap of faith. Hoping he really will quit and tell me if he can't. We're still opening up to each other. I told him how I couldn't be that girl, and how my sister's husband is on speed because he can't afford coke. I wanted to say more but we were talking a lot and all Brooklyn's shit didn't come up. Except that I've seen too many people I care about become that girl and I won't be a victim. He said look what it did after one time and I know you probably want to kill me right now. And he asked if I was going to break up with him. I said no, but I'm really mad at you and he said he would be too. He knows he was wrong and he always finds a way to screw things up. So then I said why would you sabotage our relationship and he said he didn't mean to. So I said you took psychology, look at it, and I grilled him till he said stop grilling me Betty. But he also said after, I thought you were going to hit me and scream and yell. I said Brooklyn and Rant smack each other and I don't agree with it. I think it's barbaric and immature. He said he wished he was dead when I told him that I thought he was dead last night. I asked him if it was that bad living back here, and he looked up at me with his brown eyes and just nodded yes. And I've been there. I've been so upset and no one understands and there's no hope, just escaping the pain. I've been there, and I know how badly he needs one good thing in his life. I don't ever want to be Brooklyn though. I can't. So he had better make his own path and not do coke. I trusted him over Lillian.

Saturday, Oct. 18, 2003 | **8:39am**

I couldn't sleep so I made myself a tea and grabbed my diary. A lot has been going on with Trent. Lillian says one thing, Wilky says another, Trent says something different, and I'm left wondering who to believe. I'm mad at all of them. Yesterday I went to the bank and my account was out $540. My debit card has been missing for three days. Trent took me to McDonalds immediately after I was innocently talking about my pin number. So I went straight to his house and we went for a drive. He said he spent too much money; he had a car payment, and line of credit stuff. I said how hard it was to believe he could go through that much money and not be doing drugs. But then we ended it with him borrowing more money for last night and mysteriously leaving the party. He told everyone it was to get me, but I had just talked to him and we were meeting up later, so Lillian and Wilky were saying he's lying. They say he's caught up in his own lies and making it out to be a big soap opera. He says he made a visa payment before the bank closed. No one believed him, and his dad was bugging him to make a payment. And so once again do I trust him and believe what he says? I had a few drinks at Suzanne's and then went to meet them all at a restaurant. Then I thought fuck you all. I want to go dancing, so I put on my army skirt and some make up and met them there. It was cool because I work with the doorman on Saturday nights so he let me and my group in ahead of the big line of people. So we drank more, I danced, and then Trent and I drove people home. Then we came to my house because I never see my dogs. Then on the way home he wanted a hoot and I thought why, to hide the coke? Then he said he believes that Lillian and Wilky were on it. He could tell and he'd bet all his money on it. So now who do I believe? Do I even care or should I just run from all of them? Trent is lying in bed next to me. Last night the last song was 'I Wish'. I had never ever heard that song and I almost wanted to bawl, but I held it in. I danced to it and went home. But I'm still sad. My whole bank account, money, lies, and alcohol day was a bad one, and I think Trent better be Mr. Fucking Wonderful from now on or I'll be very upset. I'll lose a lot of hope. Can't Lillian be wrong, and Trent and I be happy?

Sunday, Oct. 19, 2003

It turns out that Lillian and Wilky did do coke Friday night. Trent suspected them of it and they were still up when we dropped a friend off. Lillian was acting weird now that I think of it. Trent talked to people who were at their house, but Trent could tell when he saw them, so they were doing it all night. And Lillian phoned me, making no sense, high, yakking at Trent forever and dramatizing everything to avert attention from her. I spent all day with Trent in bed until I came home. Brooklyn picked me up and now I'm in the bath. Last night Trent came over after I got home from work and I know he was drunk, not high. I can't say that about Lillian. She's still in that world of hell that coke brings. Brooklyn thinks she always tries to sabotage my relationships, so she can have me to herself, and make herself feel better about having someone. Who knows? And Brooklyn thinks I should tell her Dad about the coke and throw her in detox. I'm going back over to Trent's house tonight. I like spending time with him, snuggling up close. I think he's sweet to me. You'd have to be there to see it but you can tell if someone likes you or not. The way he rubs my shoulder or kisses my head, or the way he notices me. He notices how I hold my burger and laughs and wants to see my collections.

Tuesday, Oct. 21, 2003

I can't wait to move. Ten days isn't soon enough. It's one thing after another around here. If it's not the dogs, it's the cat or the iguana, and it's always a mess around here. Sometimes I can't take it. I'm tired of being the responsible adult around here. I guess it's the whole divorce and me finally getting to live away from my parents and sisters that make me see the role I play around here. I've always tried to keep our family social and upright in the community. Being Miss Goody-Two-Shoes to all my friend's parents. Tricks I picked up from TV or movies or people along the way. I observed them all and made note on what I wanted my future to be like, because the one thing they taught me was that life is what you make it. You create your life. They taught me to believe in a dream and for some reason I've never let that dream go. It's all I've had at times, that thought of happiness in the future. Every little kid has a dream and at some point they let it go for all sorts of different reasons. The ones that hold on, they make it because the universe rewards those that believe in themselves. So keep believing it will happen. One day at a time, we somehow survive. We carry on no matter how beaten or tired we are. But sure as shit, I swear for every down there's an up. It's like the ying and yang sign, balance. The people who've made it big have usually had some downs to start. And I've had my downs now so I can share the ups with my kids. I can't wait to be June Cleaver, soccer mom. It will be a different era for sure. Trent had to go to Cityville to get his head and balance checked with a neurosurgeon. I hope everything is fine. He gets his results in three more days from his cat scan yesterday. So I'm praying that he's fine and the results are good. I don't think I've said yet, but Brooklyn caught Rant on speed again. So she gave him until the end of the month to get another place to live. Sink or swim, he's on his own. She was just waiting for him to screw up and he did. They talked all day and she said it made her sick to her stomach to go near him and he's out. Brooklyn might pick up a shift a week at the World. I think it would be so good for her self-esteem. The boys (guys I work with) will adore her. She'll feel good about herself again. I'm so excited just thinking about it. It saw a glimpse of that Brooklyn the last time she left Rant. And I know she's in there still. The Brooklyn that loves to cook, clean, eat, and do all that mom stuff. She is so better off without him. He pulls down the whole family. It's hard to say this is happening in my family because no one wants to admit that it's happening to them. No one wants to admit that they have an abusive husband, or Dad, or brother-in-law. But it can happen at any level and it's wrong.

Wednesday, Oct. 22, 2003 | 8:15am

I hate when radio stations put on too many commercials. We only want to hear music, that's it. It's been over ten minutes with no music. This week the Real Room thinks they'll need me Thursday – Saturday, so yeah and extra $200 plus. I love getting money. So many people have trouble getting it and I just get money given to me at work. Actually, people in the industry tip big, then drunks, then crackers last, well young kids last. If they're in at nineteen and they don't know, they don't tip. But they all make up for each other. It's an on average thing. I would even say that girls tip just as well on average as men. I get a lot of good tips from pretty ladies that want a good image or from cougars that want respect. So of course all I want to do is buy new clothes. I love to wear new and trendy threads. But I should sponsor a child in a third world country for $30/month before I go shopping again. It's that hope that someone in the world cares. If only more people would do it. I feel a lot better today. I just have some bad days sometimes. It's like the stress builds and builds until I go "boom" and blow over little things that I don't care about today, but was so mad about yesterday. It makes me realize I should shut my yap next time or calm down. Good thing Belle understands. Belle seems happy with Shane. And I'm happy with Trent. I just hope he feels the same. Oh, I talked to Lillian and I let her have it. I was mad at her and I said that all those things she said to Trent, she should have been saying to herself. And I said, you guys are supposed to be his support system and now it makes me not want him to hang around any of you. I see dead people walking around this town and they look gross, its' such a fucking coke town! Everyone does it. It makes me wonder who else does. How many of them? I can think of lots of people and none of them look that happy straight.

And it's more than that. They look like the corpse of a person I once knew. They're eyes get darker, they're cheeks are thinner and their look gets duller and sadder. Then you can tell. They all know not to show it to me. Especially after I talked to Lillian, now she'll hide it too. She promised to never do it again. Famous last words. I hope she can do it, but I doubt it. I hope Trent never touches it again too. Lillian said I can guarantee I'll see it Halloween, and I said great, I can think about that while I work my double shift.

Thursday, Oct. 23, 2003 | **9:37am**

I'm sitting downstairs and Trent still hasn't phoned me. I drove Brooklyn to work and we concluded that he got back with his ex who lives in Cityville. I phoned his house and his Dad said he was out, not still in Cityville, but out. So who knows, but it bothers me. Why hasn't he called me? Oh well, I still have my new place to look forward to. I can't wait to get all settled in. Just me and my dogs and maybe Elliot. I want perfect love that you don't have to work so hard at. Is that possible? Or do you always have to work? And there's always Mr.X. Brooklyn and I are going to get our show started soon on the local TV station. But I'm not going bungee jumping. I've said it before, years ago, and I'll say it again. I'm not going to scare myself like that. Brooklyn can if she wants but I'm not. It hurts Brooklyn to leave Rant, but she knows it's best for the family. And she's ready. Deep down, she's happy to finally feel free to leave.

Saturday, Oct. 25, 2003

I think I'm the saddest girl in the world right now. I think I'd better roll a couple before I begin this entry. I miss Trent and what I thought we had. I was ready for a good relationship with anyone. I just wanted him to call me and he finally did, but I missed it and then he didn't answer, didn't answer. I feel like I must have screwed up somehow, somewhere along with way. Now he wants nothing to do with me. I miss him and want him back in my life, as crazy as that may seem. I just want to talk to him. All I want is to be happy with a boyfriend. And I don't think Trent is capable of giving me what I want. He treats me like this, ignoring my calls like I'm some two dollar whore. I think of our time together and I miss him, but I think of how mean it is of him to ignore me and I think I deserve better. I deserve a man who isn't afraid to commit to me and us and share himself with me, the good and bad. I feel so dumb, just dumb. Dumb for letting myself care about someone who won't care about me back. I want it to be back the way it was. When we watched movies and talked and snuggled and were happy together. I know he must feel the same way about me. He must. I know I can't feel this and have him feel nothing over me. He doesn't want to be a cracker.

Monday, Oct. 27, 2003 | 2:10pm

Sitting at the kitchen table, puffin and listening to 'I Wish'. I keep repeating it because I feel like it. I saw the CD sitting there and I haven't listened to it for a while. It's nice to remember the boys alive, rather than as ghosts. I still hate how the last night I saw them bowling and I was going to give him (Wonder) a B-day hug, but I thought, oh I will later because I was in a hurry to put my stuff down, and I never did. I forgot to. And the next time I saw him, he was lying in his casket. I know that them being dead has taught me so much, and has given me a reason to cry. That's why I love music. It calms me when nothing else works. Some nights it's all that gets me through at work. And I'm sure a lot of people would say that music is a magical thing. I love writing because I get to escape for a while and just write. I checked my message from my agent and I don't have to go to class tonight. I'm going to a different class instead. It's 11:11 at night and I wish for Brooklyn to be happy. Lillian came and visited me tonight. We smoked and drank a couple of mudslides. We did our Russian cards and hers said make a choice. Your happiness depends on it. Mine said he's good and hers said he's not so maybe I shouldn't worry.

Tuesday, Oct. 28, 2003

Early in the morning I have to drive Brooklyn to work. She talked the people at the local TV station into giving me some air time on a show called 'the Sports Room'. So I'm going to go in and meet some people when I pick her up. It's exciting, a step in the right direction I think. She had to do some smart talking to hook me up, but if that works out we next want our own show. The show will be a 'what's fun to do around here' type of show. And we are the hosts, Brooklyn and Betty, and Belle will be our music girl. And it will be an on the road talk show. We need to brainstorm, but the first step is getting me in the TV station. The second step will be taking over the air waves. We want a funny show. We love funny, but that's just us making jokes where ever we go. Belle says she wants to host shows too, so Brooklyn will have a posse of girls to back her and help her. I'd like to do a show on struggling artists and musicians, actors and dancers. Maybe I should go shopping this morning after I drop Brooklyn off.

1:48pm

I'm in the bath. I'm going to have to meet the TV station people when I pick up Brooklyn at 4pm. I'm not sure what to wear to that meeting, or what I'm going to say. I have no idea about sports but I'm cute and funny. Should I look sexy or conservative professional? I need food. I'll feel better after I eat, do my makeup, and then I pick out my wardrobe. If I have time I might stop by Beatrice's for resume help.

Monday, Nov. 2, 2003

I'm killing time before my acting class starts at six, thirty-five minutes from now. I started painting my place today. It' a long way from being done that's for sure. But it's bigger than I remembered it, and I'll fit everything in just fine. Mom and Belle are home. Mom's happy because she just signed her divorce papers. Finally, I'm almost in my own place. It will be nice once I'm in and the dogs are there with me, and I've decided the tree might just go in my kitchen. Well I guess I don't even have time to finish my entry. Kandy needs ear drops and I have to change before class.

Nov. 5, 2003

I'm in my new place. Mindy's grandpa grew up in this house! Sometimes I think, "Will I ever get my stuff in? Ever?" The ceiling is sore on the neck (it's so low), but it looks a million times better around here and I'll keep working on it. Maybe I'll get the painting done tonight. I think I'll order cable here. If Mindy has always afforded cable, I can afford cable. I'll just drink less. And I really want a new tower for my computer so I can edit videos and make music at home. I want it to burn DVD's like Lillian's dad's computer and CD's like Buck's computer. I can keep the old key board and screen. I'm going to like it here. It's cute now that I've painted it, and it's affordable and it lets me have my pets. The little old stove takes some getting used to, and I need to fence my yard so the dogs can't escape. Trent is a nice boy most of the time but he still does this thing where he won't call for a day or three, but he always calls sooner or later and it teaches me to be more independent. I saw a friend at the mall with his new wife and baby, and they look so happy. It just made me see that I want that. I want my career too, but I want that happy family home that you see on TV.

Thursday, Nov. 6, 2003

The weirdest thing just happened. I was driving to my place just now and I saw the hummer parked on the side of the road. The only person who drives that is Carl. What is he doing here? Seems so odd, just parked there with no one in sight. I already think of him enough, why is he here? Trent hasn't called me in a couple days. He does this all the time. And that's fine, but I need someone who can be honest with me. Lillian fills my head with all these things, and I can't stand how one second I have a boyfriend and then the next I don't. I can't call him to ask him a quick question because I don't know when he'll return. Trent seems like he doesn't even care if he sees me or not. And I can't get Carl off my mind if he comes around. Hey, I need to drop off weed for people today, and I can stop at the World and do some investigating. I'd love to see him. He has a way of bringing my spirits up. The shit Lillian says about Trent, anyone would get depressed standing up for him. She won't budge, and goes on and on about what everyone else says. They just talk about each other so much and make every situation worse. I don't know why he doesn't call for days at a time and I don't know if that's normal or not.

Tuesday, Nov. 11, 2003

Work will be easy today. But there's shit going on (as always down there) with the owners/management/staff. It turns out the new manager is after a waitress and she's suing for sexual harassment. Carl phoned to talk to me about it on Sunday night. I said how I've always said a manager is a waste of money. And he is a bit of a tyrant. If he's mad the whole place feels it. And all those accidental brushes, were they on purpose I wonder? On the other side of things I haven't heard from Trent since Friday morning. Why does he disappear for days like that?

Thursday, Nov. 13, 2003

I'm in the bath, hurrying to get ready in time to pick up Brooklyn at 8:30am. I still haven't heard from Trent. What a freak, most men like to hang out with me. But not Trent, he likes to avoid me. Last night I wrote him a four-page letter because I felt like talking to him and it's been six days now since I've talked with him. His Dad says he was in Cityville but he's back now and no one knows where he is. His dad says that it's due to the head injury and he needs counseling, and he's not speculating on what else he's doing.

Friday, Nov. 14, 2003

I'm in the bath and Belle is in the shower and I'm throwing her things. It's every man's dream. Trent was found last night. Thank God. I was so worried that I'd never see him again. Now I'm not allowed to see him but at least I know he's safe. Apparently he's in bad shape and has been in a crack shack for days. The counselors say that he can't see anyone until they talk to him. His Dad says that he'll probably sleep until tonight and he might phone me when he's feeling more himself. All I know is that it sucks to be him and me right now. I wonder if he even thinks of me. I'm tired of this emptiness I feel.

Monday, Nov. 17, 2003

Wow, what a Saturday I had. I had class from 11 – 5, and then I found out after class that Trent was out, he escaped that morning. So I got home and I lost it. I was walking around in circles then I just collapsed to the floor crying. All I could think was, I have to find him, I have to find him, and I was driving around with the dogs, not even smoking I was so upset. Crying and looking and preying, and then all of the sudden there he was in front of me. I knew it was him because of the license plate (BJB, my initials). Then he pulled over and I pulled over behind him. I left the dogs in the car with the car running in case he took off. When I got to his window he was very surprised to see me. I said I wanted to go with him and I parked Brooklyn's car and took the dogs with me. Then he told me that he owed someone one hundred dollars and he swore on his mother's grave that he just had to pay it and that I couldn't go. I said it would kill me if he didn't show up, so of course he didn't show up. Brooklyn and I waited and waited and waited. Then I phoned Wilky and he told me where Trent was so Brooklyn and I drove there. We saw his car and I wanted to go in but Brooklyn and Wilky wouldn't let me. So Brooklyn and I started to drive home when Trent called my cell so we went back there and got him. I just went to the door and nicely asked for him. I walked up and said are you ready to go? We left just in time before Wilky and his thugs got there. They wouldn't have gotten in. I got in because of my cute face and that's the truth. There was a cute kitten in there that someone traded for a hoot. I took Trent to my place and held him while he slept.

Saturday, Nov. 22, 2003

Wow, am I an emotional mess right now. After everything I've been through and it doesn't seem to end. The big part today is my mom moved out. My dad stopped by and I just knew from the few minutes I spent with him that I couldn't live with him. He has an attitude. They both ask me about each other and I say I don't know to each of them. If they want to know so much maybe they should talk. I left today looking for a home and now I'm in it, back here, where I started. I started a fire and did the dishes for the last time at my house in Hemlock. Still no one appreciated it. My dad even made me help him move the washer and dryer inside. When does he help me? I told him he's going to have to get some male friends. Then I left without having a shower and I stopped at Brooklyn's. Rant was yelling at the dogs and the kids and I knew I didn't want to stay there either. When I got here it was cold and I was feeling alone, like no one even cared what I was doing. My dogs snuggled me on my bed as I cried. I phoned Trent and his voice made me feel better. At least I have him right now. We've been through a lot these last few days. I wouldn't even know where to begin. So I'll just say that I hope he cares for me like I care for him. I know I didn't handle the last few days the best I could have. I should really take the time to write the story out. Well, Tuesday Trent and I went to his counselors and places and then Tuesday night was darts. We were in the car when he found some tin foil in the passenger side door. He pulled it out and said, I bet this is drugs, and opened it and it was. So I said I'd get rid of it through Harry and keep the money. But he wouldn't let me. Then we went to Wilky's house and we were smoking and drinking and Trent wanted the bong. I knew it was to smoke crack. I watched and I actually saw the tiniest piece of white in with the weed. I didn't want to make a scene in front of Wilky, so I was waiting for Wilky to have his shower when I was going to say I saw that. Then after he hit the bong I asked for a hit. Ha ha ha. You should have seen the look on his face. He lit it again and again, and then emptied it out before giving it to me. Busted. So Wilky finally gets in the shower and I wrestled Trent for it. He managed to get this little piece and put it in the bong and I grabbed it. I had it all. Then Wilky was back and we had to leave. Actually, how I got it off of him was I started to cry and he couldn't make me cry. But then he kept bugging me for it. He wouldn't stop. So needless to say darts was no fun. Trent kept giving me guilt trips and trying to get my car keys off me so he could go get some. I didn't know what to do. He went into the drugstore next to the pub where he got pens and water, and he kept saying, "are you going to give me my shit yet?" It was crazy. I couldn't fight him so I said fine, you can do a little of it. He said he only wanted a little of the rock. So I agreed on a little because he was going to go buy it anyway. I said I wanted to leave darts, get my dogs, and stay at my place. So we made a deal. He told everyone I was sick and wanted to leave. I had to lie to Simon and tell him I was sick. We left and were on route to Hemlock when we stopped at Eagle Park. I went to the water to throw out the rock and he stayed in the car to smoke his share. The night didn't end there though. We went into town and he got more from the shack. I didn't want to stay there so we left, back to my place and he hooted more until that was gone too. Then we went back because he wanted more, only that time we stayed there. I met a lot of very interesting people there. There was a native lady named Claire, but everyone called her Mom, including me. I liked her. She opened right up to me. Trent and I stayed there for hours, with me talking to people and him off in rooms hooting tons. It was a lot for me to take in, but I'm a pretty open minded and non-judging person, and I knew all those junkies were just people too. There was a man named Marvin who was the oldest one there and he chatted with me. He actually believes time travel is possible and told me the name of a good book called Majestic. So I'll have to find that. There was a really old guy named Spider who was walking around saying five days and I still can't get high. As I left with Trent I heard Spider say, "Bye girl, we'll talk next time". I experienced a party unlike I ever have. One girl was wearing a BC ferry shirt and I can remember her I think. She said she's been homeless for two years and `Mom` said two months for her. And I said I'm sure you have a strong sense of who you are and the BC ferry lady said there's one thing about being homeless, no matter where you go, you're at home. It was a crazy place. TG was the house operator. He seemed to keep them all together.

No Such Thing As Secrets

So Trent and I went back to my place and I couldn't believe how much time we spent at that crack shack. Then Trent had to go pay TG so he left me at my place and I fell asleep after I put my phone on silent. I woke up at six and phoned Brooklyn. She came and got me and I fell asleep on her couch for the night. The next morning I was really worried about Trent so Rant drove me in to TG's. Rant was supposed to stay in the car but he came in and started threatening TG. I was calming him down and TG gave me his number and said to call and basically not come back. Rant totally made an ass of himself and almost got us killed. He should have waited in the car. So I went to the hotel where TG said Trent was and got into his room. I asked him to leave, but he didn't want to. So we left and I must say Rant handled that one wrong too. He was so loud and arrogant and embarrassing. But he meant well. He even started crying at one point. Trent and I were chatting in the bathroom and he said he had to get money off these guys for TG then he would be done, so Rant and I went home. Trent called me and came out to Hemlock. He drove me to work after Tyson fixed his tire that Rant let the air out of. Trent was so mad. He still doesn't like Rant. I went home from work because it was dead and I hadn't eaten properly in days because I was so stressed. I dropped a lot of weight. But where was I. Ok, so Trent phoned me at 6:30 and we met at my place. He had some cheesy noodle dinner and he was going to go home the next morning so I left him my house key so he could have some toast. I went home, had a bath, went to work, and I didn't feel like working so I decided to go home. All of the sudden his Dad called and said where do you live, I've got him blocked in and I'm not going anywhere. I said I'm leaving work right now. I got there and he followed me in. He tried to get Trent to leave with him but Trent said take the car and leave. He did after saying, 'have a nice life son', and slammed the door. Trent was stressed and thought I brought his dad there but his Dad found him. I went to Hemlock to get my dogs and some things and when I got back he wasn't here. So I unpacked stuff and mucked about for a bit before I went back to Hemlock for the VCR and microwave. Then I put in my favorite Christmas movie and fell asleep. At 4:30am Trent called. He just wanted to check in but I wanted to pick him up so I did. He went home today and I went to Brooklyn's, then I came back here and wrote in my diary. He called me, I picked him up, and we went to my place. He was dressed up, but told me he was staying in, so I got ready for work and left. As I was on my way to Playsville (he had my bank card) I phoned my mom and got her to phone the bank. She stopped two to three hundred from being withdrawn, but he had already taken out one hundred tonight when he was supposed to be depositing it. That low life fucker stole from me for the last time! I had to work knowing that he has my card and is most likely putting in fake envelopes and screwing me. He already owes me $1500.00. All my fucking savings! How fucking stupid am I? Ahhhhh!!! I might need to go for a drive. This is fucking horse shit! Who the fuck begs, borrows, and even steels his girlfriend's money when he makes twice as much as her on his fucking UI? I don't know what to do anymore. The world has played its last ha ha, fucking trick on me. Where the fuck is that piece of shit Trent? I fucking hate myself for ever caring about him. He has treated me like shit! He owes me so much money and he needs some help. That self centered asshole. This time I don't care if he dies. I only care about getting my money back. I'm not supporting him. That mother fucker. Should I tell his parents or Lillian first? I just wonder how on earth I was so blind. How oh how could I let him keep on using me, even tonight. I trust you, see you after work. Dumb twit I am. Soon maybe I'll be done getting mad and I'll be ready to sleep it off. I'm so sad. So very sad that Trent decided to fuck me up the ass. Now that it's over with him, maybe I should go back online? I know it's risky to be known as the internet porn star in town, but why date men and have them fuck up my head and body when I can get money from them? I'd rather be a Goddess any day over some guy's girlfriend. Maybe Belle will move in with me somewhere new. I don't feel safe here. How could Trent hurt me like he has? Mother Fucker!!

Thursday, Nov. 27, 2003

So where was I on my Hell life story? Trent put a check in my account for $800 and then took out $400, so he owes me like $1900.00 now! He came home Monday. He's sorry and will pay me it all back. Yeah right, I'll believe it when I see it. I stayed Tuesday night at Trent's and then left Wednesday morning for work early. Then I phoned for Trent after work last night and he was out "watching floor hockey". But look, no Trent last night. He didn't phone. He's probably paid G back the $600 he still owed him and fronted more, or who even knows. But why the fuck should I care about that fuck head anymore? He didn't even call me. Hey, remember me, the girl you owe $1900 to? I need someone more stable than him. I don't need to go down that road. I guess I can kiss that money goodbye and I can move on in life. I don't need this shit. Trent used me and won't stop using me. It's so fucked up. All I want is a Christmas tree and I'll work a lot to try to afford Christmas. I'm actually thinking of quitting my agent's classes. It costs me way too much money per month. Being an extra is boring and I think she likes my money more than me. I know other actresses are doing well. I'll get a different agent before I waste any more money on this one. I need to move on, and having zero money makes me look at what I'm spending my money on. I know enough people at the World alone who can help me. All my agent did was give me my confidence back. I don't know why I lost it. I can act! I can write and I can sing! And above all else, I have my dogs. I love them so very much and I know they love me. Man's best friend is right. I'm getting more and more used to it here in my hobbit hole, but I worry that Trent will try to break in and steal things from me! I wonder if my land lord would go for a security system for me. I think I'd feel safer with Molly here. I think I might get the internet again. Thank God my Mom has stuck by me and helped me pay my bills (once again). I can't wait to really pay her back one day for all her kindness. One day I'll buy her that house in Hawaii. I'm so broke right now I'm thinking about going back online. I mean why not? Why should I date a man who takes my money when I can use men for their money online? I met a lot of contacts online I never took advantage of. Trent is out and internet is back in.

Friday, Nov. 28, 2003

I talked to Trent last night. I didn't think he would even be home. But he had his cousin from out of town visiting, so last night I went to Suzanne's and got drunk with Melissa, her parents, Suzanne and her parents, and Buck. I must say I feel a bit left out from Trent's family visit. Not that I wanted to go but I wanted the invite. I go to hell and back for your son and now I'm not good enough to go out for dinner with the cousin. I'm going to curl my hair for work and wear something nice. That will make me feel better. So I guess I have to phone my agent and tell her that I won't be going tomorrow due to my busy schedule and recent lack of funding. I have to take a break from acting classes. As for Trent I'm more confused than ever. If you can't trust someone not to steel off you or pawn your dogs off then how can you have a relationship with them? And my mom has made me promise to stay away from him.

Saturday, Nov. 29, 2003 | 12:40am

Trent ditched me at the bar. What a tool! What a fucking tool. You don't treat people like that. He's a no good, shit head right about now. Trent's own cousin told me to leave him. But I've got lots going for me. Everything with the local TV is going good, and after tonight I'm going back online. I may as well go set up an account for online right now because Trent is out and money is in. I'm going smoke a doobie and email Dibbs and tell him my troubles. That will make me feel better.

Monday, Dec. 1, 2003

My mom is coming to pick me up and then we're going to the bank. I have to borrow eighty dollars for rent because I don't have enough. I really have to go back online. I went shopping on my credit card today. It was fun. I love to charge it and pay later. But now I need to work so I can pay all of my bills I'm adding up. Then Melissa came over for a visit last night. She's such a nice friend. It still hurts about Trent, I feel like I was dumped. He chose drugs over me. He doesn't care about me, he doesn't even like me. I may as well kiss my money good bye. And for my own good, I better kiss Trent goodbye too. I'll just work hard and work on my music, writing, films. I'll never go to my agent again. I strongly feel like she is only interested in making money off me taking her "acting classes" and not getting me the auditions that I have been promised. She sent me to one audition and sent me unprepared and I just don't feel like she is interested in helping my acting career at all. I gave her lots of money and time to show me auditions and I feel like I am better off focusing on the local TV.

Tuesday, Dec. 2, 2003 | 9:44am

Trent called me last night. He said he hadn't called since Friday because he was mad that we left him out that night. Now today he gets his money. I wonder who will get it, TG or me. I just don't know what to do about him. I'm tired of working so hard and getting absolutely no where. Still struggling, using my master card. But I'm happy in my hobbit hole. It took some getting used to, but it's getting comfier and comfier.

2:45pm

I've phoned Trent's house and his mom said he was out. So I said to get him to call me. But I can't help but feel that he won't call today. Who knows what he's up to, but it's his pay day. Lillian, Mom, Suzanne, and I think even Brooklyn all want me to walk away from Trent. Today is it. Today is the day because I know he has money and freedom (he's not home). Only time will tell.

11:09pm

I've been at home all day cleaning. No word from Trent. I don't know why I even listen to him at all. He's so full of shit. What a joke. I'm so tired of getting sucked back in by him, only to get let down. What was the point of me having a shower today? I should have worked online all day and made money. I'll move the computer into my room tomorrow morning. I work 2 – 6, then I can come back and work tomorrow night online. Then I still need flea stuff for my dogs and my Christmas tree and more picture frames to decorate. Hey maybe I'll curl my hair tomorrow? I need to get a car, tanning minutes, and most of all I need to be working online for cash.

Wednesday, Dec. 3, 2003

I'm working online, smoking a doob, and writing. It takes a while before you get a fan base, but I will. Where there's a will there's a way. I just need money. I might get a phone line even? You can always make more money when you offer phone with video. You can charge more per minute that way. It's a lot to be on the phone with the clients though. It's different than just sitting alone in your room watching TV and dancing around. It's actually hearing their voice and talking back. I have a sexy voice that I use that is not my normal voice at all. One time years ago I was working online doing the phone too, before I did the dominatrix, and I actually felt so much shame that tears started to silently roll down my cheeks. Of course the viewer didn't see that, they just got off all the same, but I didn't enjoy it for the record. I didn't enjoy feeling like I was only good for sex, with me telling one client after another how to pull his goalie till he explodes. No one wants to imagine the sexy Goddess reduced to tears because she feels so much judgment, and like she is only wanted for one thing.

All men just want to have sex with me, and that's ok, I get it. I guess everyone is good at something, and I'm good at being sexy and sexually confident. I'd rather be treated like fucking royalty online than like dirt as a real life girlfriend. I'm just going to go all out and make tons of cash. That's what I want for Christmas, my life back. This online job can be quite boring, waiting and waiting. I know I can't do this job forever but for now, I prefer it over having a boyfriend. At $900/month, who can afford a boyfriend? I got too close to Trent and now I really must let him go. Focus on my music and my career. I'll be more than busy at SBCtv and I'll get my control over my life back soon enough. I might go snowboarding next Wednesday with Jacquie and Zarren. That would be rad.

I went for dinner with Lillian and her Dad for Lillian's birthday. We had steak, shrimp, and crab. It was so good and a lot of fun. Lillian has been doing so much better since she left Wilky Wednesday night. And I think it was Wednesday night that I stayed over at Trent's. Lillian dropped me off at his house and rather than breaking up with him I didn't say anything, fell asleep and I left the next morning and haven't talked to him since. I went shopping Thursday morning with Brooklyn and the kids. Jordan set the fire alarm off in Winmart and started crying. Those kids were being bad and he needed a scare. At least that lesson didn't cost anything. As for Trent, well I still have my computer in my bedroom. I mean fuck, he's not putting anything into this relationship. I know there has to be a man out there who isn't all screwed up? What is wrong with me that makes me want to stay with someone who treats me so badly? There is seriously something wrong with my head because I always toss the good ones and stay with the horrible assholes. I'm tired of caring about a self-centered asshole. I think I'd better just break it off because my head is telling me to ignore my heart. I don't even know where Trent is most days. He never calls me. Lillian tells me one thing and he tells me another. It's just so confusing. I want someone who I talk to almost every day, see more often, and who I can have sex with on a regular basis. Trent doesn't give me enough. He doesn't even care about me. He's just with me because he thinks that's what he should do. I just don't think I can do it anymore. This has just gotten dumb and really sad. He probably owes so many people, so much money. How do you get through to someone? These drugs are ruining too many good people. They are taking over too many lives. Why can't these people quit? What is going on, I mean everyone thinks it's socially acceptable to do coke as long as you keep it in control. But where do we draw the line?

No Such Thing As Secrets

Sunday, Dec. 7, 2003

The Christmas shopping days are diminishing. Belle and I are going out after my staff meeting today. I'm going to take my dogs to the meeting. If I can take them I do. I've been leaving them too much lately. Then Chippy will stay here and Belle and I will shop till we drop. I still have lots of people to buy for when you really stop and think about it. I'd better make a list and check it twice. As for Trent, well he's been out of the house since Thursday. But his brother found him Friday night and took him to his place. His parents are putting him in rehab or something, detox. Karaoke tonight and we're taping it for SBCtv at a pub downtown.

Monday, Dec. 8, 2003 | **10:00am**

I'm in my little kitchen. Yesterday after the staff meeting my co-worker told me how she saw Trent with some girl with long blonde hair at Gribby`s on Saturday night and it looked odd enough that she thought she would say something. So I phoned Trent's house, talked to his Mom. She said that he did leave the night before with some girl with long blonde hair who picked him up at 9:30. So that is it. I sold his X-mas gift to Callie last night. I'm done with that piece of shit. It's so over, and I told his mom that. At least I got to break up with his mom. She's so nice. How can her son be so fucked up? I hate him so much. I'm trying to get it off my mind. But it's impossible to do. I need to yell at him. I'm going to make lots of money online. I went to karaoke last night and this old guy who took cinematography at UNP, went to Vietnam, and saw piles of dead bodies get lifted into the helicopters by nets. He said no one should see that but in the 60's the news was free and they showed everything. He also said that we were doing a fucking horrible boring job and we needed to be out in the room more. So I said I would talk to the camera man about it. He said don't bull shit people. People have been through shit, so be real.

Wednesday, Dec. 10, 2003

I'm in my kitchen again, waiting for Zarren to pick me up. I'm going boarding with Zarren, Lance, and Jacquie. I've fed the dogs, let them out for two pees, put the paper down, got all my stuff packed, and now I'm smoking my second doob because Zarren's a bit late. But I'm glad because it gives me time to write a quick one. I can't wait to hit the mountain. I just remembered a scarf. I need a scarf.

Dec. 11, 2003 | **5:45am**

I can't sleep. I've been up since 4am tossing and turning. I fell asleep too early last night. Snowboarding was fun. I couldn't see though. So I need new goggles before I go again. I'm going to the TV station with Brooklyn today to tape some Christmas thing. Then I work 2 – 6 at the World. My agent has been calling me about the checks she has for me. I think I'll get Brooklyn to go in. Someone just called me and I'm listening to a car drive around. I can't tell who it is. It came up as a private number. I think they left the phone in the car. That was fucked up. I guess I'll hang up now. This town is getting to me! I managed to fall back asleep. I got up and curled my hair and we shot a little Christmas greeting for the sports room. That was my agent calling and she's very worried about me. She doesn't want to lose me and she knows what it's like to have a guy dump all over you. She was married twice before her husband. She said she would lend me money and pay for my class on Saturday but I work all day and night. She said a lot and made me cry. She was crying. She just doesn't want to lose me. And so I have to think about all that. I have to take it in and try to see what is going on. I don't know. I promised to call her over the holidays and I will. I need to handle it. I can't run away from anything because it will find me.

Friday, Dec. 12, 2003

I'm in the kitchen again. Jose is tucked in my house coat and Kandy is in bed with Trent. Kandy just opened the door and sat in front of the heater. I don't think I'm going go to work today. I've got that flu that Brooklyn and Annie had. I've been tossing and turning all night. I am so achy. I even threw up. I couldn't sleep so I thought I'd have a tea to help my tummy. Now Kandy is in my house coat too. I put up my tree last night after work. It looks very nice. It feels more like Christmas. So I was on my way out to Melissa's (she was going to help me promote the World) but then Trent called. He called earlier when Lillian was over, and then I called him on my way to Melissa's. His parents kicked him out and he had nowhere to go. So I picked him and his hockey bag of stuff up. Now he's here and I have a lot to talk to him about. It's confusing, you don't phone me for a week then you want to move in? I don't know what I'll say. I'm so sick I don't even feel like puffin. My oven dinger rang three times last night too. Weird. I think the ghosts were saying we're helping you. I hate feeling achy and yucky. I can't sleep. I just groan and moan and feel all gross. I'm very surprised that Trent is here.

4:05pm

I feel a little better. I can't believe how sick I was today. I threw up like five times and slept off and on until about an hour ago. Trent and I got up. He just took my truck to get some cigarettes and McDonalds. I don't know when or if he'll return. Trent's friend called and I told him that Trent has to return my truck regardless. He'd fucking better come back. You know, seeing Trent's bag kind of scared me. I'm not ready to have him live with me. I don't need more shit going missing. The first thing I did when I got up was check my purse. Trent's dad called today and said he could come home. I can't imagine what it's like to be Trent. To have your life so messed up and crave only drugs. I mean I crave Mary-Jane, what if I loved coke as much as I love weed. The page opened over and yelled write on me too. So I must have more to say. Let's see. My tree looks very cute. Not as cute as – I was going to say my dogs but Trent came over with McDonalds. He got more money off his parents while I had a shower and I know he's high. Just a bit, but I can feel it in his kiss. Now he went to get me strawberries and cottage cheese, he forgot! I don't know, I can't leave him alone with my dogs. If they got out and he didn't notice they would die in a matter of minutes. Now he's using my gas, getting high, it's just dumb.

5:10am

Trent did come home at about 10pm saying that his friends weren't out. Then he went out a little bit later when the phone rang, saying I'll see you after the bar sweetie. I told him last night I was giving him rope for him to either hang himself or prove himself, and he hung himself. Mason phoned at 4:30 asking for Trent. He said I shouldn't give Trent my truck and he hadn't seen him in a couple hours. Well why would he phone then? I bet Trent was there getting Mason to phone. When he does get here I'm driving him home! I'm so sick of his shit. I'd really rather be single than treated with such disrespect. It's over.

He's not staying here. I can't even date him anymore. He keeps fucking up and fucking up. It's horrible to watch someone fuck their life up so badly, but that's his choice. He's an asshole. A self centered asshole. I can't take the stress of this relationship. I can't go to work, leave him here and trust that my valuables and dogs are safe. He couldn't even spend a night taking care of me when I'm sick. He has to get Mason over here and take off with my truck. But he has still made it hard for me to walk away. I don't want some coke head, cracker for a boyfriend. I don't want a boyfriend at all. I'm happy he didn't come home because it gives me an easy way out. I can put him and his bag in my truck and drive him home where I should have left him! Because he is fucked! I have to move on. He has lied to me for the last time. He has taken me for a fool for the last time! Why is it so hard for some people to leave an abusive relationship? Like me, right now any sane person would have pressed charges and never spoke to him again. He just got home. It's 5:40am.

2:40pm

My mom just called and she doesn't want him in my life at all. She doesn't care about the money. She thinks he'll pawn my jewelry and everything. I know I don't really want to leave him here alone. I don't even know if I want him living with me. It comes down to the trust thing. The worst part is I fear my mom is right. How many times have I said, people don't change. It's hard with my mom feeling the way she does. Lillian doesn't like him either.

Monday, Dec. 15, 2003 | **7:07am**

Lillian and Belle came over yesterday for a bit. Lillian really doesn't want me and Trent together. She says he's hooting with Mason at that girl with long blonde hair's house. So I let him stay last night after a big fight with me crying and him saying how sorry he was. He said he needed to see more of this (me crying), his parents only yell at him. I just don't know how I feel about him anymore. I'm always questioning him and where he's been. That's no life. So, do people change? Rant never did, he got worse, but Tyson did and he got way better. My Dad will never change. He will always cheat. My Mom changed when she stopped taking it from him. Brooklyn takes shit from Rant every hour. Beatrice doesn't take shit unless it's from socialites. When the fuck will I get a dime back from him. He owes me over $1800! That was all of my savings that I was going to use for a new computer. He owes me a new computer. My Mom and Lillian hate him. Suzanne said she doesn't want him at her house. Belle says he's not in her good books. Brooklyn says don't ask her, she's the biggest co-dependent around. I haven't talked to Beatrice because I'm never out at that end. And I just plain never talk to my Dad.

11:40am

Belle dropped Chip off and informed me that my Grandma B didn't wake up this morning so she's in the hospital. She has apparently come around by now but I haven't heard since. Then I just went to plug my cell in and I found a lighter that doesn't work and an empty cig pack with tin foil all ripped out in pieces. So Trent has been on crack every day. Isn't this all just fucking great. Fuck, Merry Christmas to me. I'm smoking a doob now but I'm telling him he's going home. I use mary-jane for two things; for my stomach and as an anti-depressant. I'm not looking forward to this talk with Trent. I'm just going to say that we've been going out for only two and a half months and more than half of that has been really hard to deal with. I just want crack whores out of my truck and out of my life. This problem of his won't magically go away. I can't have people like Mason and Trent in my life. They will take everything they can from me forever. They are users. They are abusers. And they can FUCK OFF!!!! It goes back to that old rule. If your family and friends hate him, dump him. Merry fucking Christmas.

Tuesday, Dec. 16, 2003

This Christmas sucks so far. I sent Trent home yesterday and today he phoned at 11:30 to go Christmas shopping, except he wanted my truck because how else would he do anything? I couldn't go pick him up and then he said do you have money for a cab, I promise I'll pay you right back. I said no.

Wednesday, Dec. 17, 2003

Trent really wanted me to stay the night last night. Then today he asked if he could use my truck while I was at work and I said no. He just called now and said he was going to counseling and I said good. He asked to use my truck again, and again I said no. I told him I don't like being stranded and my Mom took over my payments and I don't think she'd like that, but really I don't trust him.

Friday, Dec. 19, 2003

Oh my God. Carl Crane called me today. He is so hot and he asked me if I wanted to get together over lunch on Monday. And I said that would be great. I haven't talked to Trent since Wednesday when I wouldn't give up my truck. Last night I saw Clint out with Tim and Johan. They've all seen me on TV. All the time people say I saw you on TV. Everyone has seen me. That's good though. I can't believe Carl called me today. I just wonder why he's going out of his way to see me if he`s with someone. I can ask him to go snowboarding sometime, as a World promo thing of course. I just adore him. It's not fare that he's taken. Oh well, there's plenty of fish in the sea.

Sunday, Dec. 21, 2003

I have the Real Room staff party tomorrow night and my Hemlock friends Christmas party tomorrow night, but most importantly, I have lunch with Carl tomorrow. That's what makes me know I can't go back to Trent, I have too strong of feelings for another man. I will just keep it cool tomorrow. Keep it professional. But if he brings it up, I'll be honest and I'll say how I feel about him, my Mr.X. I can't wait to see Carl tomorrow.

Tuesday, Dec. 23, 2003

I went for lunch with Carl yesterday and I haven't stopped thinking about him since. I've thought of him every second, every minute, it's horrible. When he was here we talked about everything, except wing chun, the one thing we were meeting for. So he said we could go over it the next time he was in town. He'll call me when he's in town then. I really can't stop thinking about him. And I can't help but wonder what he thinks of me. I mean, what are his plans. I still haven't gotten my Christmas present from Trent and I still don't want to. I'm just not into having anything to do with him. Today is his pay day, so he's probably out spending my money.

No Such Thing As Secrets

Dec. 25, 2003

Christmas was nice except I was so sick. My head was pounding and I was lame all day! Now I'm starting to relax as I puff a puffer but I was ready to kill. The kids ran wild at Mom's for dinner. I didn't really smoke all day because I'm just a cough head. I took one of my antibiotics, I hope it stays down. I phoned Trent today to say Merry Christmas – no answer. He's probably high somewhere with his friends right now. I don't know if I feel like hanging out with everyone tonight. Jake and Mindy are having over Marty and Talon, and Lillian's on her way over here. We're supposed to hang out with Suzanne. Mindy wants us all to go over there but Marty, Lillian, and I don't work well together. And I feel sick still. Maybe I should smoke weed and watch a movie here with Lillian instead of going out. I still have to give Zeus, Melissa, and Zarren their gifts. I thought about driving them out to them. It just seems like a lot of driving around. And it's not safe to drive with the dogs. Belle and I have to find a place to live for February. I'm giving my notice and so is she. My Mom got me a DVD/VCR and my Dad got me an electric guitar that Basil is bringing out in January. My Mom says I can use Auntie Callie's amp. So I'm excited. Lillian's here.

Dec. 26, 2003

Here I am, 25 years old. Do you believe it? Lillian stopped by…

Dec. 27, 2003

Carl phoned me and wished me a Happy Birthday. I missed the call so I phoned him back, said thank you, and that I still wanted to get together tomorrow (today). So he called me at 10:30 this morning and said he was coming over and would be in town around 12:30, and would talk to me then. So Lillian and I jumped around and cleaned my place. During all that Rambo called me. It turns out that the add I called in the paper was his. So I went and looked at it and I said I would take it. I'll phone him later with damage and rent for January. Belle will be so excited. She wants a home so bad. And Rambo's done a nice job painting it. And he doesn't mind our Chihuahua's. And I'll somehow talk him into Molly too. Molly could sleep in the garage. I'm looking forward to it. I'm looking forward to Carl stopping by too.

Ok, we had a very nice visit. He stayed from one until four. I love talking to him. I love spending time with him. I totally still want my money back from Trent, but Carl helps me not care. He helps me see the kind of man I want to be with. They do exist. And they can be perfect. Only he's with someone. So I need a single Carl Crane. I wonder when we'll talk about all that. I'm going to eat cheesy noodle dinner, drink tea, finish this doob and have a nap before work tonight. Carl lent me his book 'Think and Grow Rich'. I can't wait to read it. How can I love someone that I don't even know that well? How could it be love at first sight? The moment I saw him, I thought he's hot and the more I get to know him, the more I really like. I can never stop thinking of him. People say what are you smiling at and I say nothing, but really I'm thinking about Carl. I've never been so comfortable and drawn to someone. I just want to talk more and more. It's like we cram as much into our little visits as we can. And he listens to me and talks crazy hippy talk with me and even comes up with things on his own. It's meant to be, but what will he choose? Will he choose the scary path of leaving his secure relationship and going for the girl who he "has trouble reading" or stay away always wondering. I'm going to practice what he has taught me. Practice makes perfect. Please, allow me to spend more time with Carl.

Monday, Dec. 29, 2003

Today I have been cleaning up, reading, and I took down my Christmas tree. I went for a drive with Brooklyn. I paid Rambo the rent for January and I just need to get the key tonight. I still can't find Belle. I talked to her yesterday but not yet today. I was going to work today but couldn't, the site was down. There's so many problems that it makes me wonder if it's not meant to be, going back to work. And so I'll just have to see what the universe has in store for me. I think I'm going to have a cat nap with my dogs while I wait for Belle to phone me.

Friday, Jan. 2, 2004

Life is different already in 2004. Everything is roses. Mom took the struggle out of my life. I haven't been struggling and I've been thinking more positive. Belle and Brooklyn both really like the place. I gave Belle the big room. We're going to move in as soon as possible. I just phoned Mom and she's going to look into hydro for me. Melissa is coming over and we're going to clean the new place for a bit. It will give her a chance to see it and if Rambo shows up I have a friend there. I will stop at the dollar store and buy some cleaning stuff. I'll bring some things over too. Why not start moving now. Stuff I won't use in the next week. Carl is in town, he phoned me. We'll most likely see each other today. I get so nervous when I talk to him. I get all excited and my heart beats faster and I don't know what to say, then I say something and I think, why did I say that? I like him so much and I don't know why. Why do I turn into mush when I hear his voice on my machine? I think my face goes white, my jaw drops, and I freeze. I can't wait to talk to him.

To be continued…